the second wives club

ALSO BY JANE MOORE

Fourplay

The Ex Files

Love @ First Site

jane moore

the second wives club

A Novel

BROADWAY BOOKS · NEW YORK

PUBLISHED BY BROADWAY BOOKS

Published in the United States by Broadway Books, an imprint of
The Doubleday Broadway Publishing Group, a division of
Random House, Inc., New York.
www.broadwaybooks.com

BROADWAY BOOKS and its logo, a letter B bisected on the diagonal,
are trademarks of Random House, Inc.

Book design by Amanda Dewey

Library of Congress Cataloging-in-Publication Data

Moore, Jane, 1962 May 17–
The Second Wives Club : a novel / Jane Moore.— 1st ed.
p. cm.
1. Remarried people—Fiction. 2. Divorced women—Fiction. 3. Domestic
fiction. I. Title.

PR6113.O557S43 2006
823'.92—dc22
2005058204

ISBN-13: 978-0-7679-1692-9
ISBN-10: 0-7679-1692-1

PRINTED IN THE UNITED STATES OF AMERICA

1 3 5 7 9 10 8 6 4 2

First Edition

the second wives club

a first wife is for life,
not just for christmas

Letting out an ever-so-pretty little sigh that wouldn't swell her bosom beyond the confines of her perfectly corseted dress, Alison cast her eyes up and down the table-tops, letting her gaze linger on the eye-catching arrangements of lilies from one of London's top florists. The fact that hundreds, if not thousands, of identical lilies had been available from far cheaper outlets was neither here nor there. As she had told Luca on the numerous occasions he had questioned the validity, not to mention expense, of it all, she wanted *the best* on her wedding day.

If she'd had her way, they'd have been married in St. Paul's Cathedral with a hundred-strong choir and Dame Kiri Te Kanawa warbling the bridal march. But the small matter of Luca's previous wedding had limited them to City Hall, and his refusal to shell out "London prices" meant the reception was being held at a nearby conference hotel of the kind usually associated with pullout ironing boards and a Mr. Coffee percolator in every room.

But looking at it now, she thought, you could never tell that the day before it had been a drab old room frequented by the sales team of a window manufacturing company. The cheap maroon velvet chairs were disguised with white cotton covers, gathered in by a red velvet bow tied round the back, and the four seventies-style pillars propping the ceiling up were now unrecognizable, peppered with red rosebuds and fronds of trailing ivy. Around her, their 150 guests sipped champagne, dined on delicacies, and laughed while snapping photos with the miniature Polaroid cameras they'd placed at every table.

Alison had employed the services of an event organizer, but being the product of a mother who was such a fanatical perfectionist that she put newspaper under the cuckoo clock, Alison was also a control freak. So she'd overseen every last detail herself, adamant that her wedding was going to be the fairy-tale perfect day she'd always imagined as a little girl. So far, she hadn't been disappointed.

As she turned to her left, her expression of relief and satisfaction skewered into one of dismay as she clocked Luca's six-year-old son Paolo smearing his foie gras terrine from one side of his plate to the other. Resisting the temptation to inform him that it had cost £10 per serving, she extended a gloved hand and patted him on the head, hoping to distract him from his messy task.

"All right, soldier?" she said gently, feeling him recoil slightly under her touch. He had made an angelic page boy, a vision in midnight blue velvet pantaloons with a matching soft velvet cap. At least he'd kept the latter on, she noted.

His four-year-old brother, Giorgio, sitting to his left, had dispensed with his foie gras in a muddy puddle hours before.

"When are we going to the park?" he whined.

"The park?" Alison looked puzzled.

"Yes, Daddy said he'd take us. Today." Paolo's big brown eyes looked up at her imploringly.

"Not now, darling," Alison murmured. "Another time, okay?" The park indeed! What on *earth* had Luca been thinking of, promising them that?

The sound of a fork tinkling against the side of a glass broke into her thoughts. She turned and gazed across the dance floor to where someone was standing next to the bandleader. It was David Bartholomew, getting ready to speak.

David had been Luca's best man at his first wedding to Sofia, but despite Alison's finest efforts to get him jettisoned in favor of someone new, Luca had flatly refused. "I can't just change my best friend to suit you," he'd argued, so she'd finally let the matter drop.

Luca and David had become friends because of their love of football. They had met through a mutual acquaintance several years earlier, discovered a mutual passion for David's home team of Chelsea, and bingo—a firm friendship was formed in the stands at Stamford Bridge. It was very much a season-ticket relationship, restricted to match days only. Alison had met David only a handful of times, usually when he popped in for a quick coffee while dropping Luca home.

She knew he was married to a woman named Fiona, but other than that, the details were sketchy. Like most men, Luca was very unforthcoming on the minutiae of other people's lives. Not because he was discreet, but simply because he wasn't interested enough to ask.

"Well, here we are again." David's voice boomed out of the speakers at the back of the room to a polite ripple of laughter.

Knowing all eyes were on her, Alison clamped on a beatific smile, but inside she felt her stomach drop. This was supposed to be *her* day with Luca, their own special bubble where they could pretend that his life had begun the day he met her. And now David had delivered an opening gambit that reminded everyone present that Luca had been married before. She glanced at Luca, seated next to her, to gauge his reaction. But things were about to get worse.

"We're here to celebrate the union of a man who signs his wedding certificates in pencil," he boomed, grinning at Luca, who grimaced back. Everyone in the room tittered, and Alison had to resist the urge to lunge for the six-inch knife lying idle by the side of the cake.

"He's the only guy I know who hires his wedding rings!" David plowed on, waiting for the laughter to end before delivering his next hugely unoriginal joke that painted Luca as a serial Lothario with a NEXT label stitched on his underpants.

Suddenly, a door slammed at the back of the room, somewhere near the dreaded table 9. Dreaded, because it was where Alison had seated the ghastliest of Luca's seemingly limitless relatives, supposedly out of harm's way. There was his Uncle Mauro, who still pointed at the planes flying overhead from the Nazi invasion, and his second cousin Maria, who, to put it kindly, was knitting with only one needle.

Alison scowled in the direction of the table, aware that a commotion had started there and was gradually progressing across the room in a Mexican wave of sharply drawn breaths. She craned her neck to see what it was, but a hideously large hat at table 11 obscured her view.

David, seemingly oblivious to anything other than the microphone in front of him, was halfway through some lame old anecdote about when he and Luca had both fallen asleep on a train and accidentally ended up in Cornwall, but no one appeared to be listening.

By now, Alison could see that a brown-haired woman was advancing unchallenged across the room, her face twisted in fury. As she moved closer and her features came into focus, Alison felt a chill start to prick at her forearms. She couldn't be sure, as she'd only ever seen one grainy photograph, but . . . "Luca?" she said tentatively. "Is that . . . ?"

"Mama!" Giorgio shot up from his chair and started to scramble under the table, brushing past Alison's ankles as he did so. Emerging on the other side, he clamped himself to Sofia's left leg as if she were rescuing him from some horrific ordeal. Paolo had the foresight to take a couple of chocolates with him before swiftly following suit.

By now, David had stopped speaking, his face frozen with apprehension. There were over 150 people in the room, but Alison had never heard a silence like it.

Sofia was now standing over her and Luca, her dark Italian eyes burning with a look that could curdle milk.

"So this is what you call 'going to the park,' is it?" She ignored Alison and looked defiantly at Luca, who had now risen from his chair but stood there motionless, saying nothing.

"You lied to me!" she shouted, leaning forward so her face was just inches from his.

Luca recoiled slightly, but his face remained impassive. "Sofia . . ." He spoke so softly that a woman at table 3 had to crane her neck to try to hear. "You and I both know that I had to lie or the children wouldn't have been able to come today." He gave her a helpless shrug. "Even though I'm their *father*, you would have forbidden it."

Drawing herself up to her full height of five-six, her chest and noticeable cleavage heaving with injustice, Sofia stuck her chin in the air in defiance. "What mother *would* want her children dressed like performing monkeys while their father marries some *puntana*—a dirty *whore*!" For the first time, she actually brought herself to look straight at Alison as she emphasized the last word.

A chorus of gasps swept through the guests, who then rapidly returned to silence in case they missed the next bit.

"Excuse *me*!" Alison stood up. If Luca wasn't going to put a stop to this monstrosity, she would. "How dare you call me that in front of my family and friends! You don't know the first thing about me."

Sofia's lip curled into a sneer, and she waved a slim, tanned arm around the room. "*Your* family and friends? I see very few people here that I didn't see at our wedding. You think you're the cat with the cream, but you have a secondhand day." She paused a moment and extended a pointed finger toward David, whose terrified expression suggested he thought it might be loaded. "A secondhand best man . . . ," the finger moved round to Luca, ". . . a secondhand husband . . . ," then finally to Alison, ". . . and what looks like a secondhand dress. You've even had to borrow my children." She clamped an arm round each of the boys' shoulders. "But not anymore, they're coming with me."

Her insides churning with humiliation and indignity, Alison looked at Luca to do something. But he stayed silent and motionless, apart from yet another Italian-style shrug. It was a habit she'd found incredibly sexy when they first met. Now it was overwhelmingly irritating.

"See what you've married?" scoffed Sofia, jerking her head toward her ex-husband. "He has never stood up to anyone, always takes the easy choice." With a child clamped to each leg, she resembled someone in dire need of a double hip replacement as she jerked her way across the dance floor to David. Grabbing his microphone, she tapped the end of it like a true professional, checking to be sure that what she was about to say would reach the entire room.

"My ex-husband is a coward, and she's welcome to him." Her voice seemed to hit the back wall and bounce back again, filling every corner. "But she's not having my children."

With that, she handed the microphone back to the stunned bandleader and began guiding Giorgio and Paolo back toward the door she had burst through just minutes earlier. As she walked past a table of the shell-shocked bride's friends and family, Alison's sister Louise rose tentatively to her feet.

"Excuse me," she said with an unerring British politeness that suggested she was about to ask where the lavatories were, "but you can't speak to my sister like that."

Sofia stopped in her tracks and fixed Louise with a death stare. "Oh, yes, I can. And I have. And I will again if it suits me to do so. *Capisce?*"

Louise sank back into her seat and looked helplessly at the others around the table. Emboldened by the sight of her sister's embarrassment and her enemy's retreating back, Alison bristled into action and swiveled to face her new husband. "Luca, they're *your* children too! Go after her and bring them back."

But Luca stayed where he was and just sighed. "It doesn't work like that in Italian families. The mother has all the power." He watched Sofia as she snaked her way to the back of the room, the guests parting like the Red Sea. "Let them go. At least they were there for the ceremony," he added.

"Well, yes, thank *goodness*," Alison said sarcastically. "I mean, that really does make up for the mortifying scene your ex-wife just caused at our wedding!" Her face now matched the roses decorating the pillars in front of her. "Is this how it's always going to be?"

"You should have asked that question *before* you married him, love," a woman's voice said.

Alison's head swiveled to where she thought the woman's voice had come from, but everyone at table 2 was looking innocent as roses. If idiots could fly, she thought mutinously, this place would be an airport.

Sitting back in her chair with a heavy thump, it suddenly dawned on her that she had spent so much time planning her fairy-tale wedding that she'd never actually stopped to think about the reality of what she was taking on. Namely, a man with a determined and ferociously bitter ex-wife and two children who were already poisoned against her.

She loved Luca dearly, was probably even a little obsessed with him if the truth be known. But now that the subterfuge of their initially illicit relationship had been stripped away, would her passion for him be able to sustain all the drama from his past? She'd just have to wait and see, hoping that it would.

Sofia had finally disappeared from view, and the room started to fill with noise again, the guests obviously discussing the theatrics they'd just witnessed. Alison knew that in most of their eyes—probably all, in fact, including her own friends—she had willfully stolen Luca from Sofia and therefore deserved everything she got.

Speeches over, the band Zorba—or "Ex-zorba-tant," as Alison referred to them after writing a £2,000 check for their services— struck up the first few notes of Elvis Costello's sleepy ballad "Alison."

With all eyes on them, Alison forced a smile and extended her hand to Luca, who led her to the dance floor.

"Aaaaaaalison, I know this world is killing you . . ."

Not to mention my husband's ex-wife, she thought darkly. As they swayed slowly to the music she tried to forget about Sofia, burying her head in Luca's neck and inhaling his Fahrenheit aftershave, the musky smell that had first attracted her to him. As she closed her eyes and let her mind wander away from the scrutiny of everyone's gaze, she worked to convince herself that everything was going to be all right. And it probably would be, she thought, if it were just the two of them.

"Aaaaaaalison, my aim is true . . ."

As the music trailed away Luca took a step back from her to acknowledge the applause of the room, and Alison's spell was broken. Leaving him to take the floor with a favored aunt, she thwarted the offer of other dances, pretending she needed to visit the powder room.

Heading in that direction for authenticity, she reached the door and came face-to-face with a smiling woman she didn't recognize. She looked disheveled, but in a sexy rather than slovenly kind of way, with her curly brown hair falling into her eyes.

"Hi, Alison." She grinned.

Alison smiled back but had absolutely no idea who she was.

"I'm Fiona."

She extended her hand, and Alison took it, still looking blank.

"David's wife. The best man?"

Alison theatrically slapped her palm against her forehead. "Oh, God, sorry. I guess I'm still a little shell-shocked from . . . well, you know." She simpered apologetically.

"Yes, I certainly do," Fiona said, rolling her eyes. "I wanted to talk to you about that actually."

"Oh?" Alison looked at her, confused. Was she going to apologize for David's speech?

Fiona jerked her head toward a small, empty sofa positioned to one side of the foyer. "Shall we?"

They wandered over and sat down, Alison taking care to smooth her dress underneath her and scooping her train to one side. Fiona took a quick look around her, then fixed her gray eyes on the bride's face. "That was pretty ugly back there."

Unsure of where this woman's loyalties lay, Alison did her best to effect a Luca-style shrug. "It couldn't be helped, I guess. It's over now, and I understand why she did it."

"Really?" Fiona looked unconvinced.

"Why, don't you think it was justified?" Alison threw the ball back into Fiona's court, testing the waters.

Wrinkling her nose, Fiona sighed. "Tricky one. Upset about the breakdown of her marriage? Yes, I sympathize." She checked over her shoulder again. "Causing an embarrassing scene at her husband's wedding in front of their two children? Nope, sorry. That's *so* wrong."

"Do you think so?" Alison studied her face for signs of potential betrayal but saw none. She knew that any of her friends and family who were present would wax lyrical about how disgraceful Sofia's behavior had been—in fact, many would probably be doing so for years. But she desperately wanted allies in Luca's camp too. Or at least someone with an objective view, and it seemed like Fiona might be that person.

"I must say, it has made me slightly apprehensive about the future . . . if that's the way it's going to be."

Fiona sighed. "Tell me about it."

"You sound like you've been there."

"Sort of. David . . ." She broke off as someone advanced toward them. It was Alison's mother, Audrey.

"Darling, I've been looking everywhere for you. Are you all right?"

"Mother!" Alison raised her eyes heavenward. "That's the tenth time you've asked me that. I'm fine, really."

Audrey looked unconvinced. "That dreadful Sofia needs to move on with her life, don't you think?" She looked at Fiona but didn't wait for an answer, turning back to Alison. "Anyway, your father wants another word. Stay here, I'll get him." She drifted off on a cloud of White Linen.

Fiona raised her eyebrows. "She's formidable."

Alison smiled. "She's also on another planet. The other day a homeless man came up to her in the street and said he hadn't eaten for three days, and she said: 'Dear chap, you must force yourself!' "

Fiona burst out laughing. In the distance, they could see Audrey honing back into view with her husband Alasdair in tow.

"Look, I won't keep you on your big day," Fiona said hastily. "I just wanted to give you my number." It was already scribbled on the piece of paper she handed over.

"Thanks." Alison wasn't quite sure what it meant, but she was grateful for the small gesture.

"It's just that me and a couple of friends have this little club, and I thought you might like to join. It's a kind of self-help group, I suppose." Fiona smiled reassuringly.

Alison looked baffled. "What, like a weight-loss thing?" She looked down at her enviably slim hips.

Looking down at her own wide girth, Fiona laughed. "No, although I could probably do with joining something like that . . . no, it's a sort of secret group founded by me. We've only got three members so far, four if you join us. We get together once a week for moral support."

Intrigued, Alison's mind raced with the possibilities of what it could be. "What's the criteria for joining?"

"You just have to have a small scar running from here to here." Fiona used her forefinger to trace a line from the corner of her mouth down her chin. "It comes from years of biting your lip."

Alison was starting to feel like someone whose pilot light had gone out. She shook her head. "Sorry, I still don't get it."

Fiona smiled benevolently. "Welcome to the Second Wives Club."

the trouble with children is
they are not returnable

Jake tentatively dipped his elbow into the soapy water, just like he'd seen them do in the sex-education video shown at school a couple of years before. It had been designed to show him and his classmates the enormity of the task involved in looking after a newborn baby, but instead he and his friends had simply snickered their way through it after catching a fleeting glimpse of the woman's nipple as she breast-fed.

Lily was sitting on the floor surrounded by her brightly colored plastic bath toys. At the age of one, she had recently started to crawl everywhere at high speed, so Jake's other free hand was extended to hold the back of her vest, making sure she didn't escape. "C'mon, pumpkin," he said, scooping her up and unbuttoning her Winnie-the-Pooh vest. "Time for some splishy splashing."

He affectionately rubbed his hand across the smooth, downy fluff that covered the top of her head. She'd been overwhelmed with gifts from Father Christmas, but hair hadn't been one of them.

Lowering her gently into her swivel bath seat, he leaned down and picked up a selection of toys from the floor, plopping them into the water like tiny bombs as she shrieked with delight.

Immediately, she started what she always did in the bath—placing her little plastic Teletubbies in a boat, then quickly tiring of such an idyllic scene and tipping it upside down.

Jake smiled benevolently. While his half sister's arrival had meant he was no longer the sole center of his father's attention, at sixteen he was old enough to handle it. In fact, as he saw it, her presence gave him a much-needed occasional hiatus in the seemingly endless parental nagging about schoolwork, career options, and the tidiness—or untidiness to be more precise—of his bedroom.

He looked down at his watch, an all-singing, all-dancing diver's timepiece, even though the closest he'd ever come to being submerged was when he jumped off the high board at the local swimming pool. He'd only done it because the awesomely hot Emma Davies had been watching him and he'd wanted to impress her. Trouble was, he'd swallowed half the pool and emerged spluttering so badly that the lifeguard had felt compelled to ask him if he needed assistance. Emma had ignored him ever since, apart from remarking to her friends, "Oh, look, it's marine boy," every time they passed in the school corridors.

Jake wrinkled his nose at the memory. It was now 6:00 P.M. Noting that Lily was absorbed in her game, he slowly backed out of the bathroom door and into the hallway. By his reckoning, there was just enough time to listen to the first track of Rim of Scum's new album before she'd even notice he was gone.

Jake's bedroom was right next door, identifiable by the DANGER: TOXIC TEENAGER sign nailed on it. He let out a deep sigh as he surveyed his room. The posters of Cameron Diaz in a variety of microscopic bikinis were starting to look a bit lame and desperate, and he made a mental note to change them for some Goth images and memorabilia. Likewise, his old train set was stuffed on top of the wardrobe along with all the evidence of his Pokémon obsession, which had lasted all of five minutes several years back.

The room undoubtedly suffered from the fact that Jake frequented it only every other weekend. On the few occasions he was there, he couldn't be bothered to spend time sorting through it, preferring to while away the hours on his PlayStation 2 or watching the latest ubiquitous teen flick on DVD in which some young girl in a baby-doll nightie (preferably Paris Hilton) was scared witless in the dead of night and felt the urge to go and investigate the pool house.

Tracing a finger along the neat row of CDs on his bookshelf, he quickly found the one he wanted thanks to his system of storing them alphabetically. It was the one thing in Jake's life that was ordered. He had bought the disc earlier that day, and already it was in its place with a handwritten "R" sticker, ready for its first airing. Music was Jake's greatest love. Well, *his* kind of music, not the old fuddy-duddy stuff his dad played, like Dire Straits, Van Morrison, and that country-and-western bollocks about wives leaving and dogs dying. He liked nothing better than to hike the volume up full blast and let the sound wash over him, transporting him to somewhere exciting and empowering, away from—as he saw it—his dull suburban life.

Trouble was, his dad's neighbors had complained about the din, so his last birthday present had been a state-of-the-art set of high-quality headphones that he'd promised to use every time he listened to music.

After sneaking a quick peek at Lily one more time, he darted back into his room, clamped the headphones in place, and lay back in his giant beanbag for the latest Rim of Scum experience.

• • •

Fiona felt her neck crick as she strained to see over her left shoulder. She was trying to reverse her little Ford Fiesta onto the shared driveway, but as ever, it was like trying to thread a fine needle with a piece of string.

For some reason, despite living in a semidetached house in the urban sprawl of Croydon, just outside London, her neighbors felt the need to have a monstrously large four-by-four Jeep with go-faster stripes and vast bullbars more commonly used in the wilds of northern Australia to fend off marauding kangaroos.

It ate up every inch of the neighbor's half of the drive and jutted out into Fiona and David's space to such an extent that once parked they were never able to open both their car doors.

"Bollocks!" Fiona cursed as her side mirror tapped the side of the Jeep and she had to reverse out again to reposition herself.

She rather hoped it was loud enough to wake David, snoring loudly in the passenger seat after consuming his own weight in lager at Luca and Alison's wedding. "I thought alcoholics were supposed to be anonymous," she said aloud, but he didn't even flicker.

Cranking the hand brake into position, she opened the driver's door and decided to leave him there to sleep it off. Besides, if she woke him now, he'd be disoriented and grumpy, and it would be just one more child to deal with while she was putting Lily to bed. Let snoring hogs lie, she thought, closing the car door gently.

As she fumbled to find her key, she could hear the faint sound of Lily crying and smiled to herself. Even at the tender age of one, she was already an archmanipulator and probably had Jake wrapped round her little finger at the slightest wail.

But as Fiona opened the front door, her heart skipped a beat. That wasn't an attention-seeking whine, it was a full-blown, hysterical scream. And it sounded like it was coming from the bathroom.

Jumping the stairs three at a time, Fiona reached Lily in just a few seconds. The child was only partially in her bath seat, having wriggled one leg out and twisted her torso to the side. There was a deep red welt at the top of one of her thighs, where she'd clearly been struggling to escape, and her face was puce with what Fiona recognized as fury and fright.

As soon as she saw her mother Lily's high-pitched screaming became more intense, and she extended her pudgy little arms in the air. "Mamma!"

"Jesus Christ!" She lifted her little girl out of the freezing water and wrapped her in a towel before fastening the nappy and pajamas that had been laid to one side. The child was shivering uncontrollably, presumably from a mixture of fear and cold, so Fiona just sat on the loo seat and cuddled her for a few seconds, trying to calm her down.

Her mind was racing. Where on *earth* was Jake? Something terrible must have happened to him.

Still holding Lily close, Fiona stood up and left the bathroom in search of her stepson. She felt sick with apprehension at the thought of what she might find.

Pushing open his bedroom door, she felt the cold, telltale prickle of nervousness when she saw him lying motionless on his beanbag in the middle of the room. His eyes were closed, his arms sprawled by his sides. He was wearing his headphones, and she could hear a faint, tinny noise that suggested something was still playing full blast.

"Jake?" she said tentatively, and somewhat fruitlessly, given the headphones. But she was afraid to touch him, afraid he might slump lifelessly onto the floor.

"Jake?" This time she placed her hand on his shoulder and shook him gently, fully expecting zero response.

But his arm twitched a little at first, then raised up to rub his eyes, which were now open and blearily blinking at her, full of confusion.

"Oh, hi, you're back," he said matter-of-factly.

Now Fiona wasn't fearful anymore. Jake was alive and well, and she was gut-wrenchingly angry.

"What the *fuck* do you think you're playing at?" she spat, grabbing his forearm and trying to haul him to his feet. It proved difficult, as she still had Lily clutched to her.

Jake stood up, his hands lifted in a gesture of surrender. "Whoa, okay, okay, take a chill pill, will you?" At first he looked puzzled by her outburst. Then he focused on Lily and realization dawned. "Oh, shit!"

Fiona's jaw fell open. "Oh, shit? Oh, *shit*? Is that all you have to say considering you just practically killed your sister?"

"Oh come *on*," he beseeched. "I know I shouldn't have left her in there alone, but she looks, well, fine to me."

The urge to slap his stupid, irresponsible face practically overwhelmed Fiona, but she knew that would instantly give him the moral high ground in the eyes of his mother and father. So she controlled herself.

"When I came in through the front door, Lily was screaming the place down." By contrast, Fiona's voice was dangerously low, a sign that she could snap at any time. "She had tried to climb out of her seat, and it's a miracle she didn't fall into the water and drown. And if she had, it would have been one hundred percent *your fault*."

Jake shrugged defiantly. "Yeah, well, she didn't, did she? So let's all get real and move on with our lives."

If he'd been in the slightest bit remorseful and apologized for being so irresponsible, Fiona might have started to calm down. But his obvious determination to place the matter at the same level of importance where one might view a spilled drink angered her enormously. Usually she bit her tongue when Jake behaved disrespectfully—which he often did—but this time he wasn't going to get away with it.

"She didn't drown because I came home and saved her." Fiona could hear a high-pitched, angry voice and realized it was hers. "God only knows what would have happened if your father and I had decided to stay at the wedding for longer . . ." She paused to catch her breath at the mere thought of it.

"Jake, you were out for the count, while your little sister—who was relying on *you* to look after her—was cold and wet and terrified at being left alone."

"Half sister."

"Sorry?" Fiona stopped in her tracks, momentarily puzzled by his interruption.

"She's my half sister, not my sister."

Fiona's hand had moved before she was even aware of it herself. The *thwack* of her palm striking the side of his face hung in the air between them, her glaring, him clutching his cheek with defiance in his eyes.

"You immature little brat," she yelled. "Can't you, just for *once*, take on board the enormity of what's just happened, rather than make some facile, irrelevant remark? Surely even you can take *some* responsibility for your actions?"

Jake said nothing for a few seconds, merely rubbing his cheek and staring at the floor. When he finally looked up, he avoided her stare and glanced over toward his bedroom door.

"Look, I'm a teenage boy, not Lily's mother. She's *your* responsibility, not mine, and if you're so worried about her, then you shouldn't have left her with someone untrained in baby care while you went off having a great time."

His words cut deep, straight into the Achilles' heel of every new mother who feels guilt-ridden when she indulges in an activity that doesn't involve her baby. But Fiona rallied herself, refusing to fall victim to such amateur, end-of-the-pier psychology. "Jake, you don't have to be trained in baby care to know that you don't leave a toddler unattended in water. Even a complete *moron* would know that, so cut the crap. You agreed to look after her—for money, of course—and therefore you were in charge. End of story."

He stood motionless for a couple of seconds after she'd finished speaking, then stooped down to pick up the overnight bag at his feet and started to stuff clothes into it.

"Where do you think you're going?"

"Home," he replied sullenly.

"This is your home."

"Yeah, right." He smiled slightly, but it didn't reach his eyes. "I think you'll find this is *your* home, a place where I am merely tolerated."

Fiona rolled her eyes. "Oh, don't be so bloody dramatic. You have your own room here, the fridge and cupboards are always full of the things you like, and your father and Lily love you dearly."

He zipped up the bag and threw it over his shoulder. "And what about you, Fiona? What do *you* feel about me?"

She was rather thrown by such a direct question from a boy with whom her previous attempts at conversation had invariably been returned unopened.

"Um, I'm very fond of you," she faltered.

"Fond, eh?" His tone was slightly mocking. "What, much like you are of those old slippers you keep under the stairs?"

He started to walk toward the door, but Fiona grabbed one of the handles of the bag and started to pull him backward.

"Jake, put it down. You're not going anywhere."

"I'm sixteen and can do exactly what I like." It was a regular battle cry of his, but this time it sounded far more loaded. "I'm out of here."

As he lumbered down the stairs Fiona shifted Lily to her other hip and followed him down to the small porch by the front door.

"If you walk out now, don't bother coming back any time this weekend," she said in desperation, realizing she was losing the battle to keep him in the house.

"A pleasure," he said in a clipped voice, opening the front door.

"What's going on?" David was standing outside, one hand poised to open the door, the other rubbing a bleary eye.

"I'm leaving." Jake made a move to step past him, but his father blocked the way.

"Leaving? Why? Where are you going?"

"I'm off to Mum's. And Fiona has made it quite clear that if I go, I'm not welcome back here this weekend." For the first time since their row, he glanced toward his stepmother.

David looked bemused and let out a nervous laugh. "Don't be silly. Of course you can come back." He turned to Fiona, his expression morphing into a frown. "Why did you say that?"

Fiona shook her head slowly in a gesture of hopelessness. "This needs to be put into context," she said wearily. "Jake, will you tell him or shall I?"

Jake already had one foot out the front door, but clearly thought better of being tried and convicted in his absence. He turned to face his father.

"Basically . . ."

"Hang on," David interrupted. "Can we go to the living room? I think I might need to sit down for this."

They all trooped through to the rectangular-shaped room where they spent most of their time, either eating at the large table positioned at one end or watching television from one of the two sofas at the other.

Fiona placed Lily in front of her toy box and sat down next to David, but Jake remained standing, his expression black.

"Basically," he continued, "Fiona came home and freaked out because I left Lily sitting in her bath seat while I was in my bedroom."

David waited to see if there were any further explanations from his son, then let out a sigh. "Well, you really shouldn't leave her alone for even a few seconds, but if that's all that happened, I really can't see why it's got to the stage that Jake is leaving to go to his mother's." He turned to Fiona as if seeking an explanation.

"Right," she said briskly. "We'll hear the more *accurate* version now, shall we? I came in the door, heard Lily screaming the place down, and found her trying to struggle out of her bath seat while Jake was fast asleep next door with some crap blasting through his headphones. Lily could easily have drowned, but Jake just doesn't seem to take that on board."

They lapsed into silence for a few seconds, David staring at the floor deep in thought. "Is that true?" he said finally, looking at Jake, who simply shrugged wordlessly. "Well, if it is, you really should have taken more care," he chided gently. "I know you're only sixteen yourself, but Lily is totally helpless. She needed you to watch over her."

"I know." Jake's tone was conciliatory. "I said I was sorry."

Fiona's eyebrows shot up. "Er, *no, you didn't*."

"Yes, I did."

"No, you *didn't*."

David held a hand up. "Please, please. Let's agree to disagree, shall we? There's no need to descend to playground bickering." He was looking at Fiona when he said the last bit.

"David, he's reinventing history as usual." She suddenly felt weary and rather wished Jake hadn't been prevented from leaving.

"Look." David's irritated expression made it clear he was in no mood to take sides. "Jake, you shouldn't have left Lily alone. And Fiona, you shouldn't have overreacted. After all, Jake didn't mean Lily any harm. Now let's leave it at that."

Fiona felt a biting sense of injustice. Overreacting. Hysterical.

Barking mad. All of these criticisms were often leveled at women, never at men. How on earth was it possible for a mother to "over-react" when her child's life had been placed in danger? Normally she would have let the matter drop, knowing she had nothing to gain because she'd been here before. Jake ruined many a weekend with his churlish or downright irresponsible behavior, but David rarely chastised him, preferring instead to make excuses for his feckless son, riddled with guilt that he'd walked out when the boy was only eight years old.

But this time was different. This time Fiona needed to make a stand.

"It wasn't an overreaction, David. If we'd stayed at the wedding even a few minutes longer than we did, Lily could have drowned. Now, you may think that's something that can be brushed under the carpet, but sorry, I don't."

Then Jake played his trump card.

"So if you didn't overreact, how come you slapped me across the face?" He rubbed his cheek for dramatic effect.

David turned toward Fiona, his face aghast. "You *slapped* him? Please tell me you didn't."

A gentle man, David was vehemently against smacking children or even shouting at them, and it was a hot topic they had often de-bated long into the night regarding how to control Lily as she ap-proached the infamous "terrible twos." Fiona felt the occasional spanking or stern verbal admonishment did no harm, but to David it was tantamount to child abuse. As a result, Jake had grown up largely undisciplined.

"It was hardly a proper slap," she said, but she knew the game was up. Jake's irresponsibility had now been totally eclipsed by her mo-mentary lack of control, and her husband was staring at her with the same look of horror he might have worn if it had been Charles Man-son sitting next to him on the sofa.

"Shame on you," he said softly, shaking his head in disbelief. "Please don't *ever* do that again."

Behind his head, she could see a triumphant Jake grinning gloatingly from ear to ear. She closed her eyes in despair. The next meeting of the club couldn't come soon enough.

fools rush in where angels have trodden

Red-faced and sweating, Susan dumped the four shopping bags on the doorstep and stretched out her aching, twisted fingers. She knew it would be the end of life as she'd known it, but lately she'd found herself staring longingly at those pull-along shopping carts used by the little old ladies in her supermarket.

As she fumbled for her house key, the bag containing four gallons of soda toppled over, sending a two-liter bottle of Diet Coke crashing onto her sandaled foot.

"Jesus Christ!" Her foot shot up involuntarily, and she hopped on the spot a couple of times, waiting for the pain to subside.

The sound of tutting distracted her, and she twisted her head to find Mrs. Tufnel, her Bible-thumping neighbor, standing just yards away and frowning in her direction.

"Really, dear, you should find a way to express yourself without resorting to blasphemy," she chided. "What if little Ellie heard you? We all need to set an example for the young ones."

The temptation to pull out every blasphemous word from her extensive repertoire and shout it at the top of her voice was overwhelming. But then Susan remembered the times she occasionally needed Mrs. Tufnel to keep an eye on Ellie while she popped out to run an errand. So she kept mum. She also knew that if she lingered even for a second, the old lady would take it as a prompt to start one of her interminable conversations about the bus routes.

"Watch out for Mrs. Tufnel," Nick had warned her when she'd first moved in. "She runs a self-help group for compulsive talkers called On and On Anon."

Wincing for extra effect, Susan continued rummaging through her pockets. "Sorry, Mrs. Tufnel, you're right. But a bottle fell on my foot, and I was in a lot of pain."

"That may be, dear. But 'oh gosh' or 'crikey' would do just as nicely to express your displeasure." Thankfully, she started to walk away.

"I'll remember that, thanks!" Susan called after her. My God, she thought, I haven't heard anyone use the word *crikey* since the *Bismarck* sank. Now where was that damned key?

Digging deep in her jacket pocket, she pulled out an empty toffee wrapper, an old bus ticket, and—how gross—a Flossette that still had a piece of ancient food stuck to it, extracted from between her back molars at least three months earlier.

Tidiness was not Susan's strong point. Neither was organization, planning ahead, or any kind of domesticity. Every day she descended on the supermarket or local shop in a panic, frantically searching for whatever it was that she'd suddenly run out of this time. She longed to be one of those women who had everything sorted out, one of those women who consequently led calm, unstressed lives.

Her bookshelves were stuffed full of self-help manuals on how to become organized and get your life on track, but she hadn't yet managed to find the time to read them. By the time I get my head together, she thought ruefully, my body will have fallen apart.

"Aha! There you are, you little bugger." Triumphantly, she located the elusive key in the pocket of her skirt.

Heaving the bags into the hallway, she dropped them on the floor and sat on the bottom stair for a moment, composing herself. Slipping off her sandals, she looked up and caught Caitlin's eye.

Caitlin was where she always was, hanging on the large expanse of wall that faced the front door. Unless you made an actual point of doggedly staring at the floor when you walked in, you *had* to see her. So every guest to the house always did.

"What a beautiful painting," they'd say, or words to that effect. What they *actually* meant, of course, was what a beautiful woman. Which Caitlin was, in every sense of the word.

Beautiful outside, beautiful inside. Not to mention organized, unflappable, and always immaculately dressed. In short, everything Susan wasn't.

With a wistful smile, Susan lugged the bags into the kitchen and began unpacking them, squeezing the contents into the already overflowing cupboards stuffed with her untouched panic buys such as pickled herring, cake mix, and the echinacea teabags Nick said tasted like cow dung.

She looked at the clock. It was 7:00 P.M., meaning he and Ellie would be through the door at any moment. Ellie had been at a friend's house for tea, so there was one less mouth for Susan to feed. All she had to worry about was her and Nick . . . now where *was* that can of spaghetti Bolognese?

"Hello, Mummy, we're back." Ellie ran into the kitchen, her cheeks flushed pink from fresh air. She wrapped her arms round the top of Susan's leg and gave it a hug.

"Hello, pumpkin, did you have a nice time?" Susan kneeled down in front of Ellie and started to unbutton her little pink jacket.

"Yes, fank you. Except that Jenny's mummy gave me carrots. I *hate* carrots."

"I hope you didn't *say* you hate them," Susan said softly. "Remember what I told you about having good manners? They get you a long way in life."

"But I don't want to go a long way. I want to stay *here*." At five years old, Ellie was at the stage where she took everything literally.

"Good!" Susan scooped her up into the air. "Because I want to keep you here *forever*."

The pair of them started spinning round like ice dancers, narrowly avoiding Nick as he walked into the room.

"Whoa!" He laughed. "You two need a learner's permit. Good day?" He kissed Susan on the nose.

Not really, she thought, but the details of why would have been too turgid to mention. "Fine," she replied. "You?"

He made a face. "So-so. I sold a couple of flats today, but those big juicy houses that make me a big fat commission are refusing to budge." He walked over to the cupboard in the far corner of the room. "Gin and tonic?"

It was their usual nightly routine. He'd come home from work and make them two beautifully prepared G&Ts with fresh lemon, while she prepared—or, more truthfully, heated—their evening meal. Then, while he "unwound" in front of the television from the day's toils, she would unwind from hers by running Ellie's bath, making her a cup of warm milk, and helping her into her pajamas.

Susan also worked—as a part-time PA to a small building firm up the road—but as she didn't earn as much as Nick, it was clearly assumed that she would bear the brunt of Ellie's bedtime routine.

Not that she minded, it was an honor. Ellie might not have been her *biological* child, but Susan couldn't have loved her any more than she did. She was a delightful little girl who had a sunny, contented nature despite being dealt such a cruel blow so early in her life.

Susan still remembered Nick's call as if it had been yesterday.

"Something terrible's happened to Caitlin. Will you come to the house and look after Ellie for me?"

A massive brain hemorrhage, they'd said. Nothing that Nick or anyone else could have done, they'd said. It was "just one of those things" that no one could have predicted.

On that fateful day, Nick had turned his key in the lock, just like he always did, and stepped into the hallway. But that time something had felt different. Worryingly different.

He could hear the excited chatter of some children's program coming from the television in the kitchen, but otherwise the place had felt eerily silent. There was also an overpowering smell of burning.

"Hello!" he'd shouted up the stairs. No answer.

Now the telltale chill of apprehension was pricking at his forearms. Perhaps Caitlin had popped out with Ellie on an errand, but it was very unlike her to leave the lights on and the TV blaring.

Moving swiftly through to the kitchen, he had scanned the room with lightning speed. Nothing and no one. Just a half-empty coffee cup on the table and Ellie's toys scattered around the floor, like they always were.

Then he saw it, his blood turning instantaneously cold. A pan was on the stove, the flame still flickering under it but the contents burned away to a charred crust. He flicked it off. There was absolutely no way that Caitlin would have been so careless. Something was horribly wrong.

"Caitlin?" He walked back into the hallway, projecting his voice up the stairs, willing her to reply. But instinctively he knew that she wouldn't.

His mind still racing with possible explanations for the gut-wrenching silence, he climbed the stairs slowly, one by one, each step edging him closer to an unedifying truth.

He found her in Ellie's bedroom, sprawled facedown on the carpet, her strawberry blond hair fanned out, her hand extended toward the crib, where Ellie stood inside, peering over the edge.

"Mummy." Ellie's pudgy little finger was extended toward Caitlin lying motionless below her. "Mummy." Her eyes red and puffy, she had obviously been crying at some point, but now she was calm, having been distracted by the piece of her teddy's neck ribbon she was curling round the fingers on her other hand.

Nick fell to his knees on the little rug he and Caitlin had bought only a few weeks before, with its pictures of starfish and coral. Tentatively, he reached out to brush her hair away from her face, then instantly recoiled. She was stone-cold.

"Jesus Christ. Oh, my God." Trying not to throw up with fear, he'd swiveled his head to look for the phone, then punched in 999.

"Ambulance quick. There's something wrong with my wife . . . no, she's not breathing. I think . . ." He could barely bring himself to say it. ". . . I think she's dead."

Caitlin's funeral had been the saddest day of Susan's life. Seeing the barely two-year-old Ellie toddle up to the coffin, her chubby little hand tucked inside her daddy's clenched fist, had almost been unbearable.

As she placed a small, hand-tied bouquet of her mother's favorite lily of the valley on top of the coffin, the little girl had seemed oblivious to the stifled sobs of those in the church.

"Mummy wake?" she'd asked loudly as she and Nick walked back to their seats. Immensely strong up to that point, Nick had lost it then, slumping onto the pew, his face clenched with pain.

Caitlin's father, Bill, deathly pale but dry-eyed, had stepped forward and taken Ellie's hand, distracting her from Nick's raw grief.

Although Susan had always been Nick's friend, having briefly dated him when they were studying for A levels at the same college, she'd grown incredibly close to Caitlin in the seven years they were together.

When Ellie had come along, Susan had been thrilled to be made her godmother and embraced the role wholeheartedly, taking an active role in the little girl's life right from the start. So it had felt entirely natural to everyone when Nick turned to her in his hour of need.

Susan had moved into the spare room, supposedly temporarily, while Nick got himself through the ordeal of organizing his wife's funeral and started the process of finding a full-time nanny for Ellie, who, while not showing any obvious signs of deeply damaging trauma, was clearly missing her mummy terribly. She soon switched all her affection to Susan, showing separation anxiety whenever Susan left the room and waking up crying in the middle of the night and refusing to be consoled unless she was taken into Susan's bed with her. Fortunately, Susan had just left an unsatisfactory secretarial job to find a new post, so with Nick's agreement, she offered to stay home at their house until a nanny had been found and Ellie had formed a bond with that new person.

"I don't even know the name of my own daughter's doctor," Nick had despaired during one of their many soul-searching chats shortly after Caitlin's death. "I don't know her favorite treats, the names of all her teddies, or even whether she has any allergies. I left all that stuff to Caitlin."

"You'll learn soon enough," Susan had assured him. "Children are very simple creatures really."

In the event, *she'd* been the one who'd lined up several nannies for interview, sitting in while Nick flailed around like a fish out of water, asking pointless questions such as what kind of music did they like and what part of the country they'd been born in. He'd ended up choosing a rather plain, dumpy girl called Joanne who still lived with her mother just a few roads away and showed no inclination to move.

"As Joanne won't be living here, why don't you carry on staying in the spare room?" Nick had said casually that night. "It seems silly to pay rent on your flat when you could just stay here and chip in on bills. And besides, Ellie loves having you around."

And that had been it. As simple as that, Susan's future had been mapped out for her.

a friend in need is
a friend to be avoided

Extending her left leg and raising it slightly, Julia closed her eyes and let the waves of relaxation wash over her as the masseur worked his magic. She always asked for a man, because she couldn't stand the wet lettuce effect of a woman's hands. She wanted to *feel* that pressure on her skin, massaging away life's little stresses.

Quite what Julia's stresses were was anyone's guess. Married to a hugely wealthy investment banker, James, she didn't sully her daily timetable with the dreary matter of work. Of any kind.

Her motto in life was: "I want it all and I want it delivered." A housekeeper kept her house, a cleaner cleaned it, and James's assistant did everything else, like paying those tiresome utility bills. Leaving Julia free to do exactly as she pleased, which wasn't much at all.

But then, she was worth it. Julia was quite simply stunning, with shoulder-length blond hair, endlessly groomed into straight, shiny submission. Its rich honey hue offset her pale green eyes, and she perfected the femme fatale look by always wearing a strikingly colored lipstick on her enviably full mouth. Her figure was boyishly slim thanks to thrice-weekly trips to an exclusive gym, but it was topped off by a fantastic pair of 34D bosoms bought for her by James shortly after they'd met four years ago. The overall effect, or so Julia hoped, was Barbie with brains.

Julia might be idle, but she certainly wasn't stupid. She knew the deal and always made sure she looked fantastic for her husband. It was important for him to have a beautiful woman on his arm at business functions, one who could dazzle his clients with her stunning looks and intelligent conversation.

Julia always made a point of researching subject matter on the Internet so that she could appear knowledgeable in the right area to the right people. At one achingly glamorous, high-profile function, she'd been seated next to a Texas billionaire whose vast wealth had come from investing his family oil inheritance wisely. Julia had brushed up on his history and by the end of the evening had him eating out of her hand. When she got going, she could sell underarm deodorant to the Venus de Milo.

"Any man who manages to git himself such a fine woman must have a hell of a lot going for him," he'd boomed at James as they shook hands to say good-bye. "Call me tomorrow and let's talk about me making some investments with your bank."

He'd ended up becoming one of James's most valuable clients, and Julia had been rewarded with the cute little Mercedes SLK that was now parked on the graveled driveway of their detached six-bedroom home on Bishop's Avenue, one of London's most prestigious roads.

A light tap on her shoulder stirred Julia from her daydreams.

"All done. I'll leave you to relax for a few minutes and get dressed." The masseur left the room.

Julia immediately sat up and swung her legs off the table, her freshly manicured toes recoiling as they hit the cold marble floor. She glanced in the mirror and winced slightly at the sight of her usually immaculate hair, all mussed up from the massage oil. Still, no problem, she had a hairdresser's appointment in half an hour. Just time to pop into the lingerie shop down the road and see if there was any new stock for her to welcome James home with. . . .

After stirring the roux sauce she held the spoon out in front of her and took a tiny sip. Just perfect, as ever.

Shortly after the boob job, her bid to become the perfect wife had continued apace with a weeklong course at Raymond Blanc's world-famous Le Manoir de Quatre Saisons in Oxfordshire, where she'd learned to cook à la carte. Now, unless he had a business dinner to attend, James was assured of a beautifully cooked meal when he returned home from work every night.

Julia glanced at the kitchen clock. It was 7:00 P.M. She had just enough time to nip upstairs and get ready.

Grabbing the bag from the lingerie shop as she passed through the hallway, she bounded up the stairs two at a time with great ease.

Throwing her new acquisitions onto the fur throw that enveloped their king-size mahogany sleigh bed, she wriggled out of her jeans, sweater, and T-shirt bra and deftly lobbed them into the linen basket in the corner of the en-suite bathroom. Julia was a five-star luxury kind of girl, anything less just wouldn't do. Her idea of roughing it was turning her electric blanket down to medium.

Clipping the new bra into place, she stepped daintily into the matching black lace panties and took a step back to admire herself in the full-length mirrored wardrobes. "Not bad for thirty-two, not bad at all," she said aloud, patting her flat stomach. She knew James didn't like her to look too "obvious," as he called it, so she opted for a black polo-neck sweater and black chinos. He could unwrap her later for his little surprise.

She heard the familiar click of a key turning in the front door, then the ensuing *whoosh* from the traffic noise outside.

"Hello, darling," she shouted down the stairs. "Won't be a minute."

Smoothing down her sweater and picking a stray hair off the shoulder, she headed downstairs, the wonderful smell of her home cooking assailing her nostrils. She'd lay out the table and light the candles for ambience, while James would choose a particularly good bottle of white wine from the chiller they'd had specially installed in the cellar. Then they would sit and talk about James's day, about how he'd slaughtered the opposition yet again and brought in big business. It was their routine every time they shared a night in together, and Julia loved it. She loved watching James talk, loved the thought that she was married to such a powerful and successful man.

"Here I am." She walked into the kitchen with her special welcome-home smile bolted in place. "How was your da—" She stopped in her tracks as soon as she clapped eyes on him.

"What?" He looked faintly annoyed.

"You've . . . um . . . had your hair cut."

"I have," he said crisply, removing his suit jacket and placing it over the back of a dining chair. "Ten out of ten for observation."

Julia hated it on sight. It was far too short and distinctly uneven on one side, with a large tuft protruding over his right ear while his left was unencumbered. She was unsure how to react at first.

"Where did you have it done?" Tell me, and I'll make sure you never, ever darken their door again, she thought.

"Nowhere. Well, not in a salon anyway." He looked slightly

uncomfortable. "I popped into Deborah's on the way home, and she did it."

Julia was stunned into silence for a few moments, unable to believe what she'd just heard. "You're kidding, right?"

"Er, *no*." He pointed at his haircut as evidence.

"You let *Deborah* cut it? She's an elementary-school teacher, for God's sake, not a hairdresser! Have you gone completely mad?"

James adopted a wounded expression. "Actually, I thought she'd done it rather well," he sniffed.

"Yes, well, you can't see it. I can, and it looks *dreadful*."

His face clouded. "Well, gee, darling, thanks for your support. I'll remember to call and ask your permission the next time I want a haircut." He picked up his jacket from the back of the chair and started to head toward the door to go upstairs.

But Julia blocked him, sidestepping so her body filled the doorway. "Hang on a minute." She was fuming with indignation. "Don't try to twist this round so it's my fault. You're the one who stopped off and got sheared by your ex-wife."

He stood stock-still in front of her, maintaining defiant eye contact but not attempting to walk past into the hallway.

"Just tell me this," she said, attempting to soften her tone. "*Why* did you have to go there? I thought we'd talked about this."

James let out a low sigh of resignation and walked back toward the kitchen table, replacing his jacket on the chair. "Because she rang and asked me to."

Julia felt the familiar bubble of anger rising inside her but managed to suppress it.

"Why?"

"There was a problem with the ballcock in her downstairs loo. It wasn't flushing properly."

"What, and every plumber in the yellow pages was unavailable?"

Julia's tone was hard. She didn't mean it to be, but she couldn't help herself.

"Oh, come on, Julia." He did one of those long blinks that suggested his tolerance was at a breaking point. "Let's not fall out over a loo cistern, for God's sake."

"No, James, *you* come on. How much longer is this poor, abandoned, home-alone Deborah crap going to go on? The rest of our lives? Can't she just move on and get her own life? We have."

James sank on the chair with a weary thud, clearly all too painfully aware that whatever evening they'd had planned, it was about to turn into yet another prolonged and heated analysis/discussion/argument—whatever you wanted to call it—about his relationship with his ex-wife.

"She *had* the life she wanted," he said, idly picking at a speck of dried food on the table, "and we took it away from her."

Julia made a loud scoffing noise. "That's not quite how I see it, but for the sake of argument, let's just go with that for the moment. I *know* you feel guilty, but how much longer are you going to wear that guilt like a millstone around your neck? After all, she's well educated, reasonably attractive . . . ," she couldn't bring herself to be *too* magnanimous, ". . . and you don't have children together, so there's no reason on God's earth why you shouldn't just be communicating via the occasional Christmas or birthday card by now. It's been nearly two years, for heaven's sake."

James's expression clouded slightly. "You may wish to discard people from your past as if they're some old shoe, but I don't. I happen to be very fond of Deborah, and I see absolutely no reason why I shouldn't stay friends with her. Unless, of course, you're suggesting that I'm sleeping with her?" He looked directly at Julia, his eyes burning into her. "Are you?"

She waved her hand in front of her face in a gesture of dismissal. "Of course not, don't be silly. That's not my point at all."

"Then what *is* your point?" He sighed. "Because I just don't get it."

"My point is that, in my view, for a marriage to work, you have to give it one hundred percent. And while you still have one foot in Deborah's camp—albeit a platonic one—I feel that while you're looking over your shoulder at what's gone before, it makes it harder for us to forge a strong, inclusive relationship. That's all." She tried to look conciliatory, but it was a struggle. "You and Deborah were like two bumps on a log when I came into your life. I was hardly encroaching on a grand passion."

"Precisely!" he said triumphantly. "That's why I can't understand what all the fuss is about. She's just a friend that I help out occasionally. Can't you just accept it for what it is?"

Julia let out a deep, frustrated sigh of such velocity that it rippled the pages of the *Vogue* magazine lying on the table in front of her. Right now, she could easily embark on an hour-long diatribe explaining that her "problem" with it had nothing to do with her trust in him and everything to do with the one-upwomanship between her and his ex-wife. Deborah always played the wouldn't-hurt-a-fly type, but Julia was convinced she knew that every little stop-off that James made to her house was not so much a dagger as a needle in Julia's heart—a minor irritation that was in danger of becoming a major ache purely on the grounds of principle alone. She didn't *know* this, but she felt it. She could also explain how Deborah's continued presence in their life made it virtually impossible—in Julia's view anyway—for their marriage to feel fresh and original. There was always a reminder that James had done it all before, and because she was so in love with him, she wanted their relationship to feel exhilaratingly new for both of them.

But she didn't say any of these things. After all, she'd been down this road before, countless times. While James was at the height of his profession and undoubtedly an extremely bright man, he was borderline moronic when it came to emotional intelligence. As far as he was concerned, there was no personal conversation so big that it couldn't be run away from.

So she buried her misgivings, deep down in that dark place where it was kept company by so many other unresolved issues and frustrations. She'd just have to let off steam at the club, that haven where she and the other second wives—conditioned to feel they weren't entitled to complain because of the circumstances of their marriage—unburdened themselves to like-minded friends.

"Let's just forget it." She put on her best brave smile and walked across to sit on James's knee. She ruffled his disastrous haircut, noticing that it didn't make it look any better. "Why don't you go and freshen up? Dinner will be ready in ten minutes."

He thrust his face into the soft crevice of her neck and inhaled deeply. "God, I love your smell. I can't get enough of you, you're my drug. I *hate* it when we argue."

"So do I, darling." She kissed him tenderly on the forehead and stood up. "As I said, let's forget it. We'll eat dinner, and then I have a little treat in store for dessert." She hooked a finger in the waistband of her chinos and pulled it down slightly to reveal the top of her new lingerie.

James let out a low groan and made a lunge for her, grabbing her waist and pulling her back toward him. "I can't wait until dessert, I want to have you for starters."

And there, on the kitchen table, he did just that.

men and women.
women and men.
it'll never work.

Natasha's Café was tucked into a small side street just yards from the busy high street frequented by the world and his wife . . . or second wife.

It was a favorite gathering place for the club, largely because all the food was homemade on the premises and therefore the chef could cater to the many and varied diet needs of each of the group's members.

Fiona was currently trying out the no-wheat, no-dairy diet and was surveying the butterless baked potato options. Punctuality was a virtue, she mused, but sadly there was rarely anyone around to share it with you.

Then she looked up and saw Alison enter the café, nervously scanning the other tables. She looked stunning, her stylish brown bob framing her honey-tanned face with its small smattering of freckles across the bridge of her impossibly neat nose.

"Over here!" Fiona waved and smiled broadly. "I'm so glad you were able to make it. How was the honeymoon? You look fantastic."

"Thanks." Alison sat down gratefully. "We had a great time. It's such a beautiful place. We did lots of scuba diving and saw some incredible fish."

"Sounds great." Fiona was impressed. "The only thing I saw on my honeymoon was the ceiling."

It had been just over two weeks since Alison and Luca's wedding, and they had recently returned from a trip to the one and only Kanahura resort in the Maldives. A fortnight in paradise had been just what they'd needed to get their relationship back on track after Sofia's dramatic intervention on their big day. It had been glorious to have Luca all to herself, although she suspected that there had been a few intense phone calls with Sofia out of her earshot.

Suddenly, the head of every man in the place swiveled to face the door. Julia had arrived, sashaying in like Lily Rabbit, fully aware of the effect she was having. With her blond hair swishing from side to side, she looked like one of those women in the "because I'm worth it" hair ads. Trailing behind her was Susan, wearing a T-shirt with JUST GIVE ME CHOCOLATE AND NOBODY GETS HURT on the front. She was looking as disorganized and disheveled as ever, her carrot-red hair springing out at right angles from her head.

"Hi, all," breezed Julia, placing her perfectly toned buttocks on the chair next to Fiona. "Sorry we're a bit late. Guess who got the wrong time?" She raised her eyes heavenward while nodding her head toward Susan, who had just dropped the entire contents of her handbag over the floor.

Susan and Julia had been friends for ten years, ever since meeting at a yoga class. No one had ever understood why the two women, oil and water, had hit it off and remained friends—least of all them—but by some miracle they had.

"Hello, we haven't met." Julia had turned her headlamps on to full beam and was bathing Alison in their light. She was being friendly, but in truth she also felt slightly threatened by the new-comer's prettiness and petite frame.

"Oh, yes, sorry," interjected Fiona. "This is Alison's first time at the club. I hope you both don't mind, but she was in desperate need of our support."

"Oh?" Julia visibly perked up at the whiff of a potential drama. "A little trouble with the first wife, eh?"

Alison coughed nervously. "You could say that, yes."

"She stormed into Alison's wedding and dragged the two chil-dren away," said Fiona, by way of quick explanation. "They were page boys . . . but she didn't know," she added as an afterthought.

"No! Really?" Julia's expression suggested that Alison had sud-denly gone up in her estimation. "That's a seriously bad-news bitch. What does she do for a living—sniff luggage at the airport?"

Alison flushed slightly and sipped her water. "It's difficult, I ad-mit. But I can understand why she is how she is. She's had every-thing taken away from her."

Julia looked at her with the same disdain she might show a tramp asking for a French kiss. "Oh, come *on*. She's still got her kids, right?"

Alison nodded mutely, still mildly unnerved by this forthright beauty in her midst. She was confident with people she knew and during her rare moments of self-preserving anger, but otherwise it generally took her a while to come out of her shell.

"Well, in that case, she should count her blessings and get on with her life. No one's happiness should depend on a man, including ours." Julia made a sweeping gesture around the table. "The trouble with a lot of first wives is that they don't realize the greatest revenge of all is to simply move on and find happiness elsewhere. That's *so* much sexier than lurking in dark corners plotting revenge on your ex-husband."

Silence descended for a few seconds while the others digested what she'd said. Eventually Fiona spoke.

"Oh, I don't know. What you're saying makes perfect sense, but if you've ever felt aggrieved by someone, all that 'revenge is a dish best served cold' stuff is all well and good, but there's nothing like the instant fix of getting your own back, even in some small way."

Julia sniffed loftily. "People should rise above it."

A loud snorting noise emanated from Susan's handbag, where her face was buried as she tried to find a tissue for her streaming nose. Clamping it to her face, she emerged with a look of derision.

"Julia, you are the absolute *worst* in that regard. You're the first person to seek revenge if you think someone has slighted you."

"That's not true!" Julia looked mortally wounded at such an attack on her, as she saw it, otherwise unblemished character. "Give an example," she added defiantly.

Susan pretended to rack her brain. "Oooh, now let's see, which example to choose? There are so many . . . oh, I know, the Jimmy Choo shoes!"

Julia's face flushed slightly, and she shifted uncomfortably in her seat. "I have no idea what you're talking about. Come on, let's order." She picked up the menu and started studying it intently, hopeful that the mere mention of food would serve as a distraction. But she hadn't bargained for Susan's tenacity.

"Julia and I went to Jimmy Choo to buy some shoes for one of those posh functions she's always going to, and before we'd even entered the shop she saw a pair in the window and set her heart on them."

Julia was doing her best to attract the attention of the waitress, whose arrival might thwart the onward march of Susan's story, but the girl was clearly depriving some village of its idiot, staring into space at the back of the room, oblivious to Julia's waving.

"Go on," urged Fiona, dying to hear the gory details of Julia's vengefulness.

"So we walked inside the shop, and just as Julia walked toward the shoes, another woman appeared from nowhere and snatched them right out from under her nose. Worse, they were totally Julia's size, and doubly worse, they were the last pair in the shop!" Susan flopped back in her chair as if she'd just delivered the Gettysburg Address.

"So what did you do?" Fiona directed the question at Julia, who had now given up trying to attract the attention of the waitress and had turned back to face them. "Come on, spill the beans."

Julia pursed her lips disapprovingly for a few seconds, reluctant to admit to a moment of weakness. But then she remembered their motto, "What's said at the club, stays in the club," and she broke out into a broad smile.

"Oh, what the hell." She leaned forward conspiratorially. "When the stupid cow was paying for the shoes, I noticed she had written her name and address on the store's mailing list. So I took a peek and memorized it."

She paused for dramatic effect, noting with great satisfaction that Alison had the expectant look of someone waiting to be told whether the ticket she'd mistakenly put through the wash was valid enough to secure a lottery win.

"I then spent a hugely enjoyable afternoon on the phone, requesting leaflets on her behalf from Viagra suppliers, impotence help lines, genital wart cures, and S&M mail-order catalogs."

There was an eerie silence for a couple of beats, then Fiona clapped her hands and burst out laughing. "Inspired! Truly inspired. I got the M&S catalog the other day—that wasn't from you, was it?"

"Well, I *am* dyslexic," Julia purred truthfully. "And you know what that means . . . never having to say you're syrro."

Fiona and Susan groaned loudly while Alison simply looked confused, painfully unused to Julia's politically incorrect humor.

Attracted by the noise, the gormless waitress finally materialized at their side, order book poised at the ready.

After she'd gone, Julia smoothed down her skirt and rested her elbows on the table. "Anyway, that was just a bit of harmless fun on my part. Hardly on a par with storming a wedding and dragging your kids away."

Fiona nodded. "True. But, Julia, may I humbly suggest that until you actually have children of your own, you won't understand the deep feelings motherhood stirs up. It's a protection thing."

Julia made a small scoffing noise. "Yeah, yeah, yeah, I know. If a child is trapped under a car, a mother will find the power to lift it. But kicking up a scene about her kids being page boys? That's nothing to do with protection and *everything* to do with her bitterness. She can't move on."

Susan laid a hand on Alison's forearm, indicating that she was about to speak. "Am I right in thinking she didn't know about the wedding?"

Alison, still feeling a little intimidated by Julia, was grateful for the softer approach. "Yes." She smiled nervously. "I thought the boys were there with her permission, but I found out that Luca had kept the entire thing a secret and told her he was taking them to the park."

"Well, *that's* why she was pissed off, because she'd been lied to about her own children." Susan directed the remark at Julia, who was slowly shaking her head.

"I'll bet she'd been lied to for the simple reason that . . . Luca, is it?" Julia looked at Alison, who nodded, ". . . knew full well that *if* he'd asked her permission, she would have rather marinated her own eyeballs in vegetable oil than give it. Am I right?"

Unsure about the vegetable oil bit, Alison winced slightly before speaking. "Yes. We've been together just under three years now, and the boys have only been out with us a handful of times, mostly at the start of our relationship, when they were very young."

"And unable to report back to their mother," Julia interjected. "I'll bet you as soon as they came home and uttered the words 'nice lady Alison,' it was curtains." She drew a finger across the front of her throat.

"Got it in one." Alison smiled ruefully. "Luca mostly sees them on his own these days."

The starters arrived at the table. A Caesar salad minus dressing or croutons for Julia—in other words, a bowl of lettuce—chicken soup for Alison, and two portions of prosciutto con melone for Fiona and Susan. They started to tuck in.

"Right." Fiona used her little finger to wipe away a small blob of cranberry from the corner of her mouth. "Let's officially open the meeting, shall we? Alison, as you're new to the club, let me explain that its purpose is simply for second wives to get together and let off steam."

Julia made the high-pitched noise of a whistling kettle and grinned broadly.

"It came to life six months ago," Fiona continued, "not long after Susan and I met at the local swimming pool with our kids in tow. We got to talking, rapidly established that we were both with men who had been married before, and bingo! We soon came to look forward to our meetings, just so we could let off steam." She looked to Susan for confirmation.

"We did indeed. The only difference is that I'm not married to Nick . . . we just live together," said Susan apologetically. "So I'm an honorary member of the club, if you like."

"A *founding* honorary member," corrected Fiona. "And about four months ago she brought Julia along, so then we were three."

"I came up with the concept and name for the club," said Julia proudly. "Before that we were just three women whining with no purpose."

"Purpose?" Alison looked baffled. "Is there a purpose to the club then?"

"Not as such, no." Fiona pursed her lips. "It's just a bit of therapy for us all, really, a chance to get first-wife issues off our chest. After witnessing Sofia in full flight at the wedding, I felt you might need a little support, and if you ever meet anyone else who you feel is a deserving candidate for membership, do bring them along."

"Thanks, I will."

"So." Fiona looked at Susan. "Why don't you start?"

"Um, well, dare I say it's not been a bad couple of weeks for me, but that's probably because Caitlin's parents haven't been to stay for the past couple of weekends. They're coming this Saturday, so no doubt I'll have plenty to moan about next time."

Alison looked puzzled. "Who's Caitlin?"

"Nick's wife."

"Has their divorce not been finalized yet?" Alison looked confused.

Susan had just popped an extra-large slice of prosciutto into her mouth. She swallowed hard. "I should explain. Caitlin died of a brain hemorrhage four years ago . . ."

Alison clamped a hand over her mouth. "Oh, that's terrible."

"Yes, it is." Even now, Susan felt she might cry. "She and Nick had a daughter, Ellie, who's nearly six and, quite understandably, Caitlin's parents adore her. . . . It's very hard for them, as Caitlin was their only child."

"It must be hard for you too, though." Alison's eyes were full of compassion. "That's a tough situation to be in."

"Yes." Susan nodded emphatically. "Hardest of all is that I feel I can never moan about my lot because there's always someone in the background, i.e., Caitlin, who died. So the only place I can really talk about my feelings and not feel guilty about it . . . is here." She gestured at the others.

Julia poked a finger in the air. "Well, if you *haven't* had a bad week, then get off the pot and let *me* do an almighty shit in it. Because I am just one Valium away from sending Deborah a funeral wreath, then gunning her down on the front step when she opens the door to accept it."

"That bad, huh?" Fiona shot Alison a look that intimated Julia was prone to exaggeration. "What's she done now?"

"I can hardly bring myself to tell you," Julia said dramatically, pushing her half-eaten dish of lettuce to one side. "She *cut* James's hair."

There was silence for a few moments.

"Is that it?" said Susan finally, voicing what everyone was secretly thinking.

"Excuse *me?*" Julia placed a palm flat against her chest in indignation. "I have a husband whose haircut makes Oscar the Grouch look like Orlando Bloom and you ask me if that's *it?*"

Susan wrinkled her nose. "What, he's got *green* hair?"

Julia raised her eyes heavenward. "No, it's just a hideously unattractive cut. I mean, name me another man who stops off on his way home from work so his ex-wife can cut his hair?"

She looked defiantly around the table, everyone shaking their heads to indicate that, no, none of their husbands ever did anything like that.

"It could be worse, I suppose." Alison ventured a lone, brave voice, on account of the fact that she did not know Julia as well as the others, who were wisely staying silent.

"No . . . *Alison*, wasn't it?" Julia fixed her with an icy glare. "It could *not* be worse. I'm doing my absolute best to make my marriage work, and all the time I have this drab leech hanging around, sucking the lifeblood out of it."

"Sorry," Alison simpered slightly. "Now you put it like that . . ."

Fiona smiled benevolently. "Julia, you're tall, slim, extremely beautiful, and nobody's fool. If, as you say, she's a drab little thing, why let her get to you? Rise above it."

"Easier said than done." Julia took a brush from her bag and ran it through her hair, ignoring the fact that Susan was still plowing her way through the last vestiges of her starter. "I don't for one minute think he'd go back to her, but their continued contact is very undermining."

"Inevitable, though, when children are involved." It was Alison again, and the others winced slightly at her misinterpretation. But Julia took it better than they anticipated.

"That's just it," she said. "There aren't any children involved. James chooses to stay in contact with Deborah simply because he . . . well . . . *likes* her."

"Oh, I see."

"You see my predicament?" Julia laid a hand over Alison's, seeking an understanding. "All of you around this table have husbands who *have* to stay in touch with their exes or their family, for the sake of the children. But I . . . I . . . have a husband who hangs around with his ex for no other reason than he finds her company pleasurable. It's a curse, it really is." She stopped speaking and stared off into the middle distance of the café, as if holding a moment's silence for the death of reason.

But the effect was lost amid the clatter of plates as the waitress arrived with the main courses.

"Fish?" She held the plate aloft.

Susan, Alison, and Fiona all shook their heads.

"Fish?" she repeated louder, aiming her words at the side of Julia's head.

"Did you order fish?" asked Alison, tapping Julia's shoulder.

Julia snapped out of her reverie and focused on the offering being held in front of her. "I ordered Dover sole."

"As I said," the waitress intoned defiantly. "*Fish.*" She placed the plate in front of Julia and turned on her heel back toward the kitchen.

Susan watched her go with bemusement, then turned back to the table. "Fiona, how are things with you?"

"Oooh, now there's a question." She grimaced slightly. "Not much to report, really, except that Jake nearly killed Lily."

Her throwaway remark hung in the air for a couple of seconds until it computed with the others, and they began spluttering instantaneously on impact.

"Whaaaaat?" Susan looked horrified. "You're kidding, right?"

Fiona shrugged. "Not really."

She spent the next five minutes bringing them up to speed on the events following her return from Alison and Luca's wedding, right up to the point that she and David had ended up in separate bedrooms.

"Jesus," muttered Julia. "And I thought I had problems. Thank God James doesn't have any children."

"Have you spoken to Jake since?" Susan extracted a piece of particularly sinewy steak from between her front teeth.

Fiona shook her head. "No, I still can't bring myself to. David has, but then he was never angry with him in the first place. I suppose I should, you know, rise above it . . . " She petered out, clearly unconvinced by her own suggestion now that it pertained to her own life.

"Bollocks to that," scoffed Julia. "Jake's sixteen, not six. He was totally in the wrong, and David's doing everyone a disservice if he's pretending otherwise."

"I guess so." Fiona shrugged and gave an expression of hopelessness. "But I do feel dreadful for having struck him."

"Why?" It was Julia again. "He deserved it. All that nonsense about never hitting a child in anger. When are you supposed to do it, Christmas Day when they're thanking you for their presents?"

Fiona sighed. "Anyway, I don't think an apology will be forthcoming, so eventually I'll just have to get on with it."

Neither Susan nor Julia contradicted her, knowing from previous conversations that Jake was a law unto himself.

"Funny, isn't it?" mused Fiona. "We spend the first two years of our children's lives teaching them to walk and talk, then the next sixteen telling them to sit down and shut up. I now know why some animals eat their young."

"Perhaps I'm lucky that Paolo and Giorgio aren't allowed to stay over," said Alison. Noting Julia's blank look, she added: "They're Luca's sons."

Fiona smiled but shook her head. "I appreciate why you might say that, but you're wrong. However much of a pain in the arse Jake is—and believe me, he really is—I still want him to be a strong presence in mine and David's life."

"Really?" Julia looked incredulous. "Why?"

Fiona gave a wry smile. "Because if he wasn't, it would mean that a huge part of my husband's life was closed off in his life with me. And that would never do."

She looked imploringly around the table. "If his only son wasn't a part of our life, if I made it difficult for them to have a relationship—whatever problems he causes between us—what kind of a marriage would we have?"

"A much safer, happier one by the sound of it," said Julia, stirring her mint tea. "I'm afraid I'd cast the little shit out into the wilderness."

"There speaks the earth mother." Susan laughed. The others joined in, including Julia herself.

"Seriously, though." Fiona directed her gaze toward Alison. "You really must insist that Luca stand up to Sofia about the boys staying over. Because if you don't, then it will become the accepted norm. Allowances have to be made, of course, but *your* marriage should be the central relationship now. If you allow the old broken one to call the shots, you're in a no-win situation."

Alison nodded slowly. "Thanks for that advice. I'll do my best. In fact, I should probably address the issue sooner rather than later." She held her wineglass in the air. "Sofia, watch out."

"Attagirl!" Julia banged her cup of mint tea against it. "Here's to second wives ruling the roost."

"Don't we all wish." Fiona laughed.

take a divorce letter,
miss jones

Alison padded quietly from the bed through to the spacious
bathroom of their hotel suite at the trendy Babington
House Hotel in Somerset, an antidote to a particularly stress-
ful week throughout which Sofia had outdone herself in her attempts
to disrupt their life. "You don't know a woman until you've met her in
court," Alison's father, Alasdair, had once told her, and his words now
resonated loud and clear.

The assault had started on Monday morning with the arrival of
yet another lawyer's letter, stressing that unless Luca increased his
monthly payments by another £400, Sofia wouldn't be able to cope
and would have no alternative but to return to court. Luca ran his
own telecommunications business and was, by most people's standards, well off. But his bank account wasn't—as Sofia seemed to
think—a bottomless well. There were two sets of school fees to pay,
two large mortgages, and Sofia's "living" expenses, which, much to

Alison's annoyance, seemed to include regular visits to Gucci, Chanel, and a very expensive private health club. So the thought of yet more money going in Sofia's direction was galling in the extreme.

"Refuse to pay it," she'd said to Luca as he sat, head in hands, after reading the letter. "The court will probably back you up and keep the payments as they are."

Luca had sighed, such a long, deep expiration that Alison feared he might not have any air left in his body. "No point," he'd said wearily. "Even if it went to court and, as you say, they did see my point of view, the legal fees to get to that stage would probably make it counterproductive. I may as well just cough it up. You're right, I don't have to agree, but it will be a lot quicker and a lot cheaper in the long run."

"But when will it stop? Will she be happily dipping into your bank account for the rest of our lives?" Alison kept her voice reasonable, but inside she felt like shouting the words with all the force of someone trying to protect another from an oncoming train.

"I'm afraid that's what happens when you have children with someone." Luca had shrugged. "We always knew it was going to be like this. That's the price you and I pay for being together."

Alison didn't disagree that there was a price to pay, she just didn't see why it should be such an iniquitously high one. The marriages of the other second wives didn't seem to have such an unreasonable blot on their landscape. Nevertheless, she said nothing.

Tuesday had passed by without incident. Then, on Wednesday, just half an hour before Luca and Alison were due to leave for a dinner with Patricia, a friend of Alison's from work, and her husband, the phone had rung. Alison answered.

"Get me Luca," barked the voice on the other end. It was Sofia, as usual devoid of any pleasantries whenever she encountered her successor.

Alison grimaced and stuck her tongue out at the receiver. Childish, she knew, but it made her feel better.

"It's Cruella de Ville for you." She gently threw the hands-free phone to Luca as he emerged from the bathroom, towel-drying his hair.

For the next few minutes she busied herself getting ready but kept one ear locked into their conversation, trying as always to guess what was being said on the other end and what latest problem of Sofia's making was about to jump up and bite them.

"Okay, I'll be around in half an hour," she heard Luca say before ending the call and replacing the handset on its cradle by the bed.

Alison's spirits plummeted. "Oh God, what *now?*"

Luca had been unreservedly apologetic, promising that he would make it up to her, but he had to go see Paolo because he was doubled over in pain. Sofia thought it might be appendicitis, and after all, they were *his* children too, and he had to shoulder some of the responsibility for looking after them physically rather than just financially. Words, Alison knew, that were straight from Sofia's mouth.

She hadn't even bothered to argue this time. It was a situation they'd found themselves in on numerous occasions before: unreliable babysitters, family "emergencies" that meant Sofia had to leave the children on short notice, various tummy ailments that the children mysteriously developed on certain evenings. The excuses were varied, but tellingly the timing was always the same: on a night when Alison and Luca had something special planned.

Every time Alison tried to reason with Luca and make him see that his strings were being pulled by his ex-wife, he would go very quiet before finally answering: "They're my children. What else can I do?"

And so Alison had yet again found herself going it alone at

dinner, spending most of the evening telling her friend Patricia how she envied her because her husband, Al, hadn't been married before.

"I know what you mean," Patricia had said, caressing Al's face as she said it, presumably a gesture of her gratefulness at having found such an uncomplicated man. Mind you, not many women would actually *want* Al for a husband, thought Alison, which was probably why he'd stayed single for so long. He was the kind of man who'd invite you back to his place to look at his etchings . . . then actually *show* you his etchings. He lit up a room when he left it.

"But look at it another way." Patricia interrupted her thoughts. "There are some women worse off than you. I read in the paper the other day that a second wife was actually *murdered* by her husband's ex. She put a pickax through her heart."

"Thanks for that," Alison had replied glumly. "I feel so much better now."

But a few days later, on this bright Saturday morning, she was feeling altogether more upbeat at the idyllic country hotel, being spoiled rotten by a profusely apologetic Luca. Last night they'd arrived at the hotel and enjoyed a romantic dinner for two in their room, which he'd arranged to have decorated with two huge vases of her favorite white roses. After they'd finished eating, he'd presented her with a large pink box she recognized as being from Agent Provocateur, the trendy lingerie store that served as the acceptable way for a man to get his girlfriend or wife to wear kinky underwear.

Peeling back the layers of pink tissue, she held up a white lace "peekaboo" bra and matching undies with a diamanté thong running up the back. Anything white and frilly was Luca's thing, which as "things" go was perfectly acceptable. One of Alison's first-ever boyfriends had gotten off on her spanking him while wearing a pair of dishwashing gloves, a rather unseemly, undignified peccadillo that had always placed her on the brink of hysterical giggles.

Pausing in front of the bathroom mirror now, she felt the warm flush of sexual desire as she remembered parading around the bedroom last night, modeling her new underwear for a growling Luca. He'd lunged at her, grabbing one side of the panties and snapping them in the process.

The memory reminded her that she'd sustained an injury. Lowering her hand to between her buttocks, she winced slightly as her fingers made contact with a sore line of flesh running up toward her coccyx. Or diamanté burn, to give its proper medical term. But then she always found that underwear designed to instigate hot sex rarely walked hand in hand with practicality.

Brushing her teeth, she leaned forward and grimaced at the mirror, inspecting her gums for any signs of decay. All in good shape.

In fact, despite a few minor quibbles here and there, Alison had to admit she was looking pretty good all over for a thirty-six-year-old. But then, of course, her body hadn't been subjected to the ravages of childbirth. Yet.

Her legs were slim but shorter than she would like, but there was nothing she could do about that except wear high heels at all times. Even her Wellingtons had them. Her brown eyes were kind and almond-shaped, definitely her most attractive feature, framed by obscenely long, dark eyelashes that needed little or no mascara. And her two front teeth crossed slightly, making her smile seem crooked. But the overall effect was cute rather than goofy, so she'd never bothered to have them fixed.

Her nose, however, had been tweaked from being a rather bulbous affair to the *retroussé* textbook version it was now. Luca didn't know her nasal history, and Alison had forbidden anyone from her family to tell him. On the one occasion he'd been to her parents' house, she'd even traveled down the night before so she could hide any pre-op photos before his arrival. "It'll be nice for me to spend a bit of time alone with Mum and Dad first," she'd babbled by way of excuse. If he had been surprised that there were no photographs of Alison prior to her twenty-fifth birthday, he hadn't shown it.

Spitting water into the sink, she wiped her mouth with the back of her hand and stepped back. Turning, she caught sight of herself in the full-length mirror on the back of the door.

Her breasts were small but evenly shaped. She'd been assured by various friends and bra-fitters that they were the breasts of a much younger woman. The minute they weren't, Alison was planning to get those tweaked as well.

Walking back through to the bedroom, she lifted the luxurious white cotton sheet and slipped in next to Luca. Shuffling herself into the spoon position, she laid her cheek against his surprisingly soft back and took a deep breath, inhaling the musky mixture of post-sex sweat and the last vestiges of yesterday's Issey Miyake aftershave.

Placing her hand in the curve of his waist, she started slowly caressing his smooth skin, moving up to the area around his left nipple and back down toward his groin, taking care not to actually touch his penis. It was a deliberate technique she knew Luca loved, slowly building up the sexual tension until he couldn't bear it anymore and would turn over to penetrate her.

As he lowered himself onto her and began thrusting in and out, his eyes closed in ecstasy, Alison studied the man she had been desperate to have—whatever the cost. A chink of sunlight was slicing its way through the curtains and falling on his face. With his Italian coloring and long eyelashes, he really was stunningly handsome.

She thought back to the first time she'd seen him nearly three years earlier, a chance but undeniably unique meeting that had crystallized in her mind as the moment she knew her life had changed forever. It had been in London's world-famous Hamleys toy shop, where Alison was desperate to secure the very latest fad toy for her five-year-old nephew Jack, son of her sister Louise. Alison and Jack had always been close, and she often babysat for him, once having him to stay for a whole week while his parents went on a well-earned holiday alone. She desperately hoped that one day she would have a child of her own to love. In the meantime, she lavished Jack with love, attention, and gifts.

Waiting for the elevator to the *Star Wars* department, her breath had caught in her throat as the doors opened to reveal a godlike creature rising from the basement floor, all melted-chocolate brown eyes and cheekbones you could hang your coat . . . or hopefully underwear . . . on.

He, in turn, hadn't seemed to notice her, glancing at his Patek Philippe watch, then staring down at his black suede shoes. She stepped in beside him, and as the lift jerked to life, Alison kept looking over, hoping to catch his eye and captivate him with a winning, albeit slightly crooked, smile.

Floor 1 . . . floor 2 . . . the floor 3 button was illuminated, so she knew she was running out of time.

Then the gods intervened. First came a loud, grinding noise, then the lift shuddered to a resolute halt between floors.

It was several seconds before one of them spoke, neither quite sure whether it was merely a dropped stitch in the day's rich tapestry or whether they really were stuck and going nowhere.

He looked at his watch again and tutted. "I was already late enough, and now this."

The remark was directed into the ether, but as Alison was the only other person in the lift she felt it fair to assume she should respond.

"Yes, I know what you mean. I only have an hour for lunch, so I hope it moves soon." *Not*, she thought silently. In fact, quite the contrary. I hope we're stuck in here for hours, possibly a whole day, until it gets so stiflingly hot that we have to remove all our clothes.

Her salacious thoughts were broken by the sound of him pressing a button on the brass panel and shouting, "Hello? *Hello?*"

Eventually a disembodied, bored voice answered. "Yes. What's the problem?"

"The lift is stuck. We can't get out," he said impatiently, his voice sounding more Italian in agitation.

"Okay, hang on. I'll get an engineer down. How many of you are in there?"

"Just two of us. Be quick . . . please." He took his finger off the button and sighed heavily, looking directly at Alison for the first time. "You okay?"

"Fine, thanks." She smiled. Never been better in fact. "You?"

"Fine. Except that I am supposed to be meeting my children for lunch."

Alison's face visibly fell, but she hastily disguised it as worry for his potentially abandoned offspring. "Oh dear. Perhaps you could get that man . . . ," she gestured at the brass panel, ". . . to call ahead and get someone else to meet them."

He waved his hand dismissively. "It's not massively urgent because my wife is with them."

First children, now a wife. Typically, like so many other dream men, someone else had gotten to him first. Suddenly, Alison didn't care how quickly they fixed the damned lift.

"Which means, of course," he added, "that when I don't turn up, she'll think I have forgotten or don't care about her and there'll be yet another unholy row when I eventually make contact."

Whoa, hold that engineer. Alison affected a face of quiet concern. "Rough patch, is it?"

"Not so much patch." He looked at his watch again. "More several hundred acres of overgrown wasteland."

"Oh." Alison didn't know what else to say, except perhaps hooray, and she didn't feel that would be appropriate under the circumstances.

"Sorry to bore you with my problems." He fixed his wonderfully sexy gaze on her. "But my marriage is all but over, and they do say it is sometimes easier to unburden to strangers."

Alison had never heard that before, but it suddenly felt like the best saying in the world. "That's okay. Feel free." She smiled in what she hoped was a cute way.

"Are *you* married?" He was blatantly studying her, waiting for her response.

"No. Not even close. In fact, I've just split up with my boyfriend after two years. He wanted to get married and I didn't," she lied. It had been the other way round, but there was no way she was going to admit that.

"Yes, marriage is a big thing. Very *final*." The word seemed to thud to the floor, weighted down by dread. "You have to be very sure, or you end up with someone you have nothing in common with . . . like I did," he added as an afterthought.

"But you have children together."

"Yes. We're Italian." He smiled, as if that explained everything. "Do you want children?"

It was a question she had banned even her mother from asking, feeling it was too laden with pressure. Yet here was a man she'd "known" five minutes asking her the same. She consoled herself that his inquiry was merely a politeness and not the loaded missive it was when it left her mother's lips. "Yes, I hope to. But I'm only just thirty-three, so there's plenty of time."

He didn't answer, merely pursing his lips in a fashion that, in Alison's mind anyway, suggested she'd better get on with it before her eggs shriveled to the size of pinheads.

"You said you're on a lunch break. What do you do?" he asked idly, staring up at the trap door in the ceiling.

"I'm an executive assistant." Now she looked at her watch. "And a very late one at that."

"Oh? Which executive?"

"Jack Phelps. From Impacta."

"Know it well." He leaned forward and removed a piece of fluff from the lapel of her jacket. "Actually, I'm looking for a new assistant. Interested?"

She wasn't. Not in the job anyway. Jack Phelps was an absolute poppet to work for, and she was paid and treated well.

But she *was* interested in this man who only fifteen minutes earlier she had no idea was even walking the planet. Yes, he was distractingly handsome, but there were plenty of those around and they didn't always strike such a chord in her. No, it was something more, something her mother had always said she'd feel when she met the man she was going to spend the rest of her life with.

And despite the fact that he was married with children, she just couldn't let him walk out of those lift doors and back out of her life. As she saw it, fate had thrown him into her path. The rest was up to her.

So that was why, when the lift suddenly jerked back into life and finally delivered them to the third floor, they emerged into the small crowd to shake hands on her new job. Alison was about to become a cliché: the secretary who ended up marrying her boss.

distant relatives are the best kind

Susan was dressed in a long white gypsy skirt with a sheer white cotton top, her unfettered breasts looking magnificent as she ran through the cornfield, her curtain of shining hair catching the last vestiges of the orange sunlight.

Denzel Washington, looking particularly rugged in a tight, white, capped-sleeve T-shirt and faded jeans, had just caught up with her and wrapped his arms around her tiny waist. He had lust in his eyes and started grunting: "God, I want y—" but the last word was drowned out by a loud whining noise coming from her right.

"Mumm-eeeeee! I want a drink."

Wincing, Susan opened one eye to find Ellie standing by the side of the bed, her faithful Pooh bear in one hand, empty cup in another. Denzel would just have to wait. "Okay, sweetie." Susan raised herself onto one elbow and squinted at the clock. It was 6:45 A.M. "Let me just get my bathrobe."

Nick was doing his usual trick of pretending to be asleep, even though Susan knew there was no way he actually was. Usually the man was such a light sleeper that he'd be disturbed by a pin dropping on a shag-pile carpet.

Every Saturday morning was the same. Susan would get up with Ellie, play with her for a couple of hours, then make an omelet at 9:00 A.M., when Nick would emerge bleary-eyed from upstairs complaining about how tired *he* was.

But Susan didn't mind too much. Nick had his faults, but he was fundamentally a good man and a great father. It was just the live-in-lover bit that needed work, she thought ruefully.

Swinging her legs around, she sat on the side of the bed and rubbed the sleep from her eyes. Or lack of sleep, in fact. Ellie was running a bit of a temperature, and it had been a disturbed night, with Susan racing in and out to reassure her every couple of hours.

"Come on, pumpkin, let's go get you some juice." Taking the child's hand, Susan led her down the stairs and into the kitchen.

Pouring grape juice into Ellie's cup and flicking on the kettle switch with the other hand, Susan leaned against the counter and tried to get her brain in gear. Now then, what day was it? Ah, yes, Saturday. For a blissful couple of seconds, she felt lighthearted about the day ahead. It was sunny outside, so perhaps she and Nick would take Ellie to the park, then stop off for a spot of lunch in one of those trendy cafés that had chairs and tables outside. Yes, that's what they'd do.

Then she remembered, and her heart thudded with disappointment. It wasn't an ordinary Saturday after all, it was a Bitch and Bracket Saturday, as she called it—otherwise known as the day Caitlin's parents, Genevieve and Bill, descended. Genevieve was "Bitch" in the complaining sense of the word, owing to her habit of criticizing Susan's every move regarding Ellie, and Bill was "Bracket" thanks to his fondness for DIY home repairs. Or botched DIY home repairs, to be more precise.

Without fail, on every one of their monthly visits, he insisted on carrying out some form of handiwork on their home, whether they wanted it or not. Invariably, it was so badly done that they ended up employing someone else to come in and put it right.

Susan let out a long sigh. Leaving Ellie in front of some children's TV program with the ubiquitous shrieking presenters saying, "You know?" every three seconds, she trudged upstairs to the spare room to check it over for Genevieve and Bill's arrival. Nick had crept in there a couple of nights before to escape a late-night visit from Ellie, all flailing limbs in the middle of their bed, and typically he had left it in total disarray. The extra blanket was on the floor, and the duvet was lying on top of it in a crumpled heap. The bottom sheet had peeled away from the mattress to reveal the unedifying sight of an old bloodstain. Whose blood was a mystery.

Wrinkling her nose, Susan began to make the bed. She knew she should change the sheets for Bill and Genevieve, but quite frankly, she couldn't be bothered. Besides, they looked clean enough, and it was only their own son-in-law who had slept in the bed.

Plumping up the pillows, she glanced toward the bedside table, where a photograph of Caitlin was smiling back at her. It had been taken the year before she died, and she looked radiantly happy, cradling a newborn Ellie in her arms.

Even though Caitlin's ghost haunted her in so many ways, Susan still felt an overwhelming sadness whenever she thought of how such a vibrant life could have been snuffed out so prematurely and so swiftly. And even though she had stepped into Caitlin's shoes and loved Nick and Ellie with all her heart, Susan would have happily given it all up if it would bring her dear friend back to life.

The photograph was in a solid silver frame, engraved with the words TO THE BEST MUMMY IN THE WORLD, LOVE, ELLIE, and it was buffed to perfection by Genevieve on every visit. Lifting the corner of her dressing gown, Susan wiped away a layer of dust on the bedside table, then stepped back into the doorway and inspected the bedroom. It looked fine, but she knew it wouldn't pass muster with Bitch, that there'd always be *something* she'd have to pick fault with, simply to hammer home how haphazard Nick's new partner was compared to her beloved daughter.

Susan instantly felt guilty thinking such thoughts, even if they were true. She knew it had been devastating for Genevieve and Bill to lose their only child, and Ellie, with her blond hair and big blue eyes, was the living image of her mother, a small part of Caitlin that lived on. She just wished they wouldn't trample her own feelings into the ground in the process of exorcising theirs.

Nick's parents had retired to Malta a couple of years ago, so their visits were irregular. Besides, both of them had readily accepted Susan because she'd always been on the periphery of Nick's life through school and his early twenties. And as for Susan's parents, well, she'd never known her father, and her mother was dead. So neither were around to pass judgment on her life.

She looked at her watch. It was now 7:30 A.M., just three hours of relative calm left before the inevitable storm.

Nana!" Ellie ran along the hallway and launched herself into Genevieve's outstretched arms, wrapping her little legs around her waist.

"My darling!" Genevieve hugged her tightly, then gently lifted her to the ground and took a step back to look her over. "You've gotten so big!"

"Yes," said Ellie proudly. "And look." She opened her mouth and stretched her lips back to reveal a gaping hole where, until last week, a front tooth had been.

"Oh, my word! Has the tooth fairy been here?"

"Yes." Ellie's eyes were shining with excitement. "She left me a whole five pounds!"

"Really?" Genevieve cast a disapproving look toward Susan and Nick, who were hovering in the background. "That was *overly* generous of her. She mustn't *spoil* you."

Christ, thought Susan, that's a world record. She hasn't even gotten past the front door and already she's picking fault. Nick came to the rescue.

"Things have moved on, you know, Genevieve. Sixpences aren't acceptable currency these days," he teased, a tactic he always used to temper his mother-in-law's grumblings.

"I know that, Nick," she retorted. "But twenty pence would suffice, or a pound at the very most."

"Well, it's up to the tooth fairy, isn't it?" he said lightly. "We can't interfere with her wishes, can we?"

Just as the subject seemed to be closed, Ellie piped up: "Mummy says I can spend it on sweets!"

Susan's heart sank. She knew there was a double whammy here. Firstly, Genevieve *hated* hearing Ellie call her Mummy, but it was something she'd had to get used to. And secondly, she was very reluctant about giving children sweets of any kind.

"I see." Her voice was brittle, and the look she shot Susan would have frozen hot water. "Intent on losing the other teeth as quickly as possible, are we?"

Susan felt like she was eight years old again, a scolded child standing mute before her terrifying headmistress. But thankfully, Nick was rarely intimidated by his mother-in-law.

"It'll be a small chocolate bar she buys, Genevieve, not nitric acid," he retorted. "Now let me take that upstairs for you." He grabbed the overnight bag at her feet and started to walk upstairs with it.

"Tea?" asked Susan brightly.

"Thanks, love, I could murder a cup," said Bill amiably, stepping forward to plant a kiss on her cheek.

Although his DIY skills left a lot to be desired, Susan always found Bill to be an easygoing, pleasant man who never voiced his views about how well or otherwise he thought Ellie was being brought up. If his formidable wife even allowed him to *have* any views.

He was a tall, slightly plump man with the kindly face usually associated with drawings of farmers in children's books. His shock of thick hair was blond peppered with gray, and his slightly darker, excessively bushy eyebrows overshadowed small currantlike eyes. He was fond of smiling, and it showed in the weather-beaten lines that were a permanent fixture on each side of his face. When he actually smiled, he flashed a set of strong but haphazard teeth yellowed from years of after-dinner cigar-smoking. His "uniform" was a pair of old cord trousers, either blue or brown, and a selection of soft cotton shirts with collars of varying degrees of frayed. After years of trying, Genevieve had given up trying to get him into smarter clothes.

In contrast, she was an impeccably dressed woman. About five-eight, she had done light exercise all her life and never overindulged on food. Consequently, she was slim and could carry off her favored trouser suits with great panache. All plain in color and classic in shape, she simply spiced them up with an embroidered shirt or colorful scarf. Nothing too fussy. She didn't smoke or drink, so her treat to herself was a twice-weekly visit to the local hairdresser to blow-dry her slightly graying brunette hair into a Margaret Thatcher–esque crowning glory. The overall image was very much Tory wife. She was in her midfifties, but although her figure and dress sense placed her as younger, her stiff, formal hairstyle and the ever-present grief etched on her face had aged her immeasurably.

"So." She followed Susan through to the kitchen, her pale blue eyes darting around the room, no doubt looking for faults. "How have you been, Susan?"

This was a new one. Usually, she questioned Susan intensely about Ellie's welfare, but never her own.

"Fine, thanks. You?" Susan didn't know what else to say. She and Genevieve had never shared cozy chats, and she felt uncomfortable being alone with her, so she breathed an inaudible sigh of relief when Bill ambled into the room clutching Ellie's hand. Instantly, his eyes alighted on a cupboard door that was hanging awkwardly, one hinge broken.

"Now look at the state of that," he tutted, his huge hands lifting it up to its correct position. "I'll have that fixed in no time."

"Thanks, Bill, but you really don't have to. We can call someone about it. Why don't you relax for a change?" Susan kept her tone light, but inside she was dreading the thought of him getting under her feet as she prepared lunch. "You and Genevieve could take Ellie to the park if you like."

"Of course we can," snapped Genevieve, quick as a flash. "We don't need your permission."

Susan just stood there for a few moments, stunned by the outburst. "I didn't mean . . . I mean, I didn't . . ." she stuttered, feeling like she might burst into tears at any moment.

"Right. Is the kettle on?" Nick was back from upstairs, rubbing his hands at the thought of a hot mug of tea. If he sensed any tension in the room, he didn't show it. "I thought we might take Ellie to the park while Susan throws together some lunch." He looked at Genevieve. "Fancy it?"

"That would be lovely, yes." She smiled warmly at her son-in-law, with no hint of the snappiness of just a few seconds earlier. "Are you coming, Bill?"

He ruffled his granddaughter's hair, then rubbed the back of his neck. "No, I think I'd better stay here and get this cupboard door fixed. It must be driving Susan mad."

No, thought Susan mutinously, what's driving me mad is the thought that you're going to stay here and make awkward conversation when I'd much rather you went with the others and gave me some time and space to myself. She shot Nick a knowing look that she hoped encapsulated those wishes, but it passed him by or he chose to ignore it. Either way, she was saddled with Bracket for at least the next hour.

Ten minutes later, with the others gone and having brought his ever-present toolbox in from the car, Bill was lying at her feet, squinting up at the broken hinge and trying to maneuver a screw into place.

"She doesn't mean anything by it, you know," he muttered, his voice muffled by having to filter through the cupboard door.

"Sorry?" Susan was genuinely puzzled as to who or what he was talking about.

"Genevieve. She doesn't mean to be so harsh on you. It's just her way."

Placing his cup of tea on the floor next to him, she stood back up quickly so he couldn't see the expression of surprise on her face. She knew Bill was a long way off from stupid, but she didn't have him down as a particularly deep thinker either.

"I don't find her harsh as such," she replied carefully. "It must be very hard for her. Both of you, in fact."

"There. All done." He stood up and moved the door backward and forward to indicate it worked properly.

"Thanks." Susan smiled and handed him his tea again.

"I don't deny it's been hard for me." He sighed, walking over to the kitchen table and sitting down. "But Genevieve suffered . . . ," he stopped and corrected himself, ". . . still *is* suffering, far more than me. They were so close."

"I know, Nick told me." Susan moved across and joined him, sitting on the chair opposite and resting her elbows on the table. "But don't underestimate the impact Caitlin's death had on you as well. She was your daughter too. It's just that we all grieve in different ways."

They sat in silence for a few moments, with Bill staring up at the conservatory roof. There was a small crack in it, and Susan feared he was going to spring into repair mode at any moment, but he didn't seem to notice it.

"Anyway." He let out a long, deep breath. "I just wanted you to know that it's not personal when she nitpicks at you. Whoever Nick took up with after Caitlin's death would have gotten the same treatment. She just finds it hard to let go, you know?"

Susan nodded sympathetically. "She doesn't have to let go. As long as there's breath in my body, Ellie will have a close relationship with the both of you, and I know Nick feels strongly about that too. She's already lost her mother; to lose her grandparents as well would be terribly cruel."

A small, almost indiscernible tear appeared in the corner of his eye, and he hastily brushed it away. "Thank you, Susan. You're a very special lady, do you know that? You've taken on a lot here, and you're coping admirably."

Now it was Susan's turn to try to control her emotions. For the past few years she'd soldiered on, trying to be all things to all people in what was a very difficult situation. And all she'd ever craved was for Nick to take her in his arms and say thank you, simply to *notice* her efforts.

Now that appreciation had finally come from the most unlikely source, Caitlin's father, dear old Bracket, a man who hitherto she had wrongly assumed was completely unintuitive. She felt the telltale pinpricking of potential tears as she absorbed this unexpected kindness, and the more she thought about what he'd said, the more they came.

"I'm so sorry," she sobbed, extracting an already well-used tissue from her sleeve. "I'm just feeling a bit emotional at the moment, and that was such a sweet thing to say." She was worried her outburst might make him feel uncomfortable, but if it did, he didn't show it. Instead, he leaned across and squeezed her forearm reassuringly.

"I think part of Genevieve's prickliness comes from a deep-seated fear that you and Nick might eventually try to exclude us from Ellie's life," he said quietly. "After all, you could easily do it, and as grandparents, we don't really have any rights. We've looked into it," he added, looking slightly sheepish.

"As I said, you have no worries on that front at all."

"Thanks." He smiled and studied her face, as if measuring her reaction to what he was about to say. "If you don't mind, when this weekend is over and we're back home, I'll tell Genevieve about our little chat. Put her mind at rest."

"I don't mind at all." Susan blew her nose and stuffed the tissue back up her sleeve. "Anything that helps her to cope better is fine by me. I can't imagine what it must be like to lose your daughter."

Bill's eyes, usually full of fun, suddenly turned sad. There was a newspaper on the table in front of him, and he picked up the nearby pen and started doodling on it. After a couple of elaborate swirls, he just dragged the pen back and forth, reinforcing the same straight line.

"I'll never forget the day Nick called," he said, staring fixedly at his handiwork. "I was in the shed at the bottom of the garden and heard what I thought was a wounded animal, a dog maybe." He rubbed his face with both hands. "It was a deep howl that seemed to go on for ages. Then I realized it was my name being called." His voice seemed to catch in his throat at this point, and he stopped for a moment.

"I don't remember running up to the house," he went on, "but I must have done so, because the next thing I remember was standing over Genevieve, who was sitting on the kitchen floor, her back ram-rod straight against the cupboard door. She still had the phone in her hand, but when I listened there was no one on the other end."

He drained his tea and stood up and walked over to the sink, where he started to rinse the cup.

"Leave it, Bill. I'll stick it in the dishwasher."

"It's done now. Besides, Genevieve always says they don't clean things properly." He smiled ruefully, as if to suggest it was one of many misgivings Genevieve had about the modern world.

"And the funeral," he continued. "Well, I just don't know how we got through it." His face contorted with pain, and she could see he was struggling to control himself. "It's not right, is it, burying your own child?"

Susan shook her head in agreement but stayed silent. There was nothing she could say to take away his pain, and she didn't want to insult him by uttering platitudes. Instead, she walked over and put an arm around his huge, shuddering shoulders, giving them a gentle squeeze of reassurance.

Outside in the distance she could hear Ellie's excited voice as the others approached the front of the house. Bill obviously heard the same because he straightened up and blinked a few times, clear-ing his throat in the process.

"Sorry about that. It just gets to me sometimes."

"Don't apologize. I'd be in a constant state of despair if it were me, so I admire your strength." She checked his face. "You look fine, not a trace of what's gone on. Would you like more tea?"

Bill nodded with a look of gratitude. "And one other thing," he added.

"Yes?"

"Don't be afraid to take Genevieve on when she oversteps the mark. It might not be in your nature to answer her back, but if you can manage it from time to time, it might work wonders." He allowed himself a little laugh. "I love her to bits, but she sometimes needs taking down a peg or two."

Susan pulled a scared face, then laughed too. "Thanks for the advice. I'll try to pluck up courage to give it a go."

The front door opened, and a red-faced Nick stumbled into the hallway, Ellie standing on each of his feet and walking in tandem. "Get the kettle on," he shouted down the hallway. "It's thirsty work having a passenger on board!"

"Hello, madam. Were the ducks pleased to see you?" Susan lifted Ellie into the air and planted a kiss on the end of her cold nose.

"Yes. But Nana says you're naughty for buying white bread. It's not good for me."

Bill's words still ringing in her ears, Susan knew it was now or never to try to break the victim-bully pattern of her and Genevieve's relationship. Taking a slow, deep breath, she placed Ellie back down on the floor and rolled her eyes heavenward. "Well, if Nana can get you to eat anything else, then she's more than welcome to try. In fact . . . ," she looked straight at Genevieve, ". . . there's some wholemeal in the bread bin, so why don't you butter some up for Ellie's tea and heat up some SpaghettiO's? I'll bet you five pounds the bread is still on the plate when the spaghetti's long gone."

Genevieve simply pursed her lips slightly, then turned toward the cutlery drawer to retrieve a knife.

Nick was reading the paper, and Susan's small victory had clearly passed him by. But when she looked over toward Bill, he winked, a small smile playing on his lips.

She winked back, resisting the urge to run over and hug him once again.

take my husband's ex-wife . . . please

Julia couldn't wait to get out of the cab. She was positively itching to rush through the doors of New York's famous Bergdorf Goodman store, but she forced herself to stay rooted to the spot until James had paid the driver.

"Oh, darling, I'm soooo excited," she breathed, clutching his arm and guiding him to the door. "This is my favorite store in the whole world."

"Really?" James tweaked her cheek playfully. "I could have sworn that honor went to Harvey Nichols . . . or was it Harrods?"

"No, they're my favorite *British* stores."

"Oh, I *see*. Well, I'm glad we've cleared that one up. Now then, where to first?"

Leading him through the vast selection of handbags, loftily displayed on podiums as if they were Olympic medal winners, Julia headed straight for the lift. It was her thirty-third birthday, and her present had been this trip to New York, plus the purchase of one out-fit (or possibly two if, as was usual, she managed to wrap James round her little finger) from the store frequented by New York's wealthiest.

As they stepped inside the elevator and pressed the button, a woman of indeterminate age followed them. She could have been anywhere between forty-five and sixty-five, but one thing was cer-tain, she'd had at least one facelift, possibly two. She got out on the second floor, and the doors had barely closed before Julia opened her mouth.

"Bloody hell, I'd sue if I were her. Did you *see* how overstretched her face was? I'll bet her belly button's up to here." She pointed to the middle of her chest. "I've never seen as many facelifts as there are in this town."

"Would you have a facelift?" asked James idly, staring down at his shoes.

Julia's hands shot up to her face, her expression that of a small child who'd just been told the last cookie in the jar had been eaten. "Why? Do you think I need one?"

He looked up. "Of *course* not," he said derisively. "It's just that you brought it up. Anyway, as Mark Twain once said, wrinkles merely indicate where smiles have been."

But Julia wasn't smiling now. Not even the glimmer of one. She let the matter drop, but inside she was stinging. She was a stunning woman, but like so many beauties, deep down she was a seething mass of insecurity. To Julia, her looks were almost everything, and the thought that they might be fading in James's eyes, even in some small way, filled her with trepidation.

The lift doors opened, and they stepped out onto the fourth floor, Julia's eyes doing a quick, ruthlessly professional scan of the racks in front of her. She headed straight for the designer evening gowns. James was going to pay dearly for that last remark.

Her fingers expertly rifling through the line of dresses, they stopped at a long, black, crepe de chine gown. It was so light to the touch, it was barely noticeable. Julia knew what suited her, and invariably it was black. Although shopping was her number one hobby, her wardrobe was that of a woman who was highly selective in what she bought. More important, she had regular clear-outs, jettisoning anything that was past its sell-by date. Unlike so many of her friends who probably had their old prom dresses lurking at the back of their closets, Julia never felt sentimental about clothes. Nor did she fool herself that if she hadn't worn it for a year, she might wear it the following one. Out it went, either to a secondhand store or to the ever-grateful charity shop a mile or so from their home. She was always making space for the next big thing. Or, in Julia's case, the next petite thing.

"Darling," she purred at James, "I think this is going to be the one. Won't be a moment." She headed off toward the changing rooms, knowing that her husband's boredom threshold was lower than Danny DeVito's testicles. The trick was to always swoop in quickly and make a decision almost instantaneously. Besides, she too wanted to get back to the hotel as quickly as possible—to make the most of their penthouse suite at the trendy, minimalist Royalton.

An hour later they were back in the room, Julia's new purchase laid out on the bed. She had been right the first time—the black dress fit her perfectly. Picking it up, she eased the ribbon straps onto a hotel hanger and padded across the floor to the wardrobe. Her bare toes sank into the deliciously soft, springy carpet.

James was lying on the bed, idly flicking through the dozens of American TV stations, most of which seemed to be dominated by frenetic infomercials advertising everything from popcorn makers to ab-toning machines.

"My God," he said, "it's relentless. Why do they always have to shout? It's enough to give you a splitting headache."

Julia walked over to the bed, crawling across it on all fours and grabbing the remote control from his hand. She flicked the off switch.

"Now we certainly don't want you getting a headache, do we?" She started to nibble his ear, flicking her tongue in and out. She knew it drove him crazy. "I've got half an hour before my facial, and I want to say thank you for my wonderful present."

Deftly, her manicured fingers started to undo the buttons of his shirt, her face nuzzling into his chest as she did so. James smiled languorously and tucked his arms behind his head, his demeanor that of a man who knew he was about to experience a very enjoyable ride.

Sex was Julia's specialty. She'd read dozens of books on it, devoured every magazine article she could get her hands on, and had once even attended a seminar entitled "Bringing Your Man to New Peaks." And it wasn't about mountaineering. What she lacked in emotion she more than made up for in technique, priding herself on being able to make any man putty in *her* expert hands.

James was already groaning in ecstasy as her mouth reached his groin, her tongue flicking butterfly-style up and down. Her lips resting gently at the top, she began to blow gently, teasing her prey. Then, just as James sounded as if he might explode, she drew him deep into her mouth until the telltale shudder that indicated her work was nearly done.

Seconds later she padded into the bathroom and spat into the sink. It was far too fattening to swallow.

"All right, darling?" She popped her head round the door and glanced at her husband, who hadn't moved.

"Perfect," he murmured, a dreamy smile playing on his lips.

Men, she thought. So easy to keep happy. A blow job a day keeps the divorce lawyer at bay, that was her motto.

Cleaning her teeth, she jettisoned another, more pleasant mouthful of froth into the sink and ran her fingers through her mussed hair. Sashaying back into the bedroom, she threw on a

T-shirt that said NEXT MOOD SWING: SEVEN MINUTES and a pair of trackie bottoms, then looked at her watch. "Right, I'm off to have my facial. I'll be back in an hour."

She stooped over and planted a kiss on James's cheek. He didn't react, seeming to be in a deep slumber.

Letting herself out of the suite, Julia closed the door quietly and padded down the corridor toward the lifts. The doors opened, and she was about to step inside when something popped into her head. "Shit!"

She let the elevator go and headed back toward the room to pick up a toweling headband. No doubt the salon would have one, but Julia was never quite sure how clean they were and preferred to use her own. Cleanliness was one of her obsessions. Turning the key, she pushed the door open gently so she wouldn't wake James. But as she stepped into the small anteroom outside their bedroom, she heard him speaking.

"Yes, it's a great room. It's been feng-shuied, for God's sake! And it's got a great little terrace, which is virtually unheard of in New York," he said.

Julia stood in the shadows behind the door, curious to know who he was talking to.

"And how's your day? Mind you, it's still early for you, isn't it?" he continued.

Okay, thought Julia, so it's not a U.S. business associate then. It's clearly someone back home.

"Ha ha ha. Really? When we were together, you always swore you'd never go there." He laughed.

Julia froze with latent fury. It was fucking Deborah. James had been virtually comatose when she left the room, yet nanoseconds later he had sprung into action to call his bloody ex-wife.

Creeping back toward the suite door, Julia opened it quietly, then slammed it shut again, remaining inside the room.

"Only me, darling!" she trilled, walking into the bedroom.

It might have been her imagination, but she could have sworn James visibly paled when he saw her.

"Gotta go. Great talking to you," he said, hastily replacing the receiver.

Julia stood directly in front of him, studying him intently. "I forgot my headband for the facial," she said matter-of-factly.

"Oh, right." He looked uncomfortable, perhaps unsure of what else to say.

Julia sauntered into the bathroom, grabbed her headband from the side of the sink, and reemerged. "Who was that on the phone?" She kept her voice as casual as possible.

"Oh, no one you know." He picked up the remote control and switched the TV back on. Julia had had every intention of remaining calm and waiting to see if he voluntarily owned up to the conversation with Deborah, but his perfunctory dismissal of her question made her rethink her strategy.

Leaning across the bed and grabbing the remote control, she hit the off button for the second time, prompting him to turn and scowl at her.

"Now that I have your undivided attention, I'll ask the question again. *Who* was on the phone?" She stood with her hands on her hips.

"As I said, *no one you know*," James emphasized, his expression suggesting she was deranged.

"Oh, I don't know," she murmured, pretending to idly pick at a piece of loose cotton on the bed throw. "I would say I know *fucking Deborah* quite well!"

James started, shifting himself into a more upright position. "*Deborah?* What are you talking about?" he replied, looking for all the world like a man who had been cruelly misjudged.

Julia held her hand in the air, facing him in a "stop right there" gesture. "Cut the crap, James. I was listening outside."

His mouth set in a thin line. "Oh, you were *listening*, were you? Since when have you taken to spying on me?"

Julia marveled at his ability, like most men, to twist the issue around so it suddenly became about something *she* had or hadn't done.

"I wasn't spying," she said, trying to be calm. "I merely came into the room quietly because I didn't want to wake you up. Then I heard you on the phone."

"And carried out the theatrics of the slamming door to catch me out afterward?" he asked, his eyebrows raised questioningly.

She looked at him defiantly. "I just wanted to see if you'd willingly tell me who was on the phone, or whether you'd lie . . ." She stopped, knowing they were now both fully aware of which option he'd taken.

"Well, sorry if I failed your little *test*," he said with a faintly bitter tone. "But it's hardly surprising I lied given your usual overreaction to any contact I have with Deborah."

Julia sat down on the end of the bed with an air of heaviness, her supposedly soothing, stress-relieving facial now a lost cause. "Did you call her, or did she call you?"

He frowned. "Is that relevant?"

"To me, yes."

"Why?"

Julia sighed in exasperation. "Just indulge me, James. For once. Please."

Silence. Then he sighed too.

"I called her."

"Why?" She was surprised by how level her voice sounded.

"To tell her I'd arrived safely." He at least had the grace to look mildly embarrassed.

"I see."

Silence again. James was staring at the remote control, as if

willing it to magically illuminate the television screen of its own ac-
cord, while Julia pursed her lips, deep in thought.

"So let's get this straight," she said after a few seconds. "You bring
me to New York for a birthday treat, I give you a sensational blow
job, then you ring your ex-wife to tell her you've arrived *safely*?
What is she, your fucking mother?"

James winced in disapproval. "Julia, please don't swear. It's very
unladylike."

"So is letting you come in my mouth, but I didn't notice you
complaining about *that*," she snapped.

Usually a tough nut, Julia felt inexplicably close to tears. Here she
was, doing everything in her power to be the perfect wife—beautiful,
manicured and dressed, fantastic cook, great at sex—and all the
while she was being constantly undermined by a woman who, as far
as she was concerned, was none of those things.

Blinking rapidly, she inwardly calmed herself, determined not to
let this latest little episode spoil her birthday weekend. But she still
wanted some answers.

"Okay, I'm sorry I swore at you." She attempted a small smile.
"But you have to admit it's a little peculiar to come to New York
with your second wife and call your first to let her know you've arrived safely. It's like calling Mummy from the school trip."

He looked slightly conciliatory and shrugged. "What can I say?
She worries, that's all."

There were a million reasons Julia could have given as to why it
just wasn't appropriate behavior between a divorced couple, one of
whom had supposedly moved on with his life, and as to why the
phone call couldn't be explained away that simply, particularly as it
had been conducted so furtively. But she suddenly felt very weary.

"Look, James, I don't want to fight about this. But I do want you
to understand that I consider calling your ex-wife out of line under

these circumstances. Particularly when I have vacated your bed just seconds earlier."

He turned down the corners of his mouth and protruded his lower lip, as if considering her assessment. "Okay," he said finally. "I apologize if it upset you."

"Thank you." She smiled, but it didn't reach her eyes. "And *if* Mummy needs to know you've arrived safely on any future trips, do me a favor . . . send her a text message instead." She looked at her watch. "Well, my facial's done for. So if my skin starts to look greasy in a couple of days, you'll only have yourself to blame."

It was a feeble attempt at a joke, but neither of them laughed. On the contrary, James's face suddenly looked very serious.

"Julia, I love you because of what's going on in here." He leaned forward and tapped the side of her head. "I couldn't care less whether your skin is greasy or not. You know that, don't you?"

She nodded slowly, placating him even though she suspected it wasn't strictly true. After all, her looks had been a major factor in attracting James's attention in the first place.

Julia had always liked her men rich, she'd never made any secret of that. And if they were quite handsome too, well, that was a definite bonus.

Trouble was, as she soon found out, behind every handsome and successful man there's usually a woman. So Julia had become used to being a mistress, in the hope that one day one of them might actually leave his wife.

Shortly before she met James, she had just come out of a three-year relationship with Michael, a hugely successful record producer based in London who had a wife based in his hometown of Manchester. They'd been childhood sweethearts, so consequently she was in her fifties just like him—and she looked it. Her once-dangerous curves were now extended detours, and she hadn't made much effort to keep up her appearance over the years. Clearly, the arrangement between them was that she stayed up north, he stayed down south, their grown-up children dipped between the two, and the word *divorce* was never mentioned. He just kept the money coming, and she kept quiet about his extramarital activities, of which Julia was one.

But Julia secretly harbored the hope that *she* would be the one he'd finally divorce his wife for, the one he couldn't bear to lose. After three years, she'd given up trying.

"I don't see why we can't just stay as we are," he'd beseeched during their last-ever conversation on the subject. "We're having fun."

"No, Michael," she'd hissed, before walking out on him for the last time. "*You're* having fun. I'm fucking miserable."

Julia had spent an unprecedented six months on her own after that, determined not to repeat the pattern of wasting precious time on a man who was never going to leave his wife. But the burning question was, How do you spot a married man who's likely to jump? "Instinct," said her friend Dee, newly married to Chris, who'd happily left his wife after a handful of dirty weekends.

"Yes, but you also had the added advantage of knowing he'd left two other wives previously," retorted Julia. "I always seem to meet men who got married when they were twelve and are determined to stick with the decision no matter what."

What she wanted was to meet someone who didn't leave lightly—minimizing the chances of him leaving *her* just as easily—but who, after much persuasion, decided he couldn't live without Julia by his side. Which, considering most women were merely looking for a man with his own bank account, she acknowledged was quite a tall order.

Then James had sauntered into her life, and the chase was on.

He was a striking man rather than typically good-looking, with dark blond hair and green eyes. His nose was large and, thanks to a school rugby clash, slightly crooked. But it somehow suited him.

It was his walk that first attracted her, a languorously slow but meaningful stride that suggested power. That and his chest, which was clearly extremely broad. He looked like a man who worked out, which, after Michael's man breasts, Julia was borderline ecstatic to note.

"Hello." She'd beamed, extending her hand in her capacity as "meeter and greeter" at the sports charity lunch. "You look a little lost. Can I help?"

Whoever needed meeting or greeting from that point had to fend for themselves as Julia engaged James in scintillating conversation about the charity and its "simply marvelous" work funding Saturday soccer clubs for the underprivileged. Like the professional networker that she was, in just under a minute she'd established that he was in his thirties, an investment banker, and called James Frankland.

"And didn't Mrs. Frankland want to come along today?" she inquired. Not very subtle, she knew, but this was her version of speed-dating.

"No, she's a primary-school teacher, so she's got an important job of her own to do," he'd replied.

Bugger, Julia thought. New tactics required. "So what's your involvement with the charity?"

"None as yet. That's why I'm here. I was reading about it the other day, and as a bit of a sports fan myself, I'm keen to get more involved."

Bingo. Julia had seamlessly moved in for the kill, handing over her numbers and suggesting they meet another time to discuss the charity in greater detail, "away from all this noise and distraction."

Their affair had started within a month, although James had made it clear that he felt racked with guilt for cheating on his wife, Deborah.

"But I just can't stop myself," he'd groaned during one of their many Olympian sex marathons at her flat. "You're like a drug to me."

Julia had made a secret promise to herself that she wasn't going to repeat the same mistakes she'd made with Michael. If, after eighteen months, James was showing no signs of leaving his wife, she'd walk away from him, however painful it proved to be.

When that time came, she slowly placed her foot on the pressure pedal and started to instigate the conversations about what their future held. Each time James would screw up his face in discomfort, assuring Julia that it was *her* he really wanted but that he just couldn't face hurting Deborah.

"Can't we just leave things as they are?" he'd implored one night, the same battle cry she'd heard so many times from Michael, and the same bullshit she'd promised herself she'd never swallow again.

So James's "drug" withdrew from his life, forcing him to go cold turkey, refusing to even take his phone calls. He'd lasted just three weeks before turning up unannounced at her flat and stating wearily: "Okay, I'll tell Deborah tomorrow."

Julia let out a nostalgic sigh as she remembered the euphoria she'd felt on hearing those words from her "prize," now lying on a hotel bed in New York having just called his ex-wife.

If, Julia mused, I'd known then what I know now, would I have been quite so keen to drag him away from Deborah?

"Penny for your thoughts?" James looked at her and smiled, his hand reaching out to cover hers.

Yes, she acknowledged, smiling back. I probably would have.

teenagers are god's punishment for having sex

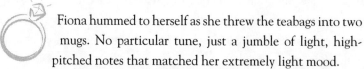Fiona hummed to herself as she threw the teabags into two mugs. No particular tune, just a jumble of light, high-pitched notes that matched her extremely light mood.

She felt uncomfortable thinking it, and wouldn't dream of saying it to David, but the Jake-free weekends were infinitely less troublesome than those when he was moping around the house and generally causing trouble.

Whenever she tentatively broached the subject with David, he always referred to it as "a phase." According to the *Concise Oxford Dictionary*, a phase is "a stage of change or development," and as far as Fiona could see, Jake had been a moody little git for the rather long stage of at least two years now.

"Adolescence," she muttered to herself. "The stage between infancy and adultery."

He hadn't always been that way. When she and David first met, four years ago, Jake had been an affable twelve-year-old, with big blue eyes and a shock of unkempt blond hair. He was angelic both in looks and nature.

In those days even Belinda had been accommodating. She and David had split up a year before he met Fiona, in a joint decision that seemed to have been arrived at through nothing more than mutual boredom.

Belinda had tried to have another baby, presumably to punctuate the tedium of her marriage, but Jake had remained the only child. The minute he started to get a life of his own—going away on football weekends or sleepovers—his parents' reason for staying together evaporated.

According to David, Belinda had instigated the conversation that led to the grand finale, but she had found him an enthusiastic participant in discussing time apart, a breathing space for them both to step back from the marriage and assess whether it had any future. By the time David met Fiona at a mutual friend's thirty-fifth birthday party, he and Belinda had been separated for two years, and for a year of that she had been dating a divorced father she'd met at one of Jake's football games.

So after six months, when David felt the time was right for Fiona to meet Jake, there had been no opposition from Belinda, who clearly relished the thought of some child-free time to spend with her new boyfriend.

The trouble started the minute Belinda discovered her "divorcé" had been economical with the truth and was in fact still married to his wife. Which meant that when he chose to return to her—leaving Belinda heartbroken—he moved seamlessly back into his old life as if he'd never been away. He also left Belinda with all the time in the world in which to be a royal pain in the arse. Suddenly, Jake became her prized possession, the precious golden child she couldn't bear to be parted from, even for one night.

Initially, Jake became like a mini Henry Kissinger, dipping between his parents' two homes, making excuses for his mother and trying to fight in his father's corner with Belinda. But just as Fiona and David were pooling what little money they had to buy a house together, a hefty chunk of his hard-earned funds began lining the pockets of a divorce lawyer who was fighting to get him greater access to his son. While Fiona and David tried their hardest to shield Jake from the ugly realities of his parents' acrimonious divorce, it seemed that Belinda wasn't being quite so fair-minded. Although she was effectively forced to allow Jake to stay with David and Fiona every other weekend, she did her utmost to make sure it was an uncomfortable experience for all of them. All too soon, Jake stopped being the diplomat and became a morose, monosyllabic teenager. Well, in Fiona's company anyway.

He remained relatively genial with his father, but whenever Fiona tried to join in the conversation, he visibly stiffened, his eyes deadening with discomfort. One Sunday afternoon, having had a bellyful of his stinking attitude, Fiona had confronted him. "What *is* your problem?" she'd demanded to know. "Anyone would think I'm the reason your parents split up. May I just remind you that when I met your father, they were already separated—so don't paint me as the witch who ruined your life."

Jake had remained silent for a few seconds, simply staring at the floor and shuffling from one grubby trainer to the other. Eventually, after Fiona had prompted with "Well?" a couple of times, he had replied: "Yeah, but if it hadn't been for you getting in the way, Mum and Dad would have gotten back together."

She had recoiled slightly, stunned by his words. "Who told you that?"

"Mum," he'd replied defiantly. "She says you're a home wrecker," he'd added as a kind of afterthought.

And there it was. Proof, if it was ever needed, that Belinda's raison d'être in life was to poison her only child against his father's new wife, even though Fiona had done nothing to deliberately hurt her.

Thus, the pattern was set for all Jake weekends: awkward, volatile visits during which almighty rows could erupt at any moment, as demonstrated by the incident with Lily in her bath.

Usually, Fiona made the effort—and it really *was* an effort—to phone Jake a couple of times a week to ask how school was going, had his team won the big game, and so on, any question she could think of to break the awkward silence at the other end. But for the past couple of weeks she hadn't bothered. She was still smarting from Jake's refusal to even acknowledge that he had left Lily unattended in such a dangerous situation, let alone apologize.

Consequently, she was secretly thrilled that he wouldn't be darkening their door this weekend. After squeezing the teabags on the sides of the mugs, she lobbed them in the bin and added a splash of milk to each mug.

"Two for tea, and tea for two, tea for me, and tea for you!" she sang.

"My, my, someone's happy."

She spun round to find David standing in the kitchen doorway, smiling at her. Fiona instantly felt guilty at expressing such obvious joy over his son's absence, but then rapidly reassured herself that he didn't actually know that was the cause.

"Yes, sunny days always put me in a good mood," she said, gesturing out of the window as the dark clouds formed. "Oh," she faltered. "Well, it was sunny a minute ago."

"Whatever." David sighed and took the mug she was offering him. "Thanks. What do you fancy doing today?"

"Well," she said brightly, "I thought we could go have lunch at that great little cheap and cheerful Italian in Kensington—you know, the one with the special children's menu where they make such a fuss over Lily." She took a sip of her tea. "And then I thought

we could go to the science museum. It's great for kids. Lily's probably a bit small, but you're never too young to learn, in my opinion."

"Yeeees." David looked thoughtful, staring out of the window.
"Sounds great, but don't you think we should wait until a weekend
when Jake is here to do that? He'd love it."

No, he wouldn't, thought Fiona mutinously. He'd slouch along—
at least twenty yards behind us—with a look of abject boredom on
his face, making it clear in no uncertain terms that he'd rather be at
home interacting with his PlayStation than with any living, breathing human being in his family.

"Darling, we can't *just* do things as a family when Jake is here.
Obviously, it would be lovely if we could . . . ," she murmured diplomatically, then paused a moment, inwardly marveling at how easily
the lies were tripping off her tongue, ". . . but we have to make the
best of the situation we're in, and that means simply getting on with
our lives. Besides, we can always go again when Jake is with us."

David let out a long, deep sigh. "Okay." He smiled, but his eyes
were sad. The toaster made a clanking noise, and two pieces of bread
popped up, one side pale and warm, the other black and crisp. It had
been a wedding present from Jake, and she was beginning to wonder
if he'd had it specially hotwired to be problematic.

"Have you spoken to him this morning?" she asked lightly, anxious
to show David that, although she was still fuming about her stepson's
irresponsibility with his little sister, she was at least mature enough to
ask after his welfare. She handed him a piece of buttered toast.

"No, not yet. I'll call him in a minute." He made a face as he took
a bite, poking out his tongue and removing a large black speck from
the end. "I just want to check that he's studying for his exams. He
really needs to work on his English."

Particularly his conversational skills, thought Fiona. But she said
nothing, once again biting her tongue as every good second wife
should.

"Right!" She wiped her hands on the tea towel. "I'll just go and get Lily dressed and we'll head off." She left the kitchen and started to walk upstairs, quietly savoring her small victory in trying to ensure that while Jake very much affected their lives when he was around, he damn well wasn't going to when he was elsewhere.

Lily was in her room, encased in the large playpen Fiona used for such times when she needed a minute to herself. There were plenty of toys and books in the playpen to keep Lily amused, and it often gave Fiona a much-needed respite from the relentless slog of monitoring every move of her extremely active daughter.

"Come on, munchkin," she murmured, lifting Lily out of the pen. Carrying her through to their bedroom, Fiona placed her on the bed next to the toddler clothes she'd laid out earlier. "We've got an exciting day ahead of us. You're going to have so much fun!"

The phone started to ring next to the bed. She left it, but then looked out of the window and saw David in the front yard, talking to the postman.

"Hello, the incontinence hotline . . . can you hold, please?" she trilled, expecting it to be Susan calling to organize a quick coffee together later in the week. She often rang on Saturday mornings for a chat. Fiona cupped the receiver between her chin and shoulder, as she needed both hands to wrestle with Lily's diaper.

"Is David there?" The disembodied voice didn't respond to her joke and didn't identify itself, but Fiona recognized it.

"Oh, hi, Belinda. He's outside at the moment. Can I help?"

"No, I need to speak to David." Her voice wasn't terse, but it wasn't exactly warm either. "Can you ask him to call me urgently?"

"Is anything the matter?" Fiona had Lily by one leg, trying to stop her from escaping.

"As I said, tell him it's urgent. I need to speak to him right away."

"Charming as ever," muttered Fiona to no one in particular.

"David!" she bellowed in the direction of the stairs. "It's Belinda for you!"

She waited for him to pick up the extension downstairs, then replaced the receiver. She was sorely tempted to stay on the line and listen in, but she'd done that once before and Belinda had sussed her out, knowing from past experience that the line quality sounded fuzzier when there were three in the conversation.

Deftly snapping Lily's clean diaper into place, she wondered what it would be this time. More money perhaps? Or maybe her car needed fixing? Despite the fact that Jake was a strapping teenager who could probably climb Kilimanjaro without breaking a sweat, Belinda still maintained he was a young weakling who needed her at home 24/7 to cater to his every whim, whether it be heating up his favorite ramen noodles or ferrying him around in her ludicrously large Jeep, paid for, of course, by David. Meanwhile, he and Fiona were driving around in a beat-up old Ford Fiesta with two doors, meaning that Fiona practically broke her neck wrestling Lily in and out of the rear car seat, the passenger seat crunching down on her ankle every five seconds. And because Belinda maintained she had to be a constant presence at home to reassure Jake, who was "traumatized" by his father's absence, it meant she couldn't possibly get a job until the lad was eighteen. In other words, she was going to wring every last penny she could out of David and Fiona's melting pot of cash.

Most of the time, Fiona rose above it, determined not to stress out over something she couldn't control. But just occasionally, when she found herself pausing over some luxurious but small purchase, anxious that it might send their joint account into freefall, she did feel an overwhelming swell of resentment.

"There you go, monkey moo." Pulling Lily's T-shirt down so it covered her little potbelly, Fiona lifted her down onto the floor. "Come on, let's go."

She took her daughter's hand and started the arduous process of descending the stairs. Since Lily had started walking, she wanted to toddle absolutely everywhere, so it took twice as long. After a couple of steps, Fiona grew impatient and scooped her up, transporting her to the bottom of the stairs while she shrieked with fury.

"We have to get a move on or the science museum will be closed," she murmured, gently patting Lily's diapered bottom.

She walked into the living room just as David was finishing up his phone call with Belinda.

"Okay, give me five minutes." He looked disturbed.

"What *now?*" Her tone belied exactly what she was thinking, that Belinda was an attention-seeking hysteric hell-bent on causing maximum disruption in their lives.

But David's expression wasn't one of irritation but of deep-seated concern. "It's Jake. He didn't come home last night."

Fiona pondered this information for a moment or two. She wasn't sure what emotions she felt, but panic or even anything approaching concern wasn't one of them. After all, he was sixteen, ferociously independent, and fond of hanging out with a gang of sallow, monosyllabic youths who thought that doing as your parents asked was "uncool." She was convinced he had probably crashed out on someone's couch, sleeping off the mother of all hangovers.

Tracing his whereabouts would require the cancelation of their plans, she knew that, but what she *didn't* get was David's obvious distress, bordering on panic. Presumably, Belinda had worked him up into a virtual frenzy, painting a very gloomy picture.

Fiona decided to bring some rational thinking to the proceedings. "So let's backtrack. Where did he go last night?"

David looked distracted, rifling through the pockets of his jacket. "Have you got the car keys or have I?" he asked, patting his jeans.

"They're in the fruit bowl." She pointed to it on the coffee table, where a bowl containing everything *but* fruit sat. "Did you hear what I said?"

"Sorry?" He had the keys in his hand now.

"I asked you where Jake went last night."

He was heading toward the door with a purposeful step but stopped in his tracks, looking slightly irritated at being delayed. "Belinda doesn't know. She says they had an argument and he stormed off. He didn't even take his mobile phone, which is unheard of. She hasn't seen him since and she's beside herself."

Yes, I'll bet she's deliberately whipped herself up into a right old frenzy, Fiona thought murderously. But she simply smiled reassuringly. "I'm sure it'll be fine. I'll lay money he's sleeping off a sore head on someone's sofa."

David scowled. "I wish I could share your optimism, but he's only sixteen and, according to statistics, in the highest-risk category of being attacked. People traditionally worry about daughters more, but it's young boys who are in the most danger."

Fiona pursed her lips, still favoring her first theory. But she could see that David was genuinely fraught.

"Go on, you get to Belinda's." She opened the door for him. "I'll stay here with Lily in case Jake calls."

"Thanks." He smiled weakly. "I hope your theory turns out to be right, but I'll never forgive myself if anything has happened to him."

Fiona couldn't quite see the logic in David blaming himself, and in any other circumstance, she would have tried to get him to see sense. But she knew all the answers before she even posed the questions. Inwardly, David would be telling himself that if he hadn't left home, Jake might not be heading off the rails, and Fiona knew there was little she could say or do to change that. She knew because she'd tried before.

• • •

After he'd gone, Fiona played with Lily for an hour or so, then popped her down for her midmorning nap.

For the umpteenth time, she checked that the main phone was on the hook and glanced at her mobile. No messages.

Making herself a cup of strong coffee and grabbing a packet of chocolate biscotti from the kitchen, she settled down on the sofa to read the latest issue of OK magazine, stuffed full of celebrities cradling their new babies while their beaming stepchildren looked on. Perhaps it's just *our* life that's blighted by teenage angst, she thought miserably. Perhaps other "blended" families, as the Americans called them, all lived happily ever after, baking cookies together and laughing raucously over board games while the ex-wife looked on, smiling benevolently.

"Nah!" she said aloud. It's a front, she consoled herself. Behind closed doors, they're all bickering, sulking, and muddling along, just like the rest of us.

love your enemies...
it'll drive them nuts

It was a beautiful sunny day, and Natasha's was bursting at the seams with grateful sun worshipers anxious to make the most of it. The owner, Emilio, had pushed most of his tables out onto the pavement overlooking the local square, and every last one was now taken.

But luckily for the Second Wives Club, Julia had rung ahead and finagled him into reserving them a prime spot at the front.

His reward was a showy hug, as she drew him into her ample bosom and wrapped her bare arms around him. As he barely scraped five feet, his eyeline was level with her cleavage, a prize so cherished he probably would have closed down the entire restaurant for her personal use.

Alison and Susan were already in place, with a bottle of sparkling water sitting in an ice bucket in the middle of the table. The waiter was uncorking a chilled bottle of rosé.

"*Hola!*" trilled Julia, pushing her chair into the shade. She was paranoid about wrinkles, which was why she didn't smoke. It was a dilemma, though. Ciggies staved off hunger pangs, so as far as she was concerned, they had a huge upside. "That's Emilio rewarded. Bless him, he's so small you can see his feet on his passport photo."

Susan laughed and shook her head. "You're incorrigible." She looked at her watch. "So we're just waiting for Fiona."

"She'll be here in a minute. I just saw her trying to park that Coke can on wheels she calls a car."

"Don't be such a snob," Susan chided. "She and David aren't loaded like you and James."

"Oh, it's not about money." Julia waved at someone inside the restaurant. "If Fiona won the lottery, she'd *still* have something similar. She's terribly practical like that, one of those 'just as long as it gets me from A to B' types. Whereas I like to go from A to B in style."

"Easy to say when it's not your money." Susan was timid about many things, but she rarely shirked from taking Julia on.

"Darling, what's his is mine, and what's mine is mine too," said Julia lightly, always happy to parody herself. "Besides, wives like me don't come cheap."

Susan raised her eyes heavenward. "Er, what do you *do* exactly?"

Julia looked surprised that she had to ask. "I'm the World Cup of trophy wives, and proud of it. I might make it look easy, but believe me, it's bloody hard work keeping up the standards expected of me. Now up yours!"

Susan laughed out loud and shook her head in disbelief. Alison simply allowed herself a small smile, still a little unsure of her place in the group. But Julia wasn't looking anyway. She was waving at Fiona, who was walking toward them.

"Sorry I'm late." She looked flustered. "I couldn't find a space."

Julia arched a finely plucked eyebrow. "You should have just dumped it and bought a new one tomorrow."

"Ha, ha." Fiona poked out her tongue, then looked at the others. "Sorry, I'll bet you're all starving. Someone pass me a menu."

Once everyone had placed their orders and the wine was poured, Fiona declared the meeting officially open.

"No more new members I note." She smiled. "Still, it's only been a week since the last get-together."

"There nearly was." Julia flicked her blond hair so it sat straight and smooth over each shoulder. "I met another second wife at the health club the other day."

"Oh?" Fiona sipped her wine and closed her eyes in bliss at the taste. "And did you tell her about our meetings?"

"I did. But she said she'd have nothing to whine about because her first wife doesn't cause her any trouble at all."

The others looked momentarily shocked by this revelation, taken aback that there *could* be such a thing as a nonproblematic first wife.

"So I take it there were no children involved?" asked Susan.

Julia shook her head. "No. But mind you, there aren't any children involved in my scenario either and look at the dreary schmuck I'm saddled with."

"True." Alison saw her chance to bond a little, and it worked. Julia rewarded her with a warm smile.

"So did she let you in on the secret of how to get to first-wife utopia?" asked Susan a little sarcastically.

Julia nodded, her mouth full of wine. "Yes. She said she killed her with kindness."

"Huh?" It was a collective expression of bafflement.

"Apparently, when the marriage split up, they were determined to stay friends, and so the other one was often hovering around in the background." Julia shifted her chair slightly so it was fully in the shade again. "So the second wife thought she could either get rattled or get clever. She chose the latter and never said one negative thing about the first wife. Not *one* thing. I mean, can you imagine that?"

They all shook their heads in agreement that, no, they couldn't.

"She even invited her to dinner at their house, for God's sake."

Fiona winced. "Oooh, that's a tall order. I'm not sure I could do that."

"That's what I thought too," Julia agreed. "But her theory was that if you take away the friction, then there's no need for subterfuge, and that means no danger or excitement. Voilà! It peters out."

"And that's what happened?" said Alison dubiously, feeling slightly nauseous at the thought of breaking bread with Sofia.

"Yep. In fact, she decided to move to France and start a new life. They severed all ties." Julia stared dreamily into the distance. "What utter, utter bliss."

"So when's Deborah coming for dinner?" Fiona laughed, intending it as a joke.

But Julia remained serious. "You may mock, but that's exactly what I'm thinking of doing. Well, that or taking her out somewhere, just the two of us. I've got to do *something*. James even rang her from New York to say he'd arrived safely, for fuck's sake."

"So please don't tell me you're actually going to try to bond with her?" said Susan derisively.

"No, I will have dinner with her purely so she can see for herself exactly what she's up against. Once she realizes what a class act I am and how happy I make James, hopefully she'll give up and bugger off. I'm going to show her that she has no effect on me whatsoever."

Fiona made a small scoffing noise. "You're going to lie, you mean?"

"Precisely." Julia raised her glass in the air. "Here's to new tactics."

They all clinked their glasses together and took a swig.

"To new tactics," parroted Fiona. "Though I'm not sure how they'll help me with Jake. We had another incident this weekend."

"God, what's he done now?" said Julia. "Microwaved the dog?"

"We haven't got a dog, but if we had, I'm sure that would be highly likely." Fiona sighed. "No, this time he went missing."

"Fabulous! Better that than moping around under your feet at home." Julia, as ever, pulled no punches. The others offered more appropriate expressions of concern.

"Where did he go?" asked Susan, presuming from Fiona's demeanor that he had eventually turned up safe and sound.

"He'd had an argument with his mother and stomped off to a friend's house, where he proceeded to get plastered and fall into an alcoholic stupor on their sofa. Which is precisely what I guessed had happened when Belinda first rang in a state of panic."

"But no one listened to you?" Alison sympathized, knowing how tough it was to make yourself heard when it came to stepchildren.

Fiona shook her head. "No. We'd had a lovely day out planned with Lily, and the whole thing went out of the window thanks to you know who. So, yes, I'd like to kill him, but with kindness? No, I was thinking of something a little more painful."

Susan waved her fork from side to side, indicating that she would like to speak but that her jaw was temporarily paralyzed by lasagna.

"If, as you say, he'd had an argument with his mother, surely this is the perfect time to step forward to be his buddy, his confidante. You can let him know that, as his stepmum, *you're* less controlling, less judgmental."

The others nodded, Julia embellishing her agreement with a thumbs-up.

But Fiona looked doubtful. "The last time I saw Jake we actually came to blows because he nearly drowned Lily. Somehow I don't think he's going to fall for the hand of friendship routine, do you?"

"Bide your time," Susan advised. "Don't force it. An opportunity will present itself, and as long as you're in that frame of mind, you can exploit it to your own ends."

Fiona wrinkled her nose in disapproval. "I hope you don't mean taking his side when he's in the wrong—which, by the way, he usually is. That would affect my relationship with David."

"Not taking his side as such. Just listen to his side of the story and don't disagree, just stay quiet. That way, you're helping Jake with his problems but not stepping on David's or Belinda's toes."

"Hmmm, well, let's see if an opportunity presents itself. But first things first, we have to start speaking again."

Julia let out a loud snort. "God, what a lot of effort. And for *what*? So you can share cozy chats about Goth bands and pimple cures until he's eighteen and then fucks off on a gap year? No thanks, I couldn't be asked."

Alison let out a snigger. She longed to be as liberated with her thoughts, but it just wasn't in her nature.

"So how about you?" Fiona turned to Susan. "Did you survive your weekend with the dreaded Genevieve?"

Susan sucked in her cheeks and crossed her eyes as if breathing her last. "It was grim. This time she wasn't even through the front door before she was finding fault. But I had a pleasant surprise and found an unlikely ally in Bill. We had a nice chat, and he told me I should stand up to her more."

"He's one to talk," Julia scoffed. "He's terrified of her himself, isn't he?"

"Not terrified." Fiona paused a moment for thought. "More apprehensive really. I think he just likes the quiet life. But anyway, she made some comment about how I shouldn't give Ellie white bread, so I challenged her to make her tea and try to get some wholemeal down her."

Even Julia, normally bored silly by children stories, looked expectant.

"And every last piece was refused. Some of it even landed in Genevieve's lap!"

"Hoorah, attagirl!" Julia clapped her hands together in delight. "I'd have paid good money to see the old bag's face."

Susan frowned disapprovingly. "No, she's not an old bag, merely a bereft mother who's terrified of losing touch with the last little piece she has left of her daughter. Bill told me as much."

They were all quiet for a moment or two, contemplating what Susan had said.

"So why don't you take her out for dinner on her own and reassure her?" Alison broke the silence.

"I've thought about it, but I don't think it would work. She's very prickly when she thinks I'm trying to, as she sees it, interfere in anything to do with her and Ellie."

Silence again, then Fiona sat upright, poking a finger in the air like a child desperate to answer a question. "I know. How about a different version of the 'kill her with kindness' philosophy? In this case, maybe a better way to approach the problem would be for you to lean on her a bit more?"

"In what way?"

"Well, rather than challenging her to do things or making it look as though you're *allowing* her time with her granddaughter, you pretend that you could do with a break and *need* her help."

Alison was nodding furiously in agreement. "That could really work."

Scooping froth from her cappuccino, Susan sucked thoughtfully on her spoon. She was about to speak, but Fiona started bouncing up and down in her chair and distracted her.

"Oooh, I know. Even better!" she squeaked. "How is Ellie about staying away from home?"

Susan shrugged. "I don't know. Nick has never allowed it. He worries she might wake up in the middle of the night and be frightened."

"Okay, here's what you do." Fiona was on a roll now. "Persuade Nick that Ellie is now old enough to try a sleepover and suggest that she stay with Genevieve and Bill for just one night. A Saturday would be ideal. Then you and Nick spend the afternoon there with her before sneaking off to a nearby hotel for the night.

"That way, Nick feels reassured that he's nearby if there's a problem, Genevieve gets to feel wanted, and you two can have a night of unbridled lust without worrying that your shrieks of pleasure might wake Ellie in the next room." She flopped back in her chair as if she'd just announced a cure for the common cold. "I'm a bloody genius."

Susan laughed. "Well, I'm not sure about the night of unbridled lust. Uninterrupted sleep sounds much more appealing. But what the hell, I'll give it a try."

Julia stretched out her long legs and yawned. "Well, my, my, aren't we making progress today? Sometimes a little bit of lateral thinking is so much smarter than all that tacky, low-rent revenge nonsense. Shall we have a group hug?"

Fiona and Susan knew she was taking the piss, but Alison looked momentarily perplexed until Julia winked at her.

"Don't worry, honey, just my little joke," she drawled. "So, three down, one to go. How's *your* giant thorn?"

Alison sighed, twirling a piece of hair round her finger. Her usually sharp cut looked a little less groomed today. "Same as ever really. She's demanding yet more money, which Luca says he's going to pay or she'll stop him seeing the boys . . . and I went to yet another dinner with friends on my own because she rang up just beforehand claiming that Paolo had appendicitis."

"And didn't he?" asked Susan.

"He had a tummyache, that's all. Luca said it was easily something she could have dealt with herself, but she wanted to make a point. Which she managed to do with consummate ease, of course."

Julia frowned and made a clucking noise with her tongue. "Maybe you need to take a leaf out of my book."

Susan shot her a look of disbelief. "What, spend all day at the hair salon?"

Julia didn't dignify her remark with a response, shifting her body slightly so she faced Alison and blocked Susan. "You should try to befriend Sofia, get her on your side."

Alison's expression suggested that she had a fear of flying and the Wright brothers had just asked her to join them for a loop-the-loop. "I'm not sure that would work," she said hesitantly, anxious not to upset Julia while she was showing such an interest in her life.

Julia tutted. "Well, you won't know if you don't try, will you? After all, it doesn't sound like things could be any worse. The only way is up."

"Have you ever met her?" Susan's eyes were wide with anticipation.

"Only when she crashed our wedding, so, no, not really."

"Do you know much about her?" asked Fiona.

"I know she's Italian. Proper Italian, born there. She came here with Luca when he got a job. They got married, had their children very quickly, and, er, that's it."

Julia made a sucking noise with her teeth. "Fuck, that's a right old bloody millstone you've got there. You'll *never* get rid of that one."

Susan punched her lightly on the arm. "You really are a help. That's made Alison feel so much better."

"Well, it's true," Julia sniffed. "She has no life of her own, so she cuckoos yours."

Fiona spluttered her coffee. "Hardly! If anything, Alison is the cuckoo in Sofia's nest." She looked at Alison apologetically. "Sorry, but it's true. We're all guilty of that to a certain extent."

"Sorry?" Julia rapped her knuckles on the side of her head. "I could have sworn this was the *Second* Wives Club, a welcome respite from the sanctimonious and moral high ground occupied by the first lot?"

Fiona's brow furrowed slightly. "It is. But we shouldn't completely bury our heads in the sand and pretend we're blameless. Only Susan can claim that."

They all looked at Susan, who blushed as if she'd just been announced homecoming queen. She picked up the bottle of sparkling water and clutched it to her chest.

"I'd like to dedicate this award to my parents for all their support, and I'd like to put an end to world poverty," she opined, pretending to wipe a tear from the corner of her eye.

They all laughed and the mood lightened again. Only Alison returned to looking serious.

"So do you honestly think I should try to talk to Sofia?" She addressed the remark to Julia, who nodded enthusiastically.

"Absolutely. What have you got to lose?"

Alison looked uncertain. "Luca perhaps?"

"Nonsense," Julia clucked. "And even if, by some remote chance, you did lose him over it, then he wasn't the man you thought he was. I'm sure that, however it turns out, he'll simply see it as you doing your best to try to make things work."

Alison tried to smile to show her gratitude, but her eyes were still full of nervous apprehension.

Susan leaned toward her conspiratorially. "So how do you think you'll approach her?"

Shrugging, Alison sighed. "Dunno, but it will have to be the element of surprise because there's absolutely no way she'll agree to meet me."

Susan raised an eyebrow. "What are you going to do? Jump out from behind the frozen peas at her local supermarket?"

"I'd wait a long time," said Alison ruefully. "She does her shopping over the Internet and has it delivered. I've seen the credit-card bills." She rubbed her eyes, sore from the bright sun. "Don't worry, I'll think of something."

"Well!" Fiona clapped her hands together. "Something tells me the next meeting is going to be a very interesting one indeed! I'm going to be all loved up with Jake, Susan and Genevieve will be swapping cake recipes, and Alison and Julia will be best buddies with the first wives."

"Christ," said Julia. "You're a bigger optimist than a banjo player with a pager." She took a sip of water. "Or failing that, Jake will be in foster care, Susan will be doing time for first-degree murder, and Alison and I will be in the ER having ice picks removed from our foreheads. Only time will tell."

sofia so bad

Alison paused on the corner of the street, glancing cautiously down toward the house.

It was an unremarkable 1930s two-story with a small, neat garden accessed via a little wooden gate, and the front windows were shielded by plain white net curtains. It was impossible to tell whether anyone was home.

A woman walking her dog strolled past and glanced back over her shoulder, clearly suspicious as to why Alison was lurking around and showing particular interest in one house. Alison smiled reassuringly at her and started to walk in the direction of the property, trying to ignore the feeling of nausea welling inside her throat. This had to be done, and if she didn't do it now, she knew she never would.

The gate creaked ominously as she pushed it open, like a sound effect from a low-budget horror movie. Rather fitting, given the cir-cumstances, she thought.

Taking a deep breath and exhaling it slowly to try to calm her nerves, she extended her finger and pressed the bell. A shrill, high-pitched buzz rang out on the other side.

Nothing happened for several seconds, and she suddenly felt calmer. For some reason, fate had intervened and it wasn't going to happen today. She'd have to galvanize herself to come back another time.

Just as she was turning to leave, there was the distinct sound of heels clicking on a hardwood floor and a silhouette appeared behind the frosted glass of the front door.

Alison froze with tension. Swallowing hard, she tried to compose her expression so she appeared friendly rather than confrontational.

As the door opened, she attempted a half-smile. "Hello. It's me," she added rather unnecessarily.

Sofia stood scowling at her for a couple of seconds, then took a determined step back and slammed the door shut with such force that the glass made a rattling noise.

Alison recoiled slightly, blinked a few times, then extended her arm again and pressed the bell, longer this time.

No answer.

She rang it again.

Still no answer.

Swiveling her head to see if anyone was watching, she noted the coast was clear and lifted the mailbox flap in the middle of the door. Peering through, she could see the hallway was empty. "Sofia, what is the point of not answering the door when I know full well you're in there?" she shouted.

No response.

"Okay, if that's the way you want to play it. I'll just stand here shouting through your mailbox until every neighbor on your street knows precisely why I'm here."

Silence. The only sound was coming from a small clock ticking on the hall table, a rather beautiful antique mahogany one. Above it, hanging on the wall, was a framed photograph of Paolo and Giorgio. Alison could see there was another frame hanging along-side it, but she couldn't crane her neck far enough to see what it was.

Her threat to cause a fuss had obviously not been taken seriously, so she let out a deep, long-suffering sigh. She'd come all this way, she knew Sofia was in there, and there was no way she was going to give up now.

Straightening her back, she stood up and turned out to face the street. As far as she could see, there was no one around.

"I'm the woman who stole Sofia's husband from her," she bel-lowed at the top of her voice. "Or at least that's how *she* sees it." Alison noticed a set of net curtains opposite had started twitching, belying the presence of whoever was furtively tucked away behind them.

"But the truth is," she continued, "that he told me their marriage was all but over anyway, that he and Sofia hadn't had sex for months, that . . ." She stopped shouting and turned as she heard the familiar click of a door opening behind her.

"Okay, stop." Sofia's face and voice were hard. "You've got five minutes to say your bit, then I want you to get the hell out of my house." She stepped aside to let Alison walk into the hallway.

Hastily extending her head out of the door and looking round, she then closed it and turned to face her sworn enemy. "What do you want?"

Alison felt awkward enough already, but when she realized she wasn't going to be allowed past the hallway, she felt even more un-comfortable. She leaned against the banister for support.

"I've come here to have a grown-up discussion with you."

"Really?" Sofia raised a thinly plucked black eyebrow, her dark brown eyes looking derisively at Alison. "About what exactly?"

She wasn't wearing any makeup, but Alison had to admit she still looked good for her age, particularly for someone facing the exhausting task of dealing with two young children on her own. Her shoulder-length black hair was swept back into a ponytail, enhancing her high cheekbones and elfin-shaped face.

The top half of her body was quite slight, with small breasts and slim arms, but her tiny waist was accentuated even more by hips that could only be described as child-bearing. She was short—about five-four—so, unusually, Alison felt quite tall by comparison.

"About the boys." Alison nodded toward the framed photograph, noting for the first time that the one alongside it was a picture taken on Sofia and Luca's wedding day. She didn't want to, but she found herself staring at it, taking in every little detail.

Luca didn't look that different from how he did now, give or take a gray hair or two. His face was less weathered and his hair slightly longer, but other than that, it was very much the man she'd woken up with this morning. She found it rather disconcerting to be looking at a picture of him marrying another woman.

Sofia looked radiant, a woman who was clearly in no doubt that this was the man she was going to spend the rest of her life with. Her hair was longer then, sleek and straight and tucked behind her neat little ears, a band of small white flowers across her head. As it was only a head-and-shoulders shot, Alison couldn't see much of the dress, other than to note that it was cream with a straight neckline.

"That's my husband," said Sofia, following her gaze. "Just in case you were wondering."

Alison looked back at her and said slowly, "*Was* your husband. He's my husband now."

Sofia made a small sucking noise with her teeth. "As far as I'm concerned, he's still my husband. He divorced me, I didn't divorce him. I take my vows very seriously."

"Whatever." Alison didn't see the point of arguing about it. She just wanted to say her piece and leave. "Look, I came here to see . . . to *ask*," she corrected herself, "whether we could come to some arrangement over the boys."

"To do with what?"

"To do with them seeing their father."

"They see him as much as they want." Her mouth was set in a firm line.

"Yes, but only when I'm not around."

"Ah." Sofia threw her head back and stared at the ceiling for a couple of seconds. "So what you mean is, you want to come to some arrangement about them spending time with *you?*"

Alison smiled uncertainly, unsure which direction their conversation was about to take. "Um, not with me as such, more with me *and* Luca. As the arrangement stands, it makes things rather difficult."

Sofia looked at her impassively, then narrowed her eyes. "Go fuck yourself."

The two women stood stock-still for a few moments, staring at each other, Sofia defiantly, Alison looking stunned. She waited to see if there was any other answer forthcoming, but after a few awkward seconds had passed she realized there clearly wasn't. "Oh, I see," she said stiffly. "Well, thanks for giving my request such deep and mature thought." Alison took a step toward the front door and opened it. "You know, Sofia, I sincerely hoped you were going to be adult about all this. After all, this situation is only damaging your children."

She was about to step outside and walk off, but she suddenly felt the door being pushed against her leg. She turned round to find a glowering Sofia attempting to pull her back into the house.

She succeeded and closed the door again before turning to Alison, her eyes blazing with rage.

"Don't you *ever* suggest that I don't know what's best for my children," she hissed. "You know *nothing* about us."

"I . . . I didn't mean it like that," faltered Alison, but the end of her sentence was trampled by Sofia's irate interjection.

"You stole their father right from under their noses." Her face was just inches from Alison's, her expression one of disgust. "So don't come round here preaching about what's best for them. You have *never* had their best interests at heart."

Alison was desperate to just open the door and run, but she stayed rooted to the spot, determined to see this out.

"Luca didn't leave his children, he left *you*," she said quietly.

"Same thing," Sofia replied huffily. "His children live here and he doesn't, which means he doesn't see as much of them anymore. That's his decision, not mine."

Alison knew she had to choose her words very carefully, as Sofia was looking perilously close to snapping completely. "He could see more of them . . . if they were allowed to stay over with us."

"Never." Sofia folded her arms defensively.

"If he wanted to, Luca could go to court to *force* you to let the children stay over," said Alison, deliberately keeping her tone light. "But he chooses not to."

"That's because he still loves me." She looked triumphant as she said it. "He doesn't want to hurt me."

A wave of weariness suddenly swept over Alison as she saw firsthand the harsh reality of what she was up against.

"Correction, Sofia. He doesn't want to hurt the *children*." She decided she'd been here long enough. "Look, how long is this going to go on for? Are you going to keep the children away from me forever?"

Sofia sniffed nonchalantly. "If that's what it takes, yes. Just tell me this, why should *you*, the woman who stole my husband away from me, just swan into my children's lives and steal them too?"

"Is that what you're afraid of?" Alison looked at her questioningly. "That I'm going to take your children away from you? I would never do that, I wouldn't be *able* to do that even if I wanted to. You're their mother, I'm just their stepmother."

Just as the conversation had started to become more measured, Alison's remark fired Sofia up again.

"You are not their stepmother! You are *nothing* to my children, and that's how it's going to stay!"

Alison let out a long sigh. "You know what? I pity you, I really do. You're a *sad*, bitter, lonely woman who just can't deal with the fact that her husband left her." She looked her up and down. "And now that I've met you, I can see why he did."

She didn't see the slap coming, merely felt its sting as Sofia's palm made contact with her cheek.

"You fucking bitch!" Alison recoiled slightly, unsure whether another attack was forthcoming, but Sofia didn't move. "That's assault!"

"Prove it." Sofia's expression was defiant. "And by the way, Alison, I don't know what shit Luca has fed you, but our marriage was an incredibly strong one. We laughed together, we supported each other through thick and thin, and we had great sex together. Then you came along, fluttered your eyelashes, and destroyed it. So forgive me, but I think of you as a dirty whore and always will." She opened the front door again. "Now get out."

Still rubbing her face, Alison picked her handbag up from the floor and stepped outside.

"Before you go, let me leave you with this thought," Sofia added matter-of-factly. "Luca adores his children, and he always will. You're always going to be second best to them, and you will *never, ever* be able to give him what I did—his firstborn son. It was a magical experience for him. And as the mother of both his sons, as long as I have breath in my body . . . ," she placed her hand on her chest, ". . . I'm going to be a giant thorn in your side, a cancer that eats away at *your* marriage the way you did mine. It will be my life's work, and don't you forget it."

With that, she slammed the door, leaving Alison standing in the front garden with little to show for her visit except a smarting cheek.

She stood staring into space, her brain whirring with analytical precision through what had just happened. She wasn't sure what she'd expected to gain from her unscheduled visit, but she had to admit that Sofia's naked aggression had disturbed her greatly.

With a heavy heart, she realized the sheer enormity of what she'd taken on in marrying Luca. If she was honest, she had hoped that, despite everything, Sofia would have started to mellow toward her. But now she could see that was a long way off, if it ever happened at all.

She was now confident in the knowledge that Luca's ex-wife would be a major irritant for years to come—she'd said as much herself. Alison felt a niggling doubt that maybe she had simply made matters worse by coming here today. What's more—and she felt a significant thump of dread in her chest as the thought struck her— did she and Luca have a marriage strong enough to sustain the continuing pressure?

went to see Sofia today."

She and Luca were watching television, having just shared a bottle of wine and a Chinese takeaway.

"You did *what*?"

He looked horrified, and Alison was surprised that Sofia clearly hadn't called to let him know first.

"I just thought it might help if I went and met her . . . you know, try to reason with her," she said apologetically.

"And I take it from your expression and demeanor that you were unsuccessful in persuading her to become your new best friend?" He raised an eyebrow questioningly.

Alison nodded, wincing slightly. "Actually, she slapped me across the face."

Luca dropped the remote control on the floor. "She *what?*" He stood up, his chair scraping on the hardwood floor. "That's completely out of order. I'm going to call her now and tell her."

"No, please don't." She half stood up and reached across to tug his arm. "That will only make matters worse."

"She *slapped* you," he retorted. "How could matters be any worse?"

Alison shrugged. "Oh, I don't know. Apparently, there was a woman in the papers the other day that stabbed her successor to death with an ice pick, so it looks like I got off lightly." She smiled in an attempt to lift the mood slightly, but Luca's face remained deadly serious.

"It's not funny, Alison. She needs to be told that it's not acceptable behavior."

How peculiar, she thought. He always seems so weak against Sofia when dealing with her irrationality over the children, yet here he is talking tough over her aggression toward me.

But even though she was sorely tempted by the thought of Sofia getting a dressing-down, she knew it would be short-term gain for long-term pain.

"Forget it," she said glumly. "If you argue with her as well, she could make it even more difficult for you to see the children, she could demand even *more* money, she could do a million things she doesn't need to do simply as a way to flex her muscles. It's not worth it."

Luca sat back down with an air of resignation. "Okay, but tell me *everything* that happened."

Alison talked him through it, careful not to leave anything out. Some of her comments to Sofia didn't place her in a favorable light, but she was determined to be fair and straightforward in her recollection. Alison had never been a bullshitter. She finished with Sofia's promise to be a thorn in their side forevermore.

"So lots to look forward to then." He smiled ruefully, then lapsed into silence for a few seconds, staring at the table.

Alison wasn't sure what reaction she was expecting from him, but she hoped he would be sympathetic to her plight.

Eventually he looked at her and slowly shook his head in a gesture of hopelessness. "What *were* you thinking of? This will set us right back to square one."

Slightly thrown by his remark, she frowned at him. "Hang on a minute, I was only trying to make things easier for us. You can't blame me for that." She was aware that the frown had now become a glare, but she couldn't help herself.

"And as for going back to square one, from where I'm standing it seems like we never left it in the first place. We're married, but your ex-wife is calling all the shots. And as you don't seem to have the balls to deal with her, I thought I'd try." She knew she'd overstepped the mark with that last dig, and Luca's face confirmed it. His mouth was set in a hard line, and his eyes were blazing with quiet anger.

"It's not about the size of my balls," he said in a controlled but patently seething voice. "It's about keeping Sofia sweet so I can spend valuable time with my sons. I'm sorry if that means seeing them without you, but I'd rather that than nothing at all."

Alison understood this point of view, but she also felt she had to fight her own corner.

"It's just that sometimes I have to remind myself that we're married." She sighed deeply. "I have a ring on my finger, and I *call* myself Mrs. Rossi, but I feel I have absolutely no rights at all. They all rest with Sofia."

She took a long but inaudible deep breath and looked directly at Luca. "To put it bluntly, I feel like a second-class citizen."

"Well, you're not." Luca gave her a small smile, but it didn't quite reach his eyes. "But you *are* a second wife, and this kind of thing goes with the territory."

Alison wasn't convinced. "Perhaps it does in the early days, but there comes a time when you have to say enough is enough and grasp control. Or you never will."

"I see," Luca replied matter-of-factly. "And how would you propose I do that?"

Alison had thought about it so many times that she had her prepared answer off-pat. She had simply been waiting for the right moment to deliver it.

"Just suppose . . . ," she leaned forward earnestly, ". . . you tell Sofia that unless you are allowed to see the boys on *your* terms, then you will stop seeing them altogether? You and I both know you'd never stop seeing them, but she doesn't know whether you'd carry out the threat or not. And what mother wants to damage her children's relationship with their father just because of her own bitterness?"

Luca had already started shaking his head halfway through her little speech. "No, I would never say that."

"Why not?" Alison felt cross that he hadn't seemed to give her suggestion even a moment's consideration.

"Because I wouldn't want my boys to be told that I'd even *made* that threat, whether I carried it out or not. My relationship with them is the most important thing in my life . . . sorry," he added as an afterthought.

"More important than your marriage to me?" She felt sick as she said it.

He pursed his lips. "I regard the two things very differently. But if you put a gun to my head and said I absolutely *had* to choose between you or my boys, it would be them every time. And you'll understand what I mean when you have children."

Alison said nothing, struggling to control the tight lump forming at the back of her throat.

She understood already, and she would never ask Luca to choose between her and his boys. His devotion to his children made him even more special in her eyes. But she didn't see why the two had to be mutually exclusive. Luca could spend time with her *and* his boys if he'd only take Sofia on and brazen it out. Sofia might be a bitch, but Alison knew she wouldn't sever contact forever. She'd eventually relent, and then they could all move forward to a more satisfactory, happier phase of their lives. But now she feared that might never happen, that she would be living life in the shadows forever, unable to form any kind of bond with the two most important people in Luca's life. A wave of disturbingly deep gloom suddenly swept over her. Sofia was right. She'd been there, seen it, and done it with Luca—Alison was merely going over old, well-trodden ground with him.

A few weeks earlier, she'd been planning their wedding, full of what she now regarded as blind hope for the future. She'd jumped in with both feet, naively assuming that, given time, the situation would improve. Now she wasn't sure it ever would.

a steak through the heart

"Holy shit!" Susan usually made a point of not swearing in front of Ellie, but this time it just slipped out. In front of her, at the end of a long, private driveway, was a beautiful, white, Georgian manor house with a turning circle round an ornamental fountain. "I knew they weren't poor, but I had no idea they were *this* rich."

Nick carried on looking straight ahead, concentrating on negotiating a particularly well-tended flower bed to one side of the front door. Parking next to it, he switched off the engine. "Yes, but don't forget they've lived here for years. They bought it when Bill was made chief accountant at his firm, and it's probably worth ten times more now."

Susan peered through the car window at the immaculate lawn sweeping down the side of the house. "It looks awfully big for just the two of them."

Nick smiled. "It is really, but they bought it so Caitlin could enjoy the open space and indulge her passion for riding, and after she died they couldn't bear to sell it because all their memories of her are here." He tooted the car horn to let them know they'd arrived.

As Susan climbed out and started to unclip Ellie from her car seat in the back, she was deep in thought. It didn't matter what you achieved in life, how much you earned, where you lived . . . if something as precious as your child was taken away from you, it all meant nothing. She knew Bill and Genevieve would give it all up in a heartbeat for just one extra day with their daughter, a chance to say all the things they were robbed of telling her because of her untimely and unexpected death.

"Nana!" Ellie had spotted Genevieve coming out of the front door. She wrestled herself from Susan's grasp and ran across the gravel.

"Careful, darling!" Genevieve's face lit up with delight as she scooped her granddaughter into her arms. "We don't want you to fall and scrape those lovely knees now, do we?"

"Hello, Genevieve." Susan stood back a few feet, smiling tentatively, Ellie's overnight bag in one hand.

"Hello, Susan." Genevieve's tone was still a little stiff, but her smile seemed genuine. "Leave the bag on the step. Bill will bring it in, he's just finishing up a phone call."

Nick had materialized at Susan's side. "Hello, Genevieve. The house is looking as lovely as ever." He stepped forward and gave her an awkward peck on each cheek.

"Thank you." She flushed slightly. "Bill and I work hard on it. It helps to keep us busy." They stood there for a moment in silence. "Right then," Genevieve said. "I'll get the kettle on. I'll bet you're parched." She stood to one side to let Nick walk past her into the house.

Susan hung back, intending to follow after them, but Genevieve stayed where she was. "Come on, dear. Come inside."

Dear, thought Susan. She called me "dear." Was it sarcastic, or was it well meaning? She decided to assume it was the latter and stepped inside, hopeful that they were entering a brave new world.

Bill had finished his phone call and was lurking in the grand entrance hall with its dominant staircase leading up from a stunning black-and-white tiled floor. "Hello, love." He gave Susan a quick hug. "Good trip?"

"Great, no problems at all," she replied quickly. Actually, the traffic had been a real headache, but she didn't want to admit it, anxious not to cast any ill humor over what she hoped would be a positive new arrangement.

"So where are you staying tonight?" asked Bill, leading her through to the large, open-plan, country-style kitchen that incorporated a stunning conservatory room with two plump, stone-colored sofas and various exotic plants.

"I've booked us into the Priory Hotel," she said. "Do you know it? I think it's only about five miles away."

Bill nodded. "Know it well. It's very nice, I believe, though I've never stayed there myself."

Susan could hear footsteps in another room, approaching the kitchen. It was Nick.

"Well, that's good news," he said. "Ellie likes her room."

Bill's face brightened with pleasure. "That's good to know. I've been working on it for a fortnight."

Nick pointed upstairs. "Do you mind if I take Susan up to see it?"

"Not at all." A kettle started to whistle on the stove. "I'll just make the tea."

Following Nick back through the door he'd just emerged from, Susan found herself in a spacious, square living room with an ornate fireplace and three sofas in a doctor's surgery formation around a low, gray marble coffee table. Everywhere she looked there were side cabinets weighed down with framed photographs of Caitlin. Caitlin as a child, Caitlin at her graduation, Caitlin and Nick on their wedding day, and Caitlin with Ellie in various poses. Caitlin, Caitlin, Caitlin. Susan had expected the house to be a shrine, but seeing it with her own eyes unsettled her, and she moved swiftly across the room, following Nick to a partially hidden back staircase. If she'd thought there'd be respite there, she was sorely mistaken. A small row of hanging pictures lined the staircase, almost all of them featuring Caitlin.

"God, I remember this!" Nick had stopped in front of one and was pointing at it. "This was taken on our honeymoon. In fact, I took it."

Caitlin, as ever, was looking gorgeous, her strawberry blond hair fanning across her bronzed shoulders. She was standing ankle-deep in the shallows of the sea. Nick carried on up the stairs. While a part of Susan liked the fact that he'd felt comfortable enough to mention it, she was grateful he hadn't dwelled on it.

Caitlin and Nick's wedding had been a traditional, lavish affair with a meringue dress, four bridesmaids, and a three-tiered wedding cake made and decorated by Genevieve's Women's League friends. Susan had been invited, but it had coincided with her long-planned backpacking trip to Australia, so she'd sent a beautiful bouquet of flowers instead and made do with watching the video on her return, both of the big day and the fortnight's honeymoon in the Seychelles. It was the kind of wedding Susan herself had always dreamed of having. But right now, she thought, she'd settle for *any* wedding.

Susan had raised the subject of marriage on a couple of occasions in recent months, but Nick had always wriggled out of it, saying they couldn't afford it because the real estate market was in the doldrums and he wasn't making good commissions right now. And there was no way Susan's part-time earnings from the building firm would cover even the cost of the flowers, he'd added.

Susan had reassured him that she'd be happy with a simple city hall ceremony followed by a small lunch for family and a couple of friends, but Nick had said he wanted to wait until they could stretch to something a bit more special. Though she smiled to indicate that she accepted his point of view, deep down Susan knew there was a lot more to his reluctance than he was owning up to. Namely his in-laws and their possible reaction to the news that their daughter's husband was marrying again.

Susan didn't blame Nick for his trepidation, but she sincerely hoped that one day soon he'd bite the bullet and ask her to marry him. In the meantime, she'd just have to put up with him always insisting there was something more pressing they needed the money for, like getting the car or the boiler fixed. It was true, they did need the money for those things. But she had always thought that ultimately marriage was about love and commitment, rather than expensive display.

Turning the corner at the end of a long corridor, she followed Nick into the most beautiful child's bedroom she'd ever seen. The walls were sky blue with little painted clouds, and everything in the room had an ocean theme. There was a dolphin rug, a small wardrobe with shells painted on it, and a cabin bed with waves running along the side. Underneath was a small desk and two shelves stuffed with cuddly toys.

"They were Caitlin's," said Genevieve, following Susan's gaze. "We thought it might be nice."

"It's a lovely idea." She smiled warmly and walked across to the bed where Ellie was sitting playing with two large seashells. "Aren't you a lucky girl?"

"Yes. Nana says I can stay here whenever I want," Ellie declared proudly. Genevieve looked across at Nick slightly sheepishly.

"Of course you can, pickle." He tickled her tummy. "But let's get through tonight first."

"She'll be fine," murmured Genevieve.

"I hope so." Nick smiled, but it was a fleeting one. "She's never spent a night away from me since . . . since . . . ," he shot a look across at Ellie, ". . . well, you know . . ."

"Since Caitlin died, Nick," Genevieve said very precisely. "We must never avoid saying it. She's dead but not forgotten."

A small, imperceptible shiver ran down Susan's back. The room suddenly felt chilly, and they all fell silent for a few seconds. Ellie hadn't seemed to notice the mention of her mother's name.

"Yes, well, anyway." Nick cleared his throat. "Susan and I are staying at the Priory, so if there is a problem, we're close at hand. Just call us."

Susan knew that it would take a suicide bomb attempt on their house for Genevieve to call them. She was going to be in charge of Ellie for just one night, and she wasn't going to relinquish a second of it to anyone. But Susan didn't blame her for her intransigence; she knew she would probably act the same way in similar circumstances. It was human nature after all.

"Right." Nick clapped his hands together awkwardly. "We'll be off then. Bye, sweetie, you be a good girl for Nana."

"I will." Ellie carried on playing with the shells, clearly untroubled by their leaving.

Nick disappeared out of the door, but Susan hung back slightly, an expectant look on her face. "I just want to say how grateful I am for this," she said carefully to Genevieve. "It's hard sometimes, and it's good to know Ellie can come somewhere that she feels so comfortable. It gives Nick a much-deserved break." She deliberately mentioned his name alone.

"The pleasure is all mine." Genevieve's face lit up with joy, and Susan noticed for the first time how attractive she was when her features weren't etched with suppressed grief.

When Susan got downstairs, Bill was waiting with two cups of strong tea.

"Sorry," Nick was saying as he took a polite sip from one of the cups. "Hmm, that's delicious, but I think Susan and I are going to get moving. It's been a hell of a long time since we had any time to ourselves, so we're going to make the most of it. We'll see you tomorrow."

Edging out of the driveway and onto the main road a few minutes later, Nick smiled at Susan. "So, how was it for you?"

She thought for a minute. "So-so. A little better, I think. She called me 'dear' when we arrived."

"Nicely or sarcastically?"

"Nicely, I think. She seems more relaxed somehow, probably because she's on her own territory and knows she's got sole charge of Ellie for a short while."

Nick's face suddenly clouded with doubt. "Do you think she'll be okay?"

Susan leaned across and gave his left arm a little squeeze, pressing her cheek against it. "She'll be absolutely fine. In fact, she'll be spoiled rotten and probably want to stay even longer."

"Fingers crossed." Nick grinned, and took his left hand off the steering long enough to make the gesture.

The Priory was a small stately home that had been converted into a hotel about ten years previously. It hadn't been refurbished since, so it was a little frayed around the edges. But what it lacked in style it more than made up for in service, with friendly, efficient staff who couldn't do enough for their guests.

Susan and Nick's room was in a prime position at the back of the house, overlooking the award-winning gardens with a small orchard, a hedge maze, and a beautiful grove of orange trees.

Susan stood in the bay window surveying the view and let out a long sigh of contentment. She adored Ellie, but like all "mums," bi-ological or otherwise, the thought of having some time alone was de-licious. She could read a magazine uninterrupted, enjoy a long soak without a little person trying to climb into the tub fully clothed, and knock back a few glasses of wine over dinner without fear of being awakened at 6:00 A.M. with a thumping hangover. And sex! Glori-ous, uninhibited sex without Ellie wandering in and saying, "What are you doing?" as had happened one time.

Nick had replied, "I'm helping Mummy look for her earring," which they had laughed about many times since.

Turning away from the window, Susan looked over at Nick, who was lying on the bed reading the sports pages of the complimentary newspaper they'd found in the room. At thirty-six, his brown hair was still thick and shiny, with no signs of receding. He wore it slightly long, brushed back close to his ears, curling into the nape of his neck. She fancied him like mad, and always had.

At school he'd been a bit of a heartthrob, the captain of the foot-ball team, and quite a mover at the annual school dance. Susan, by contrast, had always had an exaggerated idea of her own unimpor-tance. Freckly, ginger-haired, and flat-chested, she had enviably long, slim legs. But such was her insecurity about the rest of her body that she didn't make the most of them. Susan wasn't a wallflower—she was the seed that still hadn't dared poke its head out into the open.

So when Nick had asked her out at the end of their senior year, she had been as surprised as the rest of their class. It had taken him four attempts to even persuade her that his invitation to the cin-ema was serious and not part of some elaborate bet with his class-mates.

Their "relationship" had only lasted the four weeks until the summer holidays started and each drifted off on a separate family vacation, but unlike so many teenage liaisons, they had maintained a firm friendship ever since.

"Happy?" She walked across the room and rubbed the top of his head.

"Hmmm," he murmured distractedly, turning the page. "You?"

"Very." She smiled widely, but he wasn't looking. "I thought I might go for a swim. Fancy it?"

He stretched his arms above his head and buried his cheek in the plump pillow. "No thanks. I fancy a very indulgent nap before dinner."

"Okay." She kissed the top of his head. "You go ahead. I'm going to do a few laps and I'll creep in next to you later."

Powering through the cool water about ten minutes later, Susan could feel the tension ebbing from her muscles. Swimming relaxed her and she was good at it. She had what her mother had always described as "a swimmer's body," with broad shoulders tapering down to a small waist and long, slender legs.

All her life she'd fought a battle with her curly red hair. On the days when she'd won, it was a crowning glory of long, eye-catching ringlets, each lubricated and tweaked to perfection. On the days when she'd lost, it was an unkempt mass into which Lord Voldemort could have easily disappeared without fear of detection. These days it was invariably in the latter state, as hair care didn't feature highly on Susan's to-do list. She simply didn't have the time, so she settled for just hating her hair instead.

She also hated her shoulders, built for speed but not for all those cute little tops that everyone else looked so great in. On the one occasion she'd worn a fashionable, off-the-shoulder gypsy top, she had felt like a transvestite trucker. Consequently, winter was her favorite time of the year, the season of covering up. Her legs, however, were long and lithe, with definition in all the right places, toned but not too muscular. When miniskirts were in, Susan was in her element.

Lifting herself out of the water, she picked up the towel she'd left on the side of the pool and buried her face in it. Dangling her legs in the deep end, she sat there alone with her thoughts for a good twenty minutes.

The place was deserted, and she smiled as she briefly imagined herself as lady of the manor, doing her daily exercise in her own private pool, from which she would sashay through to the dining hall to eat a perfectly cooked meal served up by a butler called something like Babinger.

In truth, unlike Julia, Susan would have actually *hated* that lifestyle.

She always felt horribly uncomfortable being served by anyone, even a waiter being paid to do so in a restaurant. Each time a waiter poured her water or even moved her fork a couple of inches to the left, she would say "Thank you" to the point that, on an average night out, she might utter it more than a dozen times. So the thought of someone making her breakfast, serving it, and clearing up afterward in her own home was enough to make her sweat with discomfort.

Her thoughts turned to Whitelands and the beautiful surroundings Caitlin had grown up in, with her two devoted parents and her beloved horse. How different could two women be, thought Susan. Caitlin was the archetypal beautiful blonde, and I'm the archetypal ugly duckling, the girl with the man's shoulders whose hair has a mind of its own. She grew up on a gorgeous estate, while I was dragged up on a tenement block in what was widely recognized as one of the most crime-ridden neighborhoods in South East London.

Susan's parents had separated before she had even entered the world. They had married in an alcoholic stupor, conceived her in much the same state, and ended the ill-advised union shortly afterward. She had never met her father and wasn't even sure if he was still alive.

Her mother, Bev, had struggled to bring her up for a few months, but neighbors on the block reported her to social services after hearing Susan crying hysterically night after night. When two social workers turned up unannounced, they'd found Bev incoherent and barely able to stumble to the door. Susan had been taken into a group home and maintained a patchy relationship with her mother, consisting of irregular visits where Bev would make an effort to arrive sober and the pair would interact awkwardly while a smiling social worker looked on.

Then, when Susan was about six, the visits stopped. When she asked after her mother, she was told that Bev had moved abroad to find work. When she was twelve, she was finally told the truth, that Bev had died of an overdose in the very same flat Susan had been retrieved from. In spite of it all, Susan had done well at her inner-city public school, getting good enough grades to secure a place at a highly thought of private high school, where she'd met Nick.

Isn't nature a curious creature? she thought now, kicking her legs so the pool water rippled into a triangular formation. Caitlin had had two parents who worshiped the ground she walked on, yet she had been cruelly snatched away from them. Yet Susan, with no parents around to care whether she lived or died, was still here, living, breathing, and enjoying life.

That's why I should be thankful and make the most of it, she told herself, smiling as she looked out of the pool window to a stunning flower bed outside. This hotel had been her choice after researching the area on the Internet, and she was really pleased with it. She'd arranged for a bottle of pink champagne to be delivered to their room before dinner, and the bowl of summer fruits—Nick's favorite—was already there.

After the club's most recent meeting, she had waited a few days before broaching the subject of Ellie staying away, mentally rehearsing every word to try to maximize the chances of Nick agreeing. But when the time came, he'd been surprisingly open to the idea, particularly when she'd mentioned her plan of staying nearby. They could ill afford it, but Susan saw it as money well spent, a restorative break for them and one small step toward better relations with Genevieve.

And so far, everything was going to plan.

T his is amazing." Nick jabbed his fork downward, in the direction of the medium-rare filet mignon he had already consumed half of. "What's yours like?"

Susan cut into one of her lamb noisettes, watching the pink meat expel its dark burgundy juice. "Not bad at all," she replied.

A waitress appeared at their side and filled their wineglasses, one hand tucked behind her in deference.

"Thanks. Thank you so much." Susan smiled. "That's great."

"You're so funny," said Nick warmly after the waitress had shifted her attention to another table. "You are the politest person I know."

Susan smiled, feigning a small bow from the waist up. "My mother always said good manners cost nothing. It was one of the few . . . probably only . . . things she taught me."

"Do you miss her?" Nick studied her face closely.

She thought about the question for a moment. "Not really," she replied honestly. "How can you miss someone you never really knew?"

He stared at the table for a few seconds, clearly pondering what she'd said. "So do you think Ellie has forgotten Caitlin?"

Susan looked horrified. "Oh, no, not at all. Besides, she has us to keep her mother's memory alive. I never really had that, and to be honest, all my memories of my mother were bad ones. She was drunk most of the time."

Nick leaned across the table and clasped one of her hands in his. "It must have been really tough for you."

She wrinkled her nose and shook her head. "I don't know, not as much as you'd think. How can you find something tough if you have nothing to compare it with? I was warm, well fed, and, if my memory serves me correctly, escaped any kind of abuse, so I was probably one of the lucky ones. That's how I look at it anyway."

Nick had questioned her several times before about her childhood, as if expecting to unleash some hidden torment, but there wasn't any. Not that Susan could remember anyway. Her motto was "that was then, this is now," and she just got on with life, determined not to hang any failures on her, as some might see it, "lost childhood."

During the next two hours they chatted away happily and polished off another bottle of wine, followed by two brandies each. By the time Nick asked for the bill to sign, they were the only diners left. All the other tables were cleared, with chairs stacked on top ready for the cleaners to descend in the morning.

It took them twice as long to stagger back to their room as it had taken coming down, first taking a wrong turning and ending up in a linen closet. There, in what they referred to forevermore as their Henry Miller moment, she and Nick started to kiss, tearing at each other's clothes, passionately locked in a frenzied, child-free idyll a world away from the normality of the bedroom and their ordered lives.

As Nick penetrated her, a wooden shelf was jabbing into Susan's lower back but she didn't care. To her, this fumbled, speedy sexual encounter felt like the most passionate love scene in the world, her own private few moments with Nick that no one had shared before.

She knew it was the drink in both of them, but they really wanted each other, rather than the usual perfunctory "oh, go on then" sex that was so often part and parcel of a relationship that involved young children.

Hand in hand, they eventually found their way back to their room, both a little more sober after their unscheduled stop. Susan was feeling absolutely radiant. Her plan had been an unmitigated success, and she was definitely going to suggest they try it again, maybe making it a monthly occurrence. It might be costly, but she was happy to spend the money to share a few precious hours alone with Nick.

Because Nick and Ellie had come as a package deal, he and Susan hadn't been able to enjoy those selfish, child-free years getting to know each other. Susan had been on a crash course in motherhood, and sometimes she'd wondered whether she might get buried in the wreckage. But the respite tonight had only recharged her batteries, and she realized happily that she was really looking forward to seeing Ellie tomorrow.

"Here we are." Nick fumbled with their door key for a few seconds before falling into the room and managing to compose himself.

As they stood side by side in the bathroom, haphazardly cleaning their teeth, Susan smiled at him in the mirror. "This has been nice, hasn't it?"

"Fantastic." He nodded, squeezing a line of paste onto his toothbrush. "We must do it again."

"My thoughts exactly." Susan grinned broadly, delighted that they were on the same page.

"Mind you, the steak was good, but not as good as last time."

The smile evaporated from Susan's face. "Last time? What do you mean 'last time'?"

Nick suddenly looked weary, a man who clearly knew that he'd just made a huge faux pas and was about to witness tears before bed-time. He let out a long sigh. "I came here with Caitlin. Once. A long time ago, before we were married. It had just opened."

"Oh, I see." Susan gripped the sink in front of her with both hands. "Why didn't you mention it before now?"

He made a gesture of exasperation. "Because I didn't think it mattered. Because I didn't want to hurt your feelings. Because, well, just because . . ." He petered out. "Does it matter?" He looked at her via the mirror, seeming reluctant to establish real eye contact.

"Does it matter?" she parroted. "Well, to me, yes, it does actu-ally."

"Why?" His tone was growing impatient.

Susan turned to face him, but he was staring down at his bare feet. "Because I wanted us to share something that was ours alone," she said simply.

He didn't say as much, but his expression suggested he wasn't even close to understanding what she was going on about. "Susan, our conversation has been ours alone. What happened back there . . . ," he jerked his head in the imagined direction of the linen closet, ". . . was ours alone. We don't need furniture and surround-ings to give us our own experiences."

She knew that what he was saying made perfect sense. But now all she could see in her mind's eye was Caitlin laughing and joking during animated conversation in the restaurant, and Caitlin's hair fanning out on the pillow as she and Nick made love. But she couldn't tell Nick that, because she knew he'd think she was daft. It would also make her sound jealous of Caitlin, which she wasn't. It was much more complicated than that.

"You're right." It was a weak smile, but at least she managed one. "Sorry, I'm just being oversensitive."

Nick kissed her on the cheek and padded out of the bathroom. She knew that, within seconds, he'd be in a deep, alcohol-induced sleep and by morning they would carry on as if this little blip had never happened.

Applying night cream, she leaned forward and stared at herself in the mirror. The ebullient, newly confident Susan of a few minutes before, buoyed by great sex with her man and the thought of a bright new future, had now been usurped by the Susan of old with the world weighing down on her broad swimmer's shoulders, her confidence gurgling down the drain along with the last vestiges of her toothpaste.

processed versus natural

Julia checked her watch yet again. Only two minutes had passed since she last looked, but it felt like hours.

She was sitting alone in a secluded corner of London's exclusive Ivy Restaurant, where making a reservation was an exercise in psychology all its own. To Julia's thinking, it was so notoriously tricky to secure a table there that it would show Deborah exactly how important she was in this town. She might not work for a living, but she could still wield power.

Assuming that Deborah was actually going to turn up, the process of getting her out for lunch had been surprisingly easy.

Julia wasn't sure what she had expected when she made the call two nights earlier, but she had to admit that Deborah had been unquestionably dignified in her response to finding her archenemy on the other end of the phone.

"Julia! What an unexpected pleasure," she'd said in a measured tone. Of course she was being sarcastic, but at least she wasn't ranting and railing.

Julia had launched herself into a full-on charm offensive, gushing about how wonderful Deborah had been, considering the circumstances, how so much water had now gone under the bridge, and how it would be so much nicer for James if they could just get on, maybe bury the hatchet over lunch.

If Deborah wanted to bury the hatchet in the side of Julia's head, certainly no such desire had shown in her response.

"Lunch?" She'd paused a few moments. "Okay, why not. When and where?"

It had been that simple. But as Julia checked her watch yet again, she was wondering whether *this* was going to be Deborah's little revenge—standing her up in one of London's busiest, most high-profile restaurants.

But no. There she was now, standing at the door and scouring the room. Julia knew it was her because she'd seen photos in James's family albums, and she was sure Deborah would have seen a picture of her, maybe on the society page of a magazine. But she waved anyway.

As Deborah made her way to the table, squeezing past six businessmen seated near the door, Julia noted with satisfaction that not one of them gave her even a second glance.

There were two reasons for that, she pondered. First, Deborah had undoubtedly been pretty far down the line when God handed out good looks. Her figure was decent, but she had covered it with rather dowdy, shapeless clothes, and she wore the kind of solid, built-for-comfort shoes favored by nurses and flight attendants. Her shoulder-length mousy brown hair looked like it was in need of a good cut and conditioning at a decent salon, as it lacked luster and was frizzing slightly around her ears. She could look one hundred times better with a little tweak here and there, Julia mused.

Second, unlike Julia, who treated every crowded room as a show-case for her obvious attractions, Deborah was almost invisible, moving across the floor virtually unnoticed, her shoulders hunched, her head bowed. Her body language screamed apologetic. She was palpably relieved when she reached the table and slid into the chair opposite Julia. What a curious lunch date they made, Julia thought. Two very different women with absolutely nothing in common except that they both fell in love with and married the same man. More bafflingly, he had fallen in love with and married two such completely different women.

"Hello," Deborah offered with a smile. Her voice was soft, but her eyes were like granite, and Julia realized immediately that she wasn't going to be a pushover.

"Thanks for coming." Julia attempted one of her most winning smiles, but it evaporated as Deborah looked away to survey the other diners.

"Come here often, do you?" she asked.

"I try to. It's one of my favorites."

"Really?" Deborah looked disdainful. "It strikes me as somewhere that people like you come to be seen, because they think it says something about how influential they are." She had, of course, nailed Julia's motives on the head.

"Oh, no, not at all." Julia smiled thinly, inwardly shocked that mousy little Deborah could come out swinging. "The food is out of this world, and you won't find better service."

"Good." Deborah surveyed the menu. "Because I'm not staying long."

So what's this all about then?" Deborah pushed her empty plate to one side and washed the last remnants of spaghetti from her mouth with a swig of still water.

For the last half an hour, they had talked stiffly about those fa-vorite old stalwarts: the weather, who was favorite to win that year's Wimbledon, the increase in street crime, and property prices. Every-thing but the hot potato of James and his relationship with both of them.

"It's not about anything really." Julia was painfully aware that her casual, cheerful manner sounded forced. "I just thought it would be nice for us to get to know each other."

Deborah looked deeply suspicious. "Why? Have you and James just discovered some old life insurance policy that still has my name on it?"

"Sorry?" Julia was flummoxed.

"Well, you'd need me to sign away my rights, so maybe that's what this is all about?" She raised a quizzical eyebrow.

"Oh, I see." Julia laughed, an obviously false, tinkling laugh that was fooling no one. "No, no, it's nothing like that. It just struck me that James is still very fond of you, and it would make his life easier if we were friends."

"Friends?" Deborah's impassive expression slipped for a moment, and her eyes bulged at the suggestion. "You want us to be *friends*? You're kidding, right?"

Julia looked, and felt, uncomfortable. "No, I'm not kidding. I see no reason why it couldn't happen."

Deborah smiled slightly and took a long, slow intake of breath. "Oh, I can, Julia. In fact, I can think of *several* reasons why we'll never be friends."

"Really?" Julia didn't like the way things were going. She had en-visaged that *she* would be in charge of the conversation, steering Deborah in the direction she wanted. But Deborah was proving to be quite a prickly adversary and nobody's fool.

"Oh, come on, Julia, let's be frank. You met my husband, targeted him, relentlessly pursued and ultimately stole him from me. You have never . . . not *once* . . . bothered to express even the slightest bit of remorse for your behavior. In fact, from what James has told me, you have actively gone out of your way on several occasions to try to stop him from remaining friends with me . . ."

She paused a moment, taking another sip of water.

"So, forgive me, but when you suddenly step up and announce that you want to be my friend, I find it deeply suspicious, not to mention insulting. You and I would *never* be friends, even if you hadn't run off with my husband. You are self-obsessed, shallow, and, if I'm honest, just a teensy bit dull." She stopped speaking and dabbed the corners of her mouth with her napkin.

Julia sat up and gasped. "Dull? *Dull?* I don't fucking think so." Being described as self-obsessed and shallow didn't bother her in the slightest, but to be accused of being boring was a harsh blow to her.

"Spoken like a true lady." Deborah pursed her lips disapprovingly and placed her elbows on the table, leaning toward her lunch companion. "Julia, you are undoubtedly a beautiful woman . . . but beyond that? Sorry, I just don't get it. What on *earth* do you and James talk about?"

Julia blinked rapidly, inwardly reeling from this verbal onslaught from a woman who looked like she wouldn't say boo to a goose. "Are you suggesting I'm thick?" She had intended to remain quietly dignified, but she could feel anger welling up inside her.

Deborah shrugged. "No, I don't know you, so I couldn't say that for sure. But I *do* know that James is fascinated by current affairs like politics and economics, and all you ever seem to do is shop and have your nails done. So, sex aside, I really can't see the attraction."

"Fuck you!" Julia threw down her napkin. Good-bye, quiet dignity. "You're a bloody primary-school teacher, love, not some towering intellect who's discovered a cure for cancer. You know *nothing* about what makes James and me tick, so don't make wild assumptions," she hissed.

Deborah smiled triumphantly, clearly thrilled she'd riled her adversary enough to make her show her true colors. "On the contrary, I know quite a lot about you. James tells me everything."

Julia recoiled slightly, as if a heavy blow had struck her chest. But she recovered quickly. "I'm surprised you find the time, Deborah, what with the two of you discussing quantum physics and foreign policy reform. I'm deeply flattered that little old me even features on your highbrow agenda."

The pair fell silent, Deborah idly stirring her black coffee, Julia furiously rearranging her napkin, her mind whirring with what James might have said about her. *If* he'd said anything at all, of course. It could easily be a wind-up, couldn't it? She didn't know for sure, but the remark had unseated her.

Deborah cleared her throat, indicating she was about to say something. "So what has James told you about our marriage?" she asked nonchalantly.

Julia took a deep breath to calm herself, happier now that the ball seemed to be back in her court. She didn't want to waste the shot.

"Oh, you know," she hedged, hoping her vagueness would make Deborah assume she knew more than she did. "Just that you'd become a bit like brother and sister, still getting on but with no spark."

"He said that?" An expression of hurt flickered across Deborah's face, but she recovered quickly.

"Yep." Julia pulled a faux apologetic expression.

"You surprise me, because that wasn't the case at all." Her eyes were flinty again. "James and I had a fantastic marriage and still had a very active sex life right up to the point that he announced he was leaving me for you."

Again, Julia was momentarily floored by this statement. James had always assured her that, sexually, his marriage had been dead in the water long before he met her.

Deborah could be lying, of course, but how would Julia ever know who was telling the truth?

Sighing, she feigned a bored expression. "Deborah, it's a well-acknowledged fact that men don't leave happy marriages."

"Ridiculous." Deborah's tone was even. "They simply *say* it wasn't happy to justify their decision to leave familiarity behind in favor of someone who's prepared to behave like a hooker—all stockings, suspenders, and blow jobs in the back of cabs."

"Are you calling me a hooker?" Julia was breathing deeper than a woman in labor in a bid to control her mounting fury.

"Of course not. I was speaking generally."

Julia knew she wasn't, but decided not to jab her in the eye with a fork just yet. "So if that's the case, why not just brush up your own bedroom skills and persuade your husband to stay?"

The corners of Deborah's mouth turned down in distaste. "Because I wouldn't want to demean myself into behaving like some porn star just to keep a man who's *supposed* to love me for who I am. My bedroom skills are just fine, thanks, but it's hard to compete against the lure of the new and the forbidden, not to mention the surgically enhanced. Particularly someone as unashamedly tenacious as *you*, Julia." Deborah fixed her with an icy stare. "I have no doubt he would have stayed if you hadn't issued him your little ultimatum. He told me all about it and was very torn."

Realizing the conversation was starting to go round in circles, Julia raised her hand for the maitre d' to get the bill before turning back to face Deborah.

"So what I don't understand is this . . . if your marriage was so great and he *still* left you, why on earth do you want to be friends with him?"

"That's a good question," Deborah admitted. "But I like his company, and we always had . . . still have . . . lots to talk about, so I guess I'd miss that. That's one reason . . ."

"Any others?" Julia rummaged through her purse looking for a credit card.

"Yes. My main reason for staying friends with him is that I know how much it pisses you off."

Julia stopped rummaging and looked up to see if Deborah was joking. But her face was deadly serious.

"You see," Deborah continued, "that's where you have been just so damned *stupid*. Vicariously, through James, you let me know very early on that you were bothered by my continued presence in his life. I can't tell you the number of times he's asked me not to call him at home because it upsets you, so we speak behind your back, like a husband with a mistress but without the sex. Ironic, isn't it?" She paused to take a sip of coffee. Her utterly unruffled demeanor infuriated Julia.

"And the more I know it upsets you, the more I hang in there." Deborah idly extracted a small piece of food from between her front teeth. "If you'd played a smarter game and pretended to be unaffected by me, I doubt my friendship with James would be anything like as strong as it is. I would have given up on him long ago, assuming I could never win him back." She suddenly smiled. "But as it is, I'm hoping you'll fuck it up and he'll come back to me."

Julia felt sick. She now knew that her supposedly clever plan to woo Deborah had been at best naive, at worst moronically delusional. The woman was nothing like the little mouse she'd imagined—she was a formidable adversary.

Suddenly her nausea gave way to a bubble of laughter, rising up through her chest and emerging as a suppressed snort.

Deborah looked slightly baffled. "What's so funny?"

Shaking her head at her own naïveté, Julia signed the credit-card bill and handed it back to the waiter. "You know, I came here expecting you to be a pushover to my charms, pathetically and gratefully snatching at my hand of friendship. But you've turned out to be quite a revelation . . . a complete bitch, in fact."

"You say that like it's a bad thing." Deborah wasn't smiling as such, but her eyes suggested that she was amused.

Julia beamed a fake smile. "And you know what? I quite admire you for it. And the really funny thing is that, although I came here to *pretend* I wanted to be friends, in another life I think we would genuinely have gotten on rather well."

"I'm not so sure." Deborah looked doubtful.

"Oh, I am. Very sure. Physically we're very different, but in character we're a lot more alike than you might think, which is probably why James married us." She stuffed her credit card back into her handbag and clasped it shut. "Anyway, it's been a pleasure." She extended her hand across the table. "And no hard feelings, eh?"

Deborah shook her hand with an icy smile. "Thank you for lunch, but I'm afraid I can't pretend I don't have hard feelings because I do. Plenty of them."

"Totally understandable," said Julia brightly, determined to swallow her anger and end the lunch on as equal a footing as possible. "I'd feel exactly the same if it were the other way round."

As she turned to go, she heard Deborah say, "If I get my way, one day it will be."

That night Julia and James were settling down to enjoy a new Mark Bittman recipe she'd tried out with great success. It actually resembled the picture in the book right down to the sprig of rosemary perched elegantly on top.

"Darling, this is just delicious," James mumbled through a mouthful of perfectly cooked beef. "You really are a sensational cook."

"Thank you." She beamed prettily, keeping the atmosphere light in preparation for his next question. She knew what it was going to be, because they went through the same ritual every night. She'd cook an à la carte meal, he'd tell her how wonderful it was, she'd thank him, and then . . .

"So how was your day?" he'd ask.

"Interesting . . . " she paused for dramatic effect, ". . . I had lunch with your ex-wife."

The beef made a hasty reappearance, spat with powerful velocity back onto James's plate. "Julia! Please don't make jokes like that."

"It's not a joke," she said calmly. "I took her to lunch at the Ivy, and we had a lovely chat."

"About what?" He looked incredulous.

"About whether we'll ever join the Euro—what on *earth* do you think we spoke about?" She raised her eyes heavenward. "About you, of course."

"What did you say?" There was panic in his eyes.

Julia pursed her lips to look thoughtful, as if trying to remember. The truth was that she could regurgitate the entire conversation verbatim, but she didn't want to let on it was *that* important to her. "I said I thought it would be nice if she and I could be friends."

"And?"

"And she said she couldn't see that happening. She said she thought I was self-obsessed and shallow." She conveniently edited out the "dull" bit.

"Oh. So that was that then?" He looked expectant.

"*James!*" She had mentioned the character assassination because she wanted him to be indignant on her behalf. "She called me self-obsessed and shallow. Don't you think that's out of order?"

He shuffled uncomfortably in his seat. "Yes, darling, of course it is. Though it surprises me, I must admit. It's really not like Deborah to say something like that."

"Well, she did," Julia said huffily. "She also said she stays friends with you purely because she knows it irritates me."

"She said that?" A dog who'd been robbed of his favorite bone couldn't have looked more pitiful.

Julia nodded and leaned across to take his hand. "Darling, I *know* you're fond of her, but she's not the gentle, unassuming Mrs. Tiggywinkle person you seem to think she is. She has quite a harsh side to her. She really upset me . . ." Her tone was wounded, her face puckered into a faux expression of self-doubt. But James didn't seem to notice.

"Was that it? She didn't give any other reason why she stays friends with me?"

She was irritated by his blanket refusal to acknowledge that Deborah might be anything but saintlike in her character, but she didn't show it. In her new strategy of trying to kill the ex-wife with kindness, she knew that a jealous outburst had no place.

"No," she said guilelessly, shaking her head. "Nothing else. In fact, to be honest, James, I'm baffled as to why *you* stay friends with *her*. I mean, don't get me wrong, she seems really, really nice. But if I'm honest . . . ," she sighed as if the next bit was painful for her to say, ". . . she's a teensy bit dull."

He didn't respond, simply staring into space with a troubled look on his face. His meal was only half-eaten, but he carefully placed the knife and fork together and pushed the plate to one side.

"That was lovely, darling, thank you. But I've suddenly lost my appetite." He smiled sheepishly. "It's not every day a chap learns his wife has been out to lunch with his ex, and I must admit it's unsettled me slightly."

Julia pouted. "Shame. And I've made such a lovely dessert too."

"Perhaps later." He smiled weakly and cleared his throat. "So how did your lunch end? Do you think you'll become friends?"

She looked at him as if he'd lost his marbles. "Hardly! Not after what she said to me. I'd say there's more chance of Israel and Palestine walking hand in hand into the sunset than us two."

"Oh." He looked faintly relieved. "So you won't be extending any more lunch invitations in her direction then?"

"Oh, I don't know . . ." Julia stood up and started to gather their plates. "I think I might invite her to my birthday party, just to show there are no hard feelings."

In other words, Julia thought, just to show her that in the grand scheme of my life, she is merely a small speck that doesn't trouble me in any way.

best of enemies

"Right. There are bottles and food in the fridge, and you should give her lunch at about twelve-thirty. Okay?" Fiona looked at David, who resembled a man being asked to memorize a knitting pattern.

"Er, yes, think so," he replied hesitantly. "And will she need her nappy changed at all?"

"Don't be a prat," she said dismissively. "Of course she will, probably several times. Seriously, David, if I have to leave a list of instructions every time I leave you with Lily, it really is totally pathetic."

She turned to the sofa where Jake was lolling, sullenly flicking through the television channels, his teenage brain unable to concentrate on one program for more than a few seconds. "Come on, Jake, are you ready?"

He didn't move.

"I think he might be dead, but I'm afraid to ask," she added, rais-ing her eyes at David.

"Jake!" he reprimanded. "Fiona's ready, come *on*. Why do we al-ways have to ask you to do something three or four times before you do it?"

"Try asking him if he wants twenty pounds to spend. That should break through the barrier." She suppressed a deep sigh, masking it as a yawn. "Gosh, I'm tired. I'm looking forward to some fresh air."

Last night, while cuddling David on the sofa and fueled by sev-eral glasses of chardonnay, she'd had the brilliant idea of her and Jake spending some time alone together. But in the cold and sober light of morning, it was looking more and more like a bad deci-sion.

She was leaving Lily in the less than capable hands of her ner-vous father to spend the day with a moody, monosyllabic teenager who looked like he'd rather be going to the Barbie Ice Capades than hanging out with his stepmother.

"I thought we'd start at the Tate Modern," she said brightly, re-ferring to the famous art museum, "and then get some lunch." In other words, she thought sourly, we'll attempt to have a nice day like the one I had planned last weekend before you fucked it up by going on the missing list.

"Whoopee. I'm at fever pitch." Sarcasm dripped from Jake's voice, but unfortunately, David had moved into the kitchen and out of earshot and Fiona felt that verbally annihilating her charmless stepson might not be a great start to their "special" day in each other's company.

"Come on, Jake, don't be a grouch," she cajoled. "You never know, you might undergo a complete personality transformation and actually enjoy something."

•   •   •

here were some really interesting pieces, weren't there? Quite thought-provoking."

Fiona and Jake were sitting in Gastro, a small French restaurant just a couple of blocks away from the museum, dining on two vast plates of *steak pommes frites*.

He shrugged and rubbed at a blob of ketchup that had fallen onto his RIM OF SCUM'S ANAL VAPORS TOUR T-shirt. "It was okay."

This had been his demeanor for the past two hours, the reluctant companion, slouching along behind her dressed in his creased T-shirt and a pair of ripped jeans sitting half-mast on his still boyish hips. With his trainer laces dragging along the ground, he made Scooby-Doo's friend Shaggy look like a snappy dresser.

Fiona, meanwhile, had morphed into a maniacally hyperactive guide, working overtime to interest her tour party in what was on the walls of the spacious galleries.

Everything she'd dragged him to was either "all right," "okay," or "rank," and the closest she'd come to winning a smile had been when he'd clapped eyes on the size of the plate of food he was now devouring with gusto.

She was feeling excessively weary, exhausted from so much fake cheerfulness, from smiling like a grinning chimpanzee when all she felt like doing was grabbing the little shit by his throat and hissing: "Go on, punk, make my day."

"Just okay, eh?" she said testily. "Well, I thought it was fascinating. Perhaps I should have taken you to a Rim of Scum concert? Maybe then you'd be stimulated into saying something a little more expansive than one word every half an hour?" She knew she was losing it, but she couldn't help herself.

Jake continued to shovel food into his mouth for a few more seconds, then stopped to wash it all down with a swig of Diet Coke, the drink he would have bathed in if he'd been allowed to.

He fixed her with his pale blue eyes, then narrowed them to indicate suspicion. "Just what are you trying to achieve here, Fiona?"

"Hoorah! A whole sentence." She smiled nervously, taken aback by this sudden and searing question from someone who hitherto had rarely shown much depth in emotional matters. "If, by that, you mean why have I brought you out for the day on our own, then it's simply because I thought it might be good for us, give us a chance to spend some time together, to bond. But obviously I was wrong."

"*Us?*" He looked at her scathingly. "I wasn't aware there was an 'us.' "

She sighed impatiently. "Don't be difficult, you know exactly what I mean. After the incident with Lily and what followed, I wanted to spend some quality time with you and try to get back on track."

"Why?" he asked sullenly, shrugging. "I mean, why bother?"

"Because I'm married to your father, because I'm the mother of your half sister, because I'm your stepmother . . . there are lots of reasons why we should try to get on."

He tucked his lank hair behind his ears for the umpteenth time and stared down at his scruffy black trainers, drooping from his feet like two punctured old tires. "It's hardly worth the bother really, is it?" he muttered. "I'll be eighteen at the end of next year and can do what I like, so you won't be seeing so much of me. I won't be *forced* to come and stay with you." He spat the word out with sullen venom.

Fiona widened her eyes in surprise. "Forced? Is that how you feel about coming to see your father? If so, that's a real shame after everything he's done for you. He adores you, Jake, you know that."

"Really?" He looked and sounded disinterested.

"Yes, really." Fiona felt bruised on David's behalf at the injustice of it. "A lot of dads lose touch with their children when a marriage breaks up, but he was determined to fight for your relationship."

Jake smiled slightly, but it didn't reach his eyes. "Not so deter-mined, though, that he decided to stay with Mum, eh? That way, he could have seen me day in, day out, like he'd always done."

"Oh, come on, Jake, you don't seriously think that, do you?"

"Think what?"

"That it was your father's fault the marriage broke up. We've had this conversation before, and you *know* that's not true. Every story has two sides." She was careful in what she said. After all, Jake had only been eight when David and Belinda split up, and at the time his father had felt it best to shield his son from the harsh realities of adult life. But Fiona was a little foggy on whether Jake had been told a few more details over the years.

"I know that Mum and Dad decided to have a bit of a break, but then he met you and never came back." He looked at her with distaste. "If there had been no *you*, they would have gotten back together."

"So you've said, many times." She sighed. "But you clearly haven't been told everything." As soon as she said it, she could have kicked herself.

"What do you mean?"

Fiona paused for a moment, contemplating what to do next. She knew it wasn't her place to tell Jake the full story, but on the other hand, he was sixteen now—old enough to have consensual sex and certainly old enough to be told a few home truths about the demise of his parents' marriage. And besides, she thought, why the hell shouldn't I tell him when it's *me* having to put up with all the crap that stems from the half-truths? "I mean," she said slowly, "that it was your mother who instigated the break, and it was your mother who started dating someone else first."

He looked confused. "No, she didn't."

"Yes, she *did*, Jake. In fact, she was still dating him when I met your father."

"Who was he?" He looked slightly flushed.

"He was the single dad of one of your old classmates from elementary school. Now what was her name?" Fiona stared at the ceiling for inspiration, pretending to search her memory. "Tamara, I think. Does that ring a bell?"

Jake had turned deathly pale, his mouth pinched with angst. "Tamara? Mum *dated* Tamara's dad?"

Fiona simply nodded.

"If that's true, why wouldn't she have told me?" he asked suspiciously.

"I don't know, love, you'll have to ask her that. All I know is that she *was* dating him when I met David, so forgive me, but I don't feel in the slightest bit responsible for the breakup of your parents' marriage."

He took another swig of Diet Coke and used his frayed sleeve to wipe away a drop from his chin. "So what happened with Mum and Tamara's dad? Why aren't they still together?"

"Because . . . ," Fiona wasn't sure how far she should go, but she felt it was only fair to give honest answers to his questions, ". . . he decided to go back to Tamara's mother."

"Oh." Jake still looked uncertain about what she'd told him, but at least he'd stopped scowling at her.

"So," she went on, "as I said, don't blame me. Even if I didn't exist, I doubt your mum and dad would have gotten back together."

They lapsed into silence for a couple of minutes, both feigning interest in what was going on elsewhere in the restaurant, anything to prevent them from having to speak to each other. Eventually Fiona spoke.

"So do you think you and I can shake hands and be friends then?" She gave him a hesitant smile. "Call a truce?"

He didn't return the smile and stared down at the table for a few seconds. When he looked up, his expression was impassive. "No offense, Fiona, but I just don't see it happening. I mean, it's not like we're about to start going on long bike rides together, is it?"

Fiona was momentarily thrown by his response. "Er, no," she faltered. "But I wasn't expecting us to become the Waltons, I just thought we might bury the hatchet and try to get on with each other, perhaps have more days out like this one?"

He wrinkled his nose. "Even if what you've just told me is true, it doesn't change much really. The reason that you and I will never really bond is because my mum doesn't like you, so even if I wanted to, I wouldn't because I know it would upset her."

"I see." Fiona tried to keep smiling. She was disappointed by his lack of courage in standing up to Belinda, but she didn't blame him. "Oh well, never mind. At least we're on speaking terms again, so the day hasn't been entirely wasted."

He had the grace to look apologetic. "Thanks for lunch."

Fiona picked up the bill and glanced at it. She had spent a day away from Lily, had achieved virtually nothing with Jake, and was now £50 lighter.

"You're welcome." She sighed.

testing times

Alison busied herself in the kitchen, boiling the kettle for no apparent reason, wiping the already pristine work surfaces and rearranging the coffee mugs. Anything to keep from thinking about that little strip of plastic upstairs, so innocuous looking yet so crucially important to her future.

She looked at her watch. Two minutes had passed since she'd stooped over the loo and urinated on the little paddle—always such a dignified exercise—and in exactly one minute's time she'd know whether her greatest wish had been granted. Or whether her high expectation would result in her not being pregnant and yet another month of waiting and hoping.

Her period was only a day late, but it was normally as regular as clockwork. And she couldn't put her finger on why, but she just felt . . . well, different somehow. Placing both her hands on her breasts, she applied pressure. They certainly felt a little tender, so that was a good sign. And earlier that morning she had felt slightly nauseous, though whether that was simply a symptom of her apprehension she wasn't sure. "Careful, girl," she told herself aloud. "Don't get ahead of yourself. We've been here before, don't forget."

Climbing the stairs to the bathroom, she paused at the top, standing in front of a small chest of drawers with family pictures on top. There were two of Alison and Luca, both taken on their honeymoon, but the rest were of him with his boys, mucking around in a park, pulling silly faces at Disneyland Paris, and cuddling up on the sofa at Luca's parents' house.

If I could fast-forward time, thought Alison, would I be standing here and looking at photographs of my and Luca's child? Or maybe two of them . . . a boy and a girl? She ached with the possibility of it. Even the mere thought that it might not happen prompted a dull stabbing pain in her chest.

Slowly pushing open the bathroom door, she walked in and looked around, her gaze taking in everything except the top of the cistern, where she knew the answer lay. She picked up a damp flannel that was scrunched up in the sink and wrang it out, hanging it over the side of the bath to dry. She screwed the lid back on the shampoo bottle and placed it back in the cupboard. And she ran the bath taps, swilling out a dead bug. Eventually she took a deep breath and turned toward the pregnancy tester, the all-important little window facing downward.

One blue line meant disappointment. Two blue lines, euphoria.

Taking a deep breath, she flipped it over, the familiar thump of loss hitting her almost instantaneously. However much she scrutinized it, there was no getting away from the bitterly disappointing fact that there was only one blue line and not even the faintest *hint* of another.

She slumped down onto the loo seat and sat there like a rag doll, her arms lying limp by her sides, her head bowed. Within a few seconds, the tears came, at first sporadic, then building up to splash down on her skirt, accompanied by gulping sobs.

She had been so convinced that *this* time she really was pregnant, that this time she'd be looking forward to creating her and Luca's child, buying all the books and being swept along in the excitement of it.

All the signs had been there, hadn't they? Or had she simply been willing them to be there in her desperation to conceive?

Running the back of her forefinger under each eye, she wiped away the tears and tried to compose herself. After all, it wasn't the end of the world. As her mother had always told her when she'd felt sorry for herself as a child, "there are plenty of people in the world who'd like your problems."

But try as she might, Alison couldn't apply this logic to her seeming inability to conceive. She *knew* there were people worse off than her, but when she looked around, all she could see were happy mothers interacting with their children. Women who seemed to have everything she wanted.

The phone rang. She toyed with the idea of leaving it, but thought it might be Luca and was suddenly seized by the compulsion to speak to him, to hear his mellifluous voice in the hope it would have a calming effect on her.

"Hello?"

"Hi, honey. It's Fiona. What are you up to?"

"Not much," she hedged. "Just doing a few chores."

"Ugh. Don't remind me. Our laundry basket is erupting with dirty clothes, and David and I just can't face tackling it."

"Luca wouldn't even consider doing it. He's a bit traditional like that."

"Lazy you mean."

Alison didn't contradict her.

"Anyway, I just thought I'd give you a ring to see how you are. I was a bit worried about you the other day."

They had met for an impromptu coffee a couple of days earlier, after Alison had called Fiona on her mobile and learned they were shopping in the same area. Over a rather watery latte and a couple of cinnamon whirls, she had ended up confiding her fear of never conceiving a baby.

"You're only thirty-six, you've got *years* left to conceive," Fiona had replied, making a pooh-poohing noise. "Women are having babies later and later these days."

The irony was that Alison had spent all of her twenties on the pill, desperate not to get pregnant when she still had so much she wanted to do with her life. And now here she was, married and desperate to have a baby, and nothing was happening. Perhaps I never needed contraception, she thought bitterly, perhaps I'm not actually *able* to conceive.

"It's sweet of you to be worried," she said, her mind refocusing on the phone call. "But I'm fine, honest. You're absolutely right, I've still got years to have a baby." She couldn't face telling Fiona about the negative pregnancy tester now lying discarded in the bathroom bin.

"That's the spirit. Think positive!" Fiona advised. "Don't get disheartened, it's early days. Well, as long as you're okay, I'd better get on with making Lily some lunch. Ciao."

Alison clicked the off button on the phone and stood up, staring at herself in the bathroom mirror.

"Think positive, think positive," she chanted to herself. "You *will* get pregnant, you *will* get pregnant."

Deep down, though, she was scared. Scared that she would never get to experience the amazing phenomenon of childbirth, scared that she would never be able to give Luca a child, never be able to match up to his first wife.

Sofia's jibe about Alison never being able to share the thrill of Luca's firstborn son with him had cut deep. Particularly as she feared she might not be able to give him children at all.

In the dream she kept having, night after night, she and Luca had a baby daughter. That was Alison's greatest fantasy, to give him the "daddy's girl" he hadn't yet experienced. But right now she'd settle for just getting pregnant.

Luca thought she had only been trying for the past three months since their wedding, and that's what she'd told Fiona too. But Alison and her doctor knew different. She'd been to see her just the previous week, confessing her concerns.

"How long have you been trying?"

"I haven't used contraception since I first met my husband. So, um, about two years now."

"I see." The doctor had scribbled something in her notes. "Well, that's probably long enough to suggest that we should carry out a few initial tests, if that's what you want to do. When's your next period due?"

"In a couple of days. So fingers crossed."

"Well, if you're not pregnant, then come back to see me, and we'll start the ball rolling to see if we can find a problem. I'm sure it's nothing major."

Alison had left the office feeling reassured, but now, after yet another negative pregnancy test, her optimism had deserted her.

Foolishly, she had mentioned to Luca that morning that she was experiencing pregnancy symptoms, and tonight, yet again, she would have to tell him she'd been wrong.

In the three months he *thought* they had been actively trying to conceive, she had laughed off the failures, babbling something about his business trips away coinciding with her fertile days. "Don't worry, darling," he'd reassured her, perfectly confident. "These things take time. And we haven't been trying all that long."

Please God, let it happen soon, she thought. I'm running out of excuses.

unraveling alone

Susan stared into the mirror and gently prized out the earrings that had been killing her all night. She then eased her feet out of the shoes that weren't far behind in the race for maximum discomfort.

Aaaaaah, lovely, she thought to herself. Well, at least the evening has ended on a pleasurable note.

She and Nick had just returned from his company's summer party at the Kensington Roof Gardens, and it had been Susan's idea of hell. Three hundred real estate agents talking endlessly about property prices while their headband-wearing wives prattled on about school carpools and how their lives had been transformed by Internet grocery shopping.

It was the first time Susan had attended the party with Nick, and she'd so wanted to make a good impression with his colleagues, but instead she'd remained mute for most of the evening, standing on

the periphery of everyone's conversation with a smile stretched
across her face. She had absolutely nothing in common with these
people, and her one attempt at breaking the ice had fallen flat.

"Terrible music, isn't it?" she'd shouted to one horse-faced
woman above the strains of "Come On, Eileen." "I'm not saying he's
old, but this guy must have been the DJ at the Boston Tea Party."

"Actually," the woman said, scowling, "I think he's very good. He
did the music at our wedding."

Susan winced now at the thought of it, as she walked across the
bedroom to where Nick was hanging up his rented tuxedo, ready for
its return tomorrow. "Can you undo my zip? God, this dress is a
nightmare to get in and out of."

She breathed a sigh of relief as the zipper relinquished its grip on
her flesh and the green satin dress fell to the ground in a crumpled
heap. Green was Susan's favored color for clothes, mainly because
anything adventurous like pink or orange clashed with her red hair.

"It's a curse being a woman, you know."

"Oh, really?" Nick replied distractedly, trying to undo his bow tie.
"Why's that?"

"Because you have to squeeze yourself into dresses like this when
all you want to do is wear baggy pajamas," she puffed, extricating one
leg from her nylons. "And when was the last time a man turned up
at a party and said, 'Shit, I've got to go, there's another bloke in the
same dinner suit as me?' " She lost her balance and fell onto the bed
in an undignified heap. "Whereas God forbid if we see anyone else
wearing the same dress."

Nick smiled. "Well, I didn't see anyone wearing the same dress as
you tonight."

"You wouldn't. This is at least ten years old. It's a trusty favorite."

"Did you enjoy yourself?" He was standing in his boxer shorts
now, rubbing the back of his neck where the bow tie had left an in-
dentation.

She wrinkled her nose. "Truthfully? No, not really. I hate those things. I never know what to say to anyone, particularly when you're not around."

"Yeah, sorry about that." He made an apologetic face. "I like to work the room, and you know what they say, he travels fastest who travels alone."

"Hmmm." She looked doubtful. "I think that's supposed to refer to long expeditions, not social occasions."

Nick walked across to the bed and threw back the duvet, climbing in. "Anyway, Caitlin never minded being left to her own devices at those things, so I just thought you'd be the same."

Ah, yes, there it was, Caitlin, Susan thought. Perhaps *that's* why I felt so damned awkward, because deep down I knew that, as usual, she had trodden the path before me, dazzling everyone with her witty repartee and charm. They must have been bitterly disappointed by this frizzy-haired mute, wondering what on earth Nick saw in her after such an attractive and articulate first wife.

She sighed rather more heavily than she'd intended, enough to make Nick look up from his book.

"You okay?"

She nodded and smiled, climbing in next to him and cuddling into the crook of his left arm. "Nick?"

"Uh-huh?" He had returned to reading.

"I don't disappoint you, do I?"

He looked puzzled. "Disappoint me? What do you mean?"

"Maybe that's the wrong word to use," she backtracked. "It's just that sometimes I wonder why you're with me when . . . well, you know . . . you could be with someone a bit more your type."

"My *type*?" He laid his book down on the duvet and twisted his body slightly toward her, looking confused. "And what's my type exactly?"

She stared down at the back cover of his book, not wanting to look at him. "Someone a bit more outgoing . . . you know, more confident at all that social stuff."

He thought about what she'd said for a couple of seconds, then made a scoffing noise. "Don't be daft. I like you just as you are." He kissed the top of her head. "Now stop being so silly."

Susan knew she should have felt reassured, but she didn't. She felt patronized. She knew Nick loved her in his own way, but there were times when she felt like an unpaid housekeeper who got shagged occasionally. True, there were moments like the one at the Priory, but she couldn't help feeling like they were too few and far between. Shouldn't there have been more romance (not to mention sex) between a couple still in the first years of their relationship? Or was she just being overly sensitive?

Neither of them were publicly demonstrative people—in fact, this evening they hadn't even held hands. As far as his colleagues were concerned, she could easily have been Nick's sister or an old platonic school friend. The lack of affection in public didn't bother her too much, but the lack of it in private did. Lately, the only times Nick kissed her were in a perfunctory way as he left the house in the morning or, more passionately, when he was instigating sex in bed at night.

She wasn't looking for him to pin her down on the sofa for regular necking sessions, but the occasional hug, squeeze, or prolonged kiss outside the usual parameters would have been nice. She had tried to change the pattern herself, sneaking up behind him at the sink, wrapping her arms round his middle, or gently caressing the back of his neck while they watched television. But he rarely responded, usually making a joke and moving away.

Not for the first time, and even though she tried to force the thought aside, she found herself wondering what he'd been like with Caitlin when they were alone. But there was something else nagging at Susan too, something much, much bigger. She wanted to try for a baby of their own.

She had been intending—longing, in fact—to bring up the subject with him for some time, but the moment or mood never seemed
right. If they were having a nice evening, she didn't want to risk
ruining it by broaching what her gut instinct told her was going to
be a sensitive subject, and if they were having an argument about
something else, it didn't seem right to throw in the baby question for
good measure.

Now, she thought, nestling back into the crook of his arm, feeling his warmth against her cheek. Maybe now was the right time.

"Nick?"

"Uh-huh?" He sounded slightly tetchier this time, clearly wanting to read his book without interruption.

But this time she was determined to plow on and have her say. "I
was wondering . . ."

She waited for him to encourage her to ask her question, as if psy-
chologically that might have a more positive impact on the answer.
But he said nothing, just carried on reading.

"I was wondering," she repeated, "how you would feel about us
trying for a baby?"

Her words hung in midair, filling the space between them with
her expectation. Now that she had finally voiced her deepest
thoughts, she felt stiff with anxiety.

"A *baby*?" His tone and expression suggested she'd just asked if
they could buy a full-size crocodile and keep it in the bathtub.

"Yes, you know, one of those pink things that crawls around on
all fours," she quipped, hoping to lighten what she suspected was
about to become a desperately negative conversation.

"Yes, Susan." He sounded cross. "I know what a baby is. What I
mean is, why on earth would you want one when Ellie still needs so
much of our time and attention? Don't forget, she's lost her mother."

Susan bristled slightly at his unspoken suggestion that she didn't
have the little girl's best interests at heart. She adored Ellie, would

do anything for her, and she didn't see that the arrival of a new baby would change any of that.

"I don't wish to diminish what she or, for that matter, you went through when Caitlin died," Susan said slowly, carefully editing her words as she went along. "But it's been nearly four years now, and you have to move on with life at some point, don't you?"

Nick didn't answer right away but simply stared straight ahead, his mouth set in a firm line. "You can't accuse me of not moving on, Susan, that's not fair." His book fell onto the floor, but he left it there. "After all, you and I are living together as a couple, and believe me, with Genevieve and Bill to deal with, that was quite a step for me to take . . ."

"I know, love . . ." She placed a reassuring hand on his forearm.

"But another baby?" He looked perplexed. "Sorry, but Ellie is my number one concern in life, and I just don't think she's ready to share me with another child. It might make her feel rejected, and I couldn't bear the thought of that."

On the contrary, Susan probably knew Ellie better than anyone and was certain she would embrace a baby brother or sister with open arms. She knew that because, without Nick's knowledge, she had casually floated the idea past the little girl on a couple of occasions, when the timing was right.

"Look, Nick," she said earnestly, propping herself up on one elbow, "I know you have Ellie's best interests at heart, but you're crediting her with far too much emotional maturity. Young children don't sit around worrying about rejection, and particularly not happy ones like Ellie, who doesn't have any doubt about how much we both love her. And don't forget, you were also worried about how she'd react to staying overnight at Bill and Genevieve's and she didn't bat an eyelid."

She paused to see if he might respond to what she'd said so far, but he showed no sign of it.

"As far as Ellie is concerned, a baby brother or sister would be like getting a new dolly, someone to dress up and play with, a little chum if you like."

She looked at him imploringly, but he had already started to slowly shake his head.

"Sorry, Susan, but I just don't agree, and I'm not going to be persuaded otherwise. It's still a no, I'm afraid."

Flopping back down onto her pillow, Susan stared at the ceiling for a few seconds, trying to calm herself. She felt a burning sense of injustice that *her* wishes on such an important and emotional subject were being dismissed as easily as one might sweep aside someone's choice of curtain fabric for a living room.

She was lacking in confidence over many things, but when she felt disrespected or unjustly treated, she always found an inner strength to fight her corner. She could feel it rising within her now.

"Well, it's not as simple as that, though, is it?" she said quietly.

"Not as simple as what?"

"You saying no and presuming that's the end of the matter."

Nick sighed, one of those long, mannered sighs that men so often use to suggest that, as they see it, they're about to be "nagged."

"Go on," he said impatiently. "Say what you have to say, and then I really would like to get some sleep. It's been a long day."

"Nick, this is really important to me, and I refuse to speak against the clock." She sat up to show she meant business. "I'm a thirty-five-year-old, independent-minded woman who wants to have a child, or children, of her own, and you can't tell me what to do with my own body."

His face hardened. "Sorry, I thought that having a baby would be a decision we would make together."

"It is. But you won't even discuss it seriously with me. Your attitude is that *you* don't want a baby and that's final."

"Well, I *don't* want one." He let out a hollow laugh. "So I don't know what else I can say really. I can couch it in softer terms if you like, but the end result would still be the same."

"Discuss it . . . tell me *why* you don't."

"I did. I told you that I don't think it would be fair on Ellie."

She wrinkled her nose. "That's an excuse, a front for some other reason. You don't seriously think that."

"I can assure you I *do*." He looked really pissed off. "And what's more, even with the best intentions in the world, how do you know that you're not going to love our baby more than you love Ellie? She might end up feeling like second fiddle."

Susan looked horrified. "How could you say that? You know I'd never let that happen. I love that little girl as if she were my own."

"Ah, but you don't know that for sure because you have nothing to compare it to."

Susan could sense everything suddenly slipping away from her and felt overwhelmed by a wave of depression. She had never both-ered to have the "children" conversation with Nick before, because she'd just assumed he'd want more, particularly as he was such an en-thusiastic, caring father to Ellie.

Now she felt her chest tighten with panic that there could be such a fundamental difference of opinion between them. What if he never wanted more children? She passionately wanted a child of her own—the question was, could she sacrifice that dream to keep Nick? Her head spun. Right now, she was in too much emotional turmoil to even think about making such a choice.

"So is that it forever then?" Her voice cracked as the tears of dis-appointment and frustration started to fall. "We're *never* going to try for a baby?"

He saw her tears and seemed faintly irritated by them. "I really don't know, Susan. I could say that maybe I'll change my mind, just to make you feel better, but I'd be lying. Why don't we just leave it for now and talk about it again in a couple of years, when Ellie's a bit older."

"Because I'm thirty-five!" She was wailing now. "In two years my chances of conceiving will have dropped even further, and the age gap between Ellie and the baby we may or may not have will be even greater, making them less likely to be playmates. It all makes sense to start trying now."

Seeing her obvious distress, his face softened and he gathered her back into the crook of his arm, stroking her left shoulder.

"Please don't be upset. I had no idea it meant this much to you." He paused and removed a piece of hair that had stuck to her wet face. "But it comes down to a simple case of you want a baby and I don't. So where does that leave us?"

"I appreciate it's a difficult situation," she sniffed. "But I'd be the primary carer, the same as I am to Ellie. Your life wouldn't change, you'd still go to work every day, and you'd come home to a slightly bigger family, that's all."

"And what about your job?"

"I'd give it up. It's only part-time reception work, hardly a career." She was feeling slightly calmer now, daring to hope that his question about her job meant she was making headway in the discussion.

He pondered what she'd said for a moment, then removed his arm from behind her head. "I'm sorry." He looked at her imploringly. "But we'd suffer financially, and apart from that, I just don't get why Ellie isn't enough for you. She *adores* you."

"That's a cheap shot." Susan sat bolt upright, angry now. "Don't ever question my love for Ellie, it couldn't *be* any stronger. But that's not the point."

"So what is the point?" he said matter-of-factly.

"I love you, I want to marry you, and the natural progression of that is that I want to try to have a child by you. I'm not unusual in feeling like this, Nick, it's why women are given hormones, wombs, and all the reproductive workings that cause us so many problems in life." She rubbed her eyes, trying to ignore the sense of hopelessness she felt, trying to find the strength of will to see this conversation through to its conclusion. She didn't want to abandon it before she'd said everything she wanted to say.

"I love Ellie as if she were my own, but the truth is, she isn't. I have never given birth and would like to, and I want to create that child with you. It's an experience that I've longed for and dreamed about—it's one of the most powerful, profound parts of being a woman. Surely you understand that?" Her eyes were full of sadness.

Nick sighed. "Look, if I'm truthful, all this has taken me a bit by surprise. I had no idea you felt this strongly." He snuggled down next to her, his nose touching her waist. He reached up and touched her cheek. "Come on," he said softly. "Let's cuddle up and try to get some sleep, and I promise I'll have a long, hard think about what you've said."

She reached across and flicked off the bedside lamp, then lay down so her eyes were level with his. "And then what?"

"I don't know, Susan." His tone was slightly irritable again. "I've said I'll think about it, and that's a big step, so just leave it with me for a while, okay?" He rolled over so his back was facing her.

Susan lay there motionless in the dark, the familiar pinch of welling emotion pricking at her nose. The ball was now firmly in Nick's court, and from what he'd already said, she knew it would be a long time before it was thrown back. If ever.

happy birthday to me

"Having fun?" Julia sneaked up behind Fiona and squeezed her waist.

"Boy, *am* I?" Fiona raised her glass of pink champagne in the air. "Free booze, fantastic music, and this impossibly glamorous location . . ." She gestured around the Claridge's ballroom. "How could I not be enjoying myself?"

"Good," Julia declared. "I always like to celebrate my birthday in style."

"Whereas the only thing I want on my birthday is to not be reminded of it." Fiona grinned. "Ah! Here's Susan."

Susan shuffled up to them looking decidedly intimidated. "My God, Julia, you have such beautiful, glamorous friends. I feel like a right old heffalump."

"Well, you don't look it, darling. Green suits you."

"It's an old favorite." Susan had taken her green satin dress to the twenty-four-hour dry cleaners after wearing it to Nick's party. She smiled at Julia and took a step back. "And you, madam, look the most stunning of the lot."

"Oh, this old thing!" She laughed. She was wearing a pale blue sequined dress that was sleeveless and extremely tight, pushing her breasts forward and upward to resemble two ripe, blemish-free melons. The skirt was fitted snugly to her shapely bottom, tapering down to a fishtail that swished along behind her, shimmering as she walked. She had bought it the day before and paid the equivalent of a small country's national debt. Or rather, James had.

"Now then, have our men been introduced yet?" Julia swiveled her neck, looking over Susan's and Fiona's shoulders. "Ah, I see James is talking to Alison and Luca. Let's go join them."

Placing each hand in the small of Fiona's and Susan's backs, she ferried them across the room to where James was holding court, telling a joke. "And when they went into her bedroom, there were cuddly toys everywhere, on shelves right up to the ceiling . . ." He held a finger in the air to indicate to Julia that she should let him finish. "He thought she was bonkers but decided to shag her anyway, and afterwards he said, 'How was it for you?' "

Alison, Luca, Susan, and Fiona looked at him expectantly, but Julia was tapping her foot with impatience, having heard it before.

"And she just shrugged and said: 'It was average—take anything from the bottom shelf!' " James erupted into forced laughter to indicate that his punch line had been delivered and should be appreciated. The others obliged with polite laughter.

"Anyway, darling," Julia chipped in, "I see you've already met Alison and Luca, and this is Fiona. She's part of our shopping gang too."

The women all looked at one another furtively, knowing that as far as their husbands were concerned, the Second Wives Club didn't exist. One of the rules of membership was that you had to explain away the meetings as the occasional retail-therapy expedition.

"Pleased to meet you, Fiona." James shook her hand. "Is your husband here?"

Fiona nodded and surveyed the room. "He is. He's over by the bar . . . where else? . . . talking to Susan's other half, Nick."

"I'll meet them later no doubt." James smiled, turning back to Alison and Luca. "And how long have you two been married?"

"Three months. Together for two years. In fact, Fiona's husband was the best man at our wedding," replied Alison.

"Any children yet?"

She shook her head. "No, not together anyway. But Luca has two boys from his previous marriage."

"Two boys, eh?" James beamed at Luca. "What a lucky man. I'd love to have a son. Hopefully I will soon." He winked pointedly at Julia.

"Leave it, James," she quipped. "Let's not start arguing on my birthday. Now then, let me get everyone some more champagne."

As Julia went in search of more bubbly, Susan stood silently by, mulling over the irony of it all. James clearly wanted a baby, Julia clearly didn't. Nick didn't want a baby, and she did. Maybe we should just swap husbands, she thought ruefully, then we'd all get what we want.

"Penny for your thoughts?" Fiona interrupted her daydreaming.

"Oh, they're not worth *that* much, believe me."

"You okay? You seem a bit glum."

Susan sighed and checked that the others weren't in earshot. James was telling another joke to a different couple, so she surmised they weren't.

"Nick and I had a heart-to-heart the other night, during which he made it abundantly and painfully clear he doesn't want to try for a baby."

"What, *ever?*" Fiona looked stunned.

Susan shrugged, blinking rapidly to stop herself from getting tearful again. "I don't know. But he's very sure he doesn't want to try for one now or even in the next year."

"Any particular reason?"

"He said he thought it would upset Ellie."

"Nonsense!" Fiona scoffed. "Jake might hate me and David, but he's never had a problem with Lily. I think he's actually quite fond of her."

"Precisely." Susan didn't mean to sound bitter, but she couldn't help it. She was still feeling raw from the conversation. "Obviously I should have married James."

Fiona laughed. "Yes, that was an interesting little exchange, wasn't it? I knew that Julia was in no hurry to have children, but I didn't realize that James was quite so keen. I'd love to be a fly on *that* wall."

"I feel like a fly on Nick's wall sometimes," said Susan gloomily. "Worse, I keep being swatted away as irrelevant."

"Oh, now come on." Fiona patted her on the back. "You know that's not true. Nick adores you."

"Does he? I'm not so sure."

"*Susan.*" Fiona dropped her voice low. "Stop it. Don't start getting all maudlin, it doesn't suit you. You'll do nothing but upset yourself."

"What doesn't suit her?" It was Julia, returning with a full bottle of champagne to top up their glasses.

"Oh, nothing, just some old sweater I saw Susan wearing the other day," replied Fiona hastily, desperately trying to deflect Julia away from the real topic at hand. But she needn't have worried.

With the attention span of a newborn gnat, Julia had already become sidetracked.

"Talking of not suiting, have you seen the *state* of my friend Annie over there?" She nodded pointedly in the direction of a woman in the far corner, wearing a microscopic black Lycra dress that clung for dear life to every lump and bump. "I've seen more cotton in the neck of an aspirin bottle. Whatever was she thinking of?"

"Each to her own, I suppose," said Fiona diplomatically.

"Mind you, I remember when I first met her . . . we worked at the same PR firm years ago . . . I knew straightaway she was one of those 'every man for myself' women." If Julia recognized the hypocrisy of what she was saying, she didn't show it. "She's so loose, she's going to have to be buried in a Y-shaped coffin."

"If she's so dreadful, why are you friends with her?" challenged Susan.

Julia frowned slightly. "I didn't say *she* was dreadful, I said she *looked* dreadful . . . there's a difference. As a person, she's fantastic fun. Can't stand her ghastly husband, though."

"Is he here?" Susan craned her neck to see.

"Yes, see the big fat bloke with the shock of blond hair? Him." She scowled in his direction. "He's so greedy, I was thinking of installing speed bumps at the buffet." She waved a hand dismissively to indicate she had tired of that subject. "Now then, I can't be seen to be looking, but I want you to look over my left shoulder at the woman who has just walked in, with dark hair and a red dress. See her?"

Fiona and Susan nodded mutely to indicate that, yes, they could see her.

"Good. Now, first of all, I want you to describe exactly what she's wearing. Then second, what you think of her."

"What we *think* of her?" Susan frowned. "I don't even know who she is."

Julia raised her eyes heavenward as if Susan was Mrs. Stupid, living in Stupid House on Stupid Street. "It's Deborah."

"*Deborah?*" hissed Susan and Fiona in unison, both casting renewed eyes over the woman in red.

"What the bloody hell is she doing here?" Fiona rummaged in her handbag, trying to locate her glasses so she could take a better look.

"I invited her," replied Julia calmly, smiling in a patently false way at a leering fiftysomething drinks waiter walking past. "Remember 'kill them with kindness'?"

"Yes," spluttered Susan. "But I thought you were going to invite her out for lunch, not to your birthday party along with James and a roomful of people."

"I did invite her out for lunch. But just to really hammer home the point that she presents absolutely no threat to me whatsoever, I invited her here as well."

Fiona had finally found her glasses and put them on. "Well, I can report that she's wearing a plain red dress with sheer sleeves and a high neck. She's quite attractive, in a Debra Winger kind of way."

Julia scowled. Until the Debra Winger bit, she'd been reveling in the description. Susan peered across the room too. "She looks a million dollars," she observed, purely to irritate Julia. It worked.

"After tax," she muttered. "Hardly one of life's snappy dressers, is she? And let me tell you, she's also inexorably dull. God knows what James ever saw in her."

"So how was lunch then?" asked Susan, wide-eyed with expectation, her own problems forgotten for the time being. "Do tell."

"Deborah! I'm so pleased you could make it!" Julia sashayed up to her, manicured hand extended. Deborah shook it, but Julia noted she had one of those limp, lackluster handshakes that usually accompanied a similar personality. Or perhaps it was just a manifestation of her reluctance to shake the hand of the woman who stole her husband.

"Thrilled to be here," she replied archly.

Julia had to admit she secretly admired Deborah's balls in coming along on her own, particularly when the only people she knew were Julia—partially—and James.

"Have you spoken to James yet?" Julia asked her brightly. "He's holding court over there."

Deborah followed her gaze and shook her head. "No, but there's no rush. I only got off the phone with him a couple of hours ago."

Julia's mind went into overdrive. She and James were staying in a room upstairs, so he must have made the call while she was in the shower. What was it about this woman that made him want to talk to her so much?

Deborah was saying something to the waiter, who was refilling her glass, so Julia took the opportunity to study her closely. She looked slightly more glamorous this evening than she had at lunch, most notably because she was wearing makeup and had clearly blow-dried her hair into a more flattering style that softened her angular face. Her arms were well toned, but her dress didn't accentuate her best points, swamping her and hanging loosely from her hips. Made to measure . . . someone else, thought Julia.

"Oh, look!" She spotted someone a few yards away. "There's my friend Jade from college. She's a teacher too. Let me introduce you."

"College?" Deborah didn't move. "What did *you* do at college?" She made no attempt to disguise her obvious surprise that Julia had been educated beyond primary level.

"I did a PR and marketing degree," replied Julia huffily, aggrieved at such a blatant underestimation of her talents. "If you remember, I first met James when I was marketing a sports charity event." That'll show her, she thought.

But Deborah's brow furrowed. "James said you were handing out leaflets or something. I didn't think you needed a degree to do that."

"Anyway, as I was saying, come and meet Jade." Julia wanted to be rid of her now. She strode across the room with Deborah trailing reluctantly behind her. "Jade darling! Lovely to see you." She embraced her warmly. "I wanted to introduce you to another . . . er . . . friend of mine, Deborah. She's a teacher too."

"Oh?" Jade turned to Deborah and broke into a broad smile. She was a stunning, statuesque black woman, with soft, curly ringlets bouncing off her head like broken springs. Her pale green eyes looked particularly striking against her dark skin.

She and Julia had been great friends at college, making a formidable sight as they went out to pubs, clubs, and parties and were chatted up by hordes of drooling men. But while Julia always flirted outrageously, Jade had been more serious-minded. She knew what she wanted in her lifelong partner, and she didn't think she'd find him in a nightclub. All Julia wanted to do was to use her PR and marketing expertise to get a lowly job with some big organization, then gradually work her way up to marry the boss. But halfway through the required courses, Jade had announced that she was finding it all a bit unsatisfying and shallow. She'd switched her major to education and was now teaching English at a private middle school in South London.

"So where do you teach?" Jade shook Deborah's hand. The pair immediately began an animated, in-depth conversation about the state of the country's educational system, and Julia tuned out, thankful to have off-loaded her husband's difficult ex onto someone else. Smiling beatifically, she took a few steps backward, moving slowly away from them until she got to such a distance that she could safely turn and walk away without them noticing.

"Oh, God, I'm sorry!" She had trodden on someone's toe.

"Not to worry. A beautiful woman is welcome to trample me underfoot anytime."

The man standing in front of her was at least six-two, with broad shoulders that tapered down into a muscular waist and long legs. His

hair was cropped close to his head, and there was something familiar about his face, but Julia couldn't quite place him. But her memory was aided slightly by the fact that he was black.

"Jade's brother, right?"

"That's right!" He grinned. "Now how did you know *that* among
this sea of white faces?"

Julia laughed. "Just a hunch. But I'm sure I've met you before,
haven't I?"

"Ah, yes, but that was in my Bob Marley phase." He made a scis-
sors gesture with his fingers. "I've had the chop now."

"Nits are a terrible thing," she teased.

He guffawed with laughter, revealing beautifully even, white
teeth. "Actually, the dreadlocks had to go for the simple reason that
every time I went for a job interview, they thought I was either going to offer them drugs or take part in a drive-by shooting. People's
perceptions are funny, aren't they?"

"Funny?" She pursed her lips in disapproval. "Sounds narrow and
insulting to me."

"That too." He nodded. "Anyway, as soon as the hair went, so
presumably did the preconceptions, and I have been happily employed as a pharmaceutical rep for the past two years."

"So you *do* sell drugs?" She kept her face straight.

He laughed again. "You're funny, do you know that?"

"I aim to please." She smiled.

She remembered meeting Paul, as she now remembered his
name, during one of her and Jade's college nights out on the town.
But she hadn't really paid him much attention, probably because
dreadlocks had never been her thing. But now she could see his
handsome, angular face, his high cheekbones slanting down to full,
beautifully shaped lips, and those striking eyes. Not quite as pale
green as his sister's, but unusual and mesmerizing nonetheless. Yes,

thought Julia, I absolutely *would* . . . if I wasn't so happily married to lovely James, of course.

"So I hope you don't mind me being here . . ." He looked at her questioningly. "It's just that Jade's invite said plus guest, and since she's single at the moment, she suggested I accompany her."

"Not at all." She gave him one of her most winning smiles. "And what about you? Are you single too?" She inwardly chastised herself, but then again, where was the harm? Julia might consider herself happily married, but it never stopped her flirting with an attractive man.

"I certainly am." He rubbed his hands together. "But I plan to do something about that very soon. Do you have any nice friends you could introduce me to?"

Julia started to shake her head. "I'm afraid all my friends are married . . ." She swiveled her neck, looking round the room. "Oh, but hang on a minute. Come with me." She hooked her arm through his and walked the few paces back to where Jade and Deborah were still deep in conversation, probably discussing Shakespearean sonnets or logarithms, thought Julia, suppressing a yawn.

"Jade," she interrupted, "do you know Paul?" Secretly she reveled in the fact that Deborah was the only one not in on the joke.

"Vaguely." Jade shook his hand. "Although didn't you pee in my Barbie swimming pool once?"

Deborah's welcoming smile had turned into a look of confusion.

"This is my brother, Paul," Jade explained. "Paul, this is Deborah, a friend of James's and Julia's."

"In fact," Julia chipped in brightly, "she's my husband's first wife!"

If Paul was thrown by this revelation, he didn't show it. "How very grown-up." He smiled, shaking Deborah's hand.

"Fruit punch?" A smiling waitress had appeared at their sides, holding a tray of drinks.

"Sounds like a gay boxer," quipped Paul, taking one and mouthing

"Thanks." Deborah laughed, and Julia noticed she looked a lot prettier for it.

Suddenly the music stopped and there was a tapping noise on the microphone. "Ahem, listen up, everyone." It was James, standing on the small platform at one end of the room. "As you all know, we're here to celebrate the birthday of my stunningly beautiful wife, Julia . . ." He looked across the sea of heads to where she was standing at the side of the room. "Am I allowed to tell them your age, darling?" He smiled.

"Thirty-three! I'm thirty-three!" Julia shouted, picking her way through the guests to the front. She didn't mind people knowing her age, in fact, she positively encouraged it. She knew she looked a lot younger, and so it would invariably prompt the kind of "How do you keep so young?" comments that she reveled in.

"I always remember my wife's birthday," James went on drolly. "It's the day after she reminds me of it."

Polite laughter rippled through the guests as he plowed on with a blissfully short, prepared speech about Julia and how marvelous she was. Everyone clapped and raised their glasses, and Julia stood at his side, beaming throughout it all.

Susan sat on the loo seat in the women's restroom, pressing her forehead against the cold wall. She was well and truly drunk, and she knew it was time to call it a night.

Unlike Nick's company party, tonight she'd had a fantastic time, mainly because she had been surrounded by friends and hadn't felt the need to put on an act. So when Nick had done his usual thing of abandoning her to work the room, she hadn't given it a thought.

She'd spent quite a while chatting with Luca and David while they analyzed Italy's chances for the World Cup. Then for the past half an hour she had been talking to a charming man called Paul and James's ex-wife, Deborah. Susan had found Deborah to be funny, self-effacing, and incredibly nice, not at all the dull social millstone that Julia had painted her as. Deborah had also shown great interest in Susan and her life, asking lots of questions about Ellie and whether she was doing well at school. Leaving the loo and picking her way uncertainly through the straggle of remaining guests, Susan scanned the room for Nick, desperate now to go home and sleep off the effects of countless glasses of champagne.

She could see Deborah and Paul having an animated conversation where she'd left them, and Julia was slow-dancing with James to "Three Times a Lady," her head resting on his shoulder.

Susan knew Fiona and David had left already because their babysitter could only stay until midnight, but she could see Alison and Luca chatting to a man who, from behind, looked like Nick.

"Ah, there you are," she said gratefully. "I need to go. I'm a bit tipsy."

He kissed the top of her head and laughed. "Okay, I'll just go and get our coats."

"Shall I get ours too?" Luca looked inquiringly at Alison, who nodded.

"Had a good time?" she asked Susan after they'd gone.

She nodded. "Probably too much. My head is spinning, and I know that . . . ," she looked at her watch, ". . . in a few hours' time Ellie will be jumping on it."

Alison smiled, but inside she was thinking about how she'd like nothing more in the world than to have a child to wake her up in the morning, hangover or otherwise.

Earlier in the evening she had visited the ladies' room to discover that her period had officially started. She hadn't mentioned the pregnancy test to Luca, mainly because she had faintly harbored a hope that it might have been wrong. After all, she had heard stories of women having a negative test, then discovering they were pregnant.

But when the blood came, she knew it wasn't to be and casually mentioned it to Luca while, ironically, they were dancing to "Baby Love."

"Don't worry, darling," he'd said, kissing her on the cheek. "It'll happen, you'll see."

Standing next to Susan now, she blinked back a tear, her self-pity enhanced by alcohol. Luckily, Susan was too drunk to notice, and seconds later the whirlwind of distraction that was Julia had barreled straight in between them.

"Ah, my trusted late-night lieutenants," she trilled. "All those other killjoys have buggered off home." She gestured toward the virtually empty room. "I mean, it's only 2:00 A.M. What lightweights! Come on, Susan, dance with me."

Susan felt a surge of bile rise in the back of her throat. "I'm afraid," she mumbled, "that unless I am taken home right now, I will projectile vomit, not just on myself but on everyone left in this room."

"Oh, I see." Julia dropped her arm with an expression of distaste. "Not to worry. It's been a great night, hasn't it?"

Alison and Susan both nodded, enthusiastically but mutely.

"Not least," Julia muttered, looking over her shoulder, "because they are getting on so well."

Alison looked momentarily baffled. "Sorry, who?"

"Deborah and Paul." Julia jerked her head backward to where they had been standing. "He's the bloke talking to her now. With any luck, he'll ask her out and take her off our hands." She looked misty-eyed at the mere thought.

"They've disappeared," said Alison, looking over Julia's shoulder. Sure enough, Deborah and Paul were nowhere to be seen, but Jade was walking toward them.

"We're off." She smiled at Julia. "Paul's getting our coats and trying to flag down a cab, but he said to say good-bye and thanks for a great party."

"Not at all. Pleasure to see you both." Julia turned around, feigning a puzzled expression. "I can't see Deborah. Paul was chatting to her, wasn't he?"

"Yes, we're dropping her off on the way home."

"Oh, that's nice of you." Julia was desperate to know more. "They seem to get on really well, don't they?"

Jade nodded. "Yes, they've discovered a mutual passion for those various dreary foreign films Paul's always trying to drag me along to see. So it looks like he might take her to one instead and let me off the hook."

"What a good idea." Julia beamed. "It sounds like they have a lot in common." She waited until Jade had said her good-byes and left the ballroom before spinning on her impossibly thin Manolo Blahnik heels and punching the air. "Eu-fucking-reka! This is the best birthday present I could have asked for!"

the ecstasy
and the agony

Fiona stretched out, feeling the warm water envelop her stiff shoulders. She'd gone a little overkill on her favorite Crabtree & Evelyn rose foam bath, and the bubbles were up to her nose.

As the mother of an eighteen-month-old, sleeping soundly down the hall, Fiona's greatest luxury in life was to have the house to herself and enjoy a long, uninterrupted soak without David popping in and out or sitting on the loo chatting away, or Lily trying to throw her teddies into the water.

David had gone to an evening football game at Stamford Bridge with Luca, and they planned to go out for a bite afterward. So she knew the night was hers alone. Grabbing the latest chicklit, she flipped it open at the bookmark, reclined her head back onto a folded towel, and started reading.

"Ahhh!" she murmured. Life didn't get much better than this. Much as she loved family life, she also luxuriated in spending time alone without the noise of others oozing into life's precious silences. She loved David to distraction, but sometimes—particularly when yet another Jake incident was flaring up—she dreamed of the two of them having houses next door to each other, separate but linked by interconnecting doors. Lockable on her side. That way, she'd have the best of both worlds.

But she had to admit that, as life stood, she didn't have it too bad.

Wiggling her toes in the rapidly cooling water, she sat up and leaned forward to add a little extra hot. She jumped suddenly as the phone rang. Knowing that her mother would likely ring for her weekly chat, as she did every Monday night, she had placed the phone on the side of the bath. Fiona shook her hands dry and picked it up.

"Hello?"

"Hello. Is this Mrs. Bartholomew?" It was a male voice she didn't recognize.

"Yeeees." She was hesitant, fully expecting him to start selling her an insurance policy.

"I'm calling from the casualty department at St. George's Hospital in Tooting." Fiona sat bolt upright, her chest tight with fear. Something must have happened to David. "But don't worry," he continued, "your son is okay."

"My *son?*" She could hear papers being rustled.

"Yes, Jake Bartholomew. He's your son, isn't he?"

"Stepson actually. What's happened to him?"

"I don't really want to go into detail over the phone, I think it's best if you come down and I'll talk you through it. Suffice to say he's had his stomach pumped. So, while he's out of danger, he's not feeling too great."

"I see." Fiona's mind was racing. Stomach pumped. Surely that meant drugs or alcohol? She cleared her throat. "Um, I think I'd better call his mother or father. They need to know."

"Well, entirely up to you. But when we asked him who we should call, he insisted that he thought of you as his mother and became highly agitated when we suggested calling his father too."

"Okay, thanks. Leave it with me and someone will be there within the hour." She pressed the end button and lifted herself out of the bath. So much for her relaxing, uninterrupted soak. Her brain was now in overdrive, mulling over every option and wondering which was the best one to take.

Jake had known David was out at the match, so he had given the hospital this number safe in the knowledge that only Fiona would answer. Also, he had made it very clear that she was the one he'd wanted them to call. No one else.

But why? Presumably because he was utterly terrified of either of his parents finding out and Fiona had been the only other option. After all, they hadn't exactly been close these past few months.

Her dilemma was, should she go against Jake's wishes and call David to tell him what had happened?

Her initial thought was that, yes, she should. Punching in David's mobile number, she waited a few seconds, then heard it go straight to message. "Hi, it's me. I just wanted to run something by you. Speak later."

Ending the call, she pondered what she'd said. She hadn't wanted to panic him by telling him the truth, and besides, why curtail his night when she could easily deal with the situation herself and keep Jake happy at the same time? Maybe this could be a turning point for them. Maybe if she showed him that he could rely on her and come to her in a time of crisis, he wouldn't feel like he needed to cop the attitude of an adversary all the time.

But by at least trying to contact David, she felt she'd covered her backside enough to go to the hospital with impunity. She'd find out the full facts behind Jake's admittance, then make the decision afterward about what to tell his father.

ello, you." She pushed Lily's buggy alongside the bed and took a look at her stepson, who was now awake and sitting up. Luckily, her little girl was a deep sleeper.

"Hey." Jake attempted a smile, but he was ghostly pale, his usually spiky blond hair matted onto his head with sweat. He looked about twelve, a small, shivering bundle of vulnerability, and Fiona was surprised at the feelings the sight of him stirred in her. With all their recent spats and his aggressive, awkward persona, she felt protective of him just the same.

"What happened, kiddo?" She perched on the side of the bed and tousled his damp fringe away from his eyes.

He cast his eyes downward, picking at an already frayed patch of bedding. "I'm too embarrassed and ashamed to tell you," he muttered.

Fiona smiled. "Well, either you can tell me in your own words, or I can go get all the gory medical details from the nurses and doctors who dealt with you."

He swallowed hard and scratched the back of his neck, where the ties of his hospital gown were dangling down. "You haven't told Dad I'm here, have you?"

She shook her head. "Not yet. I gathered you didn't want him called, so I decided to come and hear your side of the story first, then decide what to do."

"If I tell you what happened, promise me you won't tell Dad?" He looked at her beseechingly.

"No can do, I'm afraid. No promises. As I said, I'll assess the situation when I have the full facts." She folded her arms expectantly.

Jake shuffled uncomfortably, propping himself up more comfortably in his temporary bed. She noted that his clothes were folded in a pile on the chair, and they looked relatively unscathed, so clearly he hadn't been in an accident.

"I took Ecstasy." The words came tumbling out in a rush, as if he were desperate to get rid of them, anxious that if he paused he might never say it.

Fiona recoiled in horror. "Jake, no! You didn't!"

He nodded mutely to reconfirm what he'd said.

"Why? *Where?*" She had so many questions that she didn't know where to start.

"At a friend's house. He's been trying to get me to take it for ages, but I always resisted. But this time I'd had quite a bit to drink and my defenses were down." He shrugged apologetically. "I figured that one wouldn't do any harm."

"No *harm*? It sounds like you're lucky to have survived." Unsure of how to respond to the bombshell, Fiona took a deep breath, her mind racing over what she should do or say next. "How did you end up here?"

"About half an hour after I'd taken it, I started to feel icy cold," he said, visibly shivering at the memory. "Then I started to shake really badly, and that's pretty much all I remember. Apparently, I was brought in foaming at the mouth." He had the decency to look wholly ashamed.

Fiona felt herself getting angry now. Not so much at Jake, who had just been damned stupid, but furious at whoever had persuaded him to take the drug. "Who's this friend?" she demanded.

"Why?"

"*Why?* Because they should be reported to the police for peddling drugs, that's why. God knows what might happen to the next poor kid he gives them to."

Jake looked terrified. "I can't tell you, Fiona. They'd make my life hell if I did. Seriously."

She let the matter drop for the moment, determined to return to it later. "Was it them who brought you in?"

Jake stared at the blankets miserably. "I don't really know. The hospital says someone called for an ambulance and directed them to an alleyway at the back of the cinema, where they found me lying in a pool of my own vomit."

Tears pricked at Fiona's eyes. "Oh, Jake, that's terrible. You poor thing." She felt a rush of maternal affection, picking up his hand and holding it tight. "Thank God you came through it."

"Yes." He smiled uncertainly. "Although I'm not sure I'll survive Dad's wrath when he finds out."

Fiona took a sharp intake of breath and looked at her watch. "Shit, I must call him. The game's over, so he'll be in a restaurant somewhere, but hopefully he'll have his mobile on." She started to rummage in her handbag, looking for her phone.

"Fiona?" He looked apprehensive.

"Yes?" Gut instinct told her she already knew what was coming.

"Would you consider not telling Dad about this?"

She flopped back down on the bed with a pained expression. "Jake, that's unfair. You can't ask me to do that."

He didn't respond, simply staring past her as if his life had come to an end.

"Is that why you asked them to call me?" She ducked her head to try to make eye contact with him.

He nodded. "Yes. I was hoping you might cut me some slack."

Fiona frowned and pursed her lips. "If you'd forgotten to do your homework or lost your door keys, then perhaps I could cut you some slack and not tell Dad. But having your stomach pumped after taking Ecstasy? Hardly on the same level, is it?"

His face crumpled with fear and he began to cry, slowly at first, then degenerating into huge, gulping sobs that were so loud that the woman in the next booth peered round her curtain to see what the noise was.

"Fiona, please, I'm begging you," he wailed, grabbing a tight hold on her arm. "If you do this for me, I promise faithfully that I will never cause you any problems again."

He was so distraught that she could barely make out what he was saying, but she got the gist.

"You don't have to make promises like that, sweetie . . ." She prized his hand from her arm and held it instead, stroking the back of it with her thumb. "You're a teenage boy, and they make mistakes." She let out a deep sigh. "But this is one hell of a mistake, and I'm not sure I should help you cover it up from your parents."

"Pleeeease, Fiona. It won't be forever. I promise that as soon as the time is right, I'll tell them both. I just want to come to terms with it myself first."

They sat wordlessly, just staring at each other. Fiona was pondering what he'd said, mulling over the options in her mind. Maybe this was the short, sharp shock that would steer Jake back onto the straight and narrow. She also knew that her next move might forever change her relationship with him.

"Okay, here's the deal. I'll drive you back home to your mom's, and if she asks where you've been, you can just say you've been at a friend's house." Fiona was speaking slowly, working it out as she went along. "I won't say anything to Dad tonight, but I'm going to sleep on it and see how I feel about it in the morning. But I'm not making any promises, okay?"

Jake had stopped crying and was wiping his nose on a well-used tissue. "Thanks, Fiona." He sniffed. "I just couldn't face telling them tonight. I feel terrible, really weak and shaky. I just want to go home and crash in my bed."

"Not to mention starving, eh? There's nothing left in your stomach. We'll pick up some food on the way."

He was standing now, and had moved behind the hospital-room partition to pull on his jeans, T-shirt, and sweater. After getting dressed, he turned and grabbed her awkwardly around the waist, hugging tight. "I'm sorry I've been such a pain," he mumbled.

She laughed and hugged him back. "Forget it. Let's wipe the slate clean and start from here, shall we?"

He nodded gratefully. "They said I have to wait for a doctor to look me over before I can be discharged. I'll just walk down to the nurses' office and see how long that's likely to be. Probably do me good to move around."

Fiona smiled, her eyes following him as he slowly sauntered out of the door. She knew it was psychological, but he seemed more like the Jake of old, younger, more vulnerable and eager to please.

She could only hope that it would last.

sperm warfare

"So what seems to be the problem? I'd like to hear it from you before I read your referral letter." The doctor peered across his desk at her. He was in his midfifties with thinning gray hair and bifocals.

"Um, I want to have a baby and I think I might need some help," stammered Alison. After going so long not voicing her deepest fears to anyone except Fiona, it felt odd to be telling a complete stranger.

"How long have you been trying?"

"Actively and consciously? . . . um, only since I got married about three months ago. But I haven't used contraception for the past two years, ever since I met my husband."

"I see. So you're married." He scribbled something down.

"Yes." She found it disconcerting that he wasn't looking at her. She'd been told he was one of the best fertility experts there was, which was probably why she'd had to wait two months to get an appointment, but his bedside manner left something to be desired.

"And you've been having sex regularly?"

She flushed, then laughed nervously. "Yes, we're still newlyweds."

He didn't even break a small smile. "I have to ask. You'd be surprised how many couples I get in here who are surprised they haven't conceived but then confess they only have sex about once a month . . . and probably not during the fertile period."

"No, that's not us."

"So where's your husband?" he asked brusquely. "After all, whatever the problem turns out to be, you're not going to get pregnant without him, are you?"

"No, that's true. But he's very busy at work, so I thought I could come along to the preliminary meeting without him."

He was looking at her now in a rather judgmental way. She decided she preferred it when he was making notes.

"We're all busy, Mrs. . . . ," he looked down at the file in front of him, ". . . Rossi, there are certain things in life we have to find time for, particularly if they're important to us."

"Yes, sir, I understand." Alison felt like she was sitting opposite her old headmaster, getting a scolding for being late with her homework.

He started to read the referral letter. "It says here that you have polycystic ovaries?"

She nodded. "Yes. I only know that because I had some tests when I was about eighteen . . . because my periods were so irregular."

"Hmmmm." He sucked the end of his pen. "Well, you *can* get pregnant if you have them, but as you're experiencing problems, there's a strong chance they're the cause."

"So is there a solution?" She was desperate to know.

"First things first, Mrs. Rossi," he chided. "There are lots of factors we need to determine before I can answer that question."

"Such as?" Alison was beginning to wish she'd opted for a woman specialist, someone who might understand in some small way the emotional strain she was feeling, the sheer ache of wanting to conceive and failing month after month.

"I'll need to take some blood and run a couple of other tests."

"Now?"

"Yes, now. I'll also need a sample of your husband's sperm for analysis. He can do it at home if he likes, and we'll send a messenger to collect it."

Alison suddenly felt sick. "Why does he need to do that? My husband has two children from a previous marriage . . . there's nothing wrong with his sperm."

"Things change," the doctor said distractedly, making notes again. "How old are his children?"

"Six and four."

He stopped writing and looked up at her, scrutinizing her over the top of his glasses. "I see. Second wife, are you?"

She nodded mutely, unsure what relevance it had.

"I got married for a second time too." He finally smiled. "I have two children in their twenties from my first marriage and one thirteen-year-old from my second marriage. She was IVF," he added with meaning.

"That's nice."

"Yes." He paused and looked at her searchingly. "Second marriages can be tricky though sometimes, can't they?"

She nodded and smiled gratefully. "Yes. Yes, they can."

Suddenly, she felt they had an understanding. Maybe this wouldn't be so bad after all.

God, he sounds like a nightmare." Fiona stirred her cappuccino and scooped a spoonful of froth into her mouth. "It makes you wonder why someone *that* brusque is inexplicably drawn toward a career that requires him to deal with human beings on a day-to-day basis."

Alison smiled. "Yes, particularly ones who are going through such a vulnerable and sensitive time." She sighed. "But to be honest, if he helps me to get pregnant, I couldn't care less about his personality." She stared wistfully out of the window as a young mother walked past the café with her toddler.

"I suppose you're right." But Fiona still looked dubious.

"We bonded a bit at the end because he's got a second wife too, and she had to have IVF."

"So do you reckon you'll have to have IVF too?" Fiona looked concerned.

Alison shrugged. "Not sure yet. He's taken some of my blood to test my hormone levels, and I also had some sort of X-ray to check out my uterus and fallopian tubes. We'll go over the results at my next visit."

She paused and took a sip of her mint tea, wincing slightly as the hot water burned the tip of her tongue. "That's the easy part. The hard part will be convincing Luca to give a sperm sample."

Fiona giggled. "Why, is he a bit squeamish about stuff like that?"

"No, it's not that." She looked uncomfortable, almost embarrassed. "He's just got a thing about it."

"A *thing*? What do you mean, a thing?"

Alison cleared her throat. "He . . . um . . . seems to think that babies should be conceived naturally, without any interference from doctors." She kept her voice low. "That's why he didn't go with me, because I didn't tell him I was going."

"I see." Fiona looked at a loss for words. "So you've had a proper conversation about it then?"

"Not as such, no. I had sensed for a while that he had a very macho view about these things, so I tested the water by bringing it up in a general sense after reading a newspaper article at the breakfast table."

"And?"

"And he was *very* critical about intervention, quite scathing actually. He thinks children are a gift and that if they don't happen naturally, then it's for a reason." She looked disconsolate.

"Yes, a reason like endometriosis or a low sperm count," retorted Fiona. "And both can be got round with a little bit of help."

"I know, I know. It's not likely to be low sperm count, though, is it? Paolo and Giorgio are testament to that." Alison added another spoonful of sugar to her tea, seeking an energy kick. "I suspect the problem will turn out to be all mine," she added miserably.

"Anyway," said Fiona brightly, "when he said he was against intervention, he thought you were talking about other people. When he knows that it's *you* who might need it, I'm sure he'll change his mind. Love does strange things to people's long-held beliefs, you know."

Alison's mood lifted slightly. "Do you think so?" She sighed wistfully. "I hope you're right, but I'll know soon enough. I'm going to try to broach it this weekend."

"Attagirl!" Fiona clinked her cup against Alison's. "After all, it has to be done. You can't have his child without his assistance."

"True." Alison smiled indulgently at a woman at the next table struggling to control her overactive toddler. Turning back to Fiona, she mused, "You know, it baffles me. In so many ways, I'm a confident person. But when it comes to what's probably the most important thing in my life, I'm too scared to even confront my husband and tell him how I feel."

"Courage abandons us all at some point in our lives."

"Even Julia?" Alison smiled. "I can't see *her* ever taking shit from anyone. I like her a lot, but she also terrifies me a little. She's so . . . in your face."

Fiona laughed. "She's all bark and no bite. Believe me, she's as vulnerable as the rest of us inside, she's just developed a thick-skinned veneer to disguise it."

"Maybe I should do the same." Alison paused for a moment, considering it. Then she snapped to attention. "But anyway, enough about me. I've been so wrapped up in my own worries that I haven't even asked what you've been up to."

Fiona made a pooh-poohing face. "Don't worry about it. You *should* be focused on yourself when trying to get pregnant."

"So have you got any gossip? I need cheering up."

Fiona made a face. "Yes, I have, but only of the depressing variety, I'm afraid. I had quite the drama last night and I'm dying to tell someone."

"Really? Go on." Alison leaned forward expectantly.

Fiona took a deep breath for dramatic effect. "Jake took an Ecstasy and ended up in hospital having his stomach pumped."

"Oh, my God!" Alison clamped a hand over her mouth in shock. "Is he okay?"

"Yes, he's mercifully unscathed, apart from a wounded dignity perhaps. But the interesting thing is that in spite of all our troubled history, he got them to call me."

"Presumably because he was scared shitless about his parents finding out?"

"Oh, absolutely. But it was nevertheless an ideal opportunity for he and I to get back on track."

"And did you?"

"I'll say. He had to grovel because he was desperate for me not to tell David what had happened."

Alison raised her eyebrows. "But you've told him now, right?"

Fiona shook her head. "No. I told Jake that I'd sleep on it, but when I woke up this morning I called him and said that I'd decided to say nothing on the understanding that he'd never take drugs again and that *he'd* tell his dad when he felt the time was right."

Alison frowned and made a sucking noise. "Are you sure that's wise?"

"I don't know." Fiona sighed. "But I thought about it long and hard and decided this was the ideal opportunity for Jake to take responsibility for his own actions, his first rung on the ladder to adulthood. And I've told him that if he takes one step out of line again, I'll tell David everything."

"Well, I'm sure you know what you're doing," Alison told her. "But it's a tough call to keep it a secret from his parents. I don't envy your position."

"One day you too might find yourself in the same straits." Fiona smiled ruefully. "After all, Paolo and Giorgio are still young. In a few years, you could well have double the trouble I've had."

"Great." Alison rolled her eyes. "You're supposed to be cheering me up, not making me feel even worse."

"Sorry." Fiona shrugged and smiled. "But that's the reality of life as a second wife if children are involved. The Partridge Family it ain't."

"Not much chance of that with us anyway. The way things stand, I don't see Sofia *ever* letting the boys be part of my and Luca's life. My well-intentioned visit to her house has ended up making matters worse."

"Uh-oh. In what way?"

"I asked Luca not to say anything to her about slapping me, but he did. Apparently, he really lit into her . . . and true to form, she retaliated by saying he couldn't see the children that weekend. They're her greatest weapon for fighting back."

"God, she makes Belinda sound like Mary Poppins. Is everything okay now?"

Alison shrugged. "Not really. Luca was allowed to go see the boys a couple of nights ago, but she made it clear in no uncertain terms that if they even clapped eyes on me, she would make it very difficult for him to see them again."

Silence descended for a few seconds as Fiona struggled to find something positive to say about the Sofia situation.

"Never mind," she finally said. "You'll have a baby of your own soon, and then she can piss off."

Alison gestured at their waitress for the bill. "That would definitely help," she agreed. "But it wouldn't change much for Luca. He adores those boys, so he'd never give up on them simply because he'd started another family. He's far too principled for that."

"Principles, eh?" said Fiona ruefully.

"I know. Luca's strong moral standards and beliefs were one of the reasons I fell in love with him. Now they're threatening to rob me of what I want most—a baby."

Fiona's expression clouded. "Just suppose you *do* need IVF and he flatly refuses . . . what would you give up, your desire to have a baby, or Luca?"

Alison let out a long sigh. "I have absolutely no idea, but hopefully it won't come to that."

strangers in the night

The Great Room of London's Grosvenor House Hotel was packed with well-heeled socialites, sitting rouged cheek by puffy jowl at two hundred immaculately laid out tables.

A magnificent flower arrangement adorned the center of each, as did wine buckets overflowing with Kristal champagne and Chablis Premier Cru. Alongside each place card, painstakingly written by a calligrapher, rested a menu boasting a pâté de foie gras starter followed by beef Wellington and individual chocolate soufflés served with vanilla bean sauce.

This was the kind of charity work Julia loved best. A glam frock, great food, and digging deep into James's wallet for whatever good cause they were supporting that night. The irony didn't escape her that so much of the money spent on the finest wines and stunning flowers would be better spent on the charity itself. But charity events in London were plentiful, and you had to be top-notch to attract the kind of moneyed guests who would fork over hundreds of thousands of pounds in the auction.

On the way to her table, positioned centrally in the vast room, she had air-kissed dozens of people, smiled prettily at various businessmen as they pumped James's arm in a handshake, and indulged in small talk with their wives. Yes, the charity was a wonderful cause. Yes, the flowers were beautiful. Yes, the menu was a triumph. Blah blah blah.

"Christ, I need a drink," she muttered in James's ear after enduring a monologue from one woman about what a child prodigy her four-month-old son was. "The kid probably just shits and dribbles like all other babies, yet you'd think he was quoting Chaucer verbatim."

Reaching table 35, she gratefully leaned toward the ice bucket and poured herself a glass of champagne, passing James his preferred red wine.

"Aaaah, that's better!" She closed her eyes in ecstasy as the icy cold fizz hit the back of her throat.

"Steady on there. Leave some for the rest of us."

Opening her eyes, Julia found Jade standing in front of her, smiling broadly. She looked fantastic in a clinging white dress that offset her dark skin.

"Hello! What a pleasant surprise." Julia hugged her warmly. "I don't usually see you at these things."

"I know. I'm here with my uncle and his wife. Over there somewhere." Jade looked back over her shoulder and pointed toward the back of the room.

Julia followed her gaze. "Oh, yes, I see him. The bald bloke?"

"He's not bald. He says he just has a wide part." She grinned. "Great party the other night, by the way."

"Did you enjoy it?" Julia was pleased and it showed. "Everyone seems to have had a good time."

"Yes, even my brother commented on how great it was, and he's not normally the partying type. He only came because I didn't want to go on my own."

"Ah, yes, Paul." Julia was thrilled that Jade had brought up the subject of her brother, saving her the trouble of finding a way to do so without looking obvious. "He seems like a very nice guy."

Jade nodded, gulping down a mouthful of champagne so she could speak. "He is. He had his moments of being monstrous to me when we were younger, but now we get on brilliantly."

"And he also seemed to be getting on brilliantly with Deborah." Julia inwardly congratulated herself on such a seamless introduction to what she *really* wanted to talk about.

"Yes, they really hit it off." Jade's eyes widened. "By the way, I can't believe you invited your husband's ex-wife to your party—how very modern! I'm not sure I'd be grown-up enough to do that."

Under normal circumstances, Julia would have owned up to the real reason for her seeming magnanimity, how, after two years of fruitlessly trying to cast the woman adrift, she had finally changed tack and decided that, rather than have Deborah on the outside pissing in, she'd have her inside pissing out. But something stopped her. Probably the strong chance that Jade might mention it to Paul, who might then mention it to Deborah.

"Oh, you know, live and let live and all that," she drawled casually. "Besides, she's a lovely person." She was really amazed by her own acting skills.

"Yes, she seemed nice the short time I spoke to her."

People were starting to sit down for dinner, and Jade looked toward her table. Julia knew she had just a few seconds left to ask the question that was playing on her mind, so she threw caution to the wind.

"So did Paul say anything else about Deborah?" She winked jauntily, trying to make light of her question with the deadly serious aim. "You know, like how it might be the start of a beautiful relationship?"

Jade laughed uncertainly, clearly unsure whether Julia was joking or not. "I don't know about that, but I do know he rang her a couple of days ago and they've arranged to go to the movies tomorrow night."

"The movies!" said Julia, with an enthusiasm that suggested he was taking her to the Taj Mahal via private jet. "How lovely!"

Jade waved at someone over at her table. "Anyway, I'd better go and join my hosts. Nice to see you. We'll talk soon." She air-kissed Julia and walked away.

"Bye!" Julia called after her. "Hoo-fucking-rah," she muttered when Jade was out of earshot, topping up her champagne. "I'll drink to that."

The line outside the bathrooms snaked out of the door and along the far wall of the room. As was the norm at a charity function, everyone had drunk copiously during dinner, then sat through various speeches and a lengthy auction and raffle draw before descending en masse upon the toilets with their eyes and legs crossed.

"Fuck!" cursed Julia when she saw the throng. Her figure-hugging dress wasn't made to accommodate a full bladder.

Making her way past the line to the bathroom entrance, she beamed at the woman filling the door frame with her generous hips swathed in cerise taffeta. "Hi there, could I squeeze through? I just want to use the mirrors to check my makeup."

The woman looked dubious but stepped aside to let her pass. Once inside, Julia stood in front of the sink, pretending to reapply the lipstick she had already applied back at her table and tweaking her hair. As soon as she heard the telltale click of the door to a stall being unlocked, she swiveled round and was in there before the next woman in line had even taken a step.

Outside, she could hear the sounds of disapproval rippling through the line, but she didn't care. The sheer relief of an empty bladder made it all worth it.

"Sorry! Sorry!" she burbled as she made the walk of shame along the line of pursed lips. "I have a bladder condition," she felt compelled to add after clocking the murderous look from one stern matronly type.

Back in the anonymity and therefore safety of the main room, she noted that everyone had now broken away from their tables to mingle and indulge in yet more small talk. But, still euphoric from the possibility that Deborah might finally be taken off their hands, Julia had other plans. She wanted to celebrate.

Making her way back to the center, she scanned the crowd for James. He was leaning against one of the pillars toward the back of the room, talking to a middle-aged woman who looked like she could run in the 2:30 p.m. at Belmont.

"Hello, darling," Julia purred, furtively pinching James's bottom and smiling at Smarty Jones in a dress. "I'm just going to talk to a couple of people. Could you meet me upstairs in the main hotel bar in about ten minutes?"

She didn't wait for an answer, gliding off in the direction of the grand staircase, which led to the lobby. Flicking open her mobile phone, she canceled their cab and headed for reception to book a room.

James was sitting alone at the bar when she arrived, a Bacardi and Diet Coke in front of him, his bow tie unraveled and hanging loose around his neck.

The room was half full, with a few couples scattered here and there and a large group of men sitting near the door. They were laughing loudly about something, but when Julia walked in they fell into a reverential hush, their eyes lasciviously following her every move in the cream satin Elie Saab dress that clung to every curve of her body. She sashayed toward James, who turned and was about to speak, but she surreptitiously raised a finger to her mouth, instructing him to be quiet.

"Is this seat taken?" she asked him, pointing at the bar stool.

"No, please be my guest," he replied loudly, knowing the men nearby were hanging on their every word.

It was a game he and Julia had played several times in the early, heady days of their relationship, and he fell back into it with ease.

"Can I get you a drink?"

"I'll have a glass of champagne, please." She settled herself onto the stool, wiggling her bottom provocatively for the benefit of the drooling pack behind her. The barman placed a glass in front of her and poured the champagne, his face impassive. But Julia knew he was listening to every word, and it gave her a sexual kick.

"Are you in town long?" she asked James, fixing him with a smoldering stare over the rim of her glass.

"Just a couple of days."

"What line of business are you in?"

"Film. I make films." One of the thrills of the game was that they could be whatever they wanted.

"Well, whaddayaknow?" She smiled, edging her stool slightly closer, a maneuver clearly noticed by everyone in the room. "I'm an actress and a damned fine one at that. What kind of movies do you make?"

"What kind of movies do you want to make?" He grinned, raising his glass in her direction.

Julia studied him, pretending she was considering his question. "Good ones," she replied.

"Oh, I'm good, I'm very, very good."

The barman, Julia noted, looked like he was going to explode with the effort of trying to appear oblivious to their conversation.

"Anything I might have seen?"

James pursed his lips. "*The Bums of Navarone, A-cock and Lips Now, Kelly's Dildos* . . ."

"Oh, I see . . . *that* sort of film." Julia managed to keep a straight face but could see the barman was struggling. "Do you only do war porn?"

"I did, but I'm branching out a bit now. I'm here in London setting up the finance for my next movie, an epic called *Titandick*."

"Sounds fascinating."

"We haven't cast the Kate Winslet part yet. Maybe you'd like to audition?"

Julia leaned forward and placed a hand on his knee. "I'd love to. What do I have to do?" She started to slowly rub his leg.

James cleared his throat. "Well, without going into too much detail, obviously there's a going-down theme . . ."

"Ah," Julia interjected, "my specialty." She placed her hand on his penis, rock-hard through the thin material of his suit.

The group of men had started chatting again, but as soon as Julia's hand reached James's groin, she noticed one of them blatantly point in her direction, and they all stopped talking to take in the view. Judging by the expressions on their faces, they considered James to be the luckiest man in the world.

Taking his hand, Julia guided it onto her knee, exposed through the high slit in her dress. Their legs were intertwined now, his fingers edging their way up her inner thigh, a journey watched intently by several others in the bar.

Julia started to nuzzle his ear. "I've canceled our cab and booked a room," she whispered, coming out of character for just a second.

Pressing her cheek against his, she flicked her tongue in and out of his ear and moved slowly round to his mouth. As they started to kiss passionately, one of the men let out a whoop to cheer them on.

Breaking away, Julia adjusted her dress. "Do you fancy a nightcap in my room?"

James nodded and motioned to the waiter to get the bill. Placing his hand on her waist, he helped her get down from the stool. "We can talk some more about that audition," he said, brandishing a credit card.

"Absolutely. In fact, why don't we *make* it the audition?" She smiled, guiding one of his fingers to her mouth and sucking slowly. The barman was now openly staring at her, rooted to the spot with the paid bill in his hand.

"Can't wait." James smiled. "Shall we go?"

He escorted her out of the bar as the group of men burst into spontaneous applause behind them.

some people don't hear you until you scream

"You're *what*? Are you sure it's safe?" Fiona was toweling the back of her neck after a strenuous yoga session in which she'd contorted herself like a novelty balloon at a children's party.

"Safe as houses," said Susan, stepping out of her sweatpants and grabbing her jeans out of the locker. "I'm not *that* stupid."

Fiona raised her eyebrows. "Hmmm. But cycling in *Vietnam*? Isn't that bandit country?"

Susan laughed. "The war ended more than three decades ago, dear. It's a beautiful, peaceful country now with white sandy beaches and glorious weather."

"Is it?" Fiona still looked doubtful. "But even so, you won't actually be enjoying the nice bits of it, you'll be cycling up and down steep inclines with an extremely sore arse. You're mad."

"No, I'm not mad, I'm *charitable*. It's all for a good cause. You should try it sometime."

"Whoa!" Fiona raised a hand up. "You can't say I don't do my bit for charity."

"Fiona!" Susan made an exasperated face. "You get invited to posh parties by Julia, wear nice dresses, and stuff your face with yummy food at various venues around London. Hardly a charity bike ride, is it?"

Combing her hair back and tying it into an unkempt ponytail, Fiona poked out her tongue. "A check is a check. The charity doesn't care if it's come from me and Julia having a great time or from you chafing your buttocks on some wafer-thin saddle."

"That's probably true." Susan giggled. "Have you got time for a coffee?"

Fiona nodded, and they wandered upstairs to the health club's small café bar to order two nonfat lattes.

"Of course, I'm not doing it *solely* because I want to raise money for charity," said Susan as they sat down at a table overlooking a squash court. She handed over a leaflet about the bike ride.

"Oh?" Fiona studied it incredulously.

"No, I think it'll be good for me."

"In what way?" Fiona took a sip of her coffee and winced as it burned her lip. "I mean, it's not like you've even *done* much cycling before."

Susan licked at the sweet froth gathered around the rim of her cup. "I know. It's probably an early midlife crisis thing, but I also think it will do some good for me to be away from Nick for a little while."

"What?" Fiona looked shocked. "You didn't tell me you'd been having problems."

"We're not, as such. I just feel a bit . . . well, taken for granted, I suppose."

"In what way?"

Susan felt the beginnings of tears pricking at the corners of her eyes. She hadn't expected to cry, she just couldn't help herself now that she was actually voicing her concerns to someone else.

"I just feel really small at the moment." She sniffed. "I don't know why, I just do."

Fiona leaned across the table and grabbed her hand tightly. "Darling, you're not small. You're the biggest person I know, especially in heart . . ."

"And bottom . . ." Susan smiled, dabbing her nose with a paper napkin.

"And humor. You see? You can even find something to laugh about when you're upset."

Susan had composed herself now. "Yes, I can laugh *here*, sitting with you. But at home I sometimes feel like I blend into the wallpaper."

Fiona made a scoffing noise. "Nonsense. You mean everything to Ellie."

"Yes, I know that. But what about Nick? What do I mean to him?" Susan shrugged. "I know he loves me in his own way, but sometimes I wonder if he even knows I'm a real person." She stared over the balcony, looking down at the squash players but not really seeing them. "I got together with Nick *in spite* of his difficult situation because I loved him and thought we could overcome anything. But lately I've been wondering whether he's only with me for . . . ," she stopped, uncomfortable with what she was about to say, ". . . for *convenience*."

Fiona put her cup down with such force that the latte spilled over the sides. "Get that out of your mind right now, lady," she said sternly. "That's utter nonsense and you know it."

"Sweet of you to say so." Susan smiled sadly. "But I'd be an idiot not to really ask myself this question given our situation. I can't quite put my finger on it, but there seems to be something missing between us. I just don't *feel* loved by Nick, if that makes any sense."

"How's your sex life?"

Susan balked slightly at Fiona's directness. "Um, well, we do have one, if that's what you mean."

"Yes, but is it exciting?"

"If you mean does he jump off the bed in a superhero outfit, then, no, but it's not totally dull either. My main problem is that deep down, there's a part of me that just can't ever fully believe that I'm what he really wants. Maybe it's the Caitlin thing, or maybe it's just the way our romantic relationship started, with me as Ellie's care-taker first and Nick's romantic partner second." She let out a sigh. "Besides, it's difficult to have a spontaneous sex life when you have children; they're invariably in your bed or wandering into the room."

Fiona nodded. "I know. That's why we've put a lock on our door. I can't relax otherwise!"

"Do you think you'll have any more?" Susan looked wistful.

"What, sex or children?"

"Ha ha."

Fiona pursed her lips. "Probably. Although David is keener than I am at the moment."

"Great, isn't it? David wants a baby and you're not sure, I want a baby and Nick doesn't."

"Ah. You didn't tell me *that*." Fiona's eyes widened. "That probably explains why you're feeling a bit vulnerable at the moment."

Susan nodded and told her the full extent of the late-night conversation with Nick. "I just felt like he trampled over what I wanted, as if I didn't matter," she explained miserably. "So I figured that ten days away doing something completely different from my ordinary, dull life might do me a world of good."

"And make Nick appreciate you more in your absence?"

"Precisely!"

Fiona pondered everything Susan had said for a few moments. "I think it's a fabulous idea. Have you told him yet?"

Susan grimaced. "Yes. It went over like a lead balloon. He did this real guilt trip with me about how Ellie had already lost one mother and now I was abandoning her too."

"It's only ten days," Fiona reassured her. "Hardly a lifetime. Besides, what he *really* means is that he doesn't know how *he'll* cope without you. You see? He does love you."

"But not in the way I want him to," Susan reiterated firmly. "I want to be loved outside the parameters of being Ellie's surrogate mummy." She paused. "I just feel we've become a bit like brother and sister, if you know what I mean?"

"I do." Fiona nodded. "That's what Julia reckons happened between James and Deborah. Not that Nick is going to leave *you*," she backtracked hastily.

"Oh, I don't worry about that anyway," Susan said. "There's much more chance of me leaving him."

"You're not thinking about it, are you?" Fiona was shocked.

"Not seriously, no, but obviously the thought has crossed my mind, just hypothetically, in an 'I wonder what would happen if . . .' kind of way. And that's what scares me most, truth be told. I don't want to leave, but if I *did*—even if I knew that's what was best for me—I don't know how I ever could."

"Sorry, I'm not with you . . ."

"I've taken on so much in becoming Ellie's shiny new mummy, dug myself in so deep with this child who isn't even mine . . . how could I ever leave? It could destroy her. It's not like a normal situation where the woman usually takes the children with her. Ellie's not mine, she'd stay with Nick. I wouldn't have any sort of legal rights. So it would mean I was leaving *her* too, and I couldn't do that."

"Honey, it sounds like you've thought about this really deeply." Fiona looked perplexed.

"No, no, it's not like that. Seriously," Susan replied in earnest. "But I figured that if *I* know that I would never leave for Ellie's sake, then Nick probably knows it too. And that's why, as I see it, he has a tendency to take me for granted."

Fiona closed one eye and pointed her finger at her. "Gotcha."

"So the bike ride has two purposes really," Susan continued. "First, it will give me some time to myself, some space to get my head around a few things and what I really want out of my life. What I can sacrifice and what I can't. And second, it will hopefully make Nick appreciate me a bit more."

"In which case . . . ," Fiona raised her mug in the air as a toast, ". . . it all makes perfect sense, and I support you wholeheartedly. Although I think I would personally prefer to make the same point while spending two weeks at a spa in the Caribbean. But if a bike ride's what you want to do . . ."

"Thanks." Susan smiled gratefully.

"So much so that I will sponsor you generously in your quest to raise money for . . . ," she frowned, ". . . what *are* you raising money for? A pied-à-terre vacation home in Tuscany?"

"No, it is not!" Susan laughed. "It's for Breakthrough, the breast cancer charity."

"Good for you. When she gets older, Ellie will be really proud of you for doing it."

"Do you think so? Trouble is, she's only six right now, and she's probably not going to understand why I'm disappearing for ten days."

"Then it's up to her father to make sure she's kept busy and doesn't suffer," said Fiona swiftly. She looked at Susan curiously. "Don't hate me for asking this, but do you think you feel the same way about Ellie as you would your own child?"

The question took Susan by surprise. "Um . . . yes, I *think* so. Without actually having a child of my own, it's difficult to say, but I can say that I love Ellie beyond anything I ever could have imagined. I can honestly say I would give up my own life to save hers."

"Wow." Fiona raised her eyebrows. "That certainly says it all. I'd like to *think* that I would do that for Jake, but if push came to shove, I'm not sure whether I would. I'd do it for Lily in a heartbeat, though."

Susan looked at her watch. "That also reminds me that I should get going if I want to be home to give her a kiss before bedtime." She scooted back her chair and stood up.

"Thanks so much for the coffee, and most of all, thanks for backing me on this." She held the leaflet in the air. "It means a lot."

"No problem, sweetie. I just hope that getting a sore arse proves worthwhile and that you cure that other pain in the butt at home." Fiona grinned.

Susan smiled back. "Oh, he's not a pain in the butt." She sighed. "He's just a little misguided at times. I do love him, you know."

"I know you do. But I think they all need a reminder from time to time of how much they'd miss us if we weren't around." Fiona idly placed a finger on her chin. "In fact, I might even go away myself."

Susan's face lit up. "Come with me!" she exclaimed.

"Hmmm, let's see now. Er . . . *no!*" Fiona laughed and looked at her as though she'd completely lost her marbles. "If you were going to the spa, then I'd be right there alongside you. But Vietnam on a tandem? Let's just say there's more chance of Carson Kressley finding the right woman."

"Oh well." Susan looked mildly disappointed. "Just a thought. I'd better head off if I want to make it back before Ellie goes to sleep. Speak soon." She blew Fiona a kiss across the table and hurried out of the café.

Susan headed down the stairs to the ground floor, oblivious to those she passed along the way. Her mind was on other things, mainly the conversation she'd just had and whether or not her planned trip was going to make any difference to life at home. She hoped so. As she rummaged in her bag, her fingers encircled a lipstick, a pack of gum, and then the unpaid parking ticket she'd meant to mail in last week. Everything but her car keys.

"Damn it!" she cursed, knowing she was already pushing it to get home in time. Even though she was home every other night of the week, Susan felt guilty if she didn't make it back for a good-night kiss on yoga night too. She reached the parking lot and stood blinking into the darkness while fumbling in the pockets of her jacket, still trying to locate the elusive keys.

"Aha!" She finally pulled them from the depths of her left pocket and dangled them in the air triumphantly. Now all I have to do, she thought, is find the bloody car.

Then she remembered. "Duh!"

She headed toward the entrance to the lot. Having arrived late for the yoga session, she had found the parking lot already filled with the Volvos and SUVs of those infinitely more organized than her. So she'd had to park in a nearby side street. Mindful of an expectant Ellie, she broke into a jog, passing row after row of cars with her purse jostling against her side as she reached the exit. I know, she thought, I'll call Nick and tell him to have her wait up a few extra minutes. Now where's that mobile phone?

The traffic was heavy on the road she had to cross, so she stopped at the edge of the curb and waited for the light to turn red. Stooping down, she placed her bag on the sidewalk and rummaged again, this time seeking her sleek and tiny Motorola phone.

Head down, engrossed in her task, she didn't see the boy on the badly lit bicycle coming along the road . . . didn't see the rider wobble precariously and fall off . . . and didn't see the car behind swerve to avoid him.

The only warning she got was the shriek of tires as the car spun out of control and, two seconds after she looked up, hit her with full force.

wake-up call

Fiona came out of the bathroom stall smiling to herself. A charity bike ride indeed. Susan was so full of surprises.

Running her hands under the cold tap, she checked her reflection. She wasn't wearing a scrap of makeup, and her face was still slightly red from the exertion of yoga. Still, it beat jogging. She'd tried it once, and by the time she found out she didn't like it, it was a long walk home.

Drying her hands, Fiona studied the "laughter" lines on either side of her eyes. I must stop finding everything so damned funny, she thought ruefully. To make matters worse, the overhead lighting accentuated the imperfections.

But she wasn't unduly bothered. She knew she scrubbed up well when she wanted to, and her relationship with David was secure enough that, unlike Julia, she didn't feel the need to rush home and get made up before her husband clapped eyes on her. Julia always said it wasn't insecurity, it was self-respect, something she did to make herself feel better. But Fiona wasn't so sure.

Walking out into the parking lot, she shivered slightly and zipped her hooded sweatshirt. It was a summer's evening, but it was a slightly chilly one, and it was starting to get dark. She'd been fortunate enough to drive in just as another car was leaving, so her little Ford Fiesta was squeezed into a prime space right near the health-club door. She smiled affectionately as she approached it. Julia may laugh, she thought, but I love my little "Fifi."

Just as she was climbing in, she heard the screech of tires in the distance, followed by a sickening thud and, a few seconds later, the sound of car horns as, presumably, other drivers became caught up in the ensuing chaos.

Everyone's in such a rush these days, she thought to herself. And now it sounds like some poor sod has had his car bashed in by some impatient fool. Edging her way out of the space, she drove slowly toward the exit, where several other cars were in front of her, attempting to pull out into the road. But the traffic was gridlocked.

People had started getting out of their cars, craning their necks to see what was causing the disruption. One man had walked to the top of the road and was now returning to report his findings to the others stuck in the jam.

Fiona sat in her car for a couple of minutes, checking her mobile phone for messages, then making a quick call home to say she was stuck in traffic. David said he would try to keep Lily up until she returned.

Eventually, she climbed out of her car and wandered up to the one in front, tapping on the window. It was a woman she recognized from yoga.

"Hi there. Any idea what all this is about?" Fiona jerked her head toward the traffic.

"Apparently, there's been an accident. A car came off the road and hit some woman." She stopped talking a moment and pointed at a man farther up who was standing by the exit looking off down the road. "That guy reckons she came out of here because she's wearing workout clothes."

"Really?" Fiona felt slightly nauseous. Had Susan changed out of her workout clothes? She couldn't remember. She had sat opposite her for a good twenty minutes and she couldn't bloody remember what she was wearing.

She walked out of the parking lot and headed toward the road junction, where a small crowd had now gathered. She walked slowly at first, speeding up as the adrenaline of fear started to kick in.

A car had clearly mounted the pavement, its front end smashed in, one side sitting higher than the other. Judging by the proximity of the assembled gawkers, she assumed someone was lying in front of the car.

Then she saw it. Susan's distinctive brown Zara handbag lying abandoned on the pavement. Distinctive because Fiona had bought it for her the previous Christmas. "Oh, my God!" she blurted out, picking it up and elbowing her way through the onlookers.

Susan was lying unconscious, a small, dark pool of blood forming under the back of her head, her arms splayed out to her sides. Her right leg was trapped under the wheel, her shin an unrecognizable mess of flesh and bone.

Fiona turned her head to one side and threw up, splashing her legs and sneakers. "Is she dead?" she choked. "She's my friend," she added by way of explanation to the man kneeling at Susan's side.

His face was etched with concern. "I don't think so, but she's in critical condition. What's her name?"

"Susan." Shaking, Fiona stooped down next to him.

Instinctively, he put an arm out toward her. "Don't move her head. Her neck might be broken."

"Oh, Christ!" Fiona let out a sob. Gently, she brushed Susan's hair away from her face. Her eyes were closed and she looked peaceful. "Are you a doctor?"

He shook his head. "No, I'm a physical therapist. I've just finished work at the health club. Susan? Susan?" he said firmly, but there was no response.

"Is she going to die?" Fiona felt she was going to vomit again.

"I don't know, but an ambulance is on the way."

Fiona suddenly became aware of someone sobbing nearby and looked up. A young man, probably in his twenties, was being comforted by another passerby.

"That's the driver," the physical therapist said, following her gaze. "Poor bastard. He swerved to avoid a lad on a bike and ended up hitting your friend instead. He's in a state of shock."

Fiona lowered her face to Susan's ear. "Susan? It's me, Fiona. Can you hear me?" But again, nothing.

"If you can hear me, stay strong. Please don't die." She was thinking about Ellie now, the little girl who had already endured the death of one "mummy." To lose another would be unthinkable.

The therapist looked deathly white, his features pinched. "She's losing a lot of blood."

"Oh, God, hurry." Fiona clamped her hand to her mouth and stood up. She could hear a siren in the distance, coming closer by the second.

Putting Susan's handbag back down on the pavement for a moment, she rummaged through her own and pulled out her mobile phone. Flipping it open, she took a long, deep breath, knowing she was about to make the most difficult phone call of her life. "Hello, Nick? It's Fiona Bartholomew, from Susan's yoga class." She paused. "Yes, it was a great session, thanks. Listen, don't panic . . . but Susan's been in an accident. She's still alive, but she's in a bad way, and you need to get here as soon as possible."

• • •

A weak ray of sunshine filtered through a crack in the curtains and fell across the bed, illuminating Susan's face.

Nick stared down at it, his eyes brimming with tears. "Do you think she's going to be all right?" It was the third time he'd asked the question in as many minutes. "I don't think I can go through all this again."

He didn't specify what "this" meant, but Fiona knew he was referring to Caitlin's death. She walked round the bed and put a comforting arm around his shoulders. She didn't know him very well, but it seemed the natural thing to do. "I'm sure she'll be fine," she answered.

She knew that was what he wanted to hear, but the truth was that Fiona was just as panic-stricken as he was about Susan's chances of survival. Having traveled with her in the ambulance, she'd heard the urgency in the voices of the emergency personnel, *seen* the concern in their eyes.

She hadn't understood most of the medical jargon being fired back and forth across Susan's motionless body, but "acute" and "critical" had stuck in her mind. Now here she was, after a three-hour operation, lying comatose and wired up to various machines and IVs. Her leg had been reset, but one of the nurses had warned Fiona and Nick that there was still a chance she'd walk with a pronounced limp.

That was bad enough, she thought, but there were other worries. They had been told that, because of the loss of blood, Susan's body was in shock. She had also suffered a fractured skull, and it would be difficult to tell if there'd been any brain damage until she came to.

"Was she happy?"

"Sorry?" Fiona understood exactly what Nick was asking but feigned puzzlement to buy herself some time to think about what she could, or should, say. She knew how important it was to choose her words carefully while Susan's life still hung in the balance.

"Was she happy when you spent time with her? With me? With us? With her life?" He looked anguished. "If she dies, I need to know she was happy."

She smiled warmly, tears forming in her eyes. "She was very happy. She loves you and Ellie desperately, and for that reason, I know she'll pull through."

"God, I hope you're right." He laid his forehead on the sheet next to Susan's immobile arm. "I'll never forgive myself if she doesn't."

Fiona moved away from him and sat in the chair on the other side of the bed. "Nick, it wasn't your fault. It was a terrible accident, that's all. There was nothing you or I or anyone else could have done about it."

He lifted his head and stared miserably at the tube running from Susan's nose, supplying her with oxygen. There was also one in the back of her hand and another running into her chest, just below her left shoulder. "I know. But that's not what I feel guilty about."

She said nothing, assuming he would continue in his own good time. He walked over to the window and opened the curtains, the soft light giving the room an ethereal glow. Standing with his back to her, he stared out over the road beyond from his sixth-floor vantage point.

"It's funny, isn't it?" he murmured. "I always used to hate that cliché 'you don't know what you've got until it's gone,' but it's true. So true."

He turned and walked back to the bed, staring down at Susan.

"She's not gone," said Fiona softly. "She's just temporarily way-laid." She crossed her fingers behind her back, praying it was true.

Nick sighed. "You know what I mean, though. Ever since you first called me, I've been thinking, over and over again, about what life would be like without Susan . . ." His voice wavered and he trailed off, clearly struggling to control his emotions. "And the answer? Fucking unbearable. And not because of everything she's done to support me and Ellie since Caitlin died, but because she's my best friend. I'd miss everything about her and who she is as a person."

"We all would. She's an amazing woman."

He gave a weak smile. "She is, isn't she? I've always known that, but I don't think I ever expressed it enough, particularly to her. I never got to say the things I wanted to say to Caitlin before she died, and now, God help me, it might happen again. I can't bear the thought. I could kick myself for being such an arsehole." He kicked the chair instead.

Fiona hoped that, despite the tubes and machines, inwardly Susan was hearing every single one of the words she'd been desperate to hear from Nick for so long.

"Don't be too hard on yourself," she murmured. "As I said, she was really happy with you and your life together."

"It's very sweet of you to say so," Nick sighed, "but I suspect you're not telling me the whole truth. Or maybe you didn't know it."

"What makes you say that?"

"Oh, I don't know." He sighed. "Gut instinct, common sense, and, of course, the bloody bike ride."

"Oh yes." Fiona smiled. "She told me about that."

She looked across at Susan and contemplated for a moment the sadness of the situation. Just a few hours ago, she'd been talking about riding a bike up and down the mountains of Vietnam. Now here she was unable to move, fighting for her life.

"I don't care what anyone says. Mothers don't go on arduous treks or bike rides unless they're trying to escape an unhappiness or trying to find themselves . . . God, I hate that phrase," he added miserably.

Fiona stayed silent, her mind whirring with the details of her conversation with Susan just minutes before the accident. Nick had clearly ascertained for himself that Susan was having reservations about their relationship, so she figured there was little harm at this point in imparting some of what Susan had said to her while being sure to tread carefully.

"As I said, she wasn't unhappy as such," Fiona said slowly. "I think she just felt she needed a little space, some timeout to do something for herself."

Nick had turned his full attention on her now, obviously hungry for any snippet of information as to Susan's state of mind before she'd been hit by the car. "She did? Why?"

Why. Such a simple word, yet so loaded with pitfalls.

"She didn't really say," Fiona lied. "But if I were to put myself in her shoes and take a wild guess, I would say it's because she's running with the baton of someone else's life, and that's a really tough thing to do. I imagine it would be easy to lose sight of yourself after a while." She felt proud of having found a way to articulate Susan's feelings without actually attributing them to her and, therefore, betraying her confidence.

"Really?" Nick looked perplexed. "If that was what she was feeling, why didn't she just say?"

Fiona smiled benevolently. "We women like to make out that we're simple creatures, but really we're a complex lot."

"You can say that again," he interrupted, more with resignation than irritation.

"And one of those complexities," she continued, "is that it takes us a hell of a long time to register that we might want to change something about our lives, and even longer to actually express it."

"You think she wanted to change her life?" He looked close to tears again.

"No, no, that's not what I'm saying at all," she added hastily. "I'm talking about women in general. Susan adored her life with you and Ellie, but all I'm saying is that it's a tough gig."

"Why, because of Caitlin?"

Fiona wrinkled her nose slightly. "Not because of Caitlin as a *person*, but because of the situation, yes." She sighed. "I only have to look at my own life to understand what Susan might have been feeling."

"Go on . . ." He looked both anguished and hopeful.

"Well, when I married David, I inherited Jake, who was delightful. But of course, there's a mother and grandparents to deal with as well." She smiled ruefully. "Sometimes it just all gets to be a bit much. But at the end of the day, I have some solace in knowing that I don't have to be Jake's mother, as he already has one, and I can complain with impunity to David about Belinda because she's still alive and kicking and driving us mad."

Nick frowned slightly. "I don't get what you're saying. Susan was going on a bike ride because she couldn't complain about Caitlin?"

"No, she doesn't *want* to complain about Caitlin, she adored her. But don't you see? She's living with an angel, a woman who, in her eyes and seemingly everyone else's, was perfect in every way . . . and she probably feels inadequate from time to time." She was careful to throw in a supposition. "So she likely wanted to do something for herself, something that didn't involve anyone else, and something that would only be about her—without the shadow of Caitlin right beside her."

"And that's it? That's the reason?"

Fiona shrugged. "I don't know if it's the reason, I'm just guessing. But if I were in her shoes, that's probably why I'd be doing it."

Fiona knew there were myriad other reasons why Susan had been temporarily fleeing to Vietnam, but she didn't feel that now was the time to impart them. She was hopeful Susan would recover, and when she did, it would be up to her to tell Nick that she felt taken for granted. And that she wanted a baby. Not anyone else.

Nick was staring at Susan again, clearly willing her to wake up. But there was no response. He used a finger to wipe away the moisture under his eyes.

"I loved Caitlin deeply," he murmured. "And when she died, I seriously thought I'd never be able to feel happy again. But Susan saved me, and I love her just as much. I know they are . . . were . . . two very different women, but it doesn't mean I can't love them equally . . . does it?" He looked at Fiona for reassurance.

"Of course it doesn't. After all, people have two, three, four children and love them all the same, so why not partners?"

"Exactly."

He seemed content with her analogy, and they lapsed into silence for a few moments, the only sound the beeping of the machine monitoring Susan's heart rate.

"I suppose I have been taking her for granted a bit," he added eventually. "You know, not showing my appreciation enough for everything she does for Ellie and me." Bingo, thought Fiona. Now he had introduced the subject, and she felt comfortable continuing it.

"I suppose we're all guilty of taking our partners for granted to a certain extent. And they us." She smiled reassuringly. "I don't know the details of your relationship with Susan, so I can't really comment, but I would say that, given what she took on, Susan perhaps deserves more praise and encouragement than most."

She stared down at her friend and smiled sadly. "It's a big deal taking on such a young child, particularly when her mother has just died. She's done an admirable job."

"She has." Nick nodded in agreement and turned back to the bed. "And I haven't shown her nearly enough gratitude for that."

Fiona heard a creak behind her and turned to see a middle-aged doctor walk into the room, followed by what were presumably two medical school students judging by their earnest expressions.

"Hello," he said, extending a surprisingly smooth hand to Fiona. "I'm Dr. Pearson. I operated on this young lady." He pointed toward Susan.

"Hello, I'm Fiona, the friend who came with her in the ambulance. This is her partner, Nick."

Nick had already stood up and walked to the end of the bed, as if a closer proximity to the surgeon might bring news faster.

"Is she going to be all right?" He looked like he might be sick.

The doctor pursed his lips, rocking backward and forward on his toes. "Well, that's always a tough question to answer in cases like these," he said carefully. "But if you mean is she going to die, then I can say that, almost certainly, she won't."

"*Almost* certainly?" Nick interrupted.

"Yes, one can never be one hundred percent because of other eventualities, but as it stands, I don't think . . . ," he glanced down at his notes, ". . . that Susan's life is in danger."

"Oh, thank God!" Relief swept over Nick's face, and he looked at Fiona and smiled broadly. "Everything's going to be fine."

The doctor raised a warning hand in the air. "Hang on a minute, there's still a way to go yet."

"What do you mean?" Nick looked desolate again.

"Well, we're monitoring her to make sure that her intercranial pressure doesn't rise. Susan has sustained a head injury, and until she comes round, we won't know whether there's been any brain damage. But the good news is that it could have been much worse."

He stared down at the clipboard again, making a couple of additional notes. "It seems her legs . . . one of them in particular . . . bore the brunt of the impact, and she fell back on the pavement and hit her head. If it had been the other way round, I doubt very much that she'd have survived."

Nick's gaze left Susan's face and traveled down the bed to where her legs were covered with a tentlike structure.

"How *are* her legs?" asked Fiona. She'd realized that she and Nick had been so concerned about the possibility of Susan dying from her head injury that they hadn't even contemplated the damage to the rest of her body.

The surgeon threw back the blanket to reveal a bridge structure protecting Susan's legs, one of which was encased in plaster and encircled by a metal frame with pins jutting out.

"It was touch-and-go when she first came in, but luckily we didn't have to amputate. It's a compound fracture, and now the uphill struggle for Susan will be trying to walk again."

Nick, having initially looked heartened by the surgeon's update, was now looking pale and gaunt again. "Is there a danger she could still lose her leg?"

"I hope not, but again, I can't rule it out completely. If everything goes according to plan, it'll be fine. But it could take months for her to walk again, and she'll have substantial scarring."

"Cruel, isn't it?" Nick looked at the surgeon. "Susan wasn't . . . isn't . . . the most secure of people about her looks, but she always felt good about her legs. They were the one part of her body that she really liked . . ." He trailed off, his voice breaking with grief.

Fiona cleared her throat. "So how long do you think it might be before we have a clearer idea of when Susan might recover?" she asked the doctor.

"First things first," he replied matter-of-factly. "Let's wait for her to regain consciousness, and then we'll see." He turned to his students. "We'd better move along. We have lots of other patients to see." Pausing, he looked back at Nick. "I'll be back here tomorrow, so let's hope things are a little better then, eh?"

"There you are. I told you she wouldn't die." Fiona smiled.

Nick didn't smile back. "Yes, but I was so busy worrying about her head injury that I hadn't really thought about the damage to her leg. It sounds like coming out of the coma will be just the start of a long struggle back to health."

He started to cry, quietly at first, then louder, gulping sobs that he tried to suppress behind his hand. "I'm sorry," he mumbled.

"Don't be. It would be odd if you *didn't* get upset," she said softly.

"It's just that I don't know how we'll cope."

Fiona leaned across the bed and squeezed his hand. "It's better than having to cope with her death. You'll be just fine."

He nodded but didn't look convinced.

"I'm afraid I have to take off now," she ventured gently. "I have a very hungry little girl at home. If I left it up to David to feed her, she'd be eating baked beans for breakfast, lunch, and dinner."

"He sounds about as useless as me." Nick attempted a smile.

Fiona chuckled. "He's not that bad really, I've been teaching him along the way. Don't forget, you're never too old to learn."

"As I'm probably about to discover."

"If you ever need a break, we can have Ellie to stay with us. I'm sure she'd love helping out with Lily."

"Thanks. She seems happy enough with Caitlin's parents for the time being, but if that changes, it's nice to have an alternative." He walked around to her side of the bed and gave her a peck on the cheek. "Thanks for everything."

"You don't have to thank me." Fiona nodded toward Susan. "I love her too, you know. She's an incredible woman."

"I know." He nodded. "And I can't wait to tell her when she wakes up."

natural-born bastard

Luca took a large bite of almond croissant and chased it with a swallow of cappuccino. It was a weekday, but the breakfast table was laid out with all the care of a lazy Sunday morning, with freshly squeezed orange juice in a glass jug and his favorite newspaper, the *Financial Times*, carefully folded and placed to one side.

"This is very nice," he mumbled through a mouthful. "What's the occasion?"

"Nothing in particular. It's just nice to still have you here at . . . ," Alison glanced at the kitchen clock, ". . . nine o'clock. You're normally long gone by now."

"I know. But as long as I make the ten-thirty train, I can get to that meeting in Reading by one o'clock. It seemed stupid to go all the way into the office first."

Alison looked up at the skylight and noted that the morning

clouds were starting to spit with rain. "I can drive you to the station if you like," she offered. She was desperate to keep him in a good mood for the conversation she was about to instigate.

"Thanks." He reached across the table and squeezed her hand. "You make my life so much easier, do you know that?"

"We aim to please." She smiled and poured him some more juice. Her chest felt tight with apprehension. She knew she was running out of valuable time . . . that all too soon he'd be in "work mode," heading off to his meeting, his mind on business matters rather than personal ones. She felt like a high diver, about to hold her nose and jump off. "By the way . . . ," she tried to keep her tone as casual as possible, ". . . as long as you have a little extra time, I need to talk to you about something . . . something very important to me and, I hope, to you."

"Oh?" He was reading the front page and sounded distracted.

"It's about having a baby."

Now she had his full attention. He turned and smiled broadly. "You're pregnant!"

Her spirits sank, and she was immediately annoyed with herself for starting the conversation in a way that could be misinterpreted. Now she was going to have to disappoint him. "No, sadly, I'm not. But I'd *like* to be."

His expression clouded slightly. She was unsure whether it was through disappointment or dread because he knew what was coming next. But he recovered well. "It'll happen, *cara mia*. It's early days."

"Well, that's the thing," she ventured, determined not to lose her nerve or momentum in getting her message across. "It *isn't* early days."

He looked puzzled. "What do you mean?"

She let out a long sigh. "The truth is that I haven't used contraception since we first started sleeping together. So it's not early days at all, I'm afraid. You see, when I was young, I was diagnosed with polycystic ovaries—"

He held up his hand, baffled by a medical term outside his command of the English language. "Wait a minute. You were diagnosed with *what?*"

"Polycystic ovaries. Basically, it's a condition that means it's harder for me to get pregnant."

"I see." He looked troubled. "So why didn't you tell me this before we got married?"

Alison was taken aback by the question, and she frowned and recoiled slightly. "Does it matter?"

He looked at her, astonished. "Well, if it means you can't have children naturally, then yes, I would say it matters very much. A husband and wife need to know everything about each other, there must be no secrets."

Alison winced inwardly, thinking about her secret nose job and all the hidden photographs from her childhood that told the true story. God forbid that Luca should ever find out about it.

"I didn't deliberately keep it a secret," she countered, worried that he was accusing her of tricking him. "You *can* get pregnant naturally, and many people with the condition do, and to be honest, I thought I'd be one of them. So it didn't seem important to mention it."

"I see." His eyes had hardened. "So what are you saying—that it now seems you *are* one of those who needs extra help?"

She nodded silently, waiting for his reaction.

"And how do you know that? Is it just guesswork or has someone told you?"

"A bit of both really. My gut instinct told me I should see a specialist, which I did, and he says I *may* need help to conceive."

"So, first a medical condition you don't tell me about, now a visit to a specialist behind my back too." He was silent for what felt like an interminable amount of time, staring at his empty plate. Then he looked up at her. "What level of help?"

His face remained impassive, but Alison felt an overwhelming sense of relief that he was even expressing an interest in understanding the situation. Perhaps everything was going to be all right after all. "I'm not sure yet. I've had some preliminary tests and am getting the results this afternoon." She paused a moment, composing herself for the next bit, trying to make sure she sounded as matter-of-fact as possible. "And they'll probably need a sample of your sperm too."

In a voice that was ominously low and measured, he said, "There's absolutely nothing wrong with my sperm."

"I know, I know," she quickly reassured him. "I told the doctor that, but he said he still needed it."

Luca's mouth had set into a firm line, and a small twitch was visible in his left cheek. "Did you tell him that I have two strong and healthy boys?"

"Yes, I did, but he said that sometimes things change."

Luca stood up quickly, his chair making a sharp scraping noise on the wood floor. Alison jumped slightly.

"No, they don't," he said stiffly. "They don't change at all. As I said, there's absolutely *nothing* wrong with my sperm."

"Of course there isn't, darling," she placated. "The problem is all mine, I know that."

"Then you won't need my sample, will you?" he said with finality, grabbing the newspaper from the table and walking toward the kitchen door. "Now I have to go. I don't want to miss the train."

Alison rose from her chair and reached for her car keys, her mind racing with how she could try to change his mind during the short drive to the station.

"I thought you wanted us to have a child as much as I do," she said as they pulled away from the curb outside the house.

"I do." He didn't look at her, only stared straight ahead.

"Well, when they have identified my problem . . . ," again, she was careful to place all blame on herself, ". . . it might be something where I won't stand a chance of getting pregnant unless you are prepared to give a sperm sample. Like, you know, IVF or something."

He didn't say anything for a few seconds, and she wondered if he was going to ignore her for the rest of the journey. But then he took a deep breath.

"I do want us to have a child together, but not like *this*, with doctors poking and prodding us," he said with an expression of deep distaste. "Creating a new life should be natural, not scientific."

"The pregnancy *will* be natural." She was painfully aware that her tone was starting to sound pleading. "I'll still carry the baby and be eating for two and all that. It's just that I might need a bit of help to conceive, that's all. And then we'll have our wonderful child." She took her eyes away from the road briefly to look at him for reassurance, but it wasn't forthcoming.

"I don't know." He shook his head slowly. "I think we should carry on trying to have a baby naturally for at least another year."

Another year. While it no doubt seemed the easiest thing in the world for him, Alison knew that at the age of thirty-six, she didn't have time to wait around on the off chance that she might . . . and it was a very large "might" . . . fall pregnant. Her frustration erupted on the surface.

"For God's sake, Luca, what difference does it make whether the baby is conceived in a four-poster bed, on a beach, or in a bloody test tube? It will still be our child biologically, I'll still carry it and give birth to it, and we'll still bring it up together."

"It makes a difference to *me*," he said quietly. "A big difference."

"But why?" she pleaded. "After all, I know you love me, so why on earth wouldn't you want me to have our baby in whichever way we can?"

The station was in sight now, just beyond the set of traffic lights they were edging their way across. Alison turned into the parking lot and pulled up outside within yards of the ticket booth, leaving the engine idling.

"*Why*, Luca?" she asked again.

He opened the door and placed one foot on the ground, then turned to face her. "Because I can't guarantee that I would feel the same way about a child created by doctors as I would about my two boys created by love in a natural way."

If someone had plunged a knife straight into Alison's heart, she couldn't have felt any greater pain than she did right then. "You bastard," she whispered through the veil of tears that had filled her eyes. "That was a really cheap shot."

"It wasn't meant to be." He shrugged. "You asked me a question, and I gave you an honest answer. That's all." He got out of the car and slammed the door. "Thanks for the lift," he added through the open window. "See you tonight."

She jammed the gear shift into reverse and angrily revved the engine, making it clear to everyone in the vicinity that she was less than pleased. She backed out of the parking lot and, after turning the corner so she was out of sight, pulled over to the side of a quiet residential street, where she sat sobbing with her forehead pressed against the steering wheel.

Coming to terms with the reality that she might be unable to conceive naturally was hard enough, but her tears were less on account of her physical misfortune and more from the frustration and anger at finding herself married to a man who made her feel less of a woman because of it.

• • •

Well, I think it's good news." The doctor gave her a half-smile and then went back to studying the test results in front of him.

"Great!" Alison managed to smile back despite the dull ache in her chest that had been there ever since that morning's conversation with Luca.

"It seems you might have a problem with your fallopian tubes, in that they appear to be stuck beneath your ovaries."

"That's *good* news?" Her brow furrowed with concern.

"Yes, because it can probably be fixed with a minor operation." He looked up at her. "It's much better to know what's wrong so it can be put right. Quite often, the women who have the greatest trouble conceiving are those for whom we simply cannot detect what the problem is."

"I see." Alison knew she was supposed to feel reassured by this, but she was still uncertain. "So what happens next?"

"A laparoscopy just to confirm that the problem is what I think it is, and then, assuming that's the case, a simple surgical procedure to free your tubes."

"And after that I might have a chance of conceiving naturally?"

"If the tubes turn out to be healthy, yes. I'll be able to examine them further when I operate," he said, as if discussing something as simple as an oil change. "But we're also going to put you on a course of hormones to help you ovulate properly."

Alison digested what he'd said for a few moments. "Well, that doesn't sound so bad."

"Fingers crossed, it won't be." He flicked through her chart. "Now, what's happened to your husband's sperm sample?"

"Um . . ." Alison felt and looked uncomfortable. "You don't need it now, do you?"

"It's still worth doing, just to be sure that it's not contributing to your problems conceiving. We should still cover all the bases." He looked at her curiously. "Mrs. Rossi, does your husband even know you're *here?*"

She nodded miserably, unable to control the tears welling in the corners of her eyes. Her chest felt as tight as a trampoline. "Yes, he does. But he won't give a sperm sample."

The doctor leaned forward, his expression one of concern. He held out a box of tissues. "Why not? Am I to assume he doesn't share your enthusiasm to have a child?"

She shook her head and took a tissue, blowing her nose loudly. "No, it's not that. He's as keen to have a baby as I am, but he thinks it should be conceived naturally."

"I see."

"Silly, isn't it?" she said with a false laugh. "A grown man thinking like that."

He nodded. "Silly, perhaps, but not uncommon, I'm afraid. I get a lot of reluctant men through these doors, dragged here by their girlfriends or wives."

Alison stopped dabbing her eyes with the tissue. "Really?"

"Yes. They see any level of medical help as a threat to their masculinity."

She had already concluded that this was likely the reason for Luca's blanket refusal to give a sample, but it helped to hear that he wasn't the only overly macho fool on the planet.

"So how are they eventually persuaded to come along?" she asked.

The doctor smiled. "Usually the woman has got hold of him by the ear . . . or somewhere even more painful . . . and pulled him in here. That, or she's managed to convince him that if he really loves her, he'll give her what she wants."

Alison was pretty certain the former option would never work with her hotheaded Italian husband, though the latter option was certainly food for thought.

"But from what you've said, it sounds like I may not have to re-sort to persuasion after all?" she ventured aloud. "Because if this op-eration is a success and I do the hormone therapy, there's a strong chance I will conceive in the normal way?" She felt queasy with ap-prehension, awaiting his answer.

"I don't know about a strong chance, but there's certainly a bet-ter chance than if you don't go ahead and have the treatment," he replied.

"In that case, let's do it," Alison said. "And I'll worry about my pigheaded idiot of a husband another time."

ooh-la-la—aaaarrrgh

Standing back to admire her handiwork, Julia smiled to herself.

The hallway was covered in darkness, except for a small, scented candle flickering on each stair leading up toward the bedroom. She had been worried it might appear eerie, but the end result was exactly what she was looking for—mysterious and romantic.

James was due back at any time, having been away for the past week on a business trip to New York, and Julia wanted to show how much she'd missed him. So she planned to do it the way she expressed most of her emotions . . . through sex.

Stepping carefully past the trail of candles, she walked up into the bedroom and flicked on the lights. The bed looked pristine and inviting, with its newly laundered white bed linen and plumped-up pillows. Julia had scattered pink rose petals across it for extra effect.

She started to light yet more candles, positioning them along the mantelpiece above the fireplace and on the small tables on either side of the bed. Picking up a remote control, she aimed it toward the wooden cabinet at the foot of the bed, from which was protruding a plasma TV screen. In James's absence, she'd retired to bed early the night before and watched two Brad Pitt movies back to back.

As she pressed the close button, the TV made a whirring noise and disappeared from view into the chest. She didn't want any distractions tonight.

Opening the table on her side of the bed, she knelt down in front of a small, concealed CD system and inserted Morcheeba's "Who Can You Trust." Otherwise known as great, sensuous shagging music, she thought with a wry smile.

Padding barefoot across to the vast closets lining the far wall, she opened one door and stooped down, peering all the way into the back. Turning her head sideways, she reached in and fumbled around until her hand felt the black plastic bin liner she was searching for. Her bag of tricks.

Tipping the contents onto the bed, she contemplated the selection of outfits laid before her. Nurse perhaps? No, wore that one a couple of weeks ago. What about the dominatrix? No, she'd only tried that on James once, and he hadn't seemed as keen as other boyfriends in the past. In which case, it was the trusty old French maid.

Stuffing the other clothes and accessories back into the bag, she dropped her robe to the floor and pulled on a black thong. Next came the black corset and miniskirt, followed by the frilly white apron. She tried the small mob cap but, deciding it looked too goofy, put it back in the bag with the other rejects.

Lastly, she carefully eased on the black fishnet stockings and squeezed her feet into six-inch, black stiletto heels.

Standing back, she glanced in the mirror. The stockings and heels accentuated her long legs, and the corset showed off her breasts to great effect. Julia liked what she saw. To her, the definition of modesty was the art of encouraging others to realize how wonderful she was.

"Oooooh, monsieur, tu es trop grand!" She pouted.

Teetering across to the door, she flicked the lights off just in time to hear a cab pulling up outside and James saying thank you to the driver. She lay on the bed and waited.

Well, that was quite some homecoming!" James smiled fortyfive minutes later, picking a rose petal off his bare chest and throwing it onto the floor.

"We aim to please." Julia, naked except for her stockings and high heels, was still straddling him, her hair cascading messily but sexily over her shoulders.

"I haven't seen the French maid's outfit in a while. I'd forgotten what a turn-on it was." He grinned, idly playing with one of her nipples.

"It was that or the nurse, and if I remember rightly, Doctor, it was only a couple of weeks ago that you sent my temperature sky-high," she teased.

"Then I'll just have to take you shopping for some more. I find uniforms so sexy, though I draw the line at traffic wardens."

Julia laughed, straightened her back, and started to slowly rock backward and forward, her inner thighs brushing his penis.

He closed his eyes. "Mmmm, that's lovely."

Lifting herself up, Julia shuffled backward and started to kiss his chest, working her way slowly downward toward his groin. She found her effect on him sexually thrilling.

Grabbing the shaft of his penis, she was guiding it toward her mouth when he placed a hand on the top of her head and gently pulled her away.

"No, darling. Later. I want to talk to you."

"You want to *talk?*" she said incredulously, her mouth just centimeters from his penis. In her many dealings with the male species, this was a first.

"Yes, come back up here." He patted her pillow next to him.

Now that a giant pin had burst their sexually charged bubble, Julia felt rather self-conscious in her getup. Placing the shoes by the side of the bed, she carefully eased off the stockings, then flopped down next to James at the head of the bed.

"Come here." He smiled, reaching his arm behind her head and drawing her into his chest.

Julia lay there wordlessly for a few seconds, feeling slightly awkward. She loved sexual attention, but at the end of the day she was uncomfortable with the plain old affection that so many of her friends said they craved from their partners. She didn't understand it. It felt rather theatrical and pointless.

She sat up. "Sorry, darling, but your chest hair is making me itch."

"Oh." He looked faintly disappointed. "I didn't know you were the allergic type."

"I'm not usually." She leaned over and took another sip of the champagne she'd poured for them earlier. Anything to avoid indulging in postcoital cuddles. "So what do you want to talk about?"

She hoped he wanted to suggest a much-needed holiday for them both, somewhere hot, gloriously luxurious, and very, very expensive. But his serious expression suggested she was way off the mark.

"Children," he said firmly.

"Anyone's in particular?"

"You see?" He sat bolt upright, jabbing a finger in her direction. "That's exactly why I want to talk about it, because every time I mention the subject you either change the subject or make a bloody joke!"

Julia recoiled slightly, taken aback by his strong reaction. "Sorry, I didn't realize it was such a big deal."

"Not such a big deal?" he parroted, shaking his head. "How can discussing whether or not we want children be classified as 'not a big deal'? It's a *huge* deal."

She shrugged. "Not to me it isn't."

"Great! Glad to hear it. When can we start trying then?" He folded his arms and stared at her defiantly.

Julia didn't want to have this conversation now. Not ever, in fact. Because she knew that what she had to say would displease him greatly and start an argument. So she used a tried-and-true avoidance tactic.

"Why are you being like this?"

"Being like what?"

"So . . . so aggressive and confrontational with me. I don't deserve that." She put on her best wounded expression. It seemed to work, and he unfolded his arms, extending a hand to touch her knee.

"Darling, I don't mean to sound aggressive. I'm just speaking passionately about something that's very important to me. I *want* to have children . . . with you . . . I don't know how else to put it."

Julia pursed her lips, her mind racing with the options of how she should respond. She was quickly becoming aware that this could be a pivotal moment in their marriage.

"Darling, I *know* you want to have children. And so do I," she lied. "But not yet. We've only been married a couple of years, and I want to enjoy having you to myself for a little while longer." She smiled coquettishly, but he didn't seem to notice. "We're having fun. There's *plenty* of time to think about having children."

"But is there?" He looked dubious. "You're thirty-three, and all the articles I've read say that a woman's fertility starts to diminish rapidly after the age of thirty-five."

Her eyebrows shot up. "You've been reading *articles* about it?"

He looked slightly uncomfortable. "Yes . . . well, one or two anyway. I just don't want us to be one of those couples that leave it until it's too late. I mean, even if we started trying now, and assuming you fell pregnant quite quickly, it would still be about another year before little James or Julia Junior was lying here."

He patted the space between them, and Julia inwardly shivered. It felt as if the bedroom walls were closing in, constricting her breathing.

"So?" He tilted his head and looked at her questioningly. "How about it?"

Her bottom lip protruding, she let out a sigh of such force that it blew her bangs to one side. "I don't know, James . . . you'll have to give me some time to think about it. I can't be pressured into something so life-changing. After all, it would be *me* left holding the baby, day in, day out, not you."

He looked at her curiously. "You know, Julia, sometimes I feel incredibly close to you, and other times I feel like I don't know you at all. Most women would love to have the luxury of staying home with their children without any financial worries."

"Yeah? Well, I'm not like most women." She gestured toward the French maid's outfit crumpled on the floor to illustrate the point. "You can't have it all ways."

"Can't I?" He looked sad at the thought. "So what are you saying? That because I have a wife who's sexually imaginative and exciting, she can't also be the mother of my children? I wasn't aware the two were mutually exclusive."

Julia knew she could make a long speech about how she saw her parents' once-vibrant marriage deteriorate painfully and slowly after the birth of her much younger sister, how as an impressionable ten-year-old she'd heard the endless, late-night arguments about their virtually extinct sex life, her father shouting that he'd not wanted another child, her mother screaming back that she was "exhausted and didn't need this shit."

She knew she could attempt to explain to James that her darling "daddy" walking out for the charms of another, much younger woman had left her devastated and that, despite her mother constantly telling her otherwise, she felt *she* was the one he'd rejected in favor of Poppy, a leggy, sexually voracious twenty-six-year-old.

"Why did he really leave?" she'd asked her older brother George one night, several years after her father had walked out.

He'd shrugged nonchalantly. "No reason other than that he was suddenly getting great blow jobs again, I suppose."

It might have been intended as a flip remark, but it had lodged itself in the impressionable Julia's mind and stayed there, refusing to budge. So that was how you kept men, she thought, by being sexually insatiable and making them the sole focus of your attention.

Now here was her husband suggesting they try for a baby, the very thing that had torn her parents' marriage apart. But she knew that if she voiced her fears, he'd only assure her that he was different from her father, that *he* would never leave in pursuit of hot, uncomplicated sex.

So she didn't see the point. And in addition to her apprehension about what having a baby might do to her marriage, Julia had to admit that her biological clock clearly didn't have any batteries in it. Not once had she felt even the slightest twinge of longing for a child, and when she held other people's babies, she did so because she felt she ought to, not because she really wanted to. She knew it probably made her unusual among her friends, but she didn't feel it made her a bad person or any less of a woman . . . just different.

"As I said, I need some time," she reiterated.

"How long? After all, most women your age would find it hard to ignore the ticking of their biological clock."

She sighed again. "James, don't push me. I won't be pushed. Let's just say I'm requesting that we hit the snooze button for a while, okay?"

He shifted his position, straightening his back and crossing his legs. He wore a pained expression. "I don't mean to push you, but I need to know if this is going to be a deal-breaker."

"A *deal-breaker?*" She felt her heart rate quicken. "What do you mean?"

"I mean that if we have a difference of opinion over something so fundamental, then it's a huge problem."

Julia pondered what he'd said for a couple of seconds. "An insurmountable problem?" she asked.

He shrugged. "If you come back and say you definitely don't want kids, then yes, I'd say it's insurmountable. Because I *do* want them, very much so."

She tucked her legs up and turned to face him full-on, glowering with suppressed rage. "So if I don't give you children, I get dumped. Is that it? Is that what you're saying?"

James said nothing, simply staring down at his feet.

"And what if I find I *can't* have them? What then? Do I get sent back in a box marked 'faulty'?"

He raised his eyes heavenward. "Don't be so facetious. There are ways round that, like IVF and so on."

"It's not always successful," she interrupted.

"Well, we'll cross that bridge when we come to it. But at the moment we can't even agree to *try* for a baby."

"Or *not* try," she threw back at him. "Why do your wishes take precedence over mine?"

"So now you're saying you definitely *don't* want kids?"

"No, I'm not saying that," she backtracked, fearful of saying something now that would forever be held up in evidence against her.

She hadn't been lying when she said she just needed some time to think. She knew she could happily forgo motherhood without a second thought, but she now knew that was no longer an option. Her new dilemma was whether she could put her own reservations on the back burner and give James the child or—God forbid—children he wanted.

"I suppose I'm saying that if it's so important to you to have children, I can't believe you didn't bring it up before we got married," she ventured.

"I didn't think I needed to!" He looked incredulous. "I mean, what woman *doesn't* want to have children?"

"Quite a few actually." She sniffed. "You'd be surprised. Not everyone fancies the idea of stretch marks and fat ankles, you know, not to mention the ensuing shitty arses and sleepless nights."

He looked at her disapprovingly. "And what about the unconditional love, the wonderful cuddles, the absolute honor and privilege of creating another human being and teaching them about the world? Doesn't any of that resonate with you?"

"Yes, of course it does," she said unconvincingly. "I'm just pointing out that it can be hard work and shouldn't be entered into lightly. Compromise has to be made, and a lot of women don't want to slow down their careers."

"Well, that's hardly the case with you, is it?" he scoffed. "Unless shopping is a career."

She didn't respond to the jibe and simply stared at him thoughtfully for a few seconds. "James?" she said eventually.

"Yes." He wasn't looking at her, preferring to stare into the middle distance.

"Why did you marry me?"

"Because you were the most gorgeous thing I'd ever seen and I fell in love with you," he replied matter-of-factly. She had asked the question before, and he always gave that reply.

"And has that changed?"

He turned to her, stunned. "No. Why, do you think it has?"

She shook her head. "No, up until five minutes ago, I felt like the most wanted woman in the world. But now it seems there are conditions to your continued love for me."

"Not conditions, Julia, simply natural *progressions*. I love you, I married you, I want us to have children together. Isn't that what makes the world go round?"

She shrugged. "Sometimes. But not always. I like our relationship as it is . . . vibrant, exciting, and, yes, a little bit selfish. I don't want to share you with anyone," she said, adopting the girlish voice that always had him eating out of her hand. She leaned into him, her left hand idly stroking his chest hair, her fingers circling one nipple, then the other.

He didn't respond, staring ahead stony-faced.

Moving her mouth to his left ear, she nibbled the lobe sensually as her left hand traveled down across his stomach toward his groin. She smiled to herself as she reached his penis, rock-hard despite his seeming reluctance to reciprocate.

Grasping it, her hand started to move up and down, but she faltered as she felt something she wasn't expecting. It was James's hand, gripping her wrist.

"For fuck's sake, Julia, stop it, will you? All you ever think about is sex. There's more to life, you know."

She sat upright, feeling a mixture of annoyance and humiliation. "Actually, you can be as po-faced as you like about it, but sex *is* what life is all about. Without it, none of us would be here."

James had his back to her, pulling on a pair of jeans and a T-shirt. He made no attempt to reply.

"And as for your claim that all I do is think about sex, I didn't notice you complaining when I was wearing a French maid's outfit and you were shagging me from behind."

He turned round, his expression one of distaste. "Do you have to be so crude?"

"Oh, I get it." She snorted with derision. "You like the dirty talk in bed, but otherwise you want me to be the shy, virginal type. Right?"

"I'm not even going to dignify that with a reply." He delved into the wardrobe and pulled out a pair of battered old deck shoes.

"How convenient. Probably because you *can't* reply because you know I'm right." Julia knew she had now descended into using run-of-the-mill argument fodder, but she didn't care. Anything to avoid returning to the subject of childbearing.

James had put his shoes on and was heading for the door.

"Where are you going?" she demanded. "I've cooked us dinner."

He stopped in the doorway and turned slightly, but didn't catch her eye. "Sorry, but I've lost my appetite. I'm going for a drive to do some thinking, and I suggest you do the same. Don't wait up."

With that, he was gone, leaving Julia to pick up the remnants of both her clothing and the evening for which she'd harbored such high hopes.

a conscious effort

Nick paced the floor by the window, glancing out at the cars below, then back to the bed where Susan lay motionless, surrounded by Fiona, Julia, and Alison.

Fiona and Alison were in jeans and sweatshirts, but Julia looked typically stunning in a tailored black suit and crisp white shirt.

"It's been three days now," he said wretchedly, reaffirming what they all knew. "It's not good, not good at all."

"Did the doctor actually say that?" said Julia anxiously, stroking Susan's hair and brushing a stray piece away from her cheek.

"Not as such, no. They keep blathering on about how it's still early, and I *know* they're only trying to be nice, but it feels like a bloody lifetime to me." He fell into the chair by the window with his head in his hands.

Alison wandered over and placed a reassuring hand on top of his head. "They wouldn't give you false hope. I'm sure she's going to be fine."

He lifted his head slightly and looked directly at her, his eyes wet, the corners of his mouth wavering with signs of distress. "God, I hope you're right." Tears started to roll down his face, falling onto his jeans and forming a small, dark patch. "I love her so much that I seriously don't think I could go on if she didn't pull through."

He lowered his head again, and the three women exchanged silent expressions of concern.

"Nick, you *have* to stay strong," said Julia firmly. "For Ellie's sake."

He laughed slightly maniacally. "I'm sick of being strong, Julia. I had to be strong when Caitlin died, I had to be strong in dealing with my young, motherless daughter, and now I'm having to be strong all over again while Susan fights for her life. I'm fucking *sick* of having to be strong."

No one said anything, the atmosphere raw with emotion. After a few seconds, he stood up and walked over to Julia, placing a hand on her shoulder. "I'm sorry. I shouldn't take it out on you. I know you're only trying to keep my spirits up." He sighed, wiping his eyes. "It's just so damn hard."

"You don't have to apologize," she said softly. "And don't worry, I have the skin of a rhino. In toughness, not appearance, of course."

He smiled slightly, then turned serious again. "The first day was almost bearable, because I felt she was going to come round at any moment, and I wanted to be there when she did." He let out a long sigh. "By the second day, my optimism was beginning to fade, and now I'm afraid that it's very low indeed. I can't help thinking that the longer she stays like this, the less chance there is of her making a recovery."

"Not necessarily," Alison piped up. "I read in the paper the other day about a man who woke up from a coma after ten years."

She'd meant it as a positive story, but as Nick's face clouded over she realized immediately that it had had the opposite effect. She also realized it when she looked across the bed and saw Julia glowering at her. "Although I'm sure Susan will recover much sooner than that . . ." she added lamely.

"What's the time?" asked Fiona, theatrically consulting her watch in a blatant attempt to change the subject. "I'd better get going soon, but I'll come back tomorrow morning and sit with her—if you'd like to take a break?" She looked at Nick.

He shook his head. "Thanks, but I'm not going anywhere. I'm terrified of even going to the bathroom in case she wakes up while I'm in there." He smiled sadly. "I want to be the first face she sees when she comes round . . . *if* she comes round." His voice broke.

"Okay, well, I'll come and keep you company anyway." Fiona stepped closer to the bed and leaned over to kiss Susan's forehead. "Bye, my darling, see you tomorrow," she murmured, before looking back to Nick. "How's Ellie, by the way?"

He rubbed his chin, covered in three days' stubble. "She's fine. She's still at Bill and Genevieve's and thinks we're away working, although she has started asking when we're going to be back." His face crumpled. "Last night she asked to speak to Mummy, and I had to come up with some old song-and-dance about her being in a meeting. Thank God for the naïveté of six-year-olds."

He started to cry quietly again, and this time Alison started too. Fiona was struggling to hold back the tears; only Julia remained dry-eyed, although her face looked pinched.

They all stood in a circle round the bed, staring silently down at Susan.

"I know none of us is really religious, but shall we say a prayer?" said Alison. Julia was about to pooh-pooh the idea and opened her mouth to speak, but Nick's voice cut across her.

"That's a lovely idea, Alison, thank you. I'd like to do that."

He moved closer to the bed, his thighs pressing against the side. He closed his eyes and bowed his head.

The three women looked at one another uncertainly for a few seconds, then Alison and Fiona bowed their heads too. Julia remained where she was until Fiona scowled at her and she hastily followed suit, tucking her chin into her chest.

"Dear Lord," he began. "Please help Susan to make a full recovery from her accident. I know I don't pray very much these days . . . well, at *all*, in fact, but I hope you'll find it in your heart to forgive me and . . ."

"Oh, my God!" Fiona clamped a hand over her mouth and let out a stifled sob, her eyes welling with tears.

Nick had stopped praying and was staring at her with a puzzled expression. Then his gaze followed hers, down to Susan's face.

She was still lying in the same position, but her eyes were open and blinking rapidly. She looked faintly confused as she focused on the four serious faces peering down at her.

"Bloody hell," she croaked. "Has someone died?"

Nick was openly sobbing again, but this time through sheer relief and joy. He and Susan were now alone in the room, the others having tactfully withdrawn after their whoops of happiness and surprise had brought the medical staff running.

"Jesus, you have no idea how good it felt to see you open your eyes." Nick grinned through the tears. "I was beginning to think that I'd lost you forever."

Susan feebly touched the bandaged area of her head and winced. "I've got the mother of all headaches." She peered downward. "And what the hell happened to my leg?"

Nick looked concerned again. "Don't you remember anything?"

She narrowed her eyes. "I remember the yoga class, and I remember having a coffee with Fiona afterward, then . . ." She stopped. "Nope, nothing else."

"You were hit by a car while you were waiting to cross the road. Your leg was trapped under the wheel, but a couple of inches the other way and you would probably have been killed." He stopped talking for a moment, clearly finding even the possibility hard to contemplate. "They think you got the head injury when you fell back onto the pavement."

She widened her eyes. "What about the driver? Is he or she okay?"

Nick smiled. "Typical of you to worry about others when you're lying in a hospital bed yourself. It was a he, and, yes, he's fine. Apparently, he had swerved to avoid a young boy who'd fallen off his bicycle, so it wasn't his fault. Just a terrible, terrible accident." He jerked his head back toward the door. "The nurses tell me he's been ringing every day to find out how you are. He's overcome with guilt, I'm afraid."

"Well, he shouldn't be." Susan carefully attempted to shift herself ever so slightly. "Please let him know I don't blame him at all. I would have done exactly the same in his position."

Nick sat on the edge of the bed and leaned in, gently kissing her forehead. "By the way, Ellie's on her way with Bill and Genevieve." He looked at his watch. "They should be here soon."

Susan smiled weakly. "I can't wait. Does she know what happened?"

He shook his head. "No, I told her we were both away working."

"She must be wondering why I haven't called." Susan's face crumpled slightly at the thought. "I hate it that she might think I'd forgotten. Still, as she's coming here, we'll be able to tell her the truth now, won't we?"

He nodded and started to stroke her hair.

Susan lay back carefully. She still didn't have the full facts about her injuries, about what had really happened, but they could wait. For now, she welcomed the change in behavior that her accident had prompted.

For the first time in ages, she could *see* the love in his eyes, *feel* his concern, and enjoy the public affection he had previously shied away from expressing.

"I'm sorry I put you through this," she murmured. "It must have been hellish for you, particularly after everything you went through when Caitlin died."

He placed a finger on her lips. "Ssssh, don't say that, particularly as it wasn't your fault. I'm just grateful beyond belief that you've pulled through." He kissed her again, this time on the mouth, and grabbed her hand, clasping it tightly. "Don't ever, ever leave me again. Not even for a bike ride."

Susan looked momentarily puzzled by what he'd said, and then the realization dawned. "Ah, yes, the bike ride. Now I remember about that too." She half sat up and Nick leapt to his feet, plumping the pillows behind her back to support her. "Well, I won't be going on that now, will I?" She forced a smile.

He stared at her with a curious expression. "I know I never really asked you, because I was too busy thinking about myself and how I'd cope without you around to organize Ellie and me, but what *was* that all about?"

She smiled. "Ah, now there's a question." She paused and sighed. "It was a bid to get noticed, I suppose." Her honesty surprised even her, but she chalked it up to the strong painkillers numbing her usual cautiousness. Plus, of course, the accident itself. When you've almost died, waiting for the right time to say something suddenly seems ludicrous.

"And then you got hit by a car, which worked just as well." He smiled briefly to let her know that he was joking before his face turned serious again. "Noticed by me?"

She didn't say anything, just nodded with a wistful, almost apologetic expression.

"I see." He looked close to tears again. "God, I'm such a fool. I should have known you were feeling that way."

"How could you? I didn't exactly wear my heart on my sleeve, did I? Susan the uncomplaining people pleaser. That's me."

"That's not the point, though." He looked troubled. "I was so busy thinking about how Ellie and I had been affected by Caitlin's death that I didn't stop to consider what you'd taken on." He paused for a moment. "It can't have been easy."

They were the words Susan had waited to hear for so long, and now that she'd heard them, she couldn't quite believe it. She stayed silent, resisting her natural temptation to reassure him that it had all been smooth sailing when, clearly, it hadn't.

"How long have you been unhappy?" He looked broken.

She squeezed his hand. "I wasn't unhappy as such, I just felt I needed to remove myself from home for a while so you could realize how much you missed me." She smiled to try to soften the blow slightly.

"So I could appreciate how much you do for me and Ellie?" he asked quietly.

She looked sheepish. "Something like that, yes."

Leaning toward her, he placed his face just two inches from hers and stared into her eyes. "Susan, I am so, so sorry that it's taken you nearly being killed to make me say these things, but I feel we've been given a second chance together, so I'll say them now." He cleared his throat. "I love you to distraction, and I would fall apart if I lost you. Not because I wouldn't know how to look after Ellie or myself, but because I would truly, truly miss *you* as the person, the human being that you are."

"Thank you." The lump in her throat made it difficult for her to say anything else.

"And another thing . . . ," he jumped up, clearly excited by what he was about to say, pacing over to the window and back again, ". . . I think we should get married."

Okay, so it wasn't the dramatically romantic proposal she'd dreamed of . . . Nick on bended knee at the top of the Eiffel Tower, perhaps, while a violinist played nearby . . . but it was still a major step forward.

"That would be lovely." Susan smiled.

"And I've been doing a lot of thinking about what you said . . . you know, about us having a baby."

She nodded mutely, rendered speechless by the speed with which Nick was changing before her eyes.

"Well, I think we should."

"You do?" Her head spinning, she tried to shift her body slightly and winced as she discovered she ached all over. "Hang on a minute . . . am I dreaming? Or has the other Nick been abducted by aliens and replaced by a cloned, New Age version?"

He smiled weakly. "I know, I know. I was a jackass, what can I say?" He held up his hands in a gesture of surrender. "But as I said, I've had a lot of time to just sit here and think." He paused slightly and looked down at the floor. "To think about losing you, to think about life without you . . . and to think of all the things I wanted to say to you and hadn't said. 'Will you marry me?' being one of them."

"Well, since you ask, yes, I will!" She laughed, tears in her eyes.

"Fantastic!" He walked back to the bed and gave her a lingering kiss on the mouth. "And then we'll try for a baby."

"Nick, you don't have to do that. It's fine really."

"No, that's just it, I *want* to," he said breathlessly. "In fact, I can't think why I ever thought it was a good idea to wait. We're in love, we're going to get married, why on earth *wouldn't* we want to try for a baby?"

She laughed at his infectious enthusiasm. "Okay." But inside, she knew it was immaterial at the moment, certainly until her leg had healed enough to bear her own weight, let alone that of a pregnancy. And by then he might have changed his mind again.

"So how *do* you feel?" He was back by her side again, carefully lowering himself onto the bed. "Are you in a great deal of pain?"

"Not really. More of a dull, persistent ache." She looked at one of the tubes running into her hand. "But I suppose if I didn't have the morphine, it might be another story."

"When you were saying good-bye to the others, I had a word with the surgeon outside, and he seemed really pleased with your progress. But we have to keep an eye on you because the brain can play funny tricks."

"Particularly mine."

"No, I'm serious. I saw a documentary the other day where this guy had suffered a head injury and knew who his family was and stuff but couldn't name certain objects. It was really weird." He held up his wrist and tapped the face of his watch. "What's this?"

"That's easy." She grinned. "It's a cucumber."

one bump or two?

"Do you think she's forgotten?" Alison looked at her watch and scanned Natasha's for the fifth time in as many minutes. "It's not like her to be late."

"Yes, it is," said Julia derisively. "She's always late, except this time she's actually got the excuse that she can't get around that easily."

Fiona looked worried. "I offered to pick her up, but she refused. She got quite cross with me actually, and said she wasn't an invalid."

"Susan cross?" Julia raised a perfectly plucked eyebrow. "Now that *really* isn't like her."

"I know." Fiona sighed, smoothing out a crease in her skirt. "I think a lot has changed about Susan since the accident, but it's all good. She just seems much more confident and decisive somehow."

"Well, let's hope I don't have an accident then," said Julia. "I'd be even more of a nightmare afterward."

Neither Fiona nor Alison responded, their silence indicating that they agreed with Julia.

"Aha!" she added, pointing along the street. "Here comes Hopalong Cassidy now."

They all craned their necks to watch Susan's painstaking progress along the sidewalk toward where they were sitting at a table positioned in the open French windows at the front of the café.

She was walking slowly but purposefully, leaning on a walking stick in her left hand, her left foot still lightly bandaged. She was wearing a pink driving moccasin on her right foot, but her left was encased in a large, burgundy slipper.

"Sorry, love, but it'll never catch on." Julia grinned, nodding toward Susan's feet as she hobbled up to the table. "Didn't they have one in pink?"

"Fuck off." Susan smiled, easing herself into the empty chair between Fiona and Alison. "Sorry I'm late. The traffic was so bad that I would have had time to change a flat tire without pulling over."

Fiona reached over to an ice bucket at her side. "As it's a special occasion, we have taken the liberty of ordering champagne." She poured Susan a glass and passed it to her. "Welcome back to the Second Wives Club. We've missed you."

Susan raised her glass and smiled. "Thank you. I've missed coming." It had been six months since she'd regained consciousness, and it had been a long, slow, limping plod along the road to recovery. She was still attending regular physical therapy sessions as well as doing exercises at home, much to Ellie's amusement. Fiona, Julia, and Alison had all been regular visitors to Susan and Nick's house over the course of the past few months, but this was the first time she had ventured out alone.

"It must be really hard," said Alison, nodding toward her leg. "I remember I broke my leg once, skiing on a school trip . . . it was a novelty at first, getting out of gym class and having everyone fuss over me. But then it quickly became a boring inconvenience."

"I broke a leg while skiing too," Julia piped up. "Fortunately, it wasn't mine. By the way, your phone's flashing." She pointed at it lying on top of Susan's handbag.

"It'll be Nick." She sighed heavily. "He's already rung me about ten times on the way here, to see if I'm all right. I've put it on silent, as I can't stand hearing it anymore." She picked it up and pressed the answer button. "Hi, darling. Yes, I got here safely. I'll call you later."

"It's nice that he's so worried about you," said Fiona, remembering all too well where Susan's relationship with Nick had been before that fateful day.

"Yes, it is," Susan acknowledged. "But it's also bloody irritating. Hopefully, once I'm fully recovered, things will settle down a bit and I'll be able to leave the house without a search-and-rescue team checking on my every move."

"So when might that be?" Alison peered down at Susan's bandaged foot and looked dubious.

"Not long. The bandage comes off for good next week. Then I just have to wear one of those elastic support socks for a while . . ."

"Sexy!" interrupted Julia.

". . . and then I can start to put weight on my foot without using the cane and, hopefully, attempt a brief vacation. Nick and I thought Florida might be nice. It's the perfect time of year there, in the eighties at the moment . . ."

"Like most of the population," Julia quipped.

Fiona was on her second glass of champagne, and as she looked at Susan she felt the alcohol making her emotional all over again. "I can't believe you're sitting here." She smiled. "Having seen you lying on that road, I wasn't sure if you'd pull through."

"Yes, I was a bit of a mess, wasn't I?" Susan grinned, trying to lighten the mood. She'd spent the past few months surrounded by people with worried expressions, and the last thing she wanted to do was discuss the accident one more time. "But I have bounced back to fight another day." She held up her glass. "*Salut!*"

"*Salut!*" they parroted, and all took a swig.

Susan simply sipped hers and placed it back on the table.

"I suppose you have to be careful, do you?" asked Alison, nodding toward the glass.

"Yes. I find it hard enough keeping my balance as it is, so I'm taking it easy." She smiled before turning to Fiona. "But enough of my woes, I want to hear about someone else's! How's life with Jake?"

Her mouth full of olive bread, Fiona chewed a few times before swallowing. "Knock on wood . . . ," she reached over and tapped the back of Alison's chair, ". . . everything is really good. He's much nicer to me these days, but I think being the keeper of his little drug secret may have something to do with it."

"*May* have?" Julia scoffed. "I'd say it has everything to do with it."

Fiona laughed. "You're probably right. Regardless, it has improved life immeasurably. He even cooked breakfast for us on Sunday."

"Isn't David suspicious as to why you and Jake have suddenly gone from butting heads to a regular lovefest?" asked Alison, looking amused.

"He doesn't seem to be. If he is, he certainly hasn't said so. I think he's just relieved not to be dragged into the middle of our arguments anymore."

"Excellent!" Susan beamed, patting Fiona on the back. "I now have a husband-to-be bending over backward to show how much he adores me, and your stepson is finally toeing the line. What a difference six months can make! Can things *get* any better?"

"Yes, they can!" Julia looked fit to burst. She paused for dramatic effect. "Deborah's pregnant!"

"Wow," said Alison, taken aback. "Who's the father?"

"Paul."

They all looked at her blankly.

"You remember, my friend's brother at my party, the one I introduced her to . . . the black guy."

"Ah, yes!" Fiona nodded, recognition dawning. "Gosh, that's quite quick work, isn't it?"

"I'll say!" Julia was beaming ear to ear, her eyes shining with the scandal of it all. "James came home and told me the other night, and he didn't look too pleased with the news. I couldn't wait for him to leave for work this morning so I could call my friend Jade and get the scoop."

"And?" Fiona raised her eyebrows expectantly.

"And Paul's family are absolutely furious . . . they're *seething*, in fact."

"Why? Just because it's so soon?" Alison looked puzzled.

"A bit of that, yes, but also because his parents had high hopes he'd settle down with a nice black girl, perhaps someone from their local church. Instead, they get the drab, agnostic Deborah, and apparently they feel she has deliberately trapped him."

"Ho-hum." Fiona theatrically patted her palm against her mouth. "I hate all that crap about women trapping men. If he didn't want to become a father, he should have taken responsibility for the situation and worn a condom."

Julia shrugged. "Apparently he's told his family that he did, but it must have been a dodgy one."

"Hmmm." Fiona looked unconvinced. "Sounds sketchy to me. So is he going to stand by her?"

"Yes," mumbled Julia through a mouthful of Caesar salad. "Apparently, he's a very principled man. He's told Jade that after the baby's born, he and Deborah will get married."

"He sounds really decent." Alison had a wistful expression.

"Decent? The man's a fucking saint," said Julia so loudly that a woman at a nearby table shot her a disapproving look. "He's taken Deborah off my hands, and for that I will be eternally grateful."

"It won't stop her and James being friends, though, will it?" asked Fiona.

"Not immediately. But it will mark the beginning of the end. After all, I can't see Paul putting up with James popping in for dodgy haircuts, can you?" Julia rubbed her hands together in glee. "No, my plan has paid off beyond even *my* wildest dreams."

Alison was staring into her champagne glass, a sad look in her eyes.

"You all right?" Fiona touched her arm.

"Fine, thanks. Or no, maybe not. I was just thinking how weird fate can be. Here I am, desperate to have a baby with Luca, I've had the surgery, I'm taking the hormones—which don't exactly make me feel wonderful, by the way—and it *still* doesn't seem to be happening. And here Deborah manages to get pregnant with someone she's known five minutes and wasn't even living with. It just doesn't seem fair, does it? Nature can be very cruel."

"It can indeed," Susan agreed, placing an arm around her shoulders. "But you must try to stay positive. There are other ways to enjoy motherhood, you know, without actually giving birth. What about adoption?"

Alison nodded. "I hear what you're saying, and I do know I have lots in my life to be thankful for, but it's been hard. Luca was so adamantly against IVF that I feel like he'd be even less likely to agree to adoption. He's very opposed to having children and becoming parents by any means that aren't truly natural."

"It won't come to that anyway," said Fiona firmly. "Keep taking the pills, and believe me, you'll soon be wearing the I'M NOT FAT, I'M JUST PREGNANT T-shirt. I can feel it in my bones."

"I hope you're right." Alison forced a smile. "God knows I'm doing everything to maximize my chances . . . temperature charts, peeing on fertility sticks, and lying with my legs in the air after we have sex. It's not exactly spontaneous or romantic, is it?"

Susan laughed. "Who cares? As long as you end up making a baby."

"I wish Luca shared that attitude," Alison said wistfully. "I try to hide most of the shenanigans from him, but I can't really avoid him seeing me with my legs in the air, and he hates it."

"I'm sure he doesn't hate it when your legs are in the air for the sex, though, does he?" Julia snarked. "Tell him to get over himself. God, men are *such* babies. In their world, growing old is mandatory, but growing up seems to be optional."

They all laughed, Alison included.

"So what's James done now?" Susan asked.

Julia rolled her eyes. "He's pressuring me for a baby."

Alison said nothing but threw her hands in the air to indicate that, once again, here was an example of the injustices of married life.

"And you don't want one?" Fiona took another chunk of bread and smeared butter on it.

"Darling, if I *wanted* to hear the pitter-patter of tiny feet, I'd put shoes on the cat . . . if I had one." She took a sip of champagne. "I've told him I'll think about it in the hope he won't mention it again."

"Of *course* he'll mention it again," Fiona scoffed. "Sounds like he's dead set on the idea. The crucial question is, will you give him what he wants?"

"I'll worry about that when the time comes." Julia waved her hand dismissively. "Now can we talk about something else, please? I'm even boring *myself* here."

Taking note of Alison's crestfallen expression, Susan leaned forward and, with some difficulty, hoisted her bandaged foot onto the table. "See that?" she said, meeting Alison's gaze. "*That*, bizarrely, is the best thing that has ever happened to me."

Alison looked puzzled.

"You and Julia don't really know about this," she continued. "But just before the accident, Fiona and I had a coffee together, and I was telling her how unloved I felt, how I thought Nick took me for granted. That's why I decided to go on that trip to Vietnam, because I hoped he would miss me and actually feel moved enough to say so."

She paused a moment and gently lifted her foot back down to the floor. "My accident had an incredible effect on him, and I now have the man I always knew he could be. He's kind, considerate, unbelievably loving, and actually *notices* everything I do. If I could just stop him ringing me every ten minutes, he'd be perfect." She grinned.

"I'm really pleased for you." Alison smiled wistfully.

"The point I'm making," Susan added, "is that six months ago I was in despair about it all, and now I couldn't be happier. Things can change very quickly. And hopefully the same will happen for you."

"Hopefully without the life-threatening accident," added Julia, topping off Alison's champagne glass. She went to fill Susan's, but Susan covered the rim with her hand. "What's the matter? Surely you can have a little bit more without falling over?"

Susan said nothing for a few moments, simply looking at them all, a thoughtful expression on her face. "Look, I wasn't going to say anything because it's very early days, but . . ."

"Oh, my God!" Fiona leapt to her feet. "*You're* pregnant, aren't you?"

Susan nodded, an enormous smile spreading across her face. "Yes. That's why I'm not drinking. Forget the stupid leg!" She laughed.

Fiona and Julia both reached across and embraced her while Alison held back and waited her turn. When it came, she gave Susan a small hug.

"I'm so pleased for you."

Susan winced slightly. "I'm sorry to announce it off the back of what we were just talking about, but I figured you'd have to know sometime. And it's really tough to not share such good news with your friends."

"I'd have been furious if you hadn't told us." Alison did her best to reassure her. "When are you due?"

"Well, that's just it. I'm only about six weeks in, so we're not supposed to be telling anyone until I've passed the three-month mark. I only did the test yesterday, so my doctor doesn't even know yet, and I know he's going to say it's not ideal because of putting so much weight on my leg. But I'll cope." She let out a sigh of contentment. "We had intended to wait until after the wedding before actively trying, but now it seems the wedding will have to wait until after this." She patted her stomach. "I don't want to walk down the aisle looking like I've got a watermelon up my dress."

Fiona couldn't stop grinning. "I'm so, so pleased for you. I know how much you wanted this baby."

Susan turned toward Alison again. "Just before the accident, I had told Nick I wanted to try for a baby. He was really against it and wouldn't be persuaded otherwise, and I poured my heart out to Fiona about it." She popped a cracker in her mouth. "And now look at me. That's why I would say don't get too disheartened about Luca being difficult—because people can and do change their minds about things."

Alison smiled and nodded but stayed quiet, raising her glass with the others in a toast.

"To Susan and Nick's new baby," declared Fiona. "And Ellie's new brother or sister."

"Hear, hear!" cheered Julia. "And here's to Alison's future pregnancy, Fiona's exemplary stepson, and Paul, the man who is the answer to my prayers. Now let's eat, drink, and be merry—for tomorrow we diet!"

the ice man waiteth

Fiona was still smiling about Susan's news when she arrived home and put her key in the front door.

She had stopped at the supermarket on the way home. It was already 6:00 P.M., and David had said he would cook them dinner this evening, but there were no delicious smells assailing her nostrils as she walked through the hallway into the kitchen. It was devoid of any activity, with every saucepan still pristine and hanging from the rack above the butcher-block island cabinets. Perhaps he was waiting for one of the ingredients in her shopping bags? Puzzled, she placed the bags down on the work surface and walked through to the living room. David was sitting with his back to her, in one of the armchairs near the fireplace. He didn't move.

"Hi there," she said casually, glancing around the room. "Where's Lily?"

David's head moved slightly, but he didn't turn round. "Jake's taken her to feed the ducks."

"Oh." She hooked her handbag over one of the dining chairs. "Do you want a drink?"

"No thanks."

She still couldn't see his face, but his voice sounded stiff.

"You okay? You sound a little tense."

This time he turned round and looked directly at her. His expression was stone-cold.

"He told me."

Fiona frowned, genuinely baffled. "Who told you what?"

"Jake," he replied flatly. "He told me all about the little incident at the hospital."

Her insides did a somersault. The secret was finally out, and clearly it hadn't gone down too well. "I see." She tried to sound calm, but inwardly she was panicking, feeling herself losing control of the situation. "So what did he say?"

David looked away and stared down at his bare feet. "He said he's been wanting to tell me ever since it happened, but he's been waiting for the right time."

Fiona was pleased that Jake had finally told his father, but she was disappointed he hadn't called her mobile to warn her before she'd walked into this emotional ambush. "It happened six months ago, Fiona," continued David, his tone furious and measured. "*Six months* ago. Why didn't you tell me?"

She stood stock-still, paralyzed by a mixture of uncertainty and, suddenly, guilt. "Um, I just thought it was up to Jake to tell you about such a big thing in his life," she replied lamely. "You know, he should take responsibility for his actions." Silence. "How did you react when he told you?" She was desperate to move the subject away from her involvement and onto friendlier ground.

"I was very supportive. It's important to be, I think." He stood up and walked across to the window, his short, graying black hair looking slightly unkempt. "I want him to know he can always tell me things, especially when he's in trouble . . . and not to have any secrets."

"Absolutely." She nodded supportively, trying to keep the mood light, but she knew what was coming next.

"And then I find out that he hasn't kept it totally secret, that my wife has been in on it and just hasn't bothered to tell me!" His tone was anguished and accusatory.

Fiona lowered her eyes and stared into the depths of her handbag, wishing she could jump inside and disappear from view. "As I said, I felt it was his place to tell you, not mine."

David spun round, his eyes blazing. "He's my *son*, Fiona. And you're supposed to be my wife. What on earth were you thinking of?"

It annoyed her that the more important issue of Jake taking drugs was being overtaken by the rights or wrongs of her own behavior, but she didn't say so. She understood that David was angry with her—this was hardly unexpected, after all—and she just needed to let him get it off his chest.

"It's complicated," she answered carefully, running a hand through her hair. "My absolute, overpowering instinct was to tell you straightaway. In fact, as I recall, I left a message on your mobile phone . . . admittedly a vague one. But Jake begged me not to. I felt stuck in the middle. If I didn't say anything, I was letting you down. If I did say something, I was letting him down at a really crucial stage in what you know has been a very difficult relationship."

His expression was less angry now, but his eyes still regarded her with suspicion. "I could have pretended not to know."

"Could you?" She looked at him questioningly. "Could you *really* have been told that Jake had taken Ecstasy and wound up in hospital and not have said anything to him?"

"Yes. But you've only got my word for that, haven't you?" he said sarcastically.

She took a step toward him but thought better of reaching out and touching him. "David, I'm truly, truly sorry. But I had to make a decision at the time, and if you think it was the wrong one, then I apologize. I saw an opportunity to help repair the relationship between me and Jake, to make this family stronger, and I took it. All I can say is that it was only ever done with the best of intentions."

His mouth was still set in a firm line. "You deprived me of the chance to help my son when he needed me the most," he said bitterly.

"Oh, come on, David, that's a bit harsh."

"Really?" He looked defiant. "Fast-forward a few years and put the shoe on the other foot. Imagine it's Lily in hospital for the same thing and I kept it from *you*. That would be fine, would it?"

She hadn't thought of it that way, and the analogy hit her with full force. "No, I'd be horrified," she whispered.

"Precisely!" bellowed David, slamming his fist down on the coffee table with such venom that it made her jump. "God, I'm so bloody *angry* with you!"

Fiona stared at him with abject horror. David had never so much as raised his voice at her before. This violent outburst was totally out of character, and it unnerved her.

"Look," she beseeched, taking another step toward him and trying to look conciliatory, "I have clearly messed up big-time here, but all I can say is that it wasn't done with any malice . . . how could it be? I love you."

He looked at her, and the cold indifference in his eyes made her breath catch in her throat.

"If that's love, then you can keep it," he said in a low voice.

"Don't be like that . . . please." She moved toward him, her arms extended, but he took a sharp step backward, recoiling from her gesture.

"Don't. I need time to think."

"Think about what?" A cold panic was creeping across her flesh. Even the anger was preferable to this.

He walked over to the side cabinet and opened the top left-hand drawer where they kept the spare car keys. The originals were still in Fiona's handbag.

"Can I take the car?" he asked, looking everywhere but directly at her.

"Yes, of course, you . . . can . . . you don't have to ask," she faltered, frowning slightly. "David, what's happening?"

Distractedly, he threw the keys a few inches into the air and caught them again. "I'm going to go away for a couple of days to do some serious thinking."

"Thinking about *what?*" she repeated, the cold panic giving way to nausea.

"To think about whether I want to continue in this marriage." This time he looked straight at her.

Fiona felt disoriented, like a child who's been blindfolded and spun round, the ground seeming to give way under her feet. She blinked rapidly, a look of deep puzzlement on her face. "David! I don't get it. What are you saying? You're acting like I've had an affair or something."

"Same problem in a way," he replied matter-of-factly, wandering around the room, stuffing some paperwork and two books into a duffel bag. "An affair is all about deceit, and so is withholding important information like this."

Under any other circumstances, Fiona would have guffawed loudly at what she perceived to be such a ludicrous comparison, but she felt winded by the sight of the husband she adored packing his bag to leave her . . . temporarily or otherwise. "You can't be serious" was all she could manage.

"Deadly serious," he retorted quickly. "Trust is an incredibly important part of a marriage, and when you start keeping secrets from each other . . . well . . ." He trailed off, reaching down the side of the armchair to retrieve another duffel, this one full of clothes.

Fiona almost choked. "I see you were planning to go regardless of what explanation I gave."

He smiled, but it didn't reach his eyes. "That's because I knew there *wasn't* an explanation that would make everything okay. God knows I played it over and over in my head enough times, trying to think of one, *hoping* I could think of one. I can't for the life of me imagine how you could have made such a colossal error in judgment. Jake is *my* son, and as parents, we're supposed to be a team. It's unfathomable."

She collapsed onto the sofa, a wave of hopelessness washing over her. Her fighting spirit had abandoned her.

She sat there for what seemed like an eternity, with David moving around behind her, presumably gathering whatever things he needed for his time away.

"Don't think I'm doing this lightly," he said into the middle distance. "I was on the verge of staying here and trying to work things out for the sake of Lily. But in the same way I knew it would be wrong to go back to Belinda just because of Jake, I've decided I *should* take time away from here . . . away from you . . . to think things through." There was no more conversation, only the loud hum of the washing machine coming from the kitchen. Then the sound of the doorbell.

"I'll get it," said David, somewhat irrelevantly as he was already near the door and Fiona hadn't moved.

She heard the door open and the voices of David and Jake speaking quietly. Then Lily shrieked "Mummy!" excitedly, stirring Fiona from her subdued reverie.

"Darling!" She stood up, arms outstretched, as the little girl burst into the room and ran toward her. Scooping her up, Fiona pulled her in close and inhaled the sweet smell that had become such a drug to her. "How were the ducks?"

"They thad," she lisped.

"Oh dear. Poor things." I know the feeling, thought Fiona ruefully.

David walked back into the room, followed by Jake, who looked white as a sheet.

"I told Dad," he said unnecessarily.

"I know." She smiled, not bearing him any ill will for it.

"And I'm really glad you did." David ruffled his son's hair affectionately, and for one brief, wonderful moment Fiona felt that everything might be fine, that the chilly spell was about to blow over.

"Mummy?" Lily was tugging at her jacket. "Juice."

"Yes, sweetie, okay. Mummy will get it for you in a minute." The little girl wandered off, and Fiona turned back to face Jake and David. "She'll look like a grape soon."

Jake smiled, but David's face remained impassive, his eyes telling her that no, everything wasn't fine and he was still hell-bent on leaving.

He turned to his son. "Come on, get your stuff. I'll drop you back at your mother's."

Jake looked puzzled. "I thought I was staying here tonight."

"Change of plan." David handed him his army jacket from the arm of the sofa. "Fiona and I need some time on our own tonight."

"I see." Jake narrowed his eyes in suspicion. "There's nothing wrong, is there? It's not to do with what happened, is it?"

He looked imploringly at Fiona, but David cut in first. "Don't be silly, of course not. We've just got a few things we need to discuss, that's all."

Fiona could see he'd positioned his two duffels by the door, so he'd have them with him after he'd dropped Jake off and driven to wherever it was he was planning to stay.

She knew it was now or never to stop him from going.

"Come on, David," she piped up. "Jake's old enough to know the truth, isn't he? We shouldn't keep secrets from him."

David scowled at her, his cheeks twitching with discomfort.

"What truth? What secrets?" Jake was looking from one to the other.

"Your dad is leaving me for a few days," she continued, never taking her eyes from her husband's face. "He's livid with me for not telling him about what happened to you."

"Dad, is that true? Where are you going?" Jake's eyes were wide with anxiety. He stood in the doorway, blocking his father's exit.

David let out a small sigh. "It's no big deal, Jake. I just want a little time on my own to think things through." He looked over his shoulder and shot Fiona a murderous look, before turning back. "Come on, let's get going."

But Jake didn't move. "It's not her fault. I asked her not to tell you, *begged* her, in fact."

"So she said," replied David crisply. "But that's not the issue."

"Then what is?"

Fiona resisted the urge to run across the room and hug him for asking the right question.

"It's complicated," muttered David, stooping down to pick up the duffel bags.

"What, too complicated for a sixteen-year-old to understand? Don't treat me like a kid."

His father wearily placed the bags back on the floor. "I'm not. It's just that some things are best kept private between a husband and wife."

"But this isn't strictly private, is it? This is about me and the fact that Fiona helped me through something you didn't know about."

He looked worried. "I don't want to be the cause of trouble between you."

"You're not, believe me."

Fiona raised her eyebrows at this blatant lie but stayed silent. The initial feeling of nausea had passed, and she was beginning to feel faintly annoyed by what she saw as David's theatrics.

"Don't worry about it, Jake," she said softly. "Let your dad go. I think we could all do with a cooling-down period. We can sort it out another time."

"Are you sure?" Jake looked at her plaintively. "I'm so sorry. If I had known this would happen, I would never have told Dad. I would have kept it secret forever."

She walked across the room and held out her arms, enveloping him in a hug. "As I said, don't fret over it. It was very responsible of you to tell him. You did absolutely the right thing."

"Did I?" Jake looked at his father for validation.

"You did." He smiled weakly, patting the top of his arm. "Now come on, go get anything you need from your bedroom, and we'll talk some more in the car."

This time Jake did as he was told and went upstairs. Neither David nor Fiona spoke until they heard the familiar creak of the floorboards overhead.

"Right then." David's voice was cold again. "I won't make a fuss of leaving with Lily around. Just tell her I had to go to work."

"No problem," she said icily. "You know me, the queen of deceit. It'll be easy."

He ignored her and walked out into the hallway, opening the front door and peering out toward the car.

"I'll be in touch when I've had time to think."

"Fine." Her voice sounded flat as she struggled to stop herself from reacting in a way she might later regret. She wanted to scream and wail, to pummel his back and shoulders in a burst of anger at his damned pigheadedness and stupidity. But instead she used all her emotional resources to retain a calm exterior. "We'll be here."

With that, she stepped back into the living room and closed the door, biting her lip and trying not to cry.

The tears of regret and frustration would come later, after Lily had gone to bed.

i'm alison, fly me

Gazing out of the cab window, Alison sighed with contentment as she took in the sights of Marrakech.

She loved it here. Its vibrancy and quirkiness made her feel she'd stepped straight onto the set of an Indiana Jones movie, with the stalls in the main square offering goat's head soup or the chance to be photographed with a monkey on a chain.

Pulling up outside the splendid Art Deco entrance of La Mamounia Hotel, she paid and tipped the driver and made her way inside the cool, marbled foyer, bustling with liveried staff and well-heeled guests clutching tourist maps.

She was here to meet Luca, who had traveled out a couple of days earlier for a business meeting with a Moroccan telecommunications company that was looking to update its system.

Usually his destinations were so dreary that she resisted the invitation to join him, but this one was a treat, and she'd jumped at his suggestion that she fly out for a short getaway once his business was concluded.

But unbeknownst to her husband, Alison had another, far stronger motive for her last-minute dash to the airport. Last night's fertility stick had indicated that today was a chance to conceive, and she was determined not to miss it.

Smiling at the concierge, she took the key Luca had left for her and made her way up to the room overlooking the swimming pool at the back of the hotel. It was a cloudless day with a china-blue sky, and the lounge chairs were packed with guests, some already a deep bronze color, others so white they looked pale blue. There'll be a few sore noses and shoulders in the bar tonight, she thought, smiling to herself as she unpacked her small suitcase containing enough clothes for a two-night stay.

She glanced at her watch: 5:00 P.M. Luca would be back at any moment, and being the sun worshiper he was, he was sure to suggest they go down to the pool to catch the last of the sun's rays, particularly now that they weren't quite so brutal as earlier in the day.

But Alison had other plans. She wanted sex, and her matching black lace underwear had been put on with the full intention of maximizing her chances of making it happen.

Usually Luca needed no persuading to make love. But lately, she'd noticed, he'd become slightly less enthusiastic, even occasionally rejecting her advances, saying he was too stressed, too tired, too hot, too cold.

When it happened, Alison was happy to let it rest, unless it was her fertile time. Then she persisted until he relented and they had perfunctory sex. Once or twice they'd even argued about it, with her pointing out that if they wanted a baby, then they had to have sex at her peak times.

He had replied that the sex-on-demand ritual was making him feel uncomfortable, that he wanted to make love spontaneously, not follow a timetable. After that, Alison had tried to make her demands seem spur-of-the-moment, but Luca was no fool. He said he could easily tell the difference between their normal lovemaking, at a time when there was little or no chance of Alison conceiving, and the more emotionally charged fertile period when, he said, there was quite clearly an intensity and urgency to her that wasn't apparent at other times.

But they were muddling through, and each time Alison's period started and she felt the bitter thud of disappointment, she would pick herself up, think positive, and carry on trying.

That was why she had made the enormous effort to fly out to Marrakech. The fertile times were few and far between, and she felt there was no time to lose.

She heard a tap on the hotel door and padded across the room to open it. There stood her strikingly handsome husband. "Hello, darling." She kissed him and stood aside to let him pass. "Good meeting?"

"Not bad. Not bad at all." Luca removed his tie and jacket and hung them in the wardrobe. "They'll let me know whether I've got the contract by next week. Good flight?"

"Yes, thanks."

He stooped down in front of the minibar and took out a Perrier water, which he glugged down in one go, the liquid running down his chin. Reaching into a drawer, he pulled out a pair of trunks. "Come on, let's go down to the pool. It's gorgeous out, and I'm dying for a swim. It'll cool me down." He removed his shirt and trousers and folded them over a chair, then wriggled out of his boxer shorts.

Alison walked up behind him and cupped his penis in her hand. "Hmmmm, you look great naked," she murmured in his ear. "Can't the pool wait?"

She felt him go rigid everywhere except his penis. "Is that why you're here?" he said quietly.

"Sorry?" She knew exactly what he meant.

"Are you here because it's your fertile time?" he persisted, stepping away from her and pulling on his swimming shorts.

"No. Well, yes . . ." she faltered. "It *is* my fertile time, but that's not why I'm here. I thought it would be nice for us to spend some quality time together, you know, relax a little."

"Yes, I know exactly what you mean." His face was impassive. "I was hoping we'd relax too, but instead you're acting like a bitch in heat."

She recoiled slightly at the coarseness of his remark. "Are you calling me a bitch?"

"I didn't mean it like that," he said wearily. "And you know it."

Alison sighed and flopped down onto the bed with an air of resignation. She patted the space to the side of her. "Come and sit down a minute."

With an air of reluctance, he walked across and sat next to her, leaving a two-foot gap between them. She shuffled closer and placed an arm round his shoulders.

"You *do* want us to have a baby, don't you?"

"You know I do."

"Well, that's what I'm trying to make happen," she said, with sadness in her eyes. "That's why I had surgery, and why I'm taking hormones, taking temperatures, mapping out timetables, peeing on fertility sticks . . ." She paused, wrong-footed slightly by the sight of Luca wincing at the excess of information.

". . . and flying out to Marrakech at my most opportune time," she continued. "I'm doing *all* of that for one reason . . . I want to get pregnant. And I want to get pregnant with you because I'm madly in love with you. Yet you seem to be judging me rather harshly because of it."

He continued to stare at the small patch of floor visible between his bare feet, his body facing forward. "I'm not *judging* you, Alison, I'm just not comfortable with the deliberateness of all this. I told you that before, and I haven't changed my mind."

Alison stared at the plastic panel on the back of the hotel room door telling guests where to assemble in the event of a fire. She was desperate to have sex, fearful that her fertility was dwindling by the second, but she also knew it was important to pursue their conversation and try to clear the air a little.

"I thought you were only uncomfortable with the thought of having to give sperm for the IVF," she said quietly. "Now that you don't have to do that, I assumed everything would be all right."

He interlocked his fingers and upturned his palms, studying them intently. "It is . . . kind of . . . ," he said hesitantly, ". . . if I don't think too deeply about those stick things and the pills, I am fine with it. It's just the sex to order that makes me feel awkward. It takes the pleasure out of it."

Alison said nothing, simply raising her eyebrows slowly and keeping them there. "I know it's stupid for a grown man to feel like that," he conceded, "and I know we're having sex to order for all the right reasons, but I'm sorry, that's just how I feel." They lapsed into silence for a few seconds, the only sound that of happy holidaymakers splashing around in the pool below, probably with their beautiful, effortlessly and naturally conceived children, Alison thought bitterly.

In truth, she wanted to slap one of his cheeks, then the other, repeatedly, until he realized what his stubborn, macho attitude was doing to the woman he professed to love. But she loved him too, and for that reason alone she knew that *she* would have to be the mature one and bury her misgivings.

There was so much more she still wanted to say, so many arguments she could make in an effort to change his views. But she also

knew from experience that Luca was too stubborn to come around
to anyone else's perspective, too convinced that his opinion was always the right one. So she changed tack.

"So I suppose a shag's out of the question then?" She smiled and
looked at him coquettishly.

He looked stunned for a moment, then, clearly grateful that the
conversation had moved onto easier ground, let a broad grin spread
across his face. "Oh, I don't know. I reckon I could muster the
strength!"

Alison felt a wave of relief wash over her. Perhaps everything was
going to be fine after all. "Glad to hear it." She turned to face him
and snaked her arm behind his head, pulling him to her for a kiss. It
started gently, then progressed rapidly to a passionate urgency.

Soon, Luca was tugging at her beach cover-up, the buttons yield-
ing easily until her specially chosen underwear was exposed. Glancing down, Alison noted with satisfaction that he was visibly aroused.

"Hmmm, *cara mia*," he murmured, edging his hand into the top
of her lacy thong and starting to remove it.

Alison lay back, a dreamy smile on her face. She had a good feeling about this, a gut instinct that this might just be the time their
first child was conceived. She felt a rush of euphoria.

Suddenly, Luca's fingers stopped working their magic and he sat
up. The hotel phone was ringing.

"Leave it," Alison murmured, pressing her hand on the back of
his head to push him down again.

He nodded and moved back into position, then stopped again. "I
can't. It might be important."

Looking faintly annoyed, Alison propped herself up on her elbows and looked down at him. "Whoever it is will leave a message,
and you can call them back."

It never ceased to amaze her how Luca could never leave a phone to ring. She, on the other hand, rarely answered a call, preferring to screen her messages and cherry-pick who she called back.

He was standing up now, having picked up the receiver. "Hello?"

Alison stared at him as he listened to whoever was on the other end of the phone. His penis was standing at attention, ready for action, packed full with all that sperm waiting within . . . waiting to start their journey up inside her, into her fallopian tubes and, hopefully, through the wall of an egg.

Closing her eyes, she tried desperately to block it out and think of something sexy instead, something to keep her passion simmering until Luca returned. But she needn't have bothered.

Hearing him replace the receiver, she opened her eyes and smiled at him. "Now then, where were we?"

"Sorry, I've got to go." He looked distracted.

"Go?" She sat upright. "Go where?"

"Back home. That was Sofia. Paolo has broken his arm; she's at the hospital with him now."

Coma, yes. Meningitis, of course. Even an unexplained high fever might warrant it. But dropping everything and flying home because of a broken arm? Alison didn't get it.

"Can't she deal with it on her own?"

Luca was hastily throwing his things into his suitcase, scanning the room for anything he might have missed. "He's asking for his daddy. I have to be there."

"She told you that, did she?" She didn't mean to sound scathing, but she couldn't help it.

"Yes." He looked at her strangely. "But I'm sure it's true. After all, why *wouldn't* he want to see me when he is so upset? He must be scared, poor little guy."

Alison knew she was on sensitive ground here, so she backtracked slightly. "Darling, of course he'd want to see you. But he could say that anytime and you can't be at his beck and call every second of the day. If his mother was a little less hysterical, she'd console him herself and simply tell him that he'll see you when you get back from your business trip."

Luca started to get dressed, pulling on a T-shirt and cargo pants and bending down to tie the laces on his Prada trainers. "You don't seem to understand," he said firmly. "I'm not having my strings pulled by Sofia here, I want to go and see my son. It's *my* decision."

She considered what he'd said for a few seconds, then felt an overwhelming sense of weariness. Standing up, she picked up her cover-up and started to put it on.

"Well, there's not much point in me staying here alone, is there? I might as well come with you."

He shook his head. "No, I'll have to pay for the room and flights anyway, so it's pointless wasting them. You stay here and enjoy it." He gestured outside. "Look, there's a wonderful pool and the weather is glorious."

"*Enjoy* it?" she parroted. "How can I when I came all the way here to see you and you're buggering off back home?"

"With good reason," he retorted sharply. "And by the way, just in case you're interested, he broke his arm falling off a slide. You never bothered to ask." Picking up his suitcase, he headed for the door. "I'll call you later. Ciao."

After the door had slammed shut, Alison sat stock-still on the bed, staring into space. A few seconds later, the first tear trickled down her nose and fell onto her bare leg, followed shortly by several more. Her distress was silent but heartfelt. The dull thud of disappointment was matched by the searing pain of her longing for a baby that she was beginning to doubt she would ever hold in her arms.

By the time she saw Luca again, another opportunity would have passed and the wait would begin for the next, a wait she wasn't sure she had the strength to endure.

Dealing with her husband's discomfort over her infertility was bad enough, but the telephone call that had just terminated their valuable time together had been yet another uncomfortable reminder that, as long as the first Mrs. Rossi walked the planet, the second Mrs. Rossi would never be allowed to forget it.

And that as long as Luca's precious firstborn son walked the planet, any child Alison managed to conceive might suffer the same fate too.

out with the old, in with the new

"Mummy, here you go. Bekfast," said a muffled voice from behind the bedroom door. There was the thud of a foot against wood, then Ellie walked in carrying a small tray. In pride of place right in the center was a jam jar with a dandelion in it, flanked by a plate of bread and butter and a glass of water.

"My goodness, this looks sooooo yummy." Susan beamed, taking the tray and placing it on the bedside table. She pulled Ellie onto the bed for a hug and buried her face in her hair, inhaling her sweet scent. "You're such a good girl, do you know that?"

Out of the corner of her eye she could see Nick edging into the room carrying another tray. "This is *my* breakfast," he said, winking at her when Ellie wasn't looking. "You can share some if you like, once you've had yours, of course."

She noted there were two rounds of bacon sandwiches and two

steaming cups of coffee. "Thank you, but first things first." She took a bite of the bread and a sip of the water. "Hmmmmm, delicious!"

Ellie beamed with pleasure. "I told Daddy you'd like mine better. I need to go pee-pee now."

After she'd padded out of the bedroom, Susan grimaced and hid the plate of bread and butter under the bed, reaching across to grab a bacon sandwich. "Thanks." She smiled.

Munching away, she studied Nick as he watched the morning's news headlines on the television perched on the corner of the bed. He looked the same, he dressed the same, and he sounded the same, but in every other way he was a completely different man since her accident.

The promises he'd made in hospital had been genuine, unlike so many who utter platitudes in times of distress, then swiftly return to their old ways. Before, it would never have crossed his mind that *he* could be the one to rise early on a Saturday and make the breakfast while she lingered snugly under the covers.

But thankfully, there were still traces of the old Nick that reassured her. He still dropped his dirty socks on the bathroom floor, still had the revolting habit of leaving his toenail clippings on the arm of the sofa, and still needed a map to find the washing machine. She didn't want him to be *too* perfect.

"Okay?" She leaned forward and rubbed the back of his neck.

"Fine, thanks. You?" He took hold of her hand and held it to his mouth, showering it with small kisses. It was done humorously but was still totally out of character from the Nick of a few months ago.

Ellie sauntered back in again, her nightgown tucked in the back of her underpants, dragging her beloved "blanky" with her. Actually, it was beloved blanky number two, as the first one had been accidentally left behind during a holiday to Cornwall and Nick had embarked on a frantic search of baby shops to find another. But Ellie didn't know that.

"Now then, while Ellie and I were making breakfast, we came up with a little plan, didn't we, sugar?" He grabbed his daughter and pulled her onto his knee.

"Did we?" Like most six-year-olds, she'd forgotten whatever it was that had been discussed just a few minutes ago.

"Yes, you remember," he persisted, rolling his eyes at Susan behind Ellie's back. "We made a plan for the weekends."

Ellie's eyes lit up. "Yes, we did, we did!" She jumped off his lap and ran round to Susan's side of the bed, throwing herself across the duvet in unbridled excitement. "It's *your* turn!"

"My turn?" Susan looked puzzled. "My turn to do what?"

"To choose what we do." Ellie's voice sounded shaky because she was jumping up and down as she said it.

Nick smiled at his daughter benevolently. "Ellie and I have decided that, from now on, each of us will take turns choosing what we do on a Saturday. It might be a day at a museum . . ."

"Ugh, boooooring!" interrupted Ellie, her head lolling to one side.

Nick tutted at her. ". . . or going swimming at the pool . . ."

"Yeeeeessss!" Her little fist punched the air.

"Basically, we do exactly what the person whose turn it is chooses to do," he added. "And today that person is . . . ," he circled his finger theatrically before pointing at Susan, ". . . you."

"*Moi?*" She placed a palm against her chest. "Well, I'm honored. Let's see now . . ."

"Swimming, swimming, swimming," chanted Ellie.

"Ellie!" Nick admonished. "Let Mummy choose for herself."

"I know!" Susan put her coffee cup down and sat up straight. "I'd like to take a picnic to St. James's Park. They have some lovely birds there, and we can feed them afterward with any leftovers."

"Yippee, a picnic!" Clearly, the choice had gone down well with Ellie. Nick rubbed his hands together. "Good, that's settled then. And tomorrow we can just chill out at home." He stood up and walked across to Ellie, who was pirouetting around the bedroom.

"Come on, poppet. Let's get you out of your nightgown and into something befitting a picnic."

"What does beef . . . beef . . . itting mean?"

"Follow me and I'll explain." He grabbed her hand and led her out of the bedroom.

Susan smiled to herself after they'd gone, settling back against the pillows, deep in thought.

She didn't want to tempt fate, but she could safely say she had never felt as happy as she did right at this moment. Placing a hand on her stomach, she thought about the baby growing inside her, the baby who would be a brother or sister to Ellie, the baby that would complete the circle of their family life.

Nick had thrown himself wholeheartedly into her pregnancy, buying books he thought might interest her, bringing home catalogs of baby products they might buy. In keeping with his "new man" persona, he had made it his business to learn all about the events that lay ahead. He'd already been through it once with Caitlin, to be sure, but he seemed determined to use Susan's pregnancy as yet another opportunity to show her that he had changed.

Truth be told, the transformation had been instant, starting on the day she'd stirred from her coma. When she'd arrived home, the first thing she'd noticed, as soon as she walked in the front door, was that the oil painting of Caitlin was no longer staring down at her.

"It's gone," she'd stated, looking up at the blank space of wall. Only the nail was left.

"Yes. I thought Bill and Genevieve would like it," Nick replied matter-of-factly. "It now has pride of place in their living room."

Grateful tears had pricked Susan's eyes, but she'd said nothing, struggling to compose herself. As she moved through the downstairs rooms and noticed that every photograph of Caitlin had been removed, the floodgates opened and she'd wept. "Thank you, but you don't have to eradicate her completely, you know."

"I haven't," he'd said softly. "There are still lots of pictures of her in Ellie's room and one pinned to the noticeboard in the kitchen. And she's still in the albums on the shelf over there. So she's there if you want to look for her, just not thrust in your face anymore."

Susan had shaken her head slowly, almost unable to comprehend that what she had wanted for so long had finally happened. Caitlin had not been erased from Nick's life, but she had taken a step back and become someone from the past. A much-loved, never-forgotten someone, but nonetheless someone who wasn't coming back and had less of an overwhelming presence in their day-to-day lives.

"I'll always love her, and I'll always want to keep her memory alive for Ellie, but my life is with you now, Susan. One hundred percent." Then he'd pulled her close and held her with such an intensity that she thought she might faint through sheer relief and happiness. Remembering that moment now, Susan felt her throat tightening with emotion. In the next room, she could hear Nick's muffled voice, telling Ellie to put on some shorts for the park.

A few months ago, it would undoubtedly have been Susan dressing her. And even in the unlikely event that Nick had troubled himself to do it, there would have been endless to-ing and fro-ing while he asked Susan where Ellie's shorts were kept or which shoes she should wear.

Susan now realized that because she'd rushed to help him out right after Caitlin's death, she had been so concerned about his grief that she'd perhaps done a little too much in looking after Ellie and

Nick had never really learned how to manage with her himself. Susan's accident and subsequent long stay in hospital had been a trial by fire for him. Ellie had stayed with Bill and Genevieve while Susan was unconscious, but after that she'd returned home and Nick had found himself having to bathe and dress her, cook for her, and rush in to stroke her hair when she woke crying in the night from a bad dream.

"You must have been absolutely exhausted all the time," he'd told Susan shortly after she'd returned home. "Because I know I am. Being with a child so much is trying, but it's also amazing. I can't believe what I've been missing," He'd had tears in his eyes as he said it. "The mundane time you spend with children is so much more rewarding than all the razzle-dazzle stuff. I'm ashamed to say that I've only really gotten to know my daughter these past few weeks."

And with Susan home convalescing, he'd had to look after her too because she could barely walk a few steps without his help.

Now the only visible sign of her injury was the elastic sock covering the lower part of her leg and the slight limp she hoped to rectify after a few more sessions of physical therapy. She did her exercises religiously, anxious to strengthen her leg enough to cope with the growing weight of the pregnancy.

She was now nearly eight weeks gone. Another four and they planned to tell Ellie, a moment Susan could hardly wait for. She knew the little girl was going to embrace the news wholeheartedly, and Susan planned to involve her every step of the way. Like all women pregnant for the first time, she was especially chomping at the bit to go out and buy a few bits and pieces. But she was saving it so she and Ellie could go shopping for baby clothes together.

The phone rang, stirring her from her reverie. Usually Nick was as fast as Billy the Kid in picking up the receiver, but after a couple of rings she realized he wasn't going to and did it herself.

"Hello?"

"Hi there, it's Alison."

Fiona, Julia, and Susan were always calling each other for long phone chats between meetings of the club, but it was only since Susan's accident that Alison had felt she knew them well enough to do the same.

"What a lovely surprise! Can you believe I'm still in bed?"

"Are you ill?" Alison sounded concerned.

"No, no, just lazy!" Susan laughed. "How was Marrakech?"

"Disastrous. Sofia called to say that Paolo had broken his arm, and Luca was on the plane home before you could say 'No sex for Alison.' "

"Oh, you poor thing." Susan felt her frustration. "So you must have barely stepped foot on Moroccan soil before you were on your way back here?"

"No, I stayed. Luca suggested I should, and when I thought about it, it did seem silly for both of us to miss out on a holiday. Besides, I didn't want to give bloody Sofia the pleasure."

"But wasn't it, you know . . . that time?" Susan asked. Alison had told her during a quick chat the day before she'd left.

"Yep." Alison sighed. "Another one down the drain. I even found myself looking longingly at the rather handsome pool man, wondering if he'd get me pregnant and I could just tell Luca I'd gotten my dates wrong."

Susan laughed. "Bide your time. It'll happen, you'll see."

"God, I hope so, or I might be up in court soon for snatching someone else's baby from outside the supermarket. I'm *that* desperate. Anyway, I'll let you get dressed, you lazy girl. Talk later."

Susan replaced the receiver and counted her blessings yet again.

"Mummy?" Ellie had wandered back into the bedroom wearing only her shorts. "I want to wear my reindeer sweater, and Daddy won't let me."

"That's because it's going to be a sunny day, darling." Susan smiled. "You'd boil."

"What, like an egg?"

"Yes, just like an egg. You should wear a T-shirt."

"Okay." She seemed to accept the explanation and wandered back out again, passing Nick on the way.

"I think she's gone to get a T-shirt," said Susan.

"Well done." He grinned, lying down on the bed next to her and propping himself up on his elbow. "Ducks, here we come. Though I'm not sure they'll be too impressed with our moldy old white sliced stuff. It's quite posh round there, they're probably more used to organic wholemeal."

She smiled. "In which case, they might like a change. Anyway, whose turn is it to choose next weekend?"

"Ellie's. Which means we'll undoubtedly start with lunch at Pizza Express followed by swimming. Or maybe the other way round . . . and then it's my turn."

"Any thoughts yet? And *please* don't say we have to go to the bloody football match. There are limits, you know."

"Yes, I do know *exactly* what we'll be doing, and no, you'll be glad to hear it's not that."

"Oh? Go on, I'm intrigued."

He sat up slightly so his face was just centimeters away from hers. "Bill and Genevieve are coming to get Ellie and take her swimming . . . ," he kissed her on the mouth briefly, ". . . then she's going back to their house to stay the night . . . ," he kissed her again, ". . . and then I'm going to make love to you all day and all night." He kissed her longer and harder this time.

"Yuck!" Ellie was back, wearing a Minnie Mouse T-shirt and standing by the side of their bed. "You're kissing!"

"We are indeed," said Nick mildly. "And if you come here, I'll give you a big sloppy kiss too."

He lunged at her and grabbed her left arm as she shrieked with excitement, wriggling around and trying to escape.

His lips puckered, Nick made loud, slurping noises and pulled her toward him, planting a wet kiss on the side of her face.

"Get off!" she screamed, giggling helplessly.

Her laughter was infectious, and Susan sat there, smiling warmly at her surprise family and thinking that, God willing, their future together was going to be a stable, happy one.

here we babygro again

Julia reached into the Kent & Carey shopping bag and pulled out a little blue-and-white-striped Babygro sleep-suit with matching cotton hat.

"Oooh, makes you melt, doesn't it?" the woman in the shop had said as she was gift-wrapping it.

"No, not in the slightest," Julia had replied with a quick smile.

The woman had looked at her curiously after that, as if she were somehow a freak, an abnormality among the throngs of womanhood.

Am I abnormal? Julia thought now, holding the outfit up in front of her, twisting and turning it so she could view it from every angle.

Nope. Nothing. Not so much as a minuscule tweak in her ovaries. As far as she was concerned, it was what it was—a garment for one of those small things that cried and pooped a lot.

Sighing, she placed it back in the middle of the piece of blue tis-sue paper laid to one side and topped it off, exquisitely, with a blue bow. Whatever task Julia set her mind to she always carried out with perfection, but motherhood felt beyond her, a project of such enormity and longevity that it made her feel queasy.

On the occasions she thought about it these days, usually after yet another overture from James, she sincerely hoped that one day she would wake up and get that feeling other women often spoke of, that overpowering urge to create and nurture another human being. But unless she felt that passion for the cause, there was no way Julia was going to allow society—or James—to pressure her into embarking on something she didn't feel ready for. Particularly as she knew that, despite his protestations to the contrary, James's life would be the least affected by it.

He'd still go to work every day, still have his coffee made by his secretary, still enjoy à la carte "business" lunches and be surrounded by adult conversation, while she would be left juggling everything at home, eating cold meals with one hand and trying to seem stimulated by a little person whose vocabulary wouldn't stretch far past *wee-wee* and *poo-poo*. Or that's how she saw it anyway.

Placing the present on the shelf by the kitchen door, she turned back to the oven with a huge grin on her face, the same one that had been bolted there for most of the day, ever since James had called midmorning to say that Deborah had given birth to a baby boy.

Game over, thought Julia for the umpteenth time as she removed the honey-roasted parsnips from the oven and expertly flipped them over.

Now she'd had a baby by someone else, there was no *way* Deborah would continue to exert such a strong influence over James's life. She'd be occupied with changing diapers and planning nursery schools, too exhausted by sleepless nights, too wrapped up in her new life with Paul to make endless demands on James and his time. Or so Julia hoped.

Humming happily to herself, she turned down the flame under

the pan-fried steaks and wiped her hands on her apron before removing it and tucking it back in the drawer along with a pile of washed
and ironed tea towels. Oh, the joy of having a good housekeeper.
She glanced at the clock: 7:00 P.M. James would be back at any moment.

Checking her hair in the mirrored panel behind the range, she
smoothed down her skirt and double-checked the table. She had
made a special effort to make it look romantic this evening, the start
of their brave new world without Deborah's shadow lurking over
their shoulders. There was a pristine white tablecloth, three smoked-
glass night lights flickering down the middle, and a low, square glass
vase stuffed with a dozen red roses.

"Hello, darling!" she trilled as she heard the key in the lock and
the familiar thud as James put his briefcase down on the wooden
floor in the hallway. "Dinner is almost ready."

"Hi." He smiled as he strolled into the room but looked hollow-
eyed and tired. Walking across to give her a rather lackluster peck
on the cheek, he scanned the table. "Wow, you've outdone yourself."

"No, not really," she replied hastily. "I had a little bit more time
than usual, so thought I'd put it to good use."

"I see." He let out a long sigh as he flopped into his usual chair at
the head of the table.

Julia poured them both a glass of chilled French chardonnay and
placed a platter of Parma ham and assorted salamis in the center of
the table.

"So. Good day?" she said brightly.

"So-so." He shrugged. "What about you?"

"I got lots of paperwork done, and I managed to get to the dry
cleaners with your dinner suit, but I really don't know where the time
went. Oh, and while I was out I bought a present for Deborah's new
baby." She jerked her head toward the shelf where the present lay.

He glanced over toward it but didn't look terribly interested.

"It's a Babygro," she added. "You know, one of those all-in-one sleepsuits that babies wear."

"Yes, I know what a Babygro is." He pinched a large piece of Parma ham between his thumb and forefinger and popped it into his mouth.

"I thought I might take it round there . . . or do you think that's a step too far?"

"Take it round?" His expression was slightly sneering. "What would you want to do that for? You don't like Deborah, and you certainly don't like babies. You've made that patently clear. Forget it, I'll mail it from the office."

Julia was anxious to avoid another baby discussion so didn't rise to the bait. "I got age three to six months because the others looked a bit small," she said. "You didn't mention how big he was. Or what his name was for that matter."

"That's because I don't know the answer to either," he replied matter-of-factly. "I just got a text from Deborah to say she'd had a little boy and everything seemed to be fine."

Fucking hell, thought Julia, the woman's lying on her back having her nether regions stitched up and she *still* manages to text my bloody husband. Is there no end to her dogged tenacity?

They carried on eating the appetizers, James munching his way through most of the platter, Julia just picking delicately from round the edges.

After a few minutes, she cleared away the plates and replaced them with two steaming dishes of pan-fried steak.

"Thanks," he said absentmindedly, removing his tie and laying it over the back of his chair.

Julia studied him for a few seconds. "Are you all right? You seem a little quiet."

"Do I?" He looked surprised. "I don't mean to be, I've just got a lot on my mind, I suppose."

"Like what?"

"Just stuff." He waved a hand dismissively. "Boring stuff. You don't want to be bothered with it."

Normally, he was right. She didn't. But there was something about his demeanor that suggested there was more on his mind than just profit margins.

"No, go on," she persisted. "I'd like to hear about it."

He chewed for a few seconds, studying her face as he did so. "You've heard it all before," he said eventually.

She frowned, her mind whirring through any recent conversations they'd shared about his latest deals. To be honest, it was so dreary that most of the time she'd forgotten it almost as soon as she'd heard it. "Really? Well, tell me again." She pushed her half-eaten steak to one side to indicate that, this time, she was going to hang on his every word.

"Babies," he said quietly. "I have babies on my mind."

"Oh, that again." Her spirits sank. She was annoyed with herself at having now prompted a deep and meaningful conversation about something she'd been desperately trying to avoid.

"Yes, *that*," he emphasized. "Have you had any further thoughts?"

She stared out of the window, giving herself a couple of seconds to let her irritation pass. She wanted to appear reasonable, but it was a struggle when her husband kept dragging them back to the same old discussion.

"I thought we'd agreed that it was something I'd give serious thought to in the next couple of years, but not now."

"Did we? I don't remember that." He looked genuinely puzzled. "All I know is that I don't want to be an old dad."

"James, you're thirty-seven, for God's sake. Hardly eligible for a bus pass just yet."

"No, I know that. But even if we agreed to start trying now, who knows what might happen? We might have trouble conceiving, we might need help . . . and that might take a couple of years to sort out. Then I'll be forty, and you'll be in that stage of a woman's life when her fertility plummets."

Julia stared at him open-mouthed for a few seconds. "Well, thanks for that cheerful thought."

"Sorry, but it has to be said." His expression was grave. "Neither of us is getting any younger, so why waste any more time *thinking* about something that in most marriages would be a complete no-brainer?"

"Because this isn't *most* marriages," she snapped. "Perhaps it's escaped your attention, but I look damn good for my age. I don't have wrinkles, my stomach is flat, and there isn't any cellulite on even *one inch* of my body."

James looked confused. "What does that have to do with our marriage?"

"Everything! It means you still fancy me, it means we have a sex life that would be the envy of most couples *everywhere*—never mind the ones that are married—and it means you have a wife you like to show off to your work colleagues. You always say how much more attractive I am than their wives."

"Yes, darling, but I still don't see what that has to do with having children."

She raised her eyes heavenward. "Because if I had a baby, my breasts and stomach would sag, I'd get wrinkles because of the sleepless nights, and I'd become one of those terrible drudges you always profess to loathe."

He didn't reply, simply staring at her with a deeply puzzled expression.

"What are you thinking?" she demanded after a few seconds.

"If you must know, I'm thinking about Elle McPherson, Cindy Crawford, and Elizabeth Hurley."

In short, Julia's worst nightmare. Her insecurity threatened to envelop her, but she resisted the urge to tip the remains of James's steak over his head and stayed outwardly calm. "Why?" she managed to utter.

"Because they all have children, and they all still look gorgeous . . . and so would you," he added wisely.

She felt slightly mollified by this. "That may be, darling, but my concern isn't just about my figure, it's about what would happen after the baby was born . . . how *our* relationship might be affected." She was giving a lot of her deepest fears away now, but she figured she had nothing to lose.

He frowned. "It would undoubtedly be strengthened. What greater high is there than to create a child together?"

Julia could think of plenty, like flying by private jet to Tahiti, or bagging a limited-edition Versace evening dress before anyone else. But she appreciated this probably wasn't the time to mention other possibilities.

"Besides," he pleaded, "you once said you'd do anything for me." He leaned across the table and grabbed both of her hands in his. "So do the ultimate for me, Julia . . . have my baby."

She felt sick inside. Even though everything he'd said had made perfect sense, even though she knew it was usually the natural progression of any happy marriage, and even though it was the one thing she could share with James that would finally set her apart from Deborah, she still couldn't bring herself to jump in with both feet.

"As I said, darling," she purred, moving round the table, "I'll think about it." She pushed him backward in his chair and straddled his lap, nuzzling his neck with her mouth. "In the meantime, there's something much more pressing I'd like to discuss with you." She grabbed one of his hands and placed it on her erect nipple, but as soon as she let go of his hand, it fell back to his side.

"Don't," he muttered. "Get off . . . please."

Julia stayed where she was, certain she could persuade him and move their evening on from the doldrums it was now entrenched in. But James clearly had other ideas.

"I said don't!" he snapped, jumping to his feet and spilling Julia onto the floor in the process.

She sat there for a couple of seconds, feeling horribly undignified, waiting for him to help her to her feet. But he didn't, taking a couple of paces away from her, then spinning round.

"There you go again. Does *everything* have to be about sex with you?"

Pulling herself onto a chair, she allowed herself a small smile at this comment, which was usually made by a woman and directed at a man. Similarly, it was rare for a man to be pressing for children with his reluctant wife. Not for the first time, Julia mulled over her peculiarities that, were it not for her extremely feminine face and body, would make her question her hormone balance.

"I haven't noticed you complaining about my fondness for sex before," she said quietly, looking up at him.

"It's just that there's a time and a place for it. And I hate it when you blatantly use it to change a subject you're not happy with."

She knew he had a valid point, but to admit as much would be to reopen the topic she had been so keen to move away from. So she said nothing.

But as it happened, he returned to it anyway.

"You know, what *really* gets me is that the woman I left for you has just had a baby with a man she's known five minutes, and yet I can't persuade my own *wife* to even try to get pregnant."

"Well, sorry if I want to give serious consideration to bringing another human being into the world, but that's just the way I am." She looked at him defiantly, her mouth set in a firm line.

"I take it very seriously too. Just as I did when I made the decision to marry the woman I *hoped* would become the mother of my children. Now it seems I should have gotten it in writing." He lifted his coat from the back of the chair. "I'm going to have a long, hot bath."

"Shall I come and scrub your back?" She smiled, desperate for them to get back on familiar territory, away from all the gloom and doom she found so suffocating in relationships.

"No thanks," he said firmly. "I'd like some time alone."

After he'd left the room, Julia sat staring at the floor for several minutes. Fucking Deborah, she thought. Just when she thought the new baby would sever the umbilical cord between James and his ex, it was turning out to be an even greater source of grief.

Inwardly, she started to panic. If she was honest about her deepest feelings, she knew damn well she never wanted to have children and thinking about it some more wasn't going to change that. She knew the "serious thought" she'd promised to give the topic was really about whether she could or, more to the point, *would* bury her own reservations and have a baby simply to please—and keep—her husband.

Right now, she hadn't a clue.

honey, i'm home

Jake was sitting at the kitchen table when Fiona walked in, still rubbing the sleep from her eyes. Despite her constantly reassuring him on the phone that she was fine, he'd insisted on coming over to stay the night, even though his father wasn't there.

She put Lily down near her little Fisher Price oven set and glanced at the clock. It was 6:30 A.M.

"I know why *I'm* up at this ungodly hour," she said, jerking her head toward Lily. "But why on earth are *you* up with the birds?"

"I couldn't sleep," he said miserably.

Fiona walked across to the kettle and opened the lid. It was full, so she flicked the switch on. "I know what you mean. There was some obnoxious party going on down the road. The noise was terrible."

He shook his head. "No, it wasn't that. I couldn't stop thinking about you and Dad."

She sat down adjacent to him at the table, moving a newspaper from the chair and dropping it onto the floor. "Now look," she said softly but firmly, "I've told you before. It's *not* your fault."

He smiled reluctantly. "Very nice of you to say so, but I'm not an idiot. One minute you and Dad are ticking along nicely. The next, I've told him about how you helped me through the drug thing and he's left home."

"What I meant was, it's not your fault that your dad reacted that way. If it hadn't been the *drug thing*, as you call it, it probably would have happened over something else. That's marriage for you . . . shit happens."

He nodded but didn't look convinced. "When did you last speak to him?"

"Last night." She stood up and returned to the kettle, pouring water into two mugs. "He rang to say good night to Lily, but she couldn't really get her little head round the fact that she could hear Daddy but not see him."

"Daddy!" At the mention of the word, Lily turned round from her plastic pots and pans and stood staring at the kitchen door.

"No, darling, Daddy's not here. He's at work." She sighed and glanced over at Jake. "For the record? I understand why he's annoyed with me, but I think walking out on us . . . particularly *her* . . . ," she pointed at Lily, ". . . is a complete overreaction."

"I agree. Did you know that Mum used to call him Jigsaw?"

Fiona shook her head, looking bemused.

"Because she said every time he was faced with a problem he went to pieces." He smiled wryly. "Do you know where he is?"

"No." She shrugged. "And I haven't asked because I don't want to pander to his stupid behavior."

"I know where he is. He told me."

"Well, don't tell me. I wish to remain in the dark about it." She gave a half-smile and placed a mug of tea in front of him.

"Thanks." He took a sip. "It's been a week now. When do you think he'll be back?"

"Don't know, and I don't care." She looked at him and winced. "Okay, I *do* care, of course I do. I care tremendously. But I've just got to get on with it, haven't I? If we both flounced around having sulks, what would happen to poor Lily?"

They sat quietly for a couple of minutes, the only sound the clattering of Lily's pots and pans and the occasional hum of the refrigerator.

"I'm so sorry," he murmured, looking for all the world like a lost puppy.

"If you say that one more time, I'm going to stick your head in Lily's toy oven." Fiona smiled. "It's . . . not . . . your . . . fault." Extending a forefinger, she jabbed it lightly in the center of his forehead with each word.

"Actually, this time I was apologizing for being such a pain over the years. There must have been times when you wished me dead."

Fiona pursed her lips. "Not dead. Maybe just roasted slowly over an open fire." She smiled again and pinched his cheek. "Actually, Jake, you're a good kid, you've just been caught between a mother and father who don't get on that well."

" 'They fuck you up, your mum and dad, / they may not mean to but they do, / they fill you with the faults they had, / and add some extra just for you . . .' "

"Language . . ." she admonished with a twinkle in her eye.

"It's not swearing, it's poetry." He laughed. "Philip Larkin, to be precise."

Fiona grabbed a tissue from the nearby box and stooped down to wipe Lily's runny nose, an exercise that took longer than one might expect because of the little girl's aversion to being cleaned up and her aptitude for wriggling out of her mother's grasp.

"Your father is a good man," she said, once the task was done.

"He feels horribly guilty that he and your mum split up, but it truly was a mutual decision at the time. And ever since he's always had you as his top priority."

"I know." Jake nodded gratefully. "In fact, I told him as much last night. We finally got round to having a longer chat about the drugs, and it kind of led on to other things."

"Like what?" She leaned across to the bread bin and pulled out a packet of croissants. Taking one for herself, she pushed them across to Jake.

"Stuff about him and Mum . . . stuff about school . . . I told him there was a girl I liked at school, but she let it be known in no un-certain terms that she fancied someone else . . ." He paused and broke off a piece of croissant. "It was no big deal, but it made me re-alize that you can't make people love each other and that if things don't work out, you just have to make the best of it that you can."

Fiona's eyebrows shot up. "Wow. You sound more mature about relationships than most adults I know."

"And I told him that I thought you were great," he added. "That you've coped remarkably well with all my shit and that he should be grateful to have you and not be sulking in some seedy hotel room."

Standing up, she leaned forward and gave him a grateful hug. "Thank you. That was very sweet of you."

"My pleasure. I just hope he listens."

They continued enjoying the croissants in silence, Fiona tending to Lily and refilling their mugs of tea every now and then. As the sun rose higher in the sky, it burned off the morning mist and sent warm, broad sunbeams streaming across the kitchen floor. Suddenly, in the distance, they heard the familiar sound of the front door slamming, then David's voice in the hallway. "It's only me!"

Fiona looked across the table at Jake, the corners of her mouth turned down in mock dread. "I think we're about to get our answer," she whispered.

"Daaaadeeee!" Lily flung herself at David's legs as he walked into the room, and he scooped her up into his arms. "Hello, pumpkin pie. Oooh, I've missed you." He kissed the side of her head, looking down at Fiona and Jake as he did so. He was expressionless, and Fiona still wasn't sure whether he had arrived back home as a friend who was staying or a foe who had come to collect his things.

"Jake?" He placed Lily back down on the floor. "Would you mind taking your sister upstairs to play? I'd like to talk to Fiona alone."

"Sure." Jake, usually so fond of the teenager's "in a minute" answer to everything, leapt to his feet without hesitation. "Come on, Lil. Let's go." Lifting her onto his hip, he left the room.

"Hello." David smiled sheepishly at her but didn't move from his position near the door.

"Hello." She didn't return the smile, unwilling to look conciliatory until she knew exactly where this conversation was heading.

"I have been a complete and utter idiot," he said amiably.

She beamed in spite of herself. "Yes, you have. But I totally and utterly forgive you." She rushed at him, her arms outstretched, and buried her face in his chest. "I've missed you."

He held her tightly. "I've missed you too. I seriously don't know *what* I was thinking of." He held her away from him and looked into her eyes. "And I can't believe you're letting me off this lightly."

Fiona sat back down. "Oh, you know me. Once the apologies are out of the way, I don't see any point in sulking or bearing a grudge. It's a waste of time." She patted the chair Jake had vacated. "Come and sit down and I'll make you a cup of tea."

Removing his coat, he hung it over the back of the chair and sat down with a heavy sigh. "God, it feels good to be home."

"Where did you go?" She felt happy to express an interest now.

"A hotel that makes Motel 6 look like the Ritz. It had two stars, and you could see both of them through the ceiling."

"That bad, huh?"

"Let's put it this way, it was so bad the rats were throwing *themselves* on the traps."

She chuckled and handed him a mug of his favorite Earl Grey tea. "Good. I'm glad it was hellish. Serves you damn well right."

"Mea culpa." He held his hands up. "I'm so sorry."

Fiona rolled her eyes. "You sound like your son. He's been apologizing to me every five minutes as well."

"He gave me absolute hell on the phone last night." David took a sip. "I must say, it felt weird being dressed down by my sixteen-year-old son. But he made perfect sense and, more important, made me realize what a fool I was being."

"We should listen to him more often. He's a smart boy."

"Apart from when he decides to try Ecstasy."

"Ah, yes, *that*." She made a face.

David took her hand and squeezed it. "You did what you thought was right at the time, and I see that now. It did help build trust between you, and he did step up like a man and tell me what happened. I've got no excuse for overreacting, but I suppose it was all part and parcel of the shock of hearing that Jake had taken drugs and ended up in hospital. You bore the brunt of it."

She placed a finger up against his mouth. "Sssssh, let's just put it behind us as one of those things."

He moved her hand away from his face but held on to it, stroking her thumb. "Okay, but first of all I just want to say that actually, in retrospect, I really appreciate what you did that night. I've been saying for ages that I want you and Jake to get on, and the minute you actually formed a bond over something, I came stomping along and ruined it all."

Fiona smiled benevolently. "Don't worry, you haven't ruined anything. In fact, Jake and I have become even closer since you walked out. He's actually been worried about me, and about us, and calling all the time. Last night he said he wanted to come and stay here to make sure I was all right. He wouldn't take no for an answer."

David glowed with pride. "As you said, he's a smart boy. And a nice one too, at heart. Shall I call him back down?"

He went to stand up, but Fiona stopped him. "Hang on, I want to say something too. I've had a lot of time to think about that night, and while I appreciate everything you're saying, I *was* wrong to keep it from you. I should have trusted you not to say anything. The adult relationship—not the parent-child one—should always be the keeper of any secrets, otherwise everything else spins out of control. I see that now. And I love you." She removed her hand from his arm and let him stand up. "But that doesn't mean you weren't a complete nitwit for reacting the way you did."

"Thank you, darling." He kissed the end of her nose. "I love you too."

He walked into the living room, where she heard him shout "Jake!" up the stairs.

A couple of minutes later, he came back into the kitchen, with an excitable Lily tucked under one arm and Jake following closely behind, grinning from ear to ear. "Dad says everything's okay now?" Jake looked at Fiona for verification.

"It is. He's still a nitwit, though."

"Never doubted it for a moment." Jake smiled, then ducked down as his father tried to grab him in a playful headlock.

Fiona looked at the clock. "My God, it's still only seven-thirty. What shall we do for the rest of the day?"

"Let's celebrate," said David.

"Celebrate what?"

"The start of a new family dynamic where we all listen to one another rather than squabble and embark with enthusiasm on the things we want to do together."

Fiona and Jake both looked dubious.

"Well, do you think we could manage it just for today?" David asked with a note of desperation.

"Okay," said Jake. "I want to go to LaserQuest."

Fiona and David groaned.

"I want to go to Macy's and buy a sarong," Fiona said.

Jake and David groaned.

"And I want to check out the new Apple Mac in PC World," David said.

Fiona and Jake groaned.

"And you, little one . . ." David kissed Lily's flushed cheek, ". . . can decide what we have for lunch."

"Pia!" she shouted her word for *pizza*.

They all laughed. Pizza it would be.

daddy fool

Flicking idly through OK! magazine, Julia visibly balked at the sight of a woman dressed in what resembled an up-turned frilly lampshade. Her sturdy little legs protruded from the bottom like two tree trunks, and her feet were squeezed into a pair of cork wedges that looked at least one size too small.

She peered closely at the caption, intrigued to learn the identity of this hapless girl who appeared to have covered herself in glue and dived into a barrel marked "fashion victim."

Ah, thought Julia. The wife of a prominent football player and yet another example of the triumph of bad taste over too much money. She was a pretty girl and would have looked infinitely more stylish—and more comfortable—in a pair of well-fitting jeans and a T-shirt. Rotating her stiff neck, Julia checked her watch. Five more minutes to go before she could be freed from the overhead heater that was warming her newly applied hair highlights to perfection.

It's funny, she mused, the ridiculous lengths we go to in our bid to look as "naturally" beautiful as possible. Here she was, with a couple of dozen pieces of silver foil hanging off her head, her freshly manicured toes drying nicely with small pieces of cotton wool separating them, and her nether regions smarting slightly from the Brazilian waxing she'd had prior to the hair-on-her-head appointment.

James, she presumed, had no idea of the arduous process involved in making her appear as blemish-free, hairless, and coiffured as she normally did. If he did, he certainly didn't mention it, and Julia wasn't going to draw attention to it. More important, he never complained about the regular, undeniably steep monthly bill from the salon.

The machine above her head started to beep, bringing a junior stylist rushing to her side to inspect the progress. Gently peeling the foils apart, she peered at the curiously purplish gunk on Julia's hair and declared it "ready to come off."

Getting to her feet, Julia was just about to stroll across to the sinks when she noticed Jade sitting in the reception area.

"Excuse me," she said to the young stylist. "Would you mind hanging on for just one minute? I've spotted someone I need to talk to." Without waiting for an answer, she headed off toward the two large cream sofas where customers waited and perused the latest magazines showing a variety of dreadful "creative" hairstyles that no person in their right mind would ever dream of having.

"Jade! Fancy seeing you here."

At first, Jade looked perplexed, clearly thrown by the sight of the foil-headed Medusa looming toward her. Then she recognized her friend. "Oh, hi, Julia. How goes it?"

"It goes well, it goes *very* well, thank you. But never mind me . . ." Julia plonked herself down on the sofa next to her. "I hear you're an auntie—how exciting!"

A fleeting look of suspicion crossed Jade's face as she scrutinized Julia's smiling expression. "You don't know, do you?"

"Know what?"

"It's not Paul's baby."

Julia frowned. "Sorry, I'm not with you . . ."

"Deborah's baby . . . it's not Paul's," Jade repeated slowly, as if addressing an idiot.

This time it sank in, and Julia recoiled slightly with surprise. "*Not Paul's?*" She said it aloud to confirm she'd heard correctly, her mind whirring with confusion. "How do you know?"

Jade raised her eyebrows and made a sucking noise through her teeth. "Well, one surefire way of knowing is that the baby is as white as the driven snow."

Unable to help herself, Julia clamped a hand to her mouth. "Oh, my God, did Paul have any idea?"

"Nope. The first moment he suspected something was up was when the midwife handed him the baby and he noticed her exchanging an uncomfortable glance with the doctor."

"Madam?"

Julia felt someone tapping her on the shoulder and turned to find the junior stylist standing there with an anxious look on her face. "I really should get the foils off your hair now."

"Yes, yes, in a minute." Julia waved her away. "Don't worry, if there's a problem, it'll be my fault." She turned back to Jade.

"I'm sure I've read that sometimes a baby with one black parent *can* look as if it's white," she said. "It has happened."

Jade nodded. "But not to someone as black as Paul. He's one hundred percent Nigerian, as am I, and it would be unheard of if the baby didn't have *some* African characteristics. This one has a shock of white blond hair." She let out a long sigh. "Anyway, after holding the baby for a while, Paul took the doctor outside and asked her outright if she thought he could be the father. She said it was highly unlikely."

"Poor thing." It was Julia's gut reaction, but then it dawned on her that there might be another side to the story. "Was he upset?"

"Devastated. Although I have to say that the rest of the family doesn't exactly share that view. Honestly, we're all rather relieved. It all happened so fast, and now my parents have renewed hope that he'll now meet someone a bit more, well, God-fearing, I suppose."

"So the relationship is over?" Sensing that her chance for a Deborah-free future was about to fly out of the window, Julia felt almost as bereft as if it were *her* relationship that was in its death throes.

Jade rolled her eyes. "I'll say. Paul's a very moral person, so it's a little hard for him to see past the fact that his girlfriend has just given birth to another man's child." Another man. Up to now, the revelation had so taken Julia by surprise that she hadn't even stopped to contemplate the fact that if Paul didn't father the baby, then someone else must have.

"So who's the father then?" A small dribble of hair coloring trickled down Julia's forehead and she wiped it away with the towel.

"Dunno." Jade shrugged. "But I do know that Deborah is a dark horse. I always had a funny feeling about her."

"Well, Paul must have asked her," Julia pressed, aware of a small fluttering feeling in the pit of her chest.

"He did, but she wouldn't tell him who it was. She just kept saying how sorry she was. Sorry, my ass!" she scoffed. "It's a bit late for that."

But Julia wasn't listening anymore. She was staring into space, replaying her conversation with James from a couple of nights ago. He hadn't said anything about the baby not being Paul's. But then again, he'd said he'd only received a text message about the birth, so perhaps he didn't know?

The latter seemed like a reasonable explanation, but the minor flutter in Julia's chest had now magnified to a significant thumping. It was a gut instinct about something her mind was trying to push out, but her subconscious kept shoving it forward, filling her with panic.

She had to get out of here.

Out of the corner of her eye, she could see her stylist, Mario, looming into view, a worried look on his face.

"Julia! Julia!" he shouted while still several paces away. "It has to come off *now* or we are all in big trouble. God knows what damage has been done already." As he drew closer, he extended a hand and placed it through her arm, trying to coax her toward the basins at the back of the salon. But Julia slapped him away.

"No," she said firmly. "I have to leave."

"Leave?" He looked panic-stricken, clearly remembering what a tricky customer she could be when her hair didn't turn out exactly how she wanted it. "You can't go. Your hair will be ruined."

Another trickle of bleach ran down her face and she furiously wiped it away. "I don't care if it turns fucking green," she boomed. "There, I hope that was loud enough for everyone to hear that I take full responsibility for my actions."

Mario pursed his lips and made a zipping motion across his mouth, to indicate he had said all he was going to say. Jade said nothing, simply looking up at her with an expression of puzzlement.

"As I said, I have to go. Send me the bill and I'll get my coat another time." With that, Julia walked out of the salon, foils flapping in her hair and still wearing the distinctive black robe. She hailed a cab directly outside.

The kitchen clock clicked round to 7:00 P.M. as a car alarm wailed outside. But Julia didn't notice either.

She was sitting at the head of the kitchen table, a magazine open in front of her. But every time she tried to focus, the words and pictures seemed to distort and become fuzzy.

The cordless phone was in her right hand, and she stared at it, desperate to call Deborah but willing herself not to. She wanted to ask James first.

He'd called about half an hour ago to say he was on his way home, and with herculean effort she had managed to keep her voice normal. Fine, she'd said, dinner will be ready.

But it wasn't. It wasn't even in preparation. The beautifully lean lamb steaks she'd bought specially were still in the fridge, and the fresh asparagus was unwashed and lying in the vegetable drawer.

The Domestic Goddess was on hold, replaced by a shadow of her former self devoid of makeup and her hair, now washed free of dye, in its natural, slightly frizzy state. She was wearing jeans and an old Mickey Mouse sweatshirt she kept at the back of the wardrobe for any small, dirty jobs around the house. It was all she could do to remember to breathe in and out.

She was desperate to hear James say that someone else was the father of Deborah's baby and to believe him when . . . in fact, *if* . . . he said it.

But a sickening gut instinct in the pit of her stomach told her that her suspicions were true, that not only had James been unfaithful and sired a child, but it was with his *ex-wife*.

Her emotions were veering wildly from abject humiliation one minute to wild, betrayal-driven anger the next. In her darkest moments, she had become breathless with fear and uncertainty that he might reject her even more by deciding to go back to Deborah.

Her breath caught in her throat when she heard James's key in the lock, followed by his footsteps down the hall. As he walked in the door, she studied him carefully, not wanting to miss one small expression or reaction to what she was about to say.

"Hello." He looked slightly taken aback. "You look . . . um . . . differ—"

She cut across him. "Is it yours?"

"Sorry? Is what mine?" He looked genuinely puzzled as he walked toward her and went to plant a kiss on her forehead, as he always did. But this time she moved her head backward to avoid it.

"Deborah's baby. Is it yours?" She stared at him intently, forensically analyzing every blink and twitch.

"What on *earth* are you talking about?"

As soon as he said it, she knew it was his. His voice may have sounded calm, but she saw a fleeting flash of fear in his eyes, and his cheeks took on the flush of guilt.

"Cut the crap," she snapped, feeling an overwhelming urge to run to the kitchen sink and throw up. But she fought it back. "I *know*."

It was a hackneyed double bluff, but Julia was beyond trying to be clever. And James, it seemed, either fell for it or saw right through it but decided to afford her the respect of an honest answer.

"We only had sex a couple of times," he said wearily, lowering himself down onto the chair next to her at the table. "I'm so sorry."

Now that her greatest fear was confirmed, Julia didn't actually feel that much worse. Perhaps the anticipation had been worse than the realization, or perhaps she was getting an early start on the inevitable shock that usually followed any such confrontation. As it stood, she didn't feel angry, she didn't even feel a twinge of sadness. She simply felt numb.

"When?"

"Um . . . ," he looked unnerved, as if he expected her to explode and fly at him at any second, ". . . remember the business trip to New York?"

"Yeee-sss," she said slowly, scowling slightly. "Don't tell me it was all bullshit and you spent the week with her?"

He quickly shook his head. "No, no. There *was* a business trip, and it was for a week. But remember when I got home and we had a row about having a baby?"

Julia scowled and nodded slowly, trying to remember *that* particular row among all the others.

"And remember I said I was going for a long drive?" He looked sheepish. "Well, the first time happened then."

She made a choking noise. "And during the couple of hours you were on the missing list, you managed to conceive a child with your ex-wife . . . is that what you're telling me?"

He nodded slowly. "I was upset, and she was upset about something as well, so we comforted each other and . . . and it just happened."

Julia shot to her feet and took a couple of angry paces toward the other side of the kitchen. "Oh, for fuck's sake, she's *always* upset about something. What was it this time? Someone looked at her the wrong way in the street? Stubbed her toe on the skirting board? Whatever crap she comes up with, you *always* fall for it."

She turned back to face him, but he was staring at the floor, deep in somber thought.

"And the second time?" she demanded. "When was that?"

"A Saturday afternoon when you were at lunch with your girlfriends."

"Which one?"

He shrugged as if it were irrelevant. "The first one Susan went to after her accident."

Julia let out a small gasp. While she was at a meeting of the Second Wives Club, he was busy shagging the very first wife she was bitching about. Oh, the excruciating irony of it. "But she was six months pregnant by then."

James nodded. "Yes, she was."

She slowly shook her head, finding it hard to comprehend what she was hearing. Deborah had always been an irritant, but never in her wildest dreams had Julia imagined that James would have sex with her. She was too plain, too mousy to have even figured on Julia's radar as a sexual threat. How wrong could she have been?

She let out a hollow laugh. "You know, there's an old saying, 'no one misses a slice from a cut loaf.'"

He frowned slightly. "I'm not with you."

"It means it's very easy to fall back into bed with someone if you've already been there," she explained, her tone hard. "As you have so effectively proved."

"Look, Julia . . ." He looked at her plaintively. "I didn't plan any of this. It just happened."

She put her hand up to indicate for him to stop. "Spare me, please. Accidents *just happen*. But falling into bed with your ex-wife is a fucking *decision*, James, and don't pretend otherwise."

Closing his eyes, James leaned back in his chair and tilted his head back, saying nothing.

Julia stayed quiet for a few seconds, struggling to control her temper. She wanted to retain the moral high ground and knew that shouting and screaming wouldn't help matters. "How long have you known it was yours?"

He rubbed his eyes. "Same time as she and Paul did. Just after the birth. She always said it was his, so I took her word for it."

"Christ, mousy *and* stupid," she muttered. "And you're not much better. If you had unprotected sex with her . . . which clearly you did . . . then of *course* there was a chance it could be yours."

She walked back to the table and sat down, stretching her long legs out in front of her. James still hadn't managed to look her in the eye. He was staring down at his loafers, glancing out the window, anything to avoid connecting with her.

"Look at me," she said.

Slowly, he lifted his head and looked at her, guilt and anxiety all over his face.

"I want to know everything about when she told you, how she told you, how you *felt* when she told you, what she said, what you said . . ." she demanded.

He let out a deep sigh. "Why torture yourself with the details? It's not important."

She felt a surge of anger again, and this time she couldn't control it. "It's important to *me*, James, and you *will* tell me everything I want to know! You fucking owe me that much!" she shouted.

He recoiled slightly and put his hands up in a gesture of surrender. "Okay, okay." He paused. "You know when I came home the other night and told you she'd texted me to say she'd had the baby?"

Julia nodded, concentrating hard on his every word, syllable, and facial expression.

"Well, that was true, she had. And the text said nothing about what had gone on with Paul." He paused again and took a deep breath. "Then yesterday morning she called me at work to say that the baby was white and that the only person who could now be the father was me . . ." He rubbed his eyes again, as if he might open them again and find out it had all been a bad dream.

"So when we had dinner here the other night and you talked about trying for a baby, you still had no idea you'd already fathered one?" Julia asked suspiciously.

"No, no idea at all. Ironic really, isn't it?"

"No, James, it's not *ironic*, it's a living bloody nightmare! I can't believe you've got yourself—gotten *us*—into this mess."

The clink of the letterbox opening in the hallway made them both instinctively look toward the kitchen door. It was probably their daily consignment of junk mail, offering two dreadful pizzas for the price of one dreadful pizza.

She turned back. "So what did you say when she told you?"

"There wasn't much I could say, was there really?" He smiled ruefully. "I told her I was shocked, which I was, and that I needed time to come to terms with it." He stopped speaking and looked at her with an air of finality.

"Was that it?"

He shrugged. "Pretty much, yes."

Julia knew that a lot more must have been said, but suddenly another thought struck her and she wanted to know the answer. "Have you seen it?"

His visible discomfort at the question told her immediately that he had. "If by '*it*' you mean the baby, then, yes, I have. I popped in on my way home from work yesterday."

She snorted sarcastically. "One day you're popping in to mend a broken toilet, another you're popping in to see your new son." The final two words stuck in her throat and she felt tears pricking at her eyes. "It's the son you've always wanted, but there's just one tiny problem. It's not with me."

She started to sob openly, her tears splashing down onto the polished wooden table. He made no move to comfort her, simply staring at her with sadness in his eyes.

"I'm so sorry," he said again.

"Sorry . . . sorry." She rolled the word around a bit, mulling it over. "Nope. That doesn't make me feel any better. I don't want easy apologies, James, I want an explanation."

"An explanation?" He looked like a rabbit caught in headlights. "How do you mean?"

She reached across to the center of the table and plucked a tissue from its box, wiping her nose. "I mean that I want to know why you slept with Deborah when you're married to someone like me." She let out a small sob. "I work hard at looking good, I'm bright, I cook like a fucking professional, *and* I'm really imaginative and adventurous in bed. Most men would kill to be married to me."

He smiled sadly and nodded. "You're absolutely right, they would."

"So why the hell did you feel the need to sleep with *her?*" She looked at him with injured defiance.

"I don't know . . . it's complicated."

"Try me."

He shuffled in his seat, looking for all the world like he'd rather be having the hair on his testicles extracted with tweezers than be having this conversation. "You want the truth?"

"No, I want you to fucking string me along again," she spat. "Of *course* I want the truth."

"Okay. Well, I guess I went to her for a break."

"A *break?*" She looked at him incredulously. "A break from what?"

"From your relentless perfection." He at least had the grace to look slightly sheepish as he said it.

She let out a hollow laugh. "Well, that's a new one. You slept with another woman because I was too perfect?"

"Something like that, yes." He leaned forward earnestly. "The thing is, Julia, that yes, you *are* every man's dream, but sometimes you just don't feel real. There are moments when I feel like I don't really know who you are, or like you know who I really am. It's like being married to a fantasy . . . a . . . a blow-up doll!"

The fantasy bit she quite liked, but the blow-up doll analogy was a hurtful step too far. Her eyes filled with tears again. "You think I'm like a blow-up doll?"

"That's the wrong way to put it," he backtracked. "I shouldn't have said that, but you know what I mean."

"No, I don't," she countered. "I don't know at all. What I *do* know is that since we've been married, I have broken my back to be everything I thought you wanted me to be." She looked and felt wounded. "You once said you left Deborah for me because you found me so exciting. What changed?"

"Nothing changed. It's just that after a while the exciting inevitably becomes the familiar, I suppose."

The tears had dried up now, and she could feel another swell of anger. "Forever chasing the chase, eh, James?" she said bitterly. "I had no idea you were one of those hackneyed, 'grass is always greener' kind of guys. How fucking *sad* you are."

He made a distasteful expression.

"Oh, don't give me that sanctimonious 'women shouldn't swear' act. Fucking save it." She was aware she was sounding shrill, but she no longer cared. "My husband has just had a child by his ex-wife. I'm fucking *allowed* to swear."

"Yet another of your unladylike characteristics," he muttered.

She knew she shouldn't take the bait, shouldn't get caught up in an argument that had nothing to do with his infidelity, but she couldn't help herself. She was now in a fighting mood. "What do mean, *another?*"

"Nothing."

"James." She raised her eyes theatrically. "If you make an accusation, at least have the balls to carry it through to the end."

"Okay then." He looked directly at her, his eyes like granite. "Your refusal to try for children. What kind of woman does that make you?"

She felt his words punch right through her, temporarily winding her. "You tell me," she said quietly but ominously.

"It makes you *odd*, that's what it makes you," he said defiantly.

"Does it indeed?" Inside, she felt wounded by his accusation, but outwardly she looked appalled. "And your punishment for my 'odd' behavior is to go and get another woman pregnant, is that right?"

"It wasn't like that."

His voice broke slightly as he said it, and she looked across to find that he was crying.

"Why are *you* crying?" she asked incredulously.

"Because it's all such a goddamned mess." He sniffed, wiping his nose with an old tissue he retrieved from his trouser pocket. "I never set out to hurt you, Julia, honestly. I just felt pissed off that you wouldn't try for a baby, and I suppose I felt rejected. I started feeling like maybe you'd only married me for my money, for our lifestyle, without any real desire to connect with me on a deeper level, to take that step to create a new life together and have a baby."

"And Deborah was there to say 'Daddy' and open her legs?" she scoffed. "How pathetic. Well, you've certainly got a baby now, haven't you?"

He nodded and blew his nose again, calmer now. "I was thinking . . . I know it's a less than ideal situation, but it might just work out for the best, you know."

At first, Julia wasn't sure she'd heard him correctly and screwed up her eyes in incomprehension. "Sorry, did you just say this could all work out for the best?"

"Yes. I know it sounds crazy, but just think about it." He leaned forward on his elbows, an earnest look on his face. "You don't want to have a baby, and now I have one. Don't you see? It's perfect!"

She shook her head. "No, I don't see. And besides," she added wryly, "I thought you didn't like perfect."

He ignored the gibe. "When he gets a little bit older, Daniel . . . that's his name, by the way . . . can come stay with us once during the week and every other weekend. That way, you don't have to actually give birth, you don't have to give up your lifestyle, but I get to be a father." His expression suggested he'd just announced a workable solution to the crisis in the Middle East.

Julia stared at him open-mouthed, still angry but also bewildered by all that had gone on and been said. She didn't trust herself to answer him at this point. She needed time to think things through before making a knee-jerk decision she might later regret.

"So what do you think?" he said hopefully, looking for all the world like a man who was simply asking her to choose which of his neckties she preferred.

"What do I think?" she parroted, stalling for time. "I think that I need time to think, that's what I think."

Now it was his turn to look bewildered. "Sorry?"

"I need time to mull everything over."

"What's to mull?" He looked genuinely surprised. "Surely you're not going to let this destroy our marriage?"

Studying his face as he spoke, she realized that what he'd said was utterly devoid of irony. "*I'm* not going to let this destroy our marriage?" she said wearily, anxious for the confrontation to end so she could retreat and lick her wounds for a while. "Any potential destruction is all your doing, James, not mine. We're not talking about a run-of-the-mill marital argument here . . . not only have you been unfaithful to me, it was with your ex-wife *and* you have fathered her child. Betrayals don't come much bigger than this."

"So what are you saying?" He suddenly looked worried. "Are you saying you want a divorce?"

Julia sighed and started to walk toward the kitchen door, feeling calmer now that she knew *she* was in control of the decision-making. "I'm not saying anything at the moment. As I said, I need time to think, and then I'll let you know."

"When?" he shot after her.

"I'm going to go upstairs and pack, then go to the airport and get a standby ticket to somewhere hot, where I will spend the week alone with my thoughts. We'll talk when I get back."

She paused in the doorway. "In the meantime, I suggest you do some serious thinking of your own about what you want from life. I thought it was me, but now I'm not so sure."

"You can't live without me!" he bellowed after her retreating back.

"Oh, I don't know," she murmured quietly to herself. "I'm willing to give it a try."

end of an earache

"A glass of water, please. And a menu. I could eat a donkey." Susan lowered herself into a wicker chair in Natasha's Café, her ever-broadening hips making it difficult to squeeze in.

"Christ, if I'm the size of a bungalow now, can you imagine what I'm going to be by the time I actually have the baby?" she grumbled to Fiona. "I've put on about forty pounds."

"It's entirely normal." Fiona smiled indulgently. "Every pregnant woman puts on weight."

"Yes, but only about six pounds of it is actual baby. The rest is fat."

"And fluid. You'll lose it really quickly once it's born, you'll see."

"Very kind of you to say so, but I suspect the reality will be a little harder to shift. It can't be a coincidence that 'stressed' is 'desserts' spelled backward. I have such a craving for sugar that I virtually inhaled some yesterday."

"It'll all be worth it. Just think . . . in about six weeks' time, you're going to be cradling your very own baby."

"I know." Susan grinned. "I don't want to go on about it when Alison gets here, because I feel so awful for her . . . so I'll say it now. It's the greatest feeling in the world. I'm so excited!"

"And I'm so pleased for you. How's the leg holding up?"

Susan turned down the corners of her mouth. "Not bad. It still looks a little unattractive, hence the trousers, and I get the occasional tweak from the metal pin, but other than that I feel very lucky to have escaped with only that to grumble about." She waved toward the door. "Here's Alison now."

"Wow, you look amazing," said Fiona, looking her up and down.

Alison was dressed in a cream linen trouser suit and flat gold sandals. She had a faint suntan, just enough to bring out a smattering of freckles across her nose, and her hair shone. "Thanks. One of the benefits of my new healthy regimen . . . the one that's supposed to help me get pregnant. It's been about six months now since a drop of alcohol has passed my lips, and it's worked wonders for my skin. Sadly, it hasn't worked wonders on other fronts." Her face clouded slightly, but she rallied herself and smiled at Susan. "But I can see you're blooming very nicely."

"Yes, blooming fat. I'd swear I was giving birth to a small sofa if I hadn't seen the scan pictures."

"I want to ask you lots of questions about it," said Alison, looking around and back toward the door. "It's been so long since we've seen each other, what with holidays, work, family commitments, and so on, that there seems heaps to catch up on. But I suppose we'd better wait until Julia gets here, and then you don't have to repeat yourself." She settled herself in the chair and hung her handbag over the back of it. "Talking of which, has anyone else spoken to her since the James drama? I called a couple of times to offer support but didn't really get much out of her."

Susan nodded. "Yes I've spoken to her quite a few times. I was ringing her up every day, but she got annoyed with me and said I didn't need to keep checking up on her. She said it made her feel old, like I was on death watch."

Fiona raised her eyes. "So I take it that heartbreak hasn't dulled her acid tongue then?"

"No, in fact, she sounds like her old self. Remarkable, really. I can only assume she's been shedding her tears in private."

"Have you actually seen her?" Fiona looked up from the menu.

"No. She was away for a while, and now she seems to have thrown herself back into promotional work. So she's not exactly been sitting at home staring at the wallpaper." She pointed at the door. "Ah, here she is now . . . oh, my goodness!"

It was definitely Julia standing before them, because the eyes and the stunning smile were the same, as was the long, lithe body and full breasts. But the rest of her was very different.

Her face was devoid of makeup, and her hair, although still sleek and shiny, was combed back into a ponytail. She was wearing a pair of faded Levi's, a faded red T-shirt with WHEN YOUR IQ GETS TO 80, SELL! on the front, and a pair of white Nikes. A casual outfit she wouldn't have been caught dead in even a month ago.

"Wow, you look fantastic!" said Fiona, and she meant it too. "You look about ten years younger."

Susan was staring at her open-mouthed. "I'm sorry, you can't sit there. My old friend Julia is coming. She's very glamorous, you know, with lots of designer clothes and paint-by-number makeup."

"Really? She sounds positively ghastly," Julia drawled, sitting down.

"Seriously, though," added Susan, "are you okay?"

"If by that you mean has my husband betraying me with his ex-wife turned me into an unattractive drudge, the answer is no. I've just learned that there's more to life than looking perfect all the time, that's all." She sighed. "So at least I got something out of my marriage."

"Imperfection is quite an art form too, you know." Susan glanced down at her scruffy sweatshirt top, straining at the seams. She smiled sadly. "So it's definitely over then?"

"Oh, yes. Siring a child with your ex-wife is a step too far, don't you think?" she answered breezily.

Fiona nodded. "Well, it would certainly be the end for me."

"I mean, even poor old Jerry Hall couldn't hack it," continued Julia. "All those years of putting up with Mick behaving like one of those oversexed dogs that shags people's legs and even *she* threw in the towel when he got one of his mistresses pregnant."

"Have you seen James?" asked Alison quietly.

"Yes. He rang me probably a hundred times while I was staying in Positano . . . paid for by him, of course!" She paused and smiled quickly at the thought. "In the end, I agreed to meet him on the proviso that he stop calling. And besides, I wanted to keep the breakup as amicable as possible. I know it's hard to believe, but I really don't bear him any ill will. I just think he's rather pathetic."

"So how did the meeting go?" Susan shifted in her seat and winced slightly, feeling a twinge in her abdomen.

"It was interesting." Julia's tone was matter-of-fact. "I seriously think he thought I'd go back to him, that I couldn't live without him." She pursed her lips. "But I told him in no uncertain terms that it was over."

"What, just like that?" As someone who would have taken at least six months of to-ing and fro-ing to come to a similar decision, Susan was skeptical.

"Yes, just like that." Julia shrugged. "Not much more to say, really, is there? The bottom line is that I wasn't keen to have a child of my own, so the chances of me loving one that isn't mine are pretty remote . . ."

"Hey, don't knock it," Susan chided. "It can be fantastic, you know."

"I'm sure." Julia laid a reassuring hand on her forearm. "But even with the best will in the world, you and I are two completely different people." She moved her hand across to touch Susan's swollen stomach. "Which is why you're expecting the baby you've always wanted, and I'm not."

She sighed theatrically. "I have absolutely no idea why I don't have a maternal bone in my body, I just don't. And I could analyze myself into oblivion over it, but the end result would still be the same, so what's the point? If that makes me an oddity, then so be it."

Fiona smiled warmly. "It doesn't make you an oddity. I think you're very brave to come out and say it, because it does go against everything we're brought up to believe."

"It would be easier if I *couldn't* have children," Julia went on. "Then, when anyone asked, I could say, 'Actually, I have been trying for ten years, but I only have one ovary after a childhood accident,' or something like that. That would shut them up." She shrugged. "I might say it anyway, just for the hell of it."

Alison's brow furrowed. "Believe me, it's not easier," she muttered. "I'd rather not want children than want them and be unable to have them."

For once, Julia looked genuinely concerned. "Darling, I'm sorry. I didn't mean to be so insensitive." She sighed. "Anyway, as I said, it's over. I'm going for a quickie divorce, and then James is free to do as he pleases."

"So you're going to have that lovely big house all to yourself?" Susan smiled wistfully.

"No, I've said he can keep it. I've rented myself a little chichi flat, and all I want is a small cash sum to tide me over for a couple of years until I find my feet again." She blew a piece of stray hair away from her eyes. "I'm going to set up my own PR agency, hiring out temporary staff to companies for big events. I know the business inside out, so it seems an obvious thing to do."

"Wow." Fiona raised her eyebrows. "You sound really together. And you're really not going to punish James financially?"

Julia shook her head. "Nope. Though clearly you're surprised by that?"

Her tone wasn't aggressive, but Fiona felt the need to backtrack. "No, not at all. Seriously, I didn't mean it like that."

Julia waved a hand dismissively. "Don't worry about it. James was clearly surprised too, so I must come across as a right gold-digger."

The other three shook their heads, somewhat unconvincingly.

"I may have happily spent his money when we were together," she continued, "but I don't see that two years of a childless marriage entitles me to screw him . . . even if he did screw his ex-wife."

"Commendable." Susan raised her glass.

"Contrary to what you all may think, I'm really not a vengeful person . . . unless, of course, someone gets to a pair of Jimmy Choos before I do." She smiled at them all.

"So what do you think James will do?" asked Susan. "He must be devastated to lose you."

"So he says. But he'll get over it. After all, he wasn't thinking too much about me when he was conceiving Daniel, was he?"

"Daniel," mused Alison. "What a lovely name."

Julia looked at the other two and raised her eyes heavenward. "I suspect that as soon as it dawns on him that I really *am* pressing ahead with the divorce, he'll be back with Deborah before you can say 'Treacherous bastard.' Well, fuck it, they deserve each other."

Fiona's eyes bulged. "Do you really think he'll go back to her?"

"I'd bet my entire wardrobe on it. Which, as you all know, is *some* wager." She took a sip of wine. "He'll be rattling around that big house, opening the fridge, and—shock, horror—finding it empty, and she'll start spending more time there, mothering him, and making sure all his needs are met . . . and before you know it, she'll move in permanently."

She leaned back in her chair with an air of finality. "It's funny, but when we had that one and only lunch together, she actually said she hoped to get him back."

Susan practically choked on her breadstick. "You never told us that bit!"

"I forgot all about it, to be honest, because I just didn't take it seriously." Julia shrugged. "But all credit to her, she's pulled it off."

Fiona looked at her in bemused disbelief, like a young child viewing her mother's radical new haircut. "I can't believe you're being so chipper about it. I'd be in pieces."

"Oh, believe me, I spent the first week just sobbing my eyes out, and the second one wasn't much better either." She smiled slightly, but her eyes looked sad. "But however shitty I felt, I knew I would eventually feel stronger and that it was better than staying with such a weak man. Deborah may think she's won, but her *prize* . . . ," she made quote marks with her fingers, ". . . is a man who's always chasing the chase. He cheated on not just one but two marriages, so I wouldn't put a lot of stock in any vows he makes. He might not actually leave her again, but he'll sure as hell be unfaithful."

Fiona thought of something and made a spluttering noise before swallowing her mouthful of wine to say her piece. "Maybe *you* could become a thorn in *her* side again! That would be a delicious irony."

Julia smiled benevolently. "It would indeed, and believe me, it has crossed my mind. It would be very easy for me to tempt James into my bed occasionally on his way back home to Deborah . . . just like the old days." She paused a moment. "But why bother? I don't want him, so it would be a waste of time and effort merely to get revenge on her. And the way I see it, we're quits right now, so we should leave it that way."

They all absorbed what she'd said for a moment or two, then

Fiona looked around at the other three. "Well, all that makes *my* little drama sound ludicrously overblown."

"Ah, yes, how *is* the teenager from hell?" asked Julia.

"Heavenly, believe it or not. And he's doing really well at school again, so he's back on track to go to college. And probably a pretty good one, at that."

"What an amazing turnaround," marveled Susan. "Especially when you think about how easily he could have gone the other way."

"I know." Fiona leaned forward and rapped her knuckles on the wooden table for luck. "And according to David, the other day Jake even argued with his mother about me. Apparently the old cow said something derogatory, and he sprang to my defense. Wonders will never cease!"

"Does his mom know about the drugs thing?" Alison asked.

Fiona shook her head. "No. David thought long and hard about it, but then agreed with Jake not to say anything as long as he stayed on the straight and narrow."

"Which is pretty much what *you* agreed with Jake when you decided not to tell your overreactionary husband," Julia scoffed.

"I know." She smiled. "David sees that now. But don't forget, I'm not one of Jake's natural parents, so with hindsight I *do* think I was wrong not to say anything."

She topped off her and Julia's wineglasses. "Still, it's all water under the bridge now, and David and I are getting on better than ever before. In fact, we're going to start trying for another baby in the next couple of months."

"You can have this one if you like." Susan placed her palms on either side of her swollen belly and grimaced. "God, it's uncomfortable. The little devil is doing somersaults."

"Have you and Nick decided on any names yet?" asked Alison.

"Well, he's convinced it's a girl, so he likes Sophie or Emma." She paused a moment and studied their faces. "But I couldn't bear the suspense and forked out for one of those tests the other day . . . and it's a boy!"

Fiona gasped. "Oh, God, that's perfect! It's just what you wanted. That way, Ellie will still be Daddy's little girl."

"Exactly." Susan beamed.

"And does Daddy know?" inquired Julia.

"No. He's always said he wants it to be a surprise, so I haven't told him. But I know he'll be thrilled to bits."

"And is he still in perfect husband mode?" Julia added. "Because, as we all know, these boys *say* they've changed, but they sometimes drift back to their old ways."

"No, so far so good. He's given the oil painting of Caitlin to her parents and put a lot of the photos away. There are still a few in Ellie's room and one under a pile of stuff on the kitchen message board, but that's it. He's really making an effort to move forward."

"That's great," said Fiona. "But what about Caitlin's parents?"

Susan shook her head in happy amazement. "Actually, they've been completely marvelous, and I *never* thought I'd hear myself say that. Ellie goes to stay there a lot, and Genevieve has even said to me that when the new baby is a little bit older, they'll be happy to have him stay over too so I can have a break."

She noticed Julia's expression of surprise. "I know, it's quite a turnaround. But Genevieve and I have been having some good heart-to-hearts recently, and we've talked quite a bit about my child-hood and losing my mum. Since then she seems to have taken me under her wing."

Julia grimaced. "Isn't that a bit nauseating?"

"No, surprisingly, not at all. It's quite nice, actually. Don't forget, they live out in the country, so she's not in my face the whole time. She sent us a card to congratulate us on our engagement, and she's even knitting for the new baby!"

"Fuck, so I'm the only sad sack here then?" said Julia with her inimitable succinctness. "Fiona's nightmare stepson has turned into a choirboy, Susan's nightmare in-laws have become chocolate-box perfect . . . ," she turned and looked at Alison, ". . . and I suppose you're about to tell us that such is his miraculous change of heart that Luca is now setting up his own IVF clinic to help others."

Alison smiled sadly. "No, quite the opposite, in fact."

Susan patted her on the back. "Is he still being pigheaded?"

She nodded. "The hormones don't seem to be having an effect, and every time I instigate sex he goes all peculiar and says it's only because I'm trying to get pregnant . . ."

She was interrupted by a loud snorting noise from Julia.

"Men are bloody priceless, aren't they? When you were on the pill and instigated sex, he probably thought he'd died and gone to heaven, yet now you're trying for a baby he gets all particular about it. What a wanker."

"Julia!" chided Susan. "That's Alison's husband you're talking about. Whatever his issues, she loves him."

"No, she's right. He *is* a wanker." Alison's words were greeted with a shocked silence from the others. "Yes, I do love him, but, well . . . I know this is going to come as a surprise, but I've come to the conclusion that he doesn't love me. At least, not enough anyway."

"What do you mean?" Fiona looked concerned. "Of course he loves you. He's just being a bit of a macho prat, that's all. And, God knows, they're all capable of that from time to time."

"Yes, they are. But it's more than that." Alison's eyes filled with tears, and she struggled to contain herself. "To tell you the truth, I've had sore misgivings for a long time."

"You should get ointment for that," quipped Julia, recoiling slightly as Fiona silently made a zipping motion across her mouth and glared at her. But Alison didn't notice. "I've been burying my true feelings, desperate to hang in there," she continued. "It's hard enough facing up to the fact that your marriage might not be working, but when you actually dragged your husband away from his first wife, there's an even greater pressure not to admit failure."

"I couldn't agree more." Julia nodded. "I was so pathetically grateful that James had left his wife for me that I felt I owed him and became almost geishalike."

Alison blew her nose on a paper napkin. "But admit failure I must. Luca's attitude toward my infertility hasn't helped matters, but the bottom line is that I just don't have the energy to fight Sofia anymore. She's won."

She started to sob quietly, and Fiona reached across to grab her hand and squeeze it. "What do you mean, she's won?" she asked.

"I mean she can have him. I give up."

Susan pulled a "what to do?" face at the others over the top of Alison's bowed head. "Darling, you can't give up now," she murmured. "Not after everything you've been through. It'll all turn out okay in the end, you'll see. You're just having a bad patch. It happens to all of us."

"And don't forget those pills will be making you feel more hormonal than usual," added Fiona. "It's not a good time to make any life-changing decisions."

"Yes, it is." Alison lifted her head and straightened her back as a sign of resolve. "Particularly if the decision changes your life for the better, as I think mine will."

"So what *is* the decision, exactly?" Julia looked confused.

"It's over. I told him last night."

The other three stared at her for a couple of seconds, their faces registering disbelief. Then Fiona spoke. "So, hang on a minute. All the time we've been sitting here . . . with me banging on about Jake and Susan talking about Caitlin's parents . . . you were sitting here with this bombshell news and didn't say anything?"

Alison nodded miserably.

"Why on earth *not?*" asked Susan.

"Because I didn't want it to dominate our lunch," she replied quietly. "I wanted to hear all your news first. You know, normal stuff, just to remind me that some people have happy lives."

"Oh, yes, my husband shagged his ex-wife and got her pregnant. My life is just your average bundle of laughs," scoffed Julia.

"I was about to say that you were the exception," Alison replied, her quick smile not quite reaching her eyes.

"So tell us about last night." Fiona's face was etched with concern.

She shrugged slightly. "It was surprisingly calm, actually. I just told Luca what I have been feeling for a long time . . . that we would never shake off the specter of Sofia, that I would never be able to have a proper relationship with his sons because of their mother's hate for me, and that, of course, meant there was always going to be a huge area of his life that I was excluded from. He has made it abundantly clear over and over again that his sons come first and that he won't take a hard line with Sofia since she has the power to take them away. I said it made our marriage virtually untenable."

"And what did he say?" asked Susan, leaning forward slightly and cupping her ear because of the noise elsewhere in the café.

"Not much really. After all, we've had variations of the conversation before, when I've tried to get him to stand up more to Sofia, to insist that I be included in his sons' lives. But he never does." She let out a long sigh, then her face crumpled in distress. "He just sort of shrugged and said that if that was the way I felt, then he couldn't stop me from leaving him."

Fiona gave her a hug. "Darling, I'm so sorry. But you never know, it might just be the kick in the bum he needs. I'm sure that once it has sunk in, he'll be on the phone asking you to come back, promising you the world."

Alison drew back from her and sat up straight, managing a weak smile. "You don't know him, that's just not his style. Now that I've said it's over, in his mind there will be no going back." She took a sip of her virtually untouched wine. "But I knew that before I said it. And it wasn't an impromptu thing, I have been thinking about it for a long time. Marrakech was probably the final straw. When he gave me a hard time about wanting sex *and* flew home to yet another Sofia crisis only hours after I'd arrived, I knew it was always going to be that way. So I had to like it or lump it."

"And you've lumped it and dumped him," said Julia matter-of-factly. "Can't say I blame you."

"So where did you stay?" asked Susan.

"At the house. Luca packed an overnight bag and said he'd stay in a hotel until he could find somewhere to rent for a while. I haven't spoken to him since he left at about nine o'clock last night." She started to sob again at the thought. "I'm sorry. I know I've made the right decision, but it just feels so unbelievably painful at the moment."

"Of course it does." Fiona took her hand and squeezed it reassuringly. "And it probably will for some time to come. Are you *sure* it's the right decision?"

Alison nodded, her eyes full of sadness. "Yes. Being Luca's second wife meant constantly feeling second best, and I know it doesn't have to be that way. You're testament to that . . ."

"There are still times when I feel second best," admitted Fiona. "But I know what you mean. Overall, David always puts me before Belinda. It wouldn't work otherwise."

"Are you sure he can't change?" said Susan softly. "After all, I had the ghost of Caitlin constantly hanging over me, and Nick didn't want me to have another baby . . . and now look." She stared down at her bump. "It just takes time."

Alison shook her head. "It's time I don't have. I'm nearly thirty-seven, and I don't want to waste two more years on a man who can't stand up to his ex-wife or support me in my desire to become pregnant. And frankly, I don't want to be on a quest to get pregnant all alone—it should be something we're both equally interested in. I have to cut him loose and get on with my life."

Her eyes were still red, but she had stopped crying. "You know, I've learned so much from all this. I was so wrapped up in the whole drama of meeting Luca, having a secret affair, and getting him away from his wife that I never really stopped to think about whether he was the right husband for me. I wanted him, I got him, and that was that. I never really thought about the consequences of it all until after we'd gotten married. Marry in haste, repent at leisure, eh?" She smiled regretfully.

"So what will happen about the house?" asked Susan. "Will you have to move? You can come and stay with us for a while if you like."

"Thanks, but he says I can keep it. I'll have to go back to work, but then I reckon I can just about manage the mortgage repayments."

"Wow." Fiona pursed her lips. "So that really is it then? Do you think he'll go back to Sofia?"

"I don't know," she mused. "It would make sense, I suppose, because he adores his sons and it would make it easier for him to see them . . . and she'd *definitely* have him back tomorrow if she could."

"And how would you feel about that?" asked Susan gently.

"Gutted." Alison smiled weakly. "But in a way it would simply validate my decision, wouldn't it?" Then she shook her head. "I actually think he'll stay single and just have a string of meaningless relationships that don't encroach too much on his time with his boys. I think he too realized that he'd gotten in over his head. But I could be proved wrong, of course."

"Do *you* want to get married again?" Fiona topped off Alison's wineglass and handed it to her.

"Yes, I'd like to, but who knows?" She took a large swallow of wine for courage at the mere thought. "If I ever do meet anyone else, the poor fool will have to fill out a detailed questionnaire before I even go on the first date. Question one: 'Do you have a certifiably insane ex-wife lurking in the background?' " She held up a finger. "Question two: 'Would you like children, and if so, do you have a problem with wanking into a test tube?' "

They all burst out laughing, a welcome relief from the somber mood of the past half an hour.

"Well," said Fiona, raising her glass, "I'd like to propose a toast . . . to the wonderful friendships that have sustained us all through our various trials and tribulations over the past few months."

"To friendship!" they chorused, clanging their glasses.

"And to the Second Wives Club, a tradition we must vow to keep up, whatever happens in the future."

"To the Second Wives Club!" they shouted, causing several people in the café to turn round and see what the noise was.

Once they'd all settled down again, Julia turned to Alison. "I have an idea," she said brightly. "I'm off to my mother's house in Provence next week for a restorative few days of fine wine and lying in the sun. Why don't you come with me? We can sit and put the world to rights."

Alison, slightly taken aback by this development in a friendship that had hitherto been restricted to chats at club meetings, recovered quickly and smiled. "That would be lovely, thank you."

"And then, when we get back, you can be my partner in crime as we trawl the city's wine bars looking for delicious, available men." She tapped her forefinger on Alison's knee.

"Er . . . ," Alison looked highly uncomfortable, ". . . I'm not sure I'm ready to start dating yet."

"I was *joking*, darling . . . well, about you, anyway." She flicked her hair back behind her shoulders. "I'm more than ready to start dating. In fact, I already have my eye on someone."

"Oh, God." Susan groaned. "Who *is* this poor creature that doesn't know what . . . or should I say who . . . is about to hit him?"

"You may scoff now," Julia sniffed, "but you'll all be thanking me in a few months' time when we're enjoying free hospitality at one of the chains of luxury health spas he owns all over the world."

"You're a fast worker." Fiona laughed. "How long have you been seeing him?"

"I only met him last night, at a drinks party. But I've been around enough men to know that he's smitten. Besides, he's already called me twice today."

"You kill me." Susan laughed. "Only you could meet an available multimillionaire within days of splitting from your husband."

"Ah," said Julia, "*that's* the only slight problem. He's not available . . . yet."

They all tutted loudly.

"There's a girlfriend, is there?" said Susan with a disapproving look.

"Not exactly . . . there's a wife."

She winced as a cacophony of "Julia, no!" and "Not again!" was fired in her direction.

"A second wife, to be precise." She curled her arms over her head, pretending to shield herself from whatever torrent of abuse was coming next, but the others simply smiled and shook their heads.

"Some people never learn," remonstrated Fiona. "Don't tell me you're *actually* going to date this man?"

Julia nodded firmly. "You bet I am. I've only spoken to him for, oooh, an hour tops, but in that time I learned that his second wife is shagging her tennis instructor, he's got five kids by two women and doesn't want to have any more, and he's seriously loaded and in desperate need of a woman to travel the world with him and sample the delights of all of his resorts." She clamped her fingers together as if holding an imaginary pen. "Where do I bloody sign?"

"Well, each to her own, I suppose." Susan laughed. "As long as you don't marry him."

"*Not* marry him?" Julia looked at her incredulously. "Of *course* I'll marry him, in fact, I'll insist on it. I'm far too old to stay a girlfriend."

The others shook their heads slowly. "It's your life," Susan added.

"You're damn right it is." Julia beamed. "And I'm going to live it to the full. Now then, *Third* Wives Club, anyone?"